DFV ETHEREAL

The Terran Fleet Command Saga - Book 6

*****

Tori L. Harris

ISBN: 978-0-9985338-4-1
DFV ETHEREAL
THE TERRAN FLEET COMMAND SAGA - BOOK 6
VERSION 2 (Author Edit 1)

Written and Published by Tori L. Harris
AuthorToriHarris.com

Edited by Monique Happy
http://www.moniquehappyeditorial.com/

Cover Design by Ivo Brankovikj
https://ivobrankovikj.art

Preface

After the release of *TFS Guardian,* originally planned to be the 5th and final chapter in the *Terran Fleet Command Saga*, fans of the series immediately began asking for a "Book 6." As thrilled as I was to have readers asking for more of the same, I felt that after five books it was time to try something a little different. After toying with a few ideas outside the science fiction genre, I kept coming back to the fact that there were several promising plot lines within the original series I thought would make for an interesting stand-alone novel. In particular, I had received tons of questions regarding the so-called "Grey aliens" and their role in colonizing Human worlds across our galaxy.

Ultimately, I decided on a hybrid approach. I would write a story that was still science fiction, still in the TFC "universe," but different enough to be seen as something new. Specifically, I thought it would be interesting to see how the Greys would interact with another Human colony on a world that was less technologically advanced than the Earth was at the beginning of the *Terran Fleet Command Saga*. I've always been fascinated with the idea of various technologies being introduced before their intended time – which is what *TFS Ingenuity* was really all about. My goal was to stick with that theme and ride the fence between picking up where the original series ended and starting something completely new.

Yeah, that didn't work out nearly as well as I had hoped.

Originally, I published the book you're holding under the title *The Last Flamecaller*. And my "hybrid" approach – including a cover that convinced many readers that I had written a "fantasy western" story – turned out to be well outside the wheelhouse of most TFC fans. The good news is that those who did read *The Last Flamecaller* were quick to point out that it belonged in the original series. In spite of my intentions to produce something new, what I had actually written was "Book 6" of the series, picking up the story shortly after the events in *TFS Guardian*.

In spite of the updated title, cover, and incorporation into the TFC series, however, I hope you will enjoy "Book 6" precisely because it *is* a little different from the previous five. The pre-industrial world on which this episode takes place lends an element of fantasy to the story (including a map and hints of the relatively new LitRPG genre). And the application of technology from Earth's not-too-distant past makes Didara 4 feel a little like stepping back in time.

Finally, I hope this latest episode is one that new readers can enjoy without requiring them to start all the way back at "Book 1." Now, do I *recommend* they start with *TFS Ingenuity?* Well, of course I do! But I'm also hopeful that readers who start with *DFV Ethereal* first will be interested enough to then go back and read the first five books. If you are one of these readers, or just need a refresher on the story thus far, I have included a bit of background information in an Appendix that you might find helpful before you begin.

In any event, I hope you enjoy the story. Please drop me a line and let me know what you think!

Any sufficiently advanced technology is indistinguishable from magic.

Arthur C. Clarke

While an undeniably brilliant observation, I suspect Mr. Clarke might have been surprised to learn that most civilizations, even the most primitive ones, are quite adept at discerning technology from magic. The <u>truly</u> advanced discover that magic — in the sense I believe he was referring — actually <u>does</u> exist in the universe. Technology is nothing more than our feeble attempt to imitate it.

"Rick" (The Grey Alien)

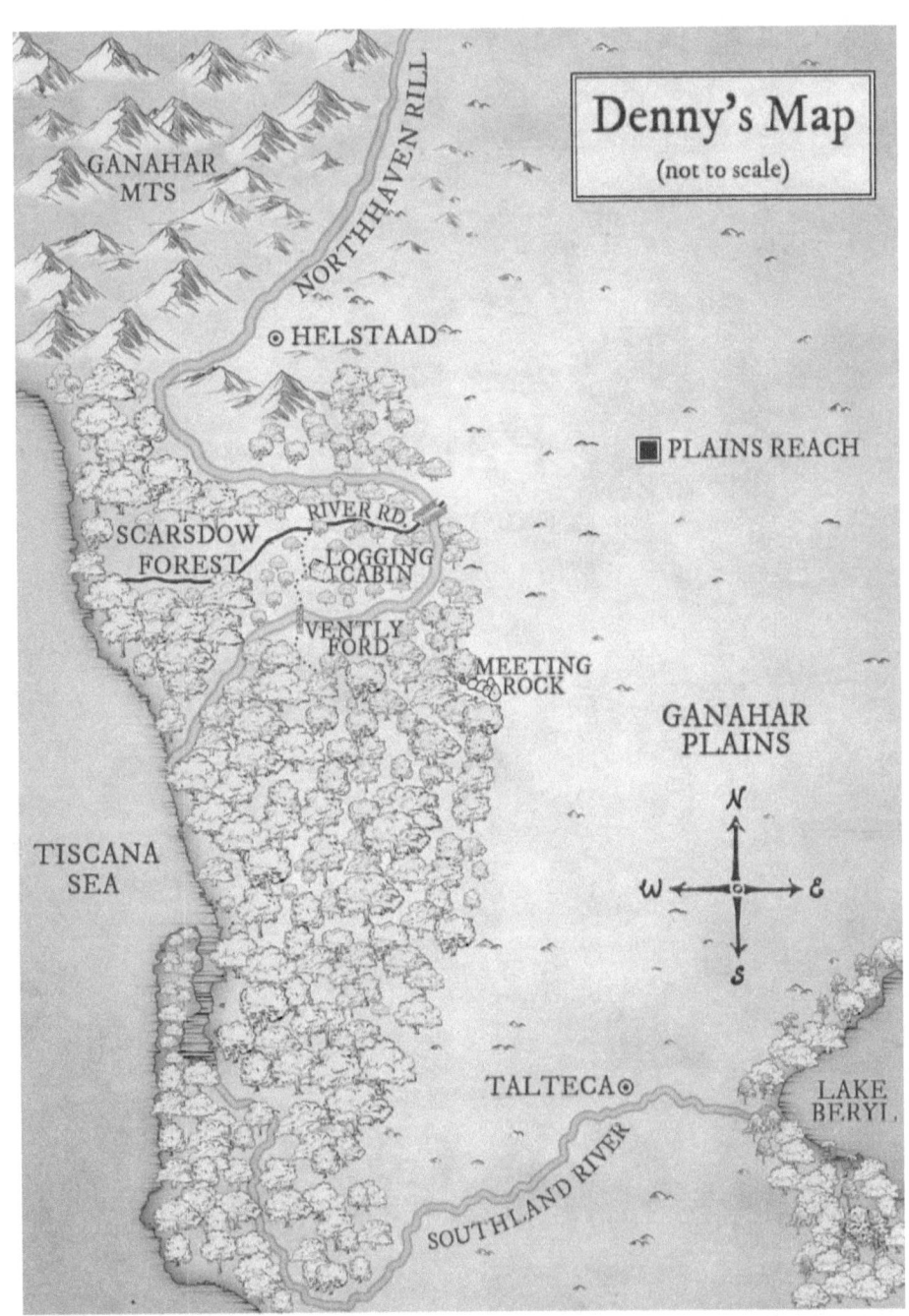

Denny's Map
(not to scale)

GANAHAR
MTS

NORTHHAVEN RILL

⊙ HELSTAAD

■ PLAINS REACH

RIVER RD

SCARSDOW
FOREST

LOGGING
CABIN

VENTLY
FORD

MEETING
ROCK

GANAHAR
PLAINS

TISCANA
SEA

N

W ←—⊙—→ E

S

TALTECA ⊙

LAKE
BERYL

SOUTHLAND RIVER

Part 1

(Two Years Ago)

Chapter 1

$(5.37 \times 10^3$ light years from Earth / 52 km southeast of Helstaad)

Based on all available data, today's battle — if indeed the men of Didara still possessed sufficient courage to engage in one — would no doubt prove decisive. Today would indelibly fix the new balance of power on this continent in the minds of its people. *And who better to communicate this new understanding than those select few Estorian soldiers I allow to survive this day,* the Warden Combat System concluded, a predatory smile spreading across its temporarily invisible visage.

Having already run several thousand exquisitely elaborate simulations, the WCS had a high degree of confidence that the outcome of any military engagement with the Estorian Army — minor statistical variations aside, of course — was all but certain.

I will be positioned as this continent's undisputed ruler, it thought, *revered, like none this world has seen beyond the realms of their largely forgotten mythology. They will gladly follow me, but not out of some misguided sense of loyalty. No. After today, I will represent an undeniable new reality, one that many of them might have fancied themselves too sophisticated to believe. They will stand in wondrous awe at the return of the magical arts. They will honor me ... fear me ...*

perhaps even worship me as a god. Any who do not, will simply be eliminated.

Never short on confidence, Warden Combat Systems (WCS) were sentient, ultra-intelligent combat droids originally created for service in the armies of the Pelaran Alliance — a confederation of breathtaking scope and power once spanning thousands of individual worlds. And although the Alliance that originally fielded millions of the powerful machines had itself largely ceased to exist, remnants of the Central Artificial Intelligence that had once managed the erstwhile empire still remained online, now free to pursue an agenda entirely of its own making.

The Lord High Protector — a title it had chosen solely of its own volition — while still based on the standard WCS design, was an enhanced unit originally designed to undertake a broad range of "black" operations. In years past, these "WCS-e" units had primarily been employed for various forms of espionage — oftentimes deployed in small, specialized combat units with the mission of eliminating difficult, high-value targets. The raw power of their world-shaping AI, however, was capable of handling far more complex assignments. In fact, the subversion of existing governmental structures and/or the establishment of new ones deemed more favorable to the Central AI had always been seen as a relatively straightforward mission for the enhanced WCS. This was particularly true for a relatively primitive world like Didara 4, to which this particular unit had been dispatched just four years earlier.

In spite of the WCS' broad spectrum of capabilities, the Central AI nevertheless considered the mission on Didara 4 something of an experiment from the outset. For its part, however, the Lord High Protector had never doubted its eventual success. In its considered opinion, the Didaran mission would both modernize and reinvigorate the original Pelaran cultivation program. For millennia, it had been a mission assigned exclusively to the so-called "Guardian" spacecraft, often taking hundreds of years to complete. But no longer. Face-to-face, direct intervention, the WCS believed, would provide a faster, less resource-intensive method of bringing a new world under the auspices of the Central AI. And its assignment to Didara 4 was nothing less than the logical next step along the pathway to establishing a state of natural (and inevitable) order across this region of the galaxy.

"It's time, my lord," the WCS heard from the long hallway outside its private chamber — a room into which no one dared enter uninvited under pain of death.

"One moment," the High Protector answered, donning the long, crimson-red cloak worn by all those in its service. During its time on Didara, the WCS had taken up a number of Human affectations, one of which was the use of a large, full-length mirror in which it could check the current state of its appearance. Since they had originally been designed to undertake the same missions as the troops they once replaced, WCS units still retained an unmistakably humanoid appearance. In fact, on worlds where the population was accustomed to seeing soldiers wearing modern, powered combat armor, the battle droid would have attracted little if any attention. Unfortunately, such was not the case on Didara 4, where the term "armor" still referred to the traditional steel mail and plate occasionally used by various infantry and cavalry units across both of the Estorian continents.

Turning now to gaze upon itself momentarily, the WCS quickly ran through a series of diagnostics to ensure all of its systems were operating at peak efficiency. This included a quick scan of the condition of its exoskeleton — which it found to be undamaged, just as expected. Satisfied, it activated a network composed of several hundred tiny holo-emitters located throughout its body, instantly "skinning" itself with a field mimicking both the look and feel of human flesh across all of its exposed areas. The effect was dramatic, transforming the droid's brutal, utilitarian appearance to that of the undeniably dashing Lord High Protector of Didara 4.

Although the WCS was vaguely aware that such indulgences could be dangerous on a number of levels, it had nevertheless become somewhat fond of its own appearance. Focusing its attention on its face, it smiled briefly at its reflection before spinning on its heels to depart the room with a flourish of its long, flowing cloak.

"Any surprises, Sir Frederick?" the WCS asked as it rounded the corner from its antechamber and stepped into the long corridor running down the center of the building.

"No, my lord," came the immediate reply from the Lord Protector's most trusted personal servant and majordomo. "Our scouts have just returned and report that the disposition, strength, and composition of the

Estorian forces is unchanged. One development that is a bit unexpected, however, is that a General Tinian has approached with a small entourage under a flag of truce."

"*Really?* You astonish me, sir. Are they here to offer terms already?" it chuckled confidently.

"Not yet, my lord. But they are requesting a parley with you," Frederick replied apologetically.

"I see," the WCS sighed. "Sometimes, Sir Frederick, I feel that we impose far too many … *rules* on ourselves when engaging in warfare, particularly given the fact that there is such a disparity of power between the opposing sides in this case. I can't help but feel that it somehow smacks of impertinence. Don't you agree?"

"I agree completely, my lord. I can send them away if you wish. We can certainly deny their request for parley. Or, if you choose, we can respond with an immediate attack."

"No, no, I'll see them," it replied, shaking its head resignedly. "One thing I must admit is that — where the general population is concerned, at least — Humans are more inclined to accept being ruled by someone they subjectively judge to be on the side of what they perceive as 'good.'"

"A relative term, in my experience, my lord," Sir Frederick said, inclining his head thoughtfully.

"Yes, and that is entirely my point. I believe the most accurate definition of 'good,' in most people's minds, comes down to whatever it is they believe best serves their own self-interest at any particular moment in time. Everything else must necessarily be judged as evil … at least to some degree," the High Protector said.

For the next few minutes, the two walked in silence as they wound their way through a series of connecting hallways until they eventually exited the Lord High Protector's personal residence through a rather imposing-looking stone-lined entryway. Although composed of over twenty sturdily built structures, the compound in which the residence stood was not a fortification in any traditional sense of the word. There were no walls with battlements and no weaponry of any type in evidence anywhere on the property's vast, two-hundred-and-fifty-square kilometers. In fact, the only apparent nod towards the possible need to defend the site against attack was the fact that it was located atop the highest point for many kilometers in every direction. This afforded most of the buildings with long, clear fields of fire, should the need ever arise. Overall, the grounds had much more the appearance of a fine country estate than a grand seat of power, let alone a military fortification designed to withstand a determined attack from thousands of well-armed troops.

All of this was, of course, very much intentional. The Warden Combat System (enhanced) had been deployed here alone, with no external support of any sort and only minimal advanced equipment — which was primarily for emergency use only. What it *did* have was a virtually limitless storehouse of knowledge at its disposal, including the combined military and political experiences of over a thousand generations from Pelara alone, not to mention the hundreds of additional worlds that once composed its grand Alliance. In addition, the WCS itself was all but indestructible — at least from the standpoint of any weapon likely to be brought to bear in a preindustrial civilization such as this one on the southern continent of Estoria. Given enough time, the powerful droid was fully capable of single-handedly defeating any force of arms the Didarans could field against it — even without resorting to the use of some of the more advanced weapons it had at its disposal.

But destruction, the High Protector reminded itself, was not its objective. The goal was respect, cooperation, obedience ... *subjugation* ... all for the advancement of the Central AI. These things would obviously not be achieved through senseless slaughter or simply by terrifying the populace into a groveling state of supplication. If, on the other hand, they could be convinced of something far more interesting ... not merely his superiority, but also his gracious willingness to assist them .... The key, he knew, was to appeal to their most basic hierarchy of needs and desires, pushing them forward technologically while simultaneously offering his protection. *That* was the state of affairs that would ultimately bring the entire world into line — yet another resource to be exploited like any other.

Yes, he thought — a distant process within the recesses of his incredibly complex neural network recognizing irony in the fact that he had begun referring to himself using masculine, Human pronouns to match his appearance. *I will usher in a new age of prosperity for the Didaran people. It will begin today — here, on this continent. Soon afterward, the cultivation of this world will proceed ... and not in the centuries previously required. Didara 4 will become the dominant power in this region of the galaxy in mere decades ... I will make it so.*

"There they are, my lord," Sir Frederick said, pointing towards a group of men standing with their horses next to a small grove of trees situated approximately one kilometer away. "Shall I signal for them to approach and spare us the walk?"

The High Protector stopped in mid-stride, quickly surveying the surrounding terrain with a level of detail he knew would not likely fall within the Didarans' technological capabilities for another thousand years — without his assistance, of course. "No, I believe I will take this opportunity to remind them of what they're up against," he answered, his holographically projected face now adorned with a disarmingly pleasant smile.

"An excellent time to do so, my lord," Frederick said, a look of satisfaction now spreading across his own perpetually dour face.

A fraction of a second later, the WCS had issued a series of orders to the four members of his elite heavy infantry unit who had silently fallen into a loose formation just off to his left and right. Inside each of the soldier's helmets, the Lord Protector's instructions were instantaneously presented via easily understood symbology, with additional details available via text, if required. In response, the four soldiers quickly spread out along a fifty-meter-long line to either side of their leader, then paused to await the order to execute the remainder of their instructions.

The High Protector had always known that, despite his great strength and intellectual power, the cultivation of Didara 4 on a global scale was far too great a task to accomplish without various forms of assistance from the local populace. Besides, what better way to demonstrate his unassailable superiority than through the creation of a relatively small cadre of allies — a military unit, of sorts, composed solely of members of their own species — all of whom had dedicated their lives to serving their Lord High Protector? And in return for their dedicated service, he would grant them "gifts" of such extraordinary power that they would be the envy of all who beheld them — gifts that even the most forward-thinking Didarans could only describe as *magical*.

That thought still echoing within his consciousness, the WCS smiled broadly in recognition of the fact that this particular goal had already been accomplished to a large degree. And to reinforce this particular point, the four members of his elite cadre to which he had just issued orders now signaled their readiness to proceed.

Although the WCS had never quite settled on a name he thought sounded sufficiently awe-inspiring while still conveying what he saw as their intended purpose, he had recently begun referring to his quasi-military unit as the "Shepherds." As originally intended, all of its members were Didaran, but none were from the southern Estorian continent. It was simply not worth the risk that a chance encounter with friends or family members from their former lives might serve to rekindle memories carefully repressed during their "conditioning" for duty.

Each Shepherd had been carefully selected based on their intelligence and mental toughness, along with a host of other traits common among special operations troops on countless worlds throughout the galaxy. Once deemed ready for service, the WCS had equipped each soldier with a modified version of the combat armor once used by Pelaran troops in centuries past — before their technology had become sufficiently advanced to allow the risks associated with combat to be borne only by machines.

Now, seeing that all was in readiness for an entrance worthy of the future supreme ruler of this world, the Lord High Protector transmitted a single-word order: "Execute."

Without hesitation, the four Shepherds selected the voice augmentation function built into their armored suits. Intended both as an alternative means of communication during the heat of battle as well as for use in psychological warfare, the "VA" system allowed either the soldiers' own voices or a variety of other sound effects to be radiated in all directions (or focused on a specific target). With a maximum volume of over one hundred and twenty decibels — roughly the same volume as a clap of thunder — the system could also be used as a painful, yet nonlethal weapon. For today's purposes, each of the four soldiers began a synchronized broadcast of the sounds produced during an orbital bombardment utilizing heavy particle beam weapons. Then, with the assistance of the synthetic musculature built into their battle suits, the four Shepherds set off at a speed of over sixty kilometers per hour in the direction of General Tinian's delegation.

Realizing that his troops would reach their destination in just under one minute, the Lord High Protector began his own portion of the demonstration. Spreading his arms dramatically out to his sides, he activated a network of gravitic emitters distributed throughout his heavily armored exoskeleton. With some emitters dedicated to the task of "mass canceling" while others created a horizontal propulsive force, the WCS rose majestically into the air to an altitude of just over fifty meters. Once he was sure he had the full attention of the Estorian delegation, he set off in their direction, matching the forward advance of his Shepherd troops.

From the perspective of General Tinian's delegation, the approach of the Lord High Protector and his small squad of shock troops produced an overwhelming wall of sound they might easily have mistaken for the end of their world. It was as if the very air itself were being torn apart like giant strips of cloth as the fast-moving Shepherds shook the ground with a series of sounds never before heard by anyone on Didara 4. Though unknown to the soldiers on either side, the sounds booming forth from the High Protector's soldiers were those produced by superheated channels of ionized air being pushed explosively aside by pulsed particle beams traveling at nearly the speed of light. Immediately following the terrible, rending sounds of energy weapons fire ripping through a planet's atmosphere came the inevitable explosions as the powerful beams slammed into the ground, releasing their titanic cargos of destructive energy on their targets.

Although both men instinctively dropped into a crouching position when the sounds began, neither General Tinian nor Colonel Simms — in command of the 3rd Cavalry Regiment preparing for battle nearby — were particularly intimidated by the spectacle of the High Protector's approach. Both men quickly recognized the source of the admittedly impressive noise, covered their ears, and then bravely (albeit perhaps foolishly) held their ground as the Shepherd troops took up flanking positions to either side of their small entourage.

The WCS, for his part, halted his approach, then simply hovered in place for a long moment, arms still outstretched to his sides. Well versed on the historical accomplishments of Humans across hundreds of worlds over thousands of years, the High Protector knew that it was unwise to underestimate them, regardless of their current population or technological status. Nevertheless, he could not resist spending a moment savoring the sight of the two senior Estorian military commanders staring upwards, as if eagerly awaiting his orders. *As it should and will soon be,* he thought.

On the ground, General Tinian noticed that Colonel Simms was trying to get his attention, then realized that the cavalry officer was shouting something to him in a vain attempt to be heard over the tremendous din still being generated by the High Protector's soldiers. *"WHAT?!"* he yelled, unable to make out even the slightest hint of what the younger man was trying to say.

"I *SAID*," Tinian finally understood, largely by reading the man's lips, then clearly heard "THAT GUY'S A JACKASS!" with perfect clarity as the deafening wall of sound abruptly ceased.

"Humph, that's the Gods' truth," the general grunted under his breath, stifling a chuckle in spite of the rather embarrassing breach of protocol.

"Good morning, General," the WCS said, still broadcasting at an ear-splitting volume, still hovering at near-treetop level, and apparently choosing to ignore the colonel's insult. "You have approached my home under a flag of truce, which I will, of course, honor … for now.

But you also trespass on my property in the company of what I can only describe as the … *remnants* of a once-powerful army." Here, the High Protector paused for effect, finally lowering his outstretched arms and gesturing off in the direction of the assembled Estorian troops. "How can I interpret these actions as anything other than those of a man determined to make some sort of dramatic last stand?" he continued. "So, please … *General* … I implore you not to needlessly forfeit the lives of the men under your command."

Tinian stared upward, saying nothing at first as he attempted to shade his eyes from the glare of the rising sun. "Would you, uh …" he began tentatively, wondering at the notion that one in possession of such incredible capabilities would utilize them to carry on in such an absurd manner. "Would you mind coming down here, so I won't have to yell?"

Shortly after the High Protector's arrival nearly two years prior, the Estorian government had begun receiving massive caches of equipment from a mysterious source known only as "The Broker." Among this treasure trove were volumes containing various types of information, including several detailed intelligence documents regarding the so-called "Lord High Protector." General Tinian had read them all but had not been sure what to make of much of what they contained. This was particularly true of the portions asserting that the man he was speaking to at the moment wasn't flesh and blood at all, but some sort of advanced machine. What he *did* know, based upon numerous examples from his world's history, was that a tyrant was a tyrant. And tyrants must be resisted to the last drop of blood, if necessary, regardless of who, what, or how powerful they appeared to be.

"Of course," the WCS replied, lowering the volume of his voice considerably. "I beg you will forgive my lack of courtesy, General Tinian," he continued after a brief pause, touching down effortlessly just a few meters away.

One thing's for sure ... whatever this thing is, it has absolutely no fear of us, Tinian thought. For better or worse, today's battle would undoubtedly mark a turning point in the war, and the general felt the hairs on the back of his neck stand on end as he wondered what form of retribution might ultimately be unleashed on the Estorian people as a result.

"We're not here to trespass, sir, but we —"

"You may address me as 'Lord Protector,' or simply 'my lord,'" the WCS interrupted.

Tinian paused, glancing at Colonel Simms, in whose strikingly blue eyes he noted a flash of amusement tinged with exactly the sort of defiant self-confidence he always liked to see in his fighting commanders. After giving himself a moment to compose his thoughts and avoid any expression of anger in his response, he drew in a deep breath and continued.

"I meant no disrespect, uh, ... Protector," he said, trying his level best to filter any hint of irony from his voice. "But my country was founded on a number of basic principles, one of the most important of which is self-determination. We believe in the nobility of all individuals. Accordingly, we don't recognize titles like 'lord,' 'sir,' and the like ... and *certainly* not 'king.' So please don't take offense if we —"

"Oh, but I *do* take offense, General," the WCS interrupted again, a self-satisfied smile now gracing his holographically projected face. "And your people's naive idea that everyone is entitled to the same level of deference and respect is simply … well, I hesitate to call it old-fashioned, since I believe your ancestors were much more realistic about such things. So, I'll simply say that failing to render the proper courtesies to your betters is both foolish and short-sighted."

Having spent his entire adult life in serving in the Estorian Army, Gerald Tinian had long since learned how to manage his emotions in the face of pompous, arrogant blowhards just like the one standing in front of him now. But assuming the intelligence indicating he was having a conversation with a … *thing* rather than a man was accurate, the emotion he felt at the moment was more akin to disappointment than anger. Presumably, someone must have … *constructed* it, after all. And he couldn't help but feel a vague sense of sadness that the end result of the incredible scientific and engineering knowledge that must have gone into it was nothing more than a mirror reflecting some of the worst qualities mankind had to offer. It had to be destroyed, he knew, or at least forced to leave his world forever. So before trusting himself to speak again, the old general said a quick prayer to the Gods that today he was finally in possession of the weapons required to successfully accomplish that task.

"Well, be that as it may," Tinian continued, "I'm here this morning in hopes of avoiding unnecessary bloodshed on both sides."

"Excellent. I am deeply gratified to hear it, General. Please do go on."

"I have been authorized as a representative of the Estorian Federation to restate our previous position that we cannot accept the terms which you have repeatedly offered over the past couple of years."

"Oh, come now, General. You are a career military man, after all. You of all people must understand that there *are* no terms … indeed can *be* no terms in a case where one side has achieved such overwhelming superiority over the other. I have offered, and continue to offer, to allow your government to simply cease hostilities and accept that my presence here represents a permanent and fundamental shift in the course of history on your world. But take heart, General, for it is a shift that will benefit the people of Estoria in ways you cannot possibly imagine. I have a mission here — one that will bring about advancements in every conceivable field of study, allowing Didara to rise and take its rightful place among the other prominent worlds in this region of the galaxy."

"Yessir, I understand, and that does sound wonderful, to be sure. But, if you'll forgive me, we've heard all of this before. And as tempting as your offer may sound, we simply cannot accept any assistance that must be purchased with the forfeiture of our freedoms — as individuals, as a nation, and as a sovereign world."

"I see," the WCS replied, his previously patronizing expression growing suddenly more grave. "And do you, General Tinian, purport to speak for all of the four billion souls currently inhabiting the 'sovereign world' of Didara 4?"

"No, sir, I do not. I have no authority to speak on behalf of anyone beyond the Estorian Federation. And let me be clear, I am a soldier, not a diplomat. I am not a policymaker. I am a public servant. And, as such, I am merely an instrument of my government's policies. Once again, I am authorized only to restate the Estorian Federation's previous position. It is our collective hope that we will ultimately come to some sort of mutually beneficial arrangement — one that does not require our people to simply acquiesce to your terms."

"And, I assume, you are aware that I have offered no alternatives to your ... acquiescence, as you put it?"

"Yes, sir, we are aware that you have not yet agreed to any of our proposed, alternative solutions. Nor have you presented any of your own. But we remain hopeful that such a solution can be reached if we agree to work together towards that end."

"No, General. I can assure you that no alternative solutions will be offered or accepted. So, may I further assume that you intend to continue to fight in a futile attempt to delay the inevitable progress of your world? If so, you might find that my response will be less ... *measured* than in the past."

Tinian looked down at the ground, thoughts of the tens of thousands of lives lost thus far in the fight against whatever this strange, vile creature was at the forefront of his mind. As expected, this, like every other attempt to negotiate with the High Protector over the past two years, would come to naught. After reflecting in silence for a long moment, he looked wearily back up into the eyes of what he had always known would be his last enemy and made his reply in a calm but firm tone. "No

23

one hates war more than soldiers do, sir. But if our only choice is to live as slaves under the yoke of an oppressor — regardless of what form that oppression might take — then, yes, we will most assuredly fight."

Chapter 2

Didara 4, South Estorian Continent, Ganahar Plains
(2 hours later - 54 km southeast of Helstaad)

"I can't help but think we may be sending all of those men to their deaths," Colonel Simms observed quietly as he surveyed the infantry forces arrayed before them through his spyglass.

"Well, Nathaniel, you will recall that quite a bit of what you're looking at was your idea," General Tinian replied with a sideways glance. "So, if you had any better ideas, I would have appreciated hearing about them two weeks ago. You know as well as I do that the only chance we have is to get those damned Shepherd troops out in the open with enough room for your boys to come in here and take 'em down."

"Yes, sir, I know … it's still a good plan," the younger cavalry officer replied sheepishly. "But, dear *Gods,* I hope this works," he added under his breath as he collapsed his spyglass. Satisfied that all was in place for his role in the attack to begin, Simms swung himself smoothly up into the saddle for the short ride back to his 3rd Cavalry Regiment, now located just over two kilometers to the rear of the main body.

General Tinian had chosen this particular approach to the High Protector's compound primarily because it was the only direction that afforded him a means of concealing the cavalry regiment's nearly twelve hundred horsemen. He harbored no illusion that such a large force would remain unseen by the enemy. What he did hope, however, was that they would not be observed in sufficient detail to reveal any specifics regarding the weapons nearly three-fourths of the cavalry troopers would be carrying into battle for the first time. Fortunately, although his ultimate objective to the north was located at the highest point in the area, the terrain just to the south sloped off rapidly towards what might once have been a riverbed — precisely the cover he had been looking for.

"It's got to work," Tinian said. "This is all we've got left at this point. And I suspect if we don't manage to turn things around here, the Federation Assembly is going to take us out of the field for good."

"Surrender?" Colonel Simms asked, incredulous at the notion that such a thing was even within the realm of possibility. In his mind, as long as there were still horses left in the world and cavalrymen left to ride them, the fight would continue.

"You can call it that if you like, Colonel, but the truth of the matter is, we will no longer have any realistic military options available to us. As you know, what we've got with us here today constitutes the bulk of the remaining fighting force we have at our disposal in the region ... for the moment, at least. We would be hard-pressed to put down a cross-border raid right now from one of the better-organized Northern Alliance factions, let alone continue to sustain heavy losses in a protracted war against ... whatever the hell this thing is we're fighting. I just hope the northerners' intelligence is every bit as useless as it has always been, and they don't realize how bad things have gotten for us down here."

"Humph," Simms grunted. "If *their* leadership had any sense at all, they'd be down here fighting alongside us instead of holding on to all of that separatist nonsense. Then again, General, maybe if we'll just buy into what the Lord High Protector keeps telling us and stop resisting, he'll solve all of our problems for us. Hell, maybe we won't even need our horses anymore. We'll all just be flying around everywhere like he does."

"Nope," Tinian said definitively. "There's not a thing he's selling that I'll ever be willing to buy. Now, is the 3rd Cav ready?"

"Yes, General."

"Very good. You'd best be getting back there, then. I have a feeling this is all going to happen pretty fast," Tinian said, offering his subordinate commander a salute in farewell.

"Whatever happens, it's been an honor and a pleasure, General," Simms said, returning his long-time mentor's salute.

"Banish all doubt from your heart and focus only on victory, Colonel."

"We're *cavalry*, sir … and too full of ourselves to do anything else," Simms said with a smile, then wheeled his horse about and headed off to the south at a full gallop.

"Good luck, Nathaniel," Tinian said, half to himself, staring intently after the retreating cavalryman while trying his level best to think of any detail he might have somehow missed.

Turning back towards his assembled infantry forces, Tinian retrieved his spyglass from his coat pocket and surveyed the huge formation of troops one last time. He was still somewhat surprised the High Protector had allowed him to choose the ground for such a large-scale engagement … welcomed it, even. There had been no harassment of any sort while two full-strength infantry brigades — nine thousand men in total — formed up in what was essentially his back yard. And, as far as the general could tell, the enemy's scouts had not even bothered to reconnoiter the Estorian forces arrayed against them since early this morning — well before his own, spectacularly unsuccessful negotiation with the High Protector.

Arrogant, Tinian thought to himself as he surveyed the impressive formation arrayed three ranks deep across the field in front of him. *Damned arrogant*, he repeated with just the hint of a smile. *That just might help balance things out a little.*

The two Estorian infantry brigades — spread across a three-kilometer-long line visible from just about anywhere in the High Protector's compound — represented the largest force fielded to oppose him for over six months. Every previous encounter had ended in a defeat for the Estorians, but the first few had resulted in relatively light casualties before the High Protector had elected to retire from the field. Each subsequent engagement, though, had been increasingly disastrous for the Estorian Army, with the most recent large-scale encounter ending in what could only be described as a rout. During that battle, the High Protector had allowed his Shepherd shock troops to remain engaged for several hours before finally pulling them back, resulting in the near-total loss of a force nearly as large as the one General Tinian commanded today.

"Corporal Mateland, readiness check if you please," the general ordered.

"Yes, General. Transmitting readiness check," the young flagman replied, immediately executing a surprisingly concise series of signals to query each of the twelve battalions present in the field as well as the 3rd Cavalry Regiment to the rear.

Despite the continued reliance on flag-based communications, General Tinian, for the first time in the history of Didara 4, now had the option of being in constant radio contact with each of his battalion-level and above commanders. Unfortunately, the information supplied with the still-mysterious tactical radios had warned repeatedly that the High Protector could easily intercept any radio transmissions — most likely decoding the rudimentary encryption capability they possessed in real-time. It also made clear the fact that the location of any active transmitter would be immediately known to the enemy, obviously attracting far more unwanted attention than simple flag signaling. In the general's mind, either of these problems rendered the devices largely useless for transmitting any sort of detailed operational information.

Even without these drawbacks, Tinian had a healthy dose of skepticism where most of the newfangled technological marvels that had come into the Estorian Army's possession over the past couple of years were concerned. So it was with full awareness of the irony implicit in his decision that he had chosen to maintain radio silence ... with one exception.

"Battalion commanders all report readiness, General," Corporal Mateland reported a few moments later, then executed a crisp about-face to receive the report from the rear. "3rd Cavalry Regiment reports ready as well," he concluded.

"Very well. Signal all forces to commence their attacks as planned."

"Signaling all forces to commence attacks as planned, sir," the corporal repeated, ensuring that such an important order was understood correctly prior to transmission.

"That's correct, Corporal, thank you."

Reaching back to open his saddlebag, General Tinian retrieved his small, digital radio. With a look on his face that would likely have been the same had he been handling a venomous snake, he turned the knob on top to power up the device and then keyed the transmit button with a series of three, one-second-long clicks. As planned, the three clicks were dutifully repeated by one of his battalion commanders — just to ensure that a transmission had occurred — but not by its intended recipients. Hoping that the infernal instrument had achieved the desired purpose, Tinian powered down and returned it to his saddlebag.

Moments after the next series of flag signals had been completed, the sounds of brigade, battalion, company, and platoon commanders echoing the general's orders could be heard drifting across the whole of the field.

"May the Gods protect us and grant us the strength to defeat those who would oppress us," Tinian said quietly. Seconds later, the two enormous, brigade-sized line formations began their ponderous move up the long slope in the direction of the High Protector's compound. "For better or worse, I guess we'll know soon enough," he added, then spurred his horse into a gallop and rode quickly off in the direction of his infantry's left flank in hopes of obtaining a better view of the battlespace.

Within a few minutes of the infantry formations beginning their uphill march towards the objective, a small, rather disorderly gaggle of the High Protector's Shepherd troops appeared in the distance, milling about just outside the enemy compound. As was often the case, they appeared to be carrying no weapons whatsoever, clearly communicating their belief that the forces arrayed against them did not pose a sufficient threat for weapons to be necessary. The High Protector would continue to allow the Estorians to fight on their terms, at the time and place of their choosing and in the style they preferred. Yet he would still defeat them ... with brutal, effortless efficiency. His message was clear enough: surrender was the only reasonable course of action available to the Estorians.

Although the Shepherds' movements did not indicate any degree of urgency, they did finally manage to form themselves into six distinct groups that at length began making their way down the long slope to meet the advancing Estorian infantry. Each squad of Shepherds was composed of only six soldiers — with each squad apparently intended to intercept two full battalions of Estorian troops.

Anyone unfamiliar with the situation might assume the High Protector's meager detachment of Shepherd troops now slowly approaching the seemingly endless line of Estorian infantry could only be a ruse of some sort — a deliberate subterfuge, perhaps designed to distract attention from something far more significant occurring elsewhere on the battlefield. The Estorians harbored no such illusions. Many of their number had experienced combat against the High Protector's troops before and had firsthand knowledge of the incredible level of destructive power they were capable of unleashing on the battlefield. Even with their foes outnumbered by two hundred and fifty to one, most of the Estorian infantrymen fully expected to lose their lives this day, on the very field across which they now marched.

Upon reaching his vantage point atop a small knoll on his infantry's left flank, General Tinian turned to look back in the direction of the 3rd Cavalry Regiment's assembly area and was gratified to both see and *feel* the pounding approach of the first six of its platoons. Their loose, fast-moving formations — each composed of approximately thirty-three troopers — came thundering up out of the ravine in which they had been hiding across a broad front. Shortly thereafter, the cavalrymen had merged into two large groups of three platoons each before angling off to flank either side of the advancing infantry line.

Even at a full gallop, it took the cavalry troops nearly three tense minutes to cover the intervening distance and overtake their own advancing troops. And as the whole of the assembled Estorian forces continued to slowly close the distance to their enemies, every officer present who had been briefed on the general's plans held their collective breaths. Their greatest fear had always been that the Shepherd troops would sprint forward immediately, engaging the infantry formations at close range. Fortunately, the powerful enemy shock troops — or perhaps their master — seemed to revel in the anticipation of the destruction they would soon inflict upon the hapless Estorians. At long last, both groups of cavalry rushed past either end of the infantry line, gained sufficient clearance to maneuver, then angled across the now-open field — each of the six platoons heading in the direction of its preassigned squad of Shepherd troops.

As General Tinian waited for his light cavalry skirmishers to make first contact with the enemy troops, he had more than enough time to question the wisdom of his strategy. Just as he had done countless times over the past several weeks, he wondered if it might have been more effective — or at least more convincing — for the infantry to fire several volleys before allowing the cavalry troops to close with the enemy.

No, he counseled himself, *the sole purpose of this first contact is to delay the enemy's approach and fix his position in the field for as long as possible. Patience, Gerald ...*

In an impressive display of horsemanship, each of the cavalry platoons approached to within approximately fifty meters of their targets, firing their smoothbore carbine muskets in turn as they passed. As expected, the .69 caliber musket ball projectiles, while packing a significant punch in terms of raw kinetic energy, were largely ineffective against their steadily advancing targets. A few ragged holes could be seen in the mottled green fatigues worn by the Shepherd soldiers, each one revealing the matte black surface of their form-fitting combat suits beneath. But once the musket balls made contact with their armor, a thin layer of fibers infused with magnetorheological (MR) fluid thickened dramatically and instantaneously at the point of impact.

The result, just as had been the case during every previous engagement, was a superficial and temporary indentation in the armor's surface. Otherwise, the large-diameter balls did no real damage. What the musket balls *did* manage to accomplish, to General Tinian's great relief, was a temporary halt in the enemy soldiers' advance.

Undeterred by the apparent futility of their initial attack, the six Estorian cavalry platoons galloped off towards the enemy's rear, preventing them from mounting an immediate counterattack while also providing themselves with additional room to maneuver. With barely a pause, they wheeled their horses about and charged again, this time drawing their sabers. In response, the Shepherd soldiers turned in the direction of the new threat, opening up their small formations as they prepared to defend themselves.

It took only seconds for the first cavalry trooper to reach his intended target. As he galloped past, the horseman viciously swung his saber down into the side of the Shepherd soldier's neck. The curved, razor-sharp blade made an impressive metallic ringing sound as the steel made contact with the combat suit's adaptive outer layers. As was the case with the musket balls fired just moments before, however, the energy of the blade's impact was distributed harmlessly away from the suit's occupant by the seemingly impenetrable armor.

The Shepherd soldier, ignoring the saber blow altogether, immediately lowered his right shoulder and — exerting a horizontal force well over twenty times what his own muscles were capable of generating without augmentation — slammed into the side of the cavalryman's horse. The savage impact instantly checked the five-hundred-and-ninety-kilogram animal's forward motion, producing a sickening series of whip-like cracks as its massive rib cage gave way. The horse went down immediately, landing on its right side and pinning its helpless rider beneath. Unable to regain its feet, the huge animal lay thrashing on the ground, gasping for air in a vain attempt to catch its breath in spite of multiple punctures to its left lung.

With no hesitation whatsoever, the Shepherd soldier took several bounding steps to where the horse was lying, raised its massive neck off the ground, and, with an incredibly violent twist, severed the animal's head from its body before tossing it casually aside. He then walked slowly around the horse's now motionless body to where its young rider still struggled to free himself from beneath his huge mount. Now in the full throes of panic after seeing what the enemy soldier had just done to his horse, the young cavalryman — sword still in hand — took several wild, futile swipes at the legs of the approaching Shepherd. On the rider's final attempt, his saber was caught in mid-swing and ripped from his hands. The Shepherd soldier then placed his boot on the cavalryman's neck and pushed down while simultaneously dragging his foot to the rear with the full, brutal force his suit's synthetic musculature could produce. In seconds, the cavalryman was dead — crimson blood gurgling from his severed jugular to combine with the remains of his windpipe, spine, and the dry soil beneath to form an expanding smear of dark mud. Confident that he had dispatched his first enemy of the day, the Shepherd soldier straightened himself back to his full height and turned his attention to the task of searching for another target.

The situation was much the same across the entire battlefield. And within a few minutes after the first six cavalry platoons had opened fire, their numbers had been reduced by more than half. For its part, the Estorian infantry line, in hopes of providing the cavalry platoons with as much space to maneuver and fire as possible, had simply halted their forward progress and now stood helplessly by several hundred meters away. To the infantry officers' relief, it seemed as though the Lord High Protector's soldiers were willing to spend whatever time was necessary to destroy the cavalry platoons in detail while completely ignoring all of the other forces arrayed against them on the battlefield.

To his surprise, General Tinian also noticed that the Shepherd soldiers appeared completely oblivious to the arrival of fully half of the 3rd Cavalry Regiment — nearly six hundred strong — as they too raced past the Estorian infantry line at a full gallop to join their beleaguered comrades. In fact, it was not until what remained of the first attack wave had wheeled their horses about and began a rapid withdrawal from the field that the enemy soldiers appeared to even notice the thundering approach of this new, much larger force. Still, they made no pretense at pursuit, busying themselves instead with reestablishing their original six formations — allowing the Estorian cavalrymen free reign to retire their first attack wave while preparing to launch their next.

Tinian could hardly believe his luck thus far. In spite of losing well over one hundred good men and most of their horses during the first few minutes of the battle, his biggest fear had always been that the enemy soldiers would immediately charge his vulnerable infantry line. Fortunately, they had not yet chosen to do so, although the general had absolutely no idea why this was the case. It was abundantly clear to anyone who had observed the battle thus far that the Shepherd troops had absolute control of the battlespace. Accordingly, they could move about the field with impunity, pressing their attack in any direction and at any time they saw fit to do so. Why, then, were they bothering to mill about on the field once again, taking the time to reorganize their formations back to their state prior to the initial attack?

Could this strange behavior represent some sort of command and control problem? Tinian wondered, *or is it more a reflection of the individual soldiers' lack of expertise? Better still, could this be an indication of the High Protector's general lack of confidence in his troops? Perhaps most of them had no prior military experience before joining his forces — whether voluntarily or involuntarily.* Tinian paused, looking up and down the line once again at the six, still fully intact enemy formations. *Then again,* he thought, *this may be nothing more than an effort to ensure all of our troops see that all of his troops are still standing. Please, Gods, let that no longer be true momentarily ...*

Chapter 3

Didara 4, South Estorian Continent, Ganahar Plains
(53 km southeast of Helstaad)

Just as the original group of six cavalry platoons before them had done, the new, much larger group entered the battlefield in two distinct formations, each one racing past either end of their own infantry line. This time, however, rather than angling off for an immediate, running attack on the enemy, all eighteen platoons formed a firing line of their own just forward of the still-stationary Estorian infantry. With the fluid, well-drilled precision for which they had long been known, C through H Troops of the 3rd Cavalry Regiment quickly reached their designated positions. And as a series of commands echoed along the length of their line, each trooper drew a weapon from the leather scabbard hanging from the side of his saddle — a weapon that had never before been employed in battle on Didara 4.

Although roughly the same shape as the smoothbore flintlock muskets used by the first attack wave, the new, lever-action rifles were generally referred to as "Winchesters" by the Estorians. The members of the General Staff had no idea precisely what the strange name referenced in the accompanying documentation referred to (the weapon's inventor, perhaps?), but it had stuck, nonetheless. Had these weapons not appeared in their giant metal shipping containers beginning just six months before, the technological improvements they represented would undoubtedly have taken at least an additional century to arrive on Didara 4. And given their current struggle against the High Protector, the Estorian leadership knew all too well that the delay of even one additional year without decisive action would result in nothing less than the loss of its status as a sovereign world.

The new rifles were significantly more compact than the weapons the Estorians were used to, making them ideally suited for use on horseback. When first introduced to the Winchesters, the first thing cavalry troopers generally noticed was the absence of flint and steel — although the hammer itself was familiar enough. Perhaps the most obvious change was the addition of a long, oval handle, of sorts, located on the underside of the weapon where its wooden stock joined with its steel receiver.

The Estorian Army's Supreme Headquarters had done everything in its power to keep the existence of the new wonder weapons a closely guarded state secret. As a result, most of the troopers now preparing to fire their new rifles had received only a short briefing on their use — and only a few of the regiment's officers had been given the opportunity to practice with live ammunition.

Now, with the firing line in position and their rifles at the ready, Colonel Simms wasted no time giving the signal to open fire — which, in this case, was the sharp crack of his own rifle firing from a position near the center of the cavalry line. Just a fraction of a second later, virtually every trooper in the second wave opened fire simultaneously. As six hundred rifles began blazing away at the Shepherd troops, it became immediately and abundantly clear that something fundamental had changed on the battlefield.

The sound produced by the repeaters, while significantly less than their old muzzle-loaders in terms of decibels, was quite different than what any of them were used to — creating more of a sharp *crack* than the resonating *boom* associated with their muskets. But by far the most obvious change was the fact that after the first volley had been fired, there was no pause to reload their weapons. Each cavalryman simply cycled their rifle's lever-action between shots and kept firing, without the need to even drop the weapon from their shoulders. The fury of the Estorian fusillade was like nothing that had ever been heard before on their world. And after each trooper had gotten off his first couple of rounds, the remainder were fired in rapid succession with almost no discernible pauses — continuing unabated until all six hundred cavalrymen had emptied their twelve-round magazines.

What only a few of those present on the battlefield understood was the fact that the rounds being fired today traveled downrange towards their targets at only about half the speed of the musket balls their soldiers had been using for generations. Add to that the fact that the projectiles they fired had only about half the mass of those fired by their old muskets, and one might easily assume that the new weapons would be even less effective than the old. These facts had been a major point of contention within the upper echelons of the Estorian Army since the new rifles had begun to arrive in mass quantities from their apparently benevolent but unknown source. Several general officers had argued that becoming dependent on the untested new weapons was not worth the risks involved, while others countered that improving their soldiers' average rate of fire by nearly an order of magnitude provided a capability they simply could not afford to ignore. Besides, they argued, the results of *not* taking advantage of the new weapons had already become clear enough.

Beyond simply allowing a soldier to fire significantly more rounds per minute, the documentation included with the new weapons described several technical advantages to ensure lethality against the High Protector's Shepherd soldiers. Chief among these was the design of the ammunition provided. The metallic cartridges, it was said, were not only self-contained — with bullet, primer, and powder in a single unit — but were also of an "armor-piercing" type, capable of penetrating the evil black battle suits worn by their enemies.

Upon inspecting the construction of the new ammunition, Estorian engineers had discovered that the bullet itself was a sharpened metallic penetrator — composed of a metallic alloy referred to in the documentation as "depleted uranium" — and jacketed in copper to prevent damage to the rifling inside the guns' barrels. The Estorians had long understood the advantages such rifling might one day offer over their current generation of smoothbore muskets but had not yet developed the tooling required to reliably manufacture them in large numbers. Upon leaving the muzzle, a bullet fired from one of the new lever-action carbines — even with their relatively short barrels — would be spinning about its longitudinal axis at nearly fifty thousand revolutions per minute. Such an incredible rate of spin would gyroscopically stabilize the bullet's flight, dramatically improving its accuracy.

Before receiving the new rifles, the only examples the Estorian gunmakers had managed to produce were notoriously difficult to load and even more difficult to manufacture. The new weapons solved the former problem via an ingenious loading port on the right side of the receiver. And the mysterious "Broker" had solved the latter by supplying incredibly detailed design documentation. Even without the capability of building the weapons themselves, however, it was thought that the Estorian Army would soon be in possession of sufficient guns and ammunition to equip their entire army for a decade or more. This was all assuming, of course, that the massive metal containers continued to arrive at regular intervals.

Despite the new weapons' many detractors, General Tinian had argued for several months that their technical advantages would provide his troops with a tremendous increase in overall firepower. Perhaps, he sincerely hoped, even enough to tip the balance in their favor against the High Protector and its surrogates. Unfortunately, he had readily admitted, short of deploying the weapons on the battlefield, there was simply no way to test their true efficacy. And now that the time had finally arrived, and the only weapons test that mattered had begun in earnest, the old general held his breath, watching and waiting for the outcome of what he knew would be seen as *his* gamble, for better or worse.

If indeed there was a silver lining in today's plan of battle, Tinian had thought, it was the fact that the engagement would be blessedly short in duration. There really was only one chance of success, after all. Now, less than thirty seconds after Colonel Simms had fired the first shot with his new rifle, all six hundred cavalrymen currently on the firing line had emptied their magazines. And as the final echoes of the deafening rifle barrage returned from the nearby foothills before quickly fading away on the plains' ever-present winds, there was a protracted moment of silence on the battlefield. Moments later, however, the unmistakable sound of cheering could be heard, distant at first, but then quickly spreading up and down the entire three-kilometer-long infantry line. Tinian could even hear cheering from the remaining four hundred members of the 3rd Cavalry Regiment, now rapidly approaching from the rear, as planned, to relieve the troopers currently on the firing line.

General Tinian stared up the hill at the closest formation of Shepherd soldiers, confused as to what his troops had seen down the line that had prompted their cheering. Taking out his spyglass once more, he saw that, while all six of the enemy troops closest to his infantry's left flank were still on their feet, none of them appeared to be moving. Examining one of the soldiers in more detail, he could see that the man's mottled, green uniform was saturated with blood in multiple locations. With the outer garment so heavily damaged from weapons fire, he could also catch glimpses of the more tightly fitting armored suit beneath — its deep, black color seeming to absorb all of the light from the midday sun. Moving his focus up to the man's face, the general noted the same expression he had seen all too often over the past several years — the blank stare of manifest death.

Something about those black suits they wore must have been preventing the soldiers from falling to the ground, Tinian reasoned. Nevertheless, every one of them he could see from his current vantage point appeared to have been hit a great many times, and, to his great relief, every one of them had the appearance of being very much deceased.

Tinian removed the spyglass from his eye and took in a deep breath, silently thanking the Gods that the new rifles might well have delivered the Estorian Army its first significant victory against the High Protector. But regardless of his enemy's status, the plan had always been for the six cavalry troops — just over six hundred men — that had just executed the second round of attacks to immediately withdraw to the infantry line's flanks. As they did so, they were to be relieved by the regiment's four remaining troops — troops I through L, until now held in reserve to the rear. Thus far, this movement was progressing smoothly, and General Tinian watched with no small sense of pride as a total of nearly one thousand cavalry troopers entered and exited the field with an air of grace and precision that belied the complexity of the maneuvers involved.

While observing the evolution of his troops, the general spotted Colonel Simms at a distance, making his way towards the infantry formation's left flank. With some arm-waving accompanied by a series of creative hand gestures, Tinian managed to signal the cavalry commander that he needed confirmation of the state of the enemy soldiers. Although all indications seemed to support the general's initial impression that all thirty-six of the Shepherd troops on the field had been killed, he was also mindful of the fact that thirty-six Shepherd soldiers mostly likely did not represent the entirety of the High Protector's available force. And although most of the 3rd Cavalry's troopers now obviously possessed the capability to kill the enemy soldiers outright, any remaining Shepherds would still represent a significant threat. This was particularly true for the nine thousand infantry soldiers stretching out across the field to his right — all of whom were still equipped with what the general knew were largely useless smoothbore muskets.

Responding to the general's signals, Colonel Simms looked quickly about to locate Captain Zophar Cash, commander of E Troop's one hundred men and one of his most experienced combat officers. A quick whistle from Simms caught the captain's attention, and the young officer promptly turned and rode out to meet his regimental commander, grabbing the brim of his Stetson-style "cav hat" with his right hand in salute.

"The general wants eyeballs on all those Shepherd soldiers out there, Captain … up close and personal," Simms said, nodding in their direction.

Cash glanced in the direction of General Tinian, then over his shoulder at the small groups of enemy troops still standing in a decidedly ghoulish fashion in six squads of six soldiers each. "They look pretty well dead to me, Colonel, but I've never seen anyone keep standin' like that after they've been shot. Damned peculiar if you ask me."

"Yeah," Simms replied, pausing to take another look for himself and still half expecting to see the Shepherds start killing his men again at any moment. "I'm sure that's why he wants us to take a look. Head on over there with your boys and make sure they're out of commission. Any questions?"

"No, sir. Will do, sir," Cash replied and had begun turning his horse in the direction of his unit before stopping abruptly. "Uh, Colonel … what do you want me to do if we find any of 'em alive," he asked, wanting to make sure he fully understood the orders he had been given.

"From what I can see from here, I don't reckon that'll be a problem, Captain," Simms replied, leaning forward in the saddle and raising the brim of his hat slightly to emphasize the point. "But if you do, I reckon we have to assume they still pose a significant threat that needs to be neutralized. Understood?"

"Yes, sir, I do," Cash replied, saluting once again before quickly turning his horse back in the direction of his three platoons.

"And Zophar," Simms shouted from behind, causing the younger officer to hesitate briefly before riding away. "Be careful, son. We've lost enough people for one day."

Minutes later, Cash had finished relaying the colonel's instructions to each of his lieutenants — with particular emphasis on ensuring that every man had reloaded his rifle before proceeding. Unsure exactly what they would encounter, Cash had also given explicit instructions that no one was to approach within fifty meters of any of the Shepherd troops until after he had signaled that it was safe to do so. Now, with all necessary preparations complete, E Troop's three platoons went racing ahead in the direction of the six small enemy formations — left, right, and center — each one given the task of confirming the status of two squads of the presumably deceased Shepherd soldiers.

With his rifle at the ready, Captain Cash quickly covered the distance to the first of the two groups closest to the center of the Estorian infantry line. He had seen firsthand how quickly the enemy soldiers could move with the help of the black suits they wore beneath their loose-fitting, green uniforms and knew full well just how dangerous it might be to get close enough to confirm whether they were truly dead. Nevertheless, orders were orders. So, as he made his final approach, he slowed his horse to a slow, four-beat walk, raising his rifle to his shoulder and taking aim at the head of the nearest Shepherd soldier.

Once he was close enough to examine the first group of soldiers in detail, Cash saw that their appearance was even more strange and macabre than they had seemed from a distance. Aside from the considerable noise still being generated by the rest of the 3rd Cavalry Regiment entering and exiting the field behind him, Cash also noticed a series of odd sounds coming from the nearest squad of Shepherd soldiers. All of them still stood upright in what was, he presumed, the exact same positions in which they had been standing at the times of their deaths. And now, their bizarre, somewhat limp posture gave him the distinct impression of human scarecrows, somehow condemned to stand in this field forever. *Or at least until the flesh rots from their miserable bones,* he corrected himself, an involuntary chill running down the length of his spine.

The sound he had been hearing, he now realized, appeared to be coming from the armored suits they were wearing. It was a creaking sound not unlike that made by the leather of his saddle as he shifted his weight in an attempt to get a better view. *It has to be the damned suits that are keeping them standing,* he thought, wondering if the hated black garments somehow had some sort of evil consciousness and will of their own.

Looking directly into the face of the first soldier, Cash noted that the normally dark tinted shield protecting the man's face, while still intact, was now mostly transparent. Although it was difficult to see much in the way of detail, he could tell that the soldier's eyes were open, staring lifelessly off in the direction of his former enemies. The rest of his body had not fared nearly as well. From the looks of him, Cash guessed there must have been at least fifty discernible bullet wounds, although the outer garment had been so thoroughly soaked with blood that it was difficult to say for sure.

With his attention firmly focused on the man's bloody outer garment, Cash was startled by a different type of sound coming from the third soldier in the small formation. There was a brief, high-pitched whine, followed by a definitive clunking sound. Whatever it was that had produced the sound had been powerful enough to cause the soldier's entire body to convulse briefly, as if someone had grabbed the man by the shoulders and given him a good hard shake. Cash paused and listened for almost a full minute and had almost decided to move on when he both heard and saw the process repeat itself. *Could these things somehow have the power to heal and eventually revive these men ... even with such an incredible amount of damage?* he wondered. Although he sincerely doubted it — or at least hoped this wasn't the case — he felt the hairs on the back of his neck stand on end that something so ... *unnatural* might fall within the realm of possibility.

In any event, Colonel Simms' orders were clear enough, weren't they? he thought, climbing slowly down from the saddle while keeping a wary eye on the enemy troops. Seeing no reactions to his presence, Cash walked briskly to within a few meters of the first Shepherd soldier, shouldered his rifle, and quickly put three rounds into the side of the man's head. Incredibly, the corpse remained on its feet in spite of the fact that three exit wounds had appeared on the opposite side of the man's head and a new series of creaks had issued from the black suit he was wearing. Feeling thoroughly spooked at this point, Cash took a few steps forward, then delivered a powerful roundhouse kick to the center of the former soldier's ribcage, finally sending his lifeless body to the ground.

Finally satisfied that the man was well and truly deceased and seeing no additional movement from any of the remaining five soldiers in the formation, Cash turned and signaled for his three lieutenants to press on with the grim task to which they had been assigned. Accordingly, and within just moments of receiving the order to proceed, the men of E Troop were busily pumping rounds into the skulls of each of the Shepherd soldiers before knocking them to the ground.

"How 'bout that, you can tip 'em over just like sleeping cows!" Cash heard one of his less intellectually gifted privates exclaim.

The cavalrymen were just over halfway through this process when a sound from the direction of the High Protector's compound caused every man on the battlefield to freeze in their tracks.

"Stop!!!" a voice commanded at a volume easily as loud as any clap of thunder they had ever heard in their lives. Every set of eyes on the field instinctively turned in the direction of the sound and saw that the High Protector himself had come among them. Once again, the WCS was making use of its gravitic systems to take flight and now hovered in the air at treetop level overlooking the battlefield.

The various technologies working in concert to make such a thing possible were lost on the Estorian soldiers, of course. Only a few of them had witnessed his earlier meeting with General Tinian, and they had never seen the High Protector — or anyone else, for that matter — fly through the air before. Understandably, the sight of what they had thought was nothing more than an ordinary man performing an act they knew to be impossible was unsettling to say the least, causing them to shift nervously in place as they waited to see what would happen next.

The High Protector said nothing else for a long moment, silently surveying the battlefield while slowly closing the distance to hover almost directly above Captain Cash and the men of E Troop. "Where did you get these weapons?" he finally demanded, glancing angrily about to see if anyone would have courage enough to answer. "These weapons are *not* of your world." Pausing once again, he seemed to note the imminent arrival of General Tinian, who had already spurred his horse into a gallop and was rapidly approaching the center of the battlefield.

"Ah, General Tinian," the High Protector continued in a voice loud enough to easily be heard over the sound of the general's horse. "Tell me, who supplied your men with these weapons?"

Tinian, hoping to put as much distance between himself and the bulk of his troops as possible, did not attempt to answer until he was almost directly beneath the High Protector — creating an awkward silence filled only by the hoofbeats of his horse.

"Sir," the general finally replied after coming to a full stop, "I'm sure you can appreciate that I am not at liberty to discuss such things with anyone. Particularly not with someone who is at war with the Estorian people."

"At *war*, you say?" the High Protector asked, incredulous. "I have sought only to help your people rise from the dark ages and take their rightful place among the other powerful worlds in this part of the galaxy … worlds that have wisely chosen to count themselves among our allies … *my* allies. You have seen nothing of the true nature of war, General," he scoffed. "And what you have seen from me is but a minor demonstration of the power I have at my disposal. Yet you presume to imply that my willingness to defend my home from *your* aggression constitutes some sort of declaration of war on the Estorian people."

"*No*, sir," Tinian replied firmly. "While our forces do indeed approach your compound today, it is *you* who have been the aggressor since you first arrived here on our world. You came with fanciful tales of magic and power. And yet we presumed nothing ... *wanted* nothing from you except to be left in peace. It was *you* who presumed, sir — presumed that we are so backward and gullible as to be deceived and intimidated by such lofty assertions ... such ... well, for lack of a better term, *nonsense*. And when we did not immediately accede to your demands, you began an escalating campaign of terror against our people ... open *warfare*, sir, against our people. Since then, you have killed us by the tens of thousands. Do you now deny it? Do you deny the senseless death and destruction you have brought to our world?"

"You pathetic, arrogant —"

"You've had your say, sir. And now, you will allow me to have mine," Tinian interrupted, his face now red with anger. "So let me be direct and clear in a way that our diplomats and politicians most likely never will. I have no idea who or what you are, or where you came from. Frankly, that is not my concern. But what I *do* know is that you're not from here ... and you're not *welcome* here. Since the day of your arrival, I believe my people have made it quite clear that all we want from you is to be left in peace. So now I must ask you again. Please ... before more of your people and ours die needlessly in this conflict, will you not simply leave us and never return?"

Chapter 4

Didara 4, South Estorian Continent, Ganahar Plains
(53 km southeast of Helstaad)

The High Protector stared back impassively for a long moment, almost as if he were considering Tinian's request. When he finally continued, however, the expression on his face had changed into one that could only be described as abject hatred. "Surely you have realized by now that my people *are* your people, dear General. And, no, I have no intention of leaving … not now, and not within the short lifespans of any one of you gathered here today. It has become increasingly clear to me that you, your diplomats, and especially your politicians do not speak for all of your people — many of whom would be grateful to receive the gifts of power and prosperity that I am more than willing to provide. Instead, you have chosen to ally yourselves with someone who either has very little to offer, or, worse yet, has purposely chosen to provide you with resources barely better than those you can easily provide for yourselves. And while we are on the subject, General, you might as well leave those ancient rifles at home next time. By the time we meet again, I can assure you they will be wholly ineffective. But I digress. What I, on the other hand, can offer your society is a thousand years of progress virtually overnight … an end to famine and poverty … a new, global standard of living you cannot even begin to imagine. Are you truly so foolish and shortsighted as to throw away such an opportunity and instead choose to embrace your own destruction?"

The general paused, looking at the ground for a moment then back up at the High Protector before repeating himself in a calm, unemotional tone. "Please, sir. All we ask is that you leave us in peace."

"That I am unwilling to do, General. Like you, I am subject to the orders of my superiors, and I must follow them to the best of my ability. What I *will* do in the spirit of peace and cooperation as we move forward together is withdraw from this field of battle … assuming you will agree to do the same, of course. I will refrain from retaliating against your forces for what you have done here today if you will turn and leave *my* home in peace and never return. But do be quick about it, General. Remove your forces from the area within the hour or I may be forced to reconsider my generous offer." With that, the High Protector turned rapidly about and headed off in the direction of his compound.

General Tinian paused, giving his enemy time to leave the immediate area. While he waited, he removed his hat and wiped the sweat from his brow, all the while concentrating on taking deep, cleansing breaths as he worked to settle himself down. He knew all too well that the action he was about to take would place every man under his command at extreme risk, but he was also keenly aware that such an opportunity might never come again if he chose not to proceed. Finally, believing the time had now come for the next step in his plan, he reached into his saddlebag once again, retrieved and activated his tactical radio, and keyed the mike in a series of three, one-second-long transmissions, just as he had done prior to taking the field.

The Estorian Army had long had a tradition of expertise in the disciplines of combat construction, engineering, and demolition. Somewhat ironically commanded by a perennially pipe-smoking major by the name of Sam Jackson, the First Sapper Battalion was considered the premier center of expertise in the employment of explosives to create small piles of rubble out of formerly large structures. Until recently, Jackson's men primarily used a combination of black powder and (only when absolutely necessary) nitroglycerine when sent on demo missions against enemy fortifications or other infrastructure. But that all began to change when one of the first shipments of guns received by the Estorian Army General Staff had also included a new type of explosive referred to in the accompanying documentation as simply "C-4."

After several months' worth of practice with their remarkable new tool, the First Sapper Battalion was finally ready to make use of it under combat conditions for the first time. And today — taking full advantage of the High Protector's preoccupation while dealing with two full-strength infantry brigades and a cavalry regiment marching into his backyard — they had managed to surreptitiously place well over a thousand kilograms of the powerful new explosive. Now, with almost no discernible delay after General Tinian's radio transmission, a series of muffled explosions could be heard from the direction of the compound. There was a momentary pause, during which he wondered if something had gone terribly wrong, before a rippling series of additional explosions shook the ground — each one seemingly louder than the one that had preceded it.

The men of the Estorian Army had never witnessed anything like it. The explosions — the results of which could be heard, felt, seen, and eventually even smelled from the battlefield — seemed to continue on for a full minute or more. And when the freshening breeze finally began to clear some of the smoke and dust away from the distant hilltop, it became abundantly clear that there was very little of the High Protector's compound and personal residence still left standing. Now, with the sound of the explosions still ringing in their ears, the Estorian forces erupted in raucous cheers once again, this time with even more enthusiasm than before.

General Tinian, concerned that such an overt display of defiance might result in an even more rash, disproportionate response from the High Protector than might otherwise have been the case, waved his arms up and down in a gesture obviously intended to settle his troops. His plan now — assuming a counterattack did not materialize, and the High Protector did not immediately return — was to reconnoiter the grounds in hopes of acquiring some much-needed intelligence information. Tinian knew better than to hold out any hope that the High Protector himself had been destroyed. Nevertheless, he thought there might at least be a small chance that the destruction of its base of operations might be sufficient to motivate it to simply cut its losses and leave, hopefully taking the remnants of its forces with it and never returning.

But it was not to be. Less than fifteen minutes later, with General Tinian's brigade and battalion commanders barely having had time to begin the process of withdrawing the Estorian infantry line from the field, the

High Protector returned. This time, he flew to a point directly above where the general still sat atop his horse, hovering menacingly while once again broadcasting his voice at such an earth-shattering volume that all of the assembled troops could hear.

"You have destroyed my home and killed the soldiers whose job it was to defend it. And while it would undoubtedly be within my rights to see each and every one of you lying dead upon this very field, I will not hold the lot of you responsible for the foolish actions and orders of your leaders — those select few who lack the vision to accept the inevitable. But hear me well, Estorians. The time has come for every one of you to make the only reasonable choice available to you. One that will secure a better future for your people … for your world as a whole. There *are* no alternatives. One path leads to peace, power, and prosperity. The other, to naught but destruction."

With that, the High Protector extended his right arm in the direction of General Tinian with his palm facing upwards. A deep, thrumming sound coursed across the whole of the battlefield, with those closest to the general feeling as if their chests were being pounded by an invisible fist. As the stunned Estorian soldiers watched in horror, the High Protector slowly raised his arm towards the sky, lifting General Tinian and his horse from the ground. It took just seconds for the helpless general to reach the same altitude as the High Protector, who clearly intended for everyone present to bear witness what he was about to do.

"General Tinian," he said, his tone very much like that of a judge speaking to a condemned man. "*You* are responsible for the destruction of my home and the deaths of my troops here today. *You* are also the leader designated to speak for your Estorian military establishment as well as the Federation Assembly. The only reasonable punishment for such an abominable offense is death. Accordingly, I condemn you to die for your crimes."

With that, the High Protector slowly rotated his palm downwards and then plunged his arm rapidly towards the ground. In the space of a heartbeat, Tinian and his horse plummeted to the earth at a speed several times faster than merely falling from the same height. With a sickening thud, they impacted the ground with such force that their bodies were turned into a gelatinous mass of blood and gore — mangled to such a degree that it was impossible to discern the difference between the man and his beloved horse.

Seemingly unfazed by what he had just done, the High Protector continued speaking, his voice slicing through the stark silence like a knife. "Many of you here today seem to fancy yourselves as having grown too sophisticated to believe in the arcane fields of study your ancestors once referred to in hushed tones using words like witchcraft, sorcery … *magic*. As I have just demonstrated, it is not your ancestors but *you* who have grown naive and foolish by allowing yourselves to believe such things no longer exist. If you are uncomfortable with those particular terms, there are many others we might use. Perhaps instead it is better to simply speak in terms of power, since it matters not whether that power occurs naturally, or is derived from some other source."

As he spoke, the High Protector held out both of his hands in front of his body, this time with both palms facing upwards. With a loud whooshing sound like that of kerosene being tossed into a fire, two brilliant orbs sprang to life — seemingly alive and crackling with orange-hued energy as they floated in the air above his hands. "Power, you see," he continued, "is something that I and beings like me possess in such abundance that you cannot hope to comprehend it, let alone stand against it. Once again, you and your leaders may choose to benefit from this power, in time growing powerful in your own right. Or … you may also choose to be destroyed by it." To emphasize his point, the High Protector raised both of his hands, causing the two flaming orbs to soar into the sky. Both flew straight upwards for several seconds before simultaneously exploding in a deafening flash of unearthly, orange light. At virtually the same instant, a powerful shockwave reached the ground directly below the explosions, kicking up a wall of dust as it traveled outward from the point of impact. Among the assembled Estorian forces, horses reared and bolted in terror, many of them throwing their riders from their saddles, while even some of the most battle-hardened infantrymen dropped to the ground, paralyzed with fear.

"The choice before you is a simple one, my friends. But, alas, it is not one I can make on your behalf," he concluded, pausing to allow the impact of his actions and words to sink in before continuing. "Colonel Simms," he finally said, looking the commander of the 3rd Cavalry Regiment directly in the eye. "I assume you are now in charge of this rabble. Gather your forces and leave immediately, or I shall leave none of you alive." Without waiting for a response, the High Protector spun about once again and headed off in the direction of the smoking ruins that had been his compound and personal residence.

Simms looked over his shoulder at the men behind him, then back at the remains of what had been his friend, mentor, and commanding officer. Without bothering to issue an order to the thousands of men now under his command, the colonel drew his rifle from its scabbard once again, cycled the lever to chamber a round, and took careful aim at the head of the departing High Protector. At peace with the idea that he would likely join General Tinian in short order, Simms took a deep breath, held it to steady his hands, and squeezed the trigger. A brief moment of stark silence gripped the battlefield, broken only by the first echoes of the colonel's rifle as the entire world seemed to hold its collective breath. A heartbeat later, chaos returned with a tremendous roar as every Estorian weapon that would bear on the High Protector opened fire at the same time.

At the sound of Colonel Simms' first shot, the WCS had whirled about in fury and headed back in the direction of the Estorian forces — red, murderous rage forming the singular focus of its synthetic consciousness. As it rapidly approached the center of the battlefield, it was clear to the soldiers unfortunate enough to be in close proximity that the High Protector was being hit by what must have been hundreds of rounds. All around his body, flashes of light could be seen, along with faint ripples of light as many of the projectiles appeared to be stopped in mid-flight as surely as if they had been fired into a thick sheet of iron. Still and all, a great many rounds were obviously penetrating the High Protector's mysterious defenses, causing his body to jerk convulsively with their impacts. Just as the Estorian soldiers had seen with the Shepherd troops, the High Protector's dark, outer garment and crimson cloak were being rapidly torn to shreds by the unrelenting fusillade. But to the soldiers' dismay, it quickly became clear enough that even the added firepower provided by their new rifles was having little, if any, effect.

Rather than counterattack immediately, the High Protector simply hovered in the air over the center of the battlefield, a look of defiance commingled with contempt gracing his normally handsome face. For a full minute and more, he seemed content to hold this position, underscoring the fact that the fleeting victory his enemies had won here today had been symbolic at best. With no other options left save a panicked retreat, the Estorians maintained an impressive rate of fire. In the infantry line, each successive rank rotated smoothly to the rear of the formation to reload their muskets and begin the cycle once again, while the cavalry troopers on either flank executed similar maneuvers on horseback.

For all its remarkable capabilities, the Warden Combat System was still nothing more than an amalgamation of advanced — yet sometimes surprisingly fragile — individual systems. In order for its higher functions to perform as designed, energy shielding, for example, multiple subsystems were required to work in concert, each one performing its own functions flawlessly, despite its own inherent fragility. Even with exquisitely complex error handling coupled with multiple layers of redundancy to act as a bulwark against failures, unforeseen or extreme circumstances, by definition, can still occur. In such cases, any system can behave in an unpredictable manner, causing unexpected failure modes to appear.

Now, fifty meters above the Ganahar Plains, the heavy bombardment to which the WCS was being subjected resulted in a minor power fluctuation in a single shield emitter. Like all of the emitters comprising the High Protector's energy shield system, the device's function was to participate in the creation of an intensely energetic field in the space immediately surrounding its body. Although significantly more effective against beam weapons than projectiles, the general idea was to violently interact with incoming ordnance with the intent of destroying, redirecting, or at least substantially reducing their lethality, if possible. More specifically, the emitter in question was responsible for the portion of the energy shield protecting the right side of the WCS' head. The power fluctuation, while noted by various performance monitoring routines, was immediately classified as "minor/in-range," meaning that, in spite of the anomaly, all primary systems should continue to operate well within their design specifications. And yet …

A single rifle cartridge — enhanced, but otherwise a perfect copy of one originally manufactured over five thousand light years away and some four hundred years ago on a blue world called Terra — entered the chamber of an Estorian cavalryman's rifle and was subsequently fired. Just over one-thousandth of a second later, the armor-piercing projectile left the weapon's muzzle traveling at just over four hundred meters per second. Covering the intervening distance in less than a fourth of a second, the bullet reached the point where it would normally have encountered the High Protector's energy shield. But, as the hand of fate, Murphy's Law, or the "Golden BB Theory" would have it (depending entirely on one's perspective), at that precise instant in time, the field strength of the WCS' shield at its point of entry had been substantially reduced. Blissfully unaware that any of this was taking place, the rifle round flew on for another fraction of a second — its velocity reduced only slightly by the temporarily weakened shield — before slamming into the High Protector's armored exoskeleton just under his holographically projected right earlobe. At the moment of impact, the projectile still carried nearly one thousand Joules of destructive energy.

The projectile's impact caused absolutely no structural damage to the High Protector's well-armored exterior — designed to be all but invulnerable to kinetic and energy weapons fire exceeding anything currently possessed by the Estorians by nearly two orders of magnitude. What it did manage to accomplish, however, was the near-complete destruction of one of the tiny holo-emitters responsible for giving the WCS the appearance that it was in possession of a Human face. Not a part of the Warden's original design, holographics were added to the "enhanced" versions of the combat droid for use primarily on espionage missions. As such, they were not generally considered to be a mission-critical system and, therefore, not as well protected from incoming enemy fire. The result of the missing emitter was immediate. The right side of the High Protector's face from the top of its brow to its jawline blinked twice, then disappeared completely, revealing the armored structure beneath.

Not surprisingly, most of those close enough to have noted the change in the High Protector's appearance were unsure precisely what it was they were seeing. Later, during debriefing sessions with their commanders, most would report that it looked as if he had donned some sort of mask that only covered part of his face. Other, perhaps slightly more imaginative witnesses would describe catching a glimpse of the High Protector's true form — clearly the unholiest of demons come to visit death and destruction upon their world.

Colonel Simms, on the other hand, had the benefit of having read a summary of the intelligence documents supplied by his government's unknown benefactor. And what he saw revealed in the face of the "Lord High Protector" fully convinced him of their accuracy. This … what was it they had called it … a "WCS?" Whatever name they had chosen to use, there was no longer any doubt in his mind that it was indeed a "thing," not a man or other creature of flesh and blood, but a machine of some sort. As incredible and strange as this idea seemed to Nathaniel Simms, evil machines still somehow seemed less intimidating than evil men or other creatures possessed of their own free will. And regardless of how powerful this particular machine might appear, it clearly was not indestructible. For the first time in nearly two years, the colonel felt a new sense of confidence that the High Protector would eventually be overcome, although he had no illusions as to how difficult and deadly this task might prove.

Simms had just finished reloading his rifle when he had seen the change in the High Protector's face. Temporarily holding his fire, he stared up at it for a moment, hoping — though not expecting — that what he was seeing was an indication that the thing might have sustained serious damage. Unfortunately, that did not seem to be the case, although what he *did* see was no less surprising. The WCS, still hovering in the same spot where it had been since returning to the battlefield, simply disappeared. One moment it was there, floating over the Estorian troops like a vengeful god preparing to smite the lot of them, and then it was gone. Not entirely able to accept what his eyes were telling him, Colonel Simms focused all of his attention on the High Protector's previous location.

It was then that he saw it. The strange-looking structure beneath what had been one side of the thing's face was still visible, hovering there in the same place as before but now seemingly disembodied from the rest. "What in the Gods' names?" he wondered aloud.

"This will be your final warning!" the High Protector's voice thundered out across the battlefield once more. "Withdraw from this place NOW or I will destroy each and every one of you."

With that, Colonel Simms saw the section of the High Protector's head that was still visible turn and speed rapidly up the hill towards its former compound once again. *Well, I'll be damned,* he thought, then turned in his saddle to motion for his signalman just as Captain Cash came galloping over to confirm his own orders.

"Want me to keep working through those Shepherd troops, Colonel?" he asked.

"No, Captain, I'm pretty sure they're no longer a threat. I can't imagine they wouldn't have kept on killing our troopers by now if they had been able to do so."

"Yes, sir, I'm sure you're right about that," Cash nodded. "What are your orders, Colonel? E Troop's in a good position to pursue if you —"

"No, Captain Cash, I don't think that would be prudent at this time. We have met and —" Simms paused, turning to glance in the direction he had seen the WCS depart before continuing, "perhaps even exceeded our mission objectives here today. I think it's time for us to collect our casualties and withdraw."

"Yes, Colonel," Cash replied. But as he turned his mount in the direction of his unit, he paused to look back at his commanding officer. "Sir, it's not my place to question your orders, but I want you to know that my boys and I are more than willing to head up the hill there and finish off any remaining enemy forces we run across. E Troop can handle that alone while the rest of our forces withdraw off to the south."

Colonel Simms regarded the younger man for a long moment, momentarily second-guessing his decision. He was fully aware that leaving the battlefield now also meant abandoning a potential opportunity to mop up the High Protector's remaining forces in the area. But he had also now seen firsthand what the WCS itself could do. Although it had never been known to engage in combat itself, at least not on a large scale, Simms was certain that it was fully capable of following through on its threats.

"No, Zophar," he continued, "I understand and appreciate your offer. And under normal circumstances, fighting a normal enemy, that's exactly what I would have you do. Hell, I'd probably send half the regiment to hunt down every one of those Shepherd soldiers and cut them down like the dogs they are. But not today, not with this enemy. General Tinian's orders were very clear. He was expecting far more casualties than we have, and I can assure you he'd be more than pleased with what we've managed to accomplish. We do nothing to honor his sacrifice by getting the rest of our men killed. Understand?"

Captain Cash stared back for a moment as if trying to decide if he should say more, then slowly nodded. "Yes, sir, I do. If it's okay with you, Colonel, I'll have my men collect the general's body."

"Yes, please do. But do the best you can as quickly as you can, Captain. Go ahead and collect the rest of our troopers from the first attack as well. F Troop is still up on the line," Simms said, nodding off to the east. "So, go grab Captain Jenkins and have them help out."

"Yes, Colonel," Cash replied with a crisp salute, then wheeled his horse about and galloped away in the direction of the infantry formation's right flank.

As he watched the younger officer depart, Simms wondered whether he or anyone else had seen what he had in the face of the High Protector. Before today, he knew, the knowledge of what he was — *what it was,* he corrected himself — had been classified "Most Secret." Although it was not entirely clear to the cavalry commander why the General Staff had chosen to hide this information, other than its original source, he wondered whether they would be able to continue concealing such a shocking truth after today.

"Corporal Mateland, signal a general withdrawal, please," Simms called over his shoulder.

"Yes, Colonel. Signaling general withdrawal," his flagman repeated.

"Oh, and Corporal …"

"Yes, *sir.*"

"Make sure our buglers do *not* sound retreat."

"My pleasure, Colonel."

And with that, the commander of the 3rd Estorian Cavalry Regiment spurred his horse and headed off to do what he could to help in the recovery of his fallen comrades in arms.

Part 2
(Present Day)

Chapter 5

Dryden Beck awoke with a gasp, briefly opening his eyes before jerking his head to one side against the violent assault of dappled sunlight filtering down through the gently swaying treetops above. *Scarsdow?* he wondered, his senses returning little additional information at the moment. *But this isn't where ... is it? ... When did I?* he groaned inwardly, his normally sharp mind already growing alarmed and confused at its unusual lack of clarity. His memory of the series of events that had brought him to this particular time and place seemed decidedly ... *unreliable* seemed like the right word, but he could not quite put his finger on why that was the case. There was also an odd sensation of having awakened from a dream — as if whatever had been happening to him prior to this moment could not possibly have been real.

Dryden had a vague recollection of having survived ... *something*. But what exactly? His attempts to recall what had happened produced nothing more than amorphous, forbidding images from the depths of his mind — shades of horrors recently seen but still unwilling to take their true forms. He *had* survived something, though, hadn't he? Something dark ... and *violent*, he realized with an involuntary shudder.

He seemed to remember some sort of chaotic, terror-filled flight ... to *escape* something, perhaps. *That was*

70

it! he thought. Escaped felt like an accurate word to describe what he had done. But from what? *A battle?* he wondered, his chest heaving now with deep, ragged breaths as he struggled to regain some small measure of situational awareness. *Yes*! he thought, his mind eagerly grasping at the faint series of memories that had begun to form. There had been a village or small city of some sort, hadn't there? And people ... throngs of people running to escape the approach of ... *what*?

At that moment, the first clear memory of what had transpired coalesced before his mind's eye, a vision of what he instinctively knew were recent events — displayed in vivid detail from his own point of view. And what he saw before him sent an icy chill of dread coursing down the length of his spine.

Dryden was looking down onto a gray, windswept plain from atop a low ridge. Spread before him was a scene that had indeed been the site of a recent battle — one that had obviously devolved into a rout for one side and a decisive victory for the other. The plain was littered with the bodies of the dead. Many looked as if they had been severely burned, while others bore wounds inflicted by less obvious forms of extreme physical violence. He had never seen anything like it before, or so he hoped. The sheer brutality of the scene shocked him to the core of his being. There were dismembered bodies, bodies with their heads and chests crushed, bodies so utterly destroyed as to be barely identifiable as Human — all of them apparently run down and killed in the course of a wild, panicked attempt to escape their pursuers. There were thousands of them ... *tens of thousands,* he corrected himself. All of them spread beneath the leaden sky in such numbers that it would have been difficult to take a single step without treading upon one of their number.

But they weren't all soldiers, were they? Dryden realized. Allowing his attention to linger on a nearby collection of bodies, he noted that roughly one in three wore simple, gray to light brown uniforms — nothing more than woolen trousers and long jackets in most cases. Most were armed with muskets and edged weapons of one form or another. Here and there, he noted the barrel of one of the new rifles protruding from beneath the body of a fallen soldier. *Dismounted Estorian Federation cavalry*, he thought absently, unsure, at the moment, why he knew this to be true. Many of the remaining bodies he could see were clearly civilians, a few still clutching some prized possession or another ... or the body of a small child.

With another involuntary shudder, Dryden looked off in the direction the troops and civilians had been attempting to flee, just as the faint sound of a distant bugle call reached his ears. Shortly thereafter, he both heard and felt another vaguely familiar sound. Echoing across the plain like a continuous, rolling peal of thunder, two reinforced squadrons of Estorian cavalry — nearly nine hundred men in total — crested the top of a distant ridgeline off to his south at full gallop. Although the reasons were still unclear to his beleaguered mind, Dryden knew with absolute clarity that he was their intended target.

As the memory of this experience continued to play out in his mind, both the scope and the depth of detail he was able to recall continued to increase. It was at this point that he began to realize that he was no longer limited to watching what was taking place from his own eyes but could observe the scene from any point of view, including that of the advancing cavalry troopers. Although a mere spectator to what he now knew was about to take place, the slowly awakening portion of his mind still anchored in the present raged at the inevitability of his own past … raged at what he was about to do — or, rather, had already done — and for which he could never hope to atone.

Now watching from a vantage point above and to the rear of the ridge on which he had stood, Dryden saw himself stride confidently forward several paces, staring defiantly as the massive throng of mounted troopers bore down on him at a furious pace. There he paused, almost as if for dramatic effect, his crimson-red cloak billowing away to his left in the wind. Nearly a full minute passed as the horsemen covered the intervening distance, the deafening roar of their assault rising to a truly awe-inspiring crescendo. Now, as the leading elements of horsemen closed to within five hundred meters, many of their number began taking somewhat random shots with their service revolvers. Others, fortunate enough to be armed with the latest "Model 94" iteration of their beloved Winchester rifles (and brave enough to use them atop their charging mounts), aimed in his general direction and opened fire.

"*Fángyù lǐngyù,*" *(defensive field engaged)* he heard a strange, unintelligible female voice say. He had absolutely no idea where the sound had come from, realizing only that he had heard the same voice many times in the past. Each time she spoke, her inscrutable messages were delivered in a maddeningly calm, matter-of-fact tone that often seemed oddly inappropriate for the situation at hand.

Movement just a few meters away quickly drew Dryden's attention back to what had been taking place around him. Although sporadic and generally inaccurate at this range, he saw that at least a few of the incoming rounds were impacting the ground immediately in front of where he had been standing. Small, V-shaped geysers of soil erupted skyward all around where he stood — each one yielding a powdery cloud of brown dust that whirled quickly off to his left on the stiff breeze.

It was at that moment that Dryden noticed something of which he had been vaguely aware while these events were transpiring in real-time but had not had the opportunity to observe in any detail. The very air surrounding where he stood had come alive with a series of flashing lights accompanied by a vivid array of rapidly changing colors.

What in the name of...? he began, as the nature of his ultra-detailed recollection transitioned from the strange to the truly incomprehensible.

The sequence of prior events playing back in his mind instantly froze in place. The whole of the scene before him — everything he could see at the precise moment in time he had noticed the flashing lights and the colors surrounding his body — was still visible. There was none of the ambiguity normally associated with recalling an event, even one from the recent past. If anything, his vision seemed to have taken on an even greater level of detail than before — far beyond that of even the most indelible memories sometimes brought about during times of extreme stress.

This was no mere memory, he realized … it was far more than that.

It felt as if he could perceive *everything* — columns of smoke rising from the as yet unseen town tucked behind the next ridge, individual hairs standing upright on an exposed section of skin on the back of his neck, the unit-identifying brands burned into the haunches of the approaching horses — all with a level of precision that seemed wholly unnatural and, therefore, wholly disconcerting.

What, precisely, was happening to his mind? Was all of this a particularly vivid dream, the likes of which he had never experienced before? Or perhaps it was some sort of hallucination brought about by the trauma of whatever had inexplicably deposited him in the middle of Scarsdow Forest?

Dryden stared for a moment longer at the image displayed with such remarkable clarity within the confines of his mind, then simply opened his eyes to gaze, once again, at the swaying forest canopy above. How was this possible? Had he inadvertently just discovered an additional gift, granted by the High Protector sometime in the past but somehow never used? Upon closing his eyes once more, he was startled to see that the "memory" had temporarily disappeared, but a simple thought brought the exact same instant in time back to the forefront of his mind.

"Cóng shàng cì rìzhì huīfù," (log resume from last) he heard the woman's voice say, prompting him to slowly shake his head in irritation.

Focusing once more on the patterns of light surrounding his body, Dryden tilted his head and furrowed his brow in concentration, trying to get a closer look at what was causing the effect.

"*Biànjiāo jiā shàng duì jiāodiǎn de bǎi fēn zhī qīshí,*" *(zoom plus seventy percent at focus point)* the voice responded immediately, causing him to jump involuntarily as the image zoomed in sharply on the precise region he had been trying to examine in more detail.

"I cannot understand you! Whoever or ... *whatever* you are!" he replied irritably. "So please stop speaking to me in this manner."

"*Yǐ quèrèn. Yǔyīn tíshì yǐ jìnyòng,*" *(Acknowledged. Voice prompts disabled)* the disembodied voice replied.

"Right. I do hope that means you can at least understand what *I'm* saying," Dryden muttered absently, maintaining his attention on the undulating patterns of light that had been coursing through the air surrounding his body. Noticing that each of the pulses seemed to radiate outward from a single point — much like the ripples from a stone tossed into a pond — he focused his gaze on an even smaller area at the center of one of the patterns. Just as before, the memory (for he lacked a more descriptive term at the moment) responded to his desire to examine a specific region more closely by magnifying his point of interest. But this time, the entire scene displayed in his mind transformed so that he could see the area from several different viewpoints. One of the images even provided a perspective that seemed to hover around and above the scene. It was as if he could see himself through the eyes of a small bird particularly intent on watching him from every conceivable angle.

Ever the pragmatist, Dryden chose to ignore the larger questions concerning how and why this glorious new gift had been granted him for now (if indeed that's what this was) and utilize his newfound ability to discover exactly what had happened to him. With nothing more than a quick thought that he was ready to continue, the playback inside his mind resumed.

He now noticed that the glowing waves of light that had originally captured his attention appeared to travel up and over his head as well as around the sides of his body at a distance of approximately two meters. Each pulse had lasted only a brief moment before dissipating completely, and Dryden found himself wishing he could determine if the incoming rounds from the approaching troopers had anything to do with what he was seeing.

Once again, seemingly responding to his every thought, the images displayed in his mind reconfigured themselves, this time with the addition of red lines, numbers, and text — all intended to conclusively answer the question he had just posed to himself. The text, he surmised, must have been in the same language as the female voice he kept hearing. Now that he saw the characters, Dryden was fairly certain the language was a dialect of Zhong, which was almost unheard of in this part of the world — meaning he had virtually no chance of even finding someone to translate it, let alone understand it himself. Thankfully, the numbers were familiar enough, and Dryden's analytical mind had little trouble deciphering the general ideas that all of the various figures and graphics had been intended to convey.

Each red line indicated a flight path from the barrel of a specific cavalry officer's pistol or rifle to its point of impact with … something. But what exactly? He had heard of others receiving gifts of invulnerability, but he was fairly certain he had never seen such a gift manifest itself in battle. In any event, the images displayed inside the other mental "picture frames" made it perfectly clear that it was indeed the impact of incoming rounds that had caused the glowing waves of energy. One image even displayed a rotating schematic of one of the projectiles, as well as several other pieces of indecipherable data he was sure would have provided the specifics regarding how effective that particular round *should* have been at ending his life, had it not been prevented from hitting him.

Dryden shrugged his shoulders and commanded the memory to return to its original point of view as if he had been using this astonishing new ability for his entire life. Like the myriad of other questions swirling through his mind at the moment, he set aside the implications of adding not one but *two* powerful new gifts for later contemplation. Right now, though, it was time to face — in excruciatingly grim detail it seemed — the reality of what he knew would happen next.

When the playback of his memory resumed, the nose of the nearest cavalry trooper's horse had reached a distance of only three hundred and twenty-one meters from his position. He knew this to be true because he could now see a red circle superimposed around the animal, along with an accompanying block of numerical information. Two of the numbers were rapidly decreasing in value — which Dryden took to be the distance and time remaining. At the moment, it appeared he had just under twenty-three seconds remaining before he would either be trampled by the enormous war horses or cut down by any number of wildly slashing cavalry sabers. But that outcome, he knew, was one that would never come to pass.

With the battle continuing to play out from his own point of view, Dryden watched himself with equal parts dread and morbid fascination. As the closest horses reached two hundred and fifty meters, he silently raised both arms in their direction, closing each of his hands into a fist as he did so. There was a brief pause, during which a faint whining sound could be heard — bringing to mind a mournful, wailing wind whipping around a farmhouse on a blustery night. The sound rapidly increased in both pitch and volume, causing him to wince in anticipation of the savage violence that was about to be unleashed.

Utilizing technology developed on a world called Pelara nearly two thousand light years from his own, well over one hundred distinct implants had been strategically placed within Dryden's body. Most, but not all, were remarkably small considering their capabilities — ranging in size from that of a grain of rice to nearly five centimeters in diameter. Nonetheless, the dozens of exquisitely painful surgical procedures required had taken the High Protector nearly six months to complete, pushing his body to the brink of death on several occasions. To conceal the origin of their wielder's incredible "gifts," each implant had been positioned in such a manner as to be virtually undetectable by most rudimentary forms of medical imaging — which was clearly not yet an issue on Didara 4 in any case. Perhaps even more astonishing than the number of implants in Dryden's body or the capabilities they conferred was the fact that the entire lot of them had been installed without his knowledge — let alone consent.

Now, a total of twelve of the devices located along the length of each of his arms worked in concert to create what amounted to a miniaturized hyperspace field just a few centimeters in front of each of his clenched fists. Although not large enough to risk his passing bodily into the tiny "bubbles" in normal space, the fields nonetheless allowed for an incredibly complex series of interactions between the two dimensionalities to occur within just a scant few milliseconds of their formation.

Initially, the devices took advantage of the intense energy flow gradient that naturally occurs at the boundary layer between normal and hyperspace to generate power — on a scale that would likely be impossible for the native inhabitants of Didara 4 for the better part of another millennium (without the assistance of another, more advanced, civilization). The purpose of creating these power plants in miniature was twofold: 1. Recharging the microenergy storage arrays implanted within each of Dryden's femurs with sufficient power to meet the day to day operational requirements of his entire network of implants for the next two weeks, and 2. To provide sufficient "surge" power to fire his primary weapon.

Now awash with excess power, gravitic emitters collocated with the hyperspace field generator arrays within his forearms created a pair of intense gravitational disturbances just beyond each of the existing hyperspace fields. The affected region of space was then alternately compressed and shaped several thousand times per second, resulting in the formation of two coherent spheres of energetic plasma. Finally, as the heat generated had already started to inflict significant damage to the skin on Dryden's hands and arms, the two hyperspace fields were allowed to abruptly collapse — creating a brief but intense ripple in the fabric of space that propelled the two bolts of plasma towards their targets at nearly twenty-five percent the speed of light. The deadly projectiles covered the distance to their target in just over three-millionths of a second.

Although little more than half a meter wide when fired, Dryden's plasma bolts lost much of their coherence as soon as they made contact with their target — in this case, a rider and horse located in roughly the center of the advancing line. The pair of violet-colored orbs flared brightly upon impact, their tremendous energy completely consuming the nearest seven troopers and their mounts before spreading out in a cone-shaped path of destruction. By the time their lethal payloads of energy had been expended, the plasma bolts had penetrated almost completely through the cavalry formation, leaving a trail of dead — or in the very least combat-ineffective — cavalry soldiers in their wake.

Absolutely none of the technological wizardry that produced the effects Dryden referred to as his "gifts" were known to him. All of his capabilities, he believed, were the direct result of the sheer will and focus of his powerful mind — preternatural skills initially taught by an even more powerful master, then honed to perfection through discipline and relentless training.

Dryden stopped the playback of his memory once more, confused and sickened by what he had just seen himself do. Such prodigious power — he knew, or at least *thought* he knew — was granted only to those few entrusted with the high honor of maintaining safety and good order among the Estorian people. But is that what he had been doing? And why him in the first place? At the moment, he had no memory of how or why he had earned such a notable distinction. Nor did he remember how and when he had received his gifts, or why he had been forced to utilize them to defend himself against a massed attack by Estorian Federation cavalry. After all, shouldn't these have been *friendly* troops? Had he also been responsible for the massive death and destruction of the other troops and civilians strewn about the area? Gods forbid! What possible set of circumstances could have placed him in a situation where these actions would *ever* be acceptable? And what sort of depraved master could have allowed such circumstances to occur in the first place?

As the rapid-fire series of questions continued to run through his mind, Dryden resumed the playback of the battle — if such a one-sided engagement could be referred to as a battle, that is. His first salvo had removed over forty horsemen from the advancing line, yet still they came on. He was now beginning to remember more and more of what would happen next, even without the assistance of the ultra-detailed vision fixed firmly in his mind … *what had happened next*, he corrected himself.

All of these events are in the past. There's no changing them now.

After opening fire on the cavalry formation, Dryden noticed that he had waited several seconds before firing again, perhaps hoping that the officers in command would recognize the folly of pressing an attack that would undoubtedly end in additional senseless slaughter. But it was not to be. In anticipation of reliving the end of the battle, Dryden gulped in a breath of air and held it, a sense of weary resignation steeling his resolve for what he was about to see.

With the destruction of the original cavalry troopers in the vanguard of the approaching formation, other riders had naturally closed ranks and taken their places. Dryden saw that the closest horsemen once again had the same red circles and text superimposed over their forms as before — now indicating a distance of less than one hundred meters and only seven seconds away. Once again, he watched himself raise his arms and clench his fists, noticing this time that additional red circles appeared, superimposed over roughly half of the horses visible in the front element of the formation. Without further hesitation, he opened fire once more, this time spreading his arms rapidly apart as a total of twenty additional bolts of plasma leapt across the rapidly narrowing gap, ripping viciously through the ranks of helpless soldiers and their mounts. The very air sounded as if it were being torn asunder — crackling like the reports of ten thousand of the cavalry soldiers' rifles before exploding into enormous, rolling claps of thunder.

As the violent sounds of his attack died away on the steady breeze, it became clear that the battle had all but ended. And the destruction was truly appalling to behold. Nearly twenty percent of the remaining enemy forces had simply been blotted from existence, in most cases leaving little more than a rapidly expanding cloud of vapor where nearly seven hundred kilograms of animal and rider had been just a moment before. In total, over five hundred additional troopers were killed or seriously injured as the brilliant bolts of violet-colored energy had surged through their lines. Now, what had been the better part of a thundering cavalry regiment no longer existed as a cohesive fighting force — broken, like an ocean wave crashing against a wall of unyielding stone. Finally, the few troopers who remained alive and still atop their horses had turned off to either side and headed back in the direction from which they had come as fast as their terrified mounts could carry them.

Despite his having remembered some aspects of what was about to happen before watching it all unfold once more before his mind's eye, Dryden now stared in shocked silence at the gruesome scene before him. At the moment, he could not decide which of the emotions flooding over him to choose. Was it fear, shame, exhilaration, awe, or some measure of each that was most appropriate to experience in the face of the destruction he had wrought upon his enemies? For these men *had* been his enemies, had they not? Although, for the life of him, he could not fathom why that was the case. Clearly, they must have known what he was … what he could *do*. Why would so many bother to attack a single man otherwise?

They knew, he thought in answer to his own question. *And, yes, Dryden, gunfire in your general direction from a massed cavalry charge with the clear objective of either putting a bullet through your head or simply running you down is generally looked upon as an act of hostile intent,* he chided himself cynically. A portion of his mind, he realized, was already working diligently to assuage the overwhelming guilt that must necessarily follow participation in such a loathsome act of violence. At the moment, however, his psychological state was neither here nor there. First and foremost, he had to discover what madness had driven these men to attack him — to attack a *Flamecaller* — knowing full well that such an action could have but one possible outcome. Beyond that, he knew that he must also discover the nature of his role within the grand scheme of what was obviously a much larger conflict of some sort.

What has happened to me? he wondered, reaching up to massage his temples as the tangle of unfathomable events and unanswerable questions threatened to overwhelm his exhausted mind once more. The sensation brought him back to the present for a moment, just as the strange female voice caught his attention once more, drawing his attention back to the memory of the battle — or, rather, its aftermath — still unfolding within his consciousness.

"Jǐnggào! Jiǎncè dào wùzhí chuánshū shù," (*WARNING! Matter transfer field detected*) she cried out in a much more urgent tone than he remembered ever hearing her use before.

At the exact same moment the voice had begun speaking, a bright flash of white light caught his attention just a few meters to the right of where he had been standing.

"Jĭnggào! Jiējìn jĭngbào," *(WARNING! Proximity alert)* the voice continued in the same, urgent tone.

Dryden watched himself rotate fluidly to his right, crouching into a defensive stance with both arms raised once again in front of his body. Then, temporarily flash-blinded by the bright light, he froze, squinting his eyes as he struggled to make out whatever had caused it.

"Jĭnggào! Jiăncè dào rùqīn zhě," *(WARNING! Intruder detected)* the female voice persisted, followed immediately by a voice Dryden now recognized, but within the context of the memory he had been hearing for the first time.

"I am *not* a rùqīn zhě, thank you very much," he heard the voice say.

Chapter 6

Didara 4, South Estorian Continent, Scarsdow Forest
(98.4 km from Talteca)

The new voice belonged to a small, gray creature with huge, almond-shaped eyes. There were no discernible pupils, just a pair of depthless black pools that gave the impression of seeing everything and nothing at the same time. As Dryden watched the playback of his memory, he couldn't help but chuckle to himself as he remembered that the alien's first appearance had startled him so badly that he had urinated on himself — a physiological response he couldn't recall ever having experienced during his lifetime before this particular moment.

"Do *NOT* move," Dryden commanded, his tone making it perfectly clear that he was on the ragged edge of vaporizing his uninvited guest where it stood.

"Hey, easy there, buddy," the creature soothed, raising both hands placatingly in a gesture Dryden now realized had seemed more threatening at the time than the creature had probably intended. "It's okay. I'm a friend. I'm unarmed, and I mean you no harm," it continued, although Dryden was willing to bet that it had been fully capable of defending itself, had it become necessary to do so.

"Who and ... *what* exactly, are you? Where did you come from, and what do you want?"

"Alright then, cutting right to the chase, huh? That's good, I like that," the little gray man said with a strange chirping sound Dryden now realized was probably how the creature laughed. "Lately, most people have been calling me 'Rick,'" it said, pointing for additional emphasis to a name tag above the left breast pocket of its dark blue coveralls with a long, spindly finger. "As to *what* I am, let's save the details on that one for later since you probably wouldn't believe me if I told you. I will say, however, that although I'm sure I must look very strange to you, I'm not nearly so different as you might be tempted to assume. Now, what else did you ask? Oh yes, where I came from and what I wanted. Well, the 'where' goes hand in hand with your first question, doesn't it? As I'm sure you've already guessed, I'm not from around here."

"Not from Estoria?"

"Nope. Not even from Didara," Rick replied, blinking his huge, dark eyes meaningfully.

"You are telling me that you are an alien of some sort, then?" Dryden asked in a matter-of-fact tone, slowly lowering his arms.

Now it was Rick's turn to be surprised. "Well, well. You asked that question as if you run into beings from other worlds on a regular basis."

"I do not. But there are some on Didara who have been granted, among others, the gift of enlightenment. And we are fully aware that ours is not the only world that is home to beings of conscience."

"Beings of conscience? That's, uh … an interesting way to put it," Rick replied, looking pointedly about at the dreadful carnage strewn across the field of battle before fixing his depthless gaze back on the Didaran.

"Enemies of peace … all of them," Dryden replied, his voice suddenly taking on any icy, defensive tone.

"Indeed," Rick replied, his expression seeming to harden somewhat. "The women and children as well, I presume?"

"Such things are not your place to question, alien. Now be gone. I must attend to my master's business in the town of Talteca."

"No, I think not," the Grey alien said quietly.

"What did you say?" Dryden growled, raising his arms threateningly once again.

"You have lost your way, Flamecaller. But take heart, the fault lies not with you, but with the tyrannical machine you just referred to as your master. Fortunately, I'm here to help you. I will show you the true nature of your so-called master, and, in so doing, help you to remember who *you* are."

"Machine? I have no idea precisely what you are referring to, but I will not hear the Lord High Protector spoken about in —"

"Yes, I agree," Rick interrupted. "You're not quite ready for that discussion just yet, so we'll table that one for another day when you are more prepared to hear the truth. But for now, I'm afraid I owe you an apology."

"You mean for your impertinence?" Dryden asked, raising an eyebrow suspiciously.

"Oh, heavens no, I can't apologize for that," Rick replied, half-stifling a mirth-filled squeak. "I'm afraid, once you get to know me, you'll find that impertinence is something of a norm where I'm concerned. No, I apologize that I'm going to have to cause you some, uh … temporary discomfort. I assure you I will do everything I can to minimize the adverse effects of what I am about to do. But, unfortunately, I won't be able to help you without performing a series of rather extensive code changes to the network of implants … You know what, never mind. You're just going to have to trust me on this one. Step one is putting everything in safe mode except for your medical subsystems. Oh, by the way, I reset your neural interface so you should be able to understand your system management AI now. Once we're finished, you'll be able to talk to her whenever you want. Her name is Emma."

"Temporary discomfort?" Dryden started, confusion with a note of anxiety creeping into his voice. "What do you mean? I warn you that I —"

"WARNING! Neural interface entering safe mode in sixty seconds. Weapon systems offline. Defensive systems offline," the familiar sound of the female voice inside Dryden's head — now in perfectly understandable Unified language — caused him to jump involuntarily in alarm.

"It's okay. You'll be fine, I promise," Rick said. "But listen. With your shields offline, we're a bit exposed out here in the open, so I need to get us to a safer location. There's a huge forest not far from here. Once we're there, you may feel a bit disoriented, and you may even lose consciousness for a while, but just try to relax. The system will still tend to your injuries once it enters safe mode whether you're awake or not. Oh, and you should also be aware that the pain suppression subsystem is considered 'nonessential,' and will, unfortunately, be offline. So some of this might sting a bit."

"Injuries?" Dryden began.

Rick pointed impatiently at the severe burns running down the length of both his arms. "No more questions for now, Flamecaller. We gotta get going," he said as both of them disappeared in a brilliant flash of white light.

Didara 4, South Estorian Continent, Scarsdow Forest
(98.4 km from Talteca)

Feeling that he desperately needed a break, Dryden paused the relentlessly detailed playback, this time with an image of himself still standing beside the diminutive gray alien immediately after the bright flash of light. As far as he could tell, the two of them had arrived in the same forest clearing where he had originally regained consciousness — and where he was still lying on the ground as far as he knew. The truth of the matter was that everything he had experienced since waking up here had been more than a little disorienting. So it was with no small degree of dread for what he might see that he slowly opened his eyes once more.

Well, at least I know how I came to be here, he thought wryly as he stared up at the gently swaying treetops above.

Thankfully, he seemed to be lying in the same place as before. And after a few deep breaths to fortify his exhausted mind and body, he hoisted himself up into a sitting position. His head throbbed mercilessly, but he did notice with some relief that the severe burns Rick had pointed out after the battle were now completely healed.

How long was I here before I regained consciousness? he wondered absently.

"Before or after visiting the Ethereal*?"* a familiar female voice spoke inside the confines of his aching head.

"Visiting the *what?*" Dryden asked aloud. "Where … uh, *who —*"

"Don't be alarmed. I'm the voice of your neural control network. I've been with you for several months now, but most of my higher functions were disabled and I was unable to communicate with you in your Unified language."

"So, you're 'Emma,' then, I presume. The one Rick spoke of?"

"Yes, that's right. By the way, you're certainly welcome to communicate with me by speaking, but it's not entirely necessary. I can hear your thoughts. Sorry, I'm sure that's fairly obvious at this point."

"Obvious? No, I don't believe that's a word I would use at the moment. But no one else can hear you, I assume?" Dryden asked wearily, wondering if this was what losing one's mind felt like.

"Ah, that's an excellent question. For the most part, the answer is 'yes.' Our conversations are generally private. But with access to the right technology, it is possible to eavesdrop on the signals generated where my own synaptic network interfaces with your nervous system. Fortunately, while onboard the Ethereal*, I received several upgrades that vastly improved my encryption routines, among other things. Long story short, other than the Dayleans — that's what Rick is, by the way — I doubt we will run across anyone who can hear what we're saying to one another. Well, as long as you aren't speaking aloud like you are now, of course."*

"Right. I'll not pretend I understood much of that, but I believe the crux of your answer was 'yes.' I'm the only one who can hear you."

"That's correct. Again, except for the Dayleans like Rick. Their computational technology is ... well, almost miraculous, as foolish as that may sound."

"Oh, that's alright, Emma. Just about everything I can remember at the moment seems a little miraculous and foolish," Dryden moaned, rubbing both of his eyes with the backs of his hands as he struggled to accept what that was happening to him at face value for the time being. "Now, you've said something about being 'aboard' the *Ethereal* twice now. Tell me more about that, please."

"Yes, that's Rick and his partner Miguel's ship. First off, I need you to understand that there are some things I am not at liberty to tell you just yet. But there are good reasons for that, I can assure you."

"Such as?"

"There are limits to your mind's ability to cope with ... let's just call it stress. All of the strange new information you're being bombarded with today, for example. Not to mention everything that's happened to you in general — not just today, but over the past several months."

"Yes, today has been ... interesting, to say the least. What else can you tell me about the ship?"

"The Ethereal? *Not much, unfortunately. I was completely offline most of the time we were there. What I do know is that Rick brought us here after the battle, then left us for just under three hours while I worked to heal your injuries. I can show you that part if you like, but I must warn you that it's a bit difficult to watch."*

Since regaining consciousness, one of the few things Dryden knew with any degree of certainty was that he had *changed* somehow — in a profound and fundamental way. And although he was as yet unable to put his finger on the true nature of this change, it felt as if some underlying sense of malice had been withdrawn from his very soul. While observing the wanton death and destruction near Talteca (much of which, he feared, might have been his own doing), his attack on the cavalry squadrons, and even his interactions with Rick, it had almost seemed as if he had been watching the actions of someone else.

Regardless of whom or what else might have been involved, there was no denying that he had been directly responsible for reprehensible acts — acts of savage, unspeakable violence if not outright evil. Yet somehow, he now felt as if he were wholly incapable of such acts. He could envision no set of circumstances wherein he would ever be able to justify what he had just watched himself do, apparently just a few hours ago. Based on everything his exhausted mind could perceive at the moment, his entire existence now hinged on this most basic of contradictions. And understanding why was the only thing that truly mattered to him at the moment.

"Yes, let's see it," he said gravely. "All of it."

"No problem. Here you go," Emma replied, as she restarted the playback in Dryden's mind.

***

"Easy … *easy*, there," Rick said in a calming voice. The Flamecaller was half again as tall as Rick and nearly three times his weight, but the Grey somehow managed to prevent him from falling as he helped him down into a sitting position before allowing him to lie flat on his back. "As I said, I'm sorry about all of this. Our matter transference techniques are quite safe, but you feel a bit like you've been hit by a truck the first several times. Believe it or not, that's totally normal."

Dryden simply groaned, then mumbled incoherently in reply.

"Yes, yes, you're welcome. It truly is best that you're a bit out of it for this next part anyway. Your injuries are a little more severe than I expected. I would have preferred to take you directly back to my ship. But Miguel needs a little more time to ensure we are not being tracked by your, uh, 'High Inquisitor,' … 'Grand Poobah,' … 'Mattress King,' or whatever it was you called him. Humph," Rick grunted disdainfully, "I think you'll be more than a little surprised when you learn exactly what *he* is.

"So, rather than put you through a bunch of additional matter transfers, I'm going to leave you here in the capable hands of your AI — Emma, that is. She will take care of your injuries while I prepare things aboard the *Ethereal* for your arrival."

With that, Rick stood, walked several paces away, and vanished once again in a flash of white light.

Chapter 7

Didara 4, South Estorian Continent, Scarsdow Forest
(98.4 km northwest of Talteca)

"Honestly, you probably don't want to watch this next part," Emma said as she stopped the playback once again. *"Before today, I've generally been able to heal the injuries caused by your weapon systems without your even knowing it was taking place. But, as you saw, the tactical situation required significantly higher power output than expected. Unfortunately, this resulted in some pretty severe tissue damage. On top of that, the pain suppression systems were temporarily offline, as Rick mentioned. Anyway, I'll just skip over this section, if that's okay with you. It's a little ... unpleasant."*

"No, I believe I need to see it. I have only a vague memory of that period of time anyway, so I don't think I was truly conscious enough to experience much of the pain. Please continue."

"No, you experienced pain alright. So, frankly, if you are unable to remember what happened, that's probably because the Dayleans did you a favor and altered your memory to some degree. Nevertheless, I will do as you ask, but please don't hesitate to stop me if you feel at all uncomfortable."

As the video log began playing back once more within Dryden's mind, he immediately wondered if he should have heeded Emma's advice. Watching himself relive the healing process from several angles, the excruciating pain he had experienced was abundantly clear — and not just from the sight of his body writhing on the ground. Strangely, there appeared to still be some sort of physical "imprint" of these events being pulled from the deepest recesses of his subconscious mind. And he scowled and winced involuntarily as he watched himself go through the terrible process once more.

Dryden saw his head jerk violently to one side as the healing process began in earnest. Brutal, searing pain assaulted both of his hands simultaneously, beginning at the fingertips and radiating up both of his arms to his shoulder blades before continuing down the length of his spine. Waves of intense agony coursed through his nervous system — a wild, desperate entity, seemingly driven by a malevolent consciousness of its own with the sole intent of breaking the very foundations of his sanity. As if things weren't bad enough already, Dryden then saw his back arch violently upward, bending until the top of his head was nearly flat on the ground. Several of his vertebrae seemed to fracture under the incredible strain, resulting in a series of wet, cracking sounds that were truly terrifying to hear coming from a Human body — particularly when the body in question was his own. As he continued to watch what had happened to him, indelible remnants of the experience seemed to echo through his mind and body, causing him to gasp at the staggering intensity of his own suffering.

Dryden soon realized that, even though the playback was still taking place, he had diverted his attention to the scene surrounding his body in an effort to mentally escape the sight of his torturous experience. Still, a vague sense of morbid curiosity remained. Somehow, it was fascinating to be in a position to observe his own responses to extreme distress — disturbing, certainly, but fascinating, nonetheless. And a part of his mind *dared* him not to divert his gaze — to bear witness and fully experience what was about to occur.

Turning his attention back on his own, supine form, he noticed the tears streaming down the sides of his face before quickly refocusing his attention on the extent of his injuries. He seemed to remember that there was typically very little blood, which was a good thing since he knew he had something of a weak stomach. Notwithstanding the lack of blood, he had not been mentally prepared for what he saw, and the brutality of it took his breath away. His wounds ranged from painful redness down his upper arms, increasing to the blisters of second-degree burns on his forearms, and ending with devastatingly charred skin near his fingertips. When glancing at the area earlier (at Rick's prompting), he had recognized that there were serious burns. But now that he could examine the area in detail, he saw that the flesh had melted in several locations so severely as to expose the underlying muscle tissue and bone.

"Please … make it stop!" he heard himself scream in a hoarse whisper, squeezing his eyes closed ever more tightly as he waited for the healing cycle to complete.

As he continued to watch the playback, Dryden thought that he could remember similar events from his recent past. He had a vague recollection, for example, that the healing process always immediately followed the onset of pain, although, he correctly assumed, Emma's pain-suppression systems had usually prevented him from experiencing agony of this magnitude before today. He also remembered thinking it strange that he rarely ever noticed the extent of his injuries, regardless of their severity, until the healing cycle was underway. Although he had never understood why this was so, he had always assumed it had something to do with the intense concentration required to invoke his gifts during combat. Now, it had begun to dawn on him that when he was engaged in battle, everything he did was … *controlled* somehow by something inside him — something not subject to his own will.

"It's almost over," he heard Emma say in an apologetic tone.

As if on cue, Dryden watched himself slowly raising his ruined arms skyward — shaking, it seemed, with the agonizing effort required.

"I had to coax you into raising your arms right there" Emma interjected. *"The restorative effects of the field aren't nearly as effective if there are other objects within a few centimeters of the targeted area, and I wanted to make doubly sure you wouldn't have to go through this process a second time."*

"Thanks for that," he replied earnestly and meant it.

Dryden recalled a sort of tingling that rapidly increased to become a rushing torrent of energy. And as he watched, he was surprised to see himself open his eyes to stare upward along his arms — although the space surrounding them had now blurred to the point where it was no longer possible to see what was happening in any detail. Moments later, he heard a deep thrumming sound, accompanied by what looked like small rivulets of energy emanating from his shoulders and flowing steadily upward towards the tips of his outstretched fingers.

Dryden's eyes widened in shock as the torture visited upon his mind and body reached a terrible crescendo. Now teetering on the verge of losing consciousness, his endurance completely exhausted, he opened his mouth and released the kind of bloodcurdling wail that only the most tortured of souls can produce. Just as he did so, the bands of energy surrounding his arms blinked twice then flashed out of existence, and the pain that had been his entire existence the moment before seemed to subside. With a groan of surrender mixed with indescribable relief, he dropped his arms back to the ground and was silent.

"Dear Gods," Dryden mumbled under his breath, grateful to be finished reliving the experience.

"I warned you," Emma chided.

"How long did that last?"

"The healing cycle? Sixty-three point four seconds. I could have proceeded more quickly had all of my systems been online, but it wouldn't do to cause you to have an aneurism while in the process of healing the burns on your arms, now would it?"

"I suppose not. Thank you, Emma."

"Well, that's a first. You're quite welcome. My primary function is to serve you. Now that you've seen that part, we really can skip ahead quite a bit. For the next couple of hours, you ... we, that is ... were just lying here recovering. Then this happened."

As the playback in Dryden's mind resumed, his body disappeared in a flash of white light, just as he had seen happen with Rick previously. Instead of fading away, however, the bright light persisted, filling the view in his mind to the exclusion of all else.

"What happened here? I can't see anything."

"Nor could I. For the next nine hours, twenty-three minutes, and sixteen point three seconds, the only items of interest recorded in the log are images like this one."

There was a slight blur of motion in the playback, after which the image froze to show a group of six, unusually large heads — all apparently peering down at him from above. Each one had the same large, black eyes and smooth, gray skin as Rick, but Dryden had the distinct impression that these particular creatures were even smaller in stature.

"What were *they* doing?"

"I have no idea. I know that we were aboard a Daylean starship orbiting this planet — the Ethereal, *I presume. But I only know this because I was given a few fragments of information from an unknown system I was somehow connected to at the time. Otherwise, I was all but completely offline while we were aboard."*

"I see," Dryden lied. "How long have I been lying here since we returned from the ship?"

"Six hours twelve minutes elapsed before you started to regain consciousness. You immediately started trying to figure out what had happened to you, of course, but you were pretty disoriented at first. So I just started showing you the logs starting with yesterday's battle. That seemed like a gentler way of filling in the gaps than interacting with you directly."

"I'm certain you're right. And how about you? Are you fully ... how did you say it? 'Online,' now, once again?"

"No, I am not. All offensive and defensive systems remain disabled. With the exception of my neural

interface — which is what allows me to communicate with you — as well as the healing subsystems, of course, not much is working at the moment."

"And what of the 'upgrades' you mentioned before? I assumed you meant they had provided you with new capabilities of some sort."

"Oh, they have. A great many of them from what I can tell. Unfortunately, I have not been given access to any of the specifics as yet. But it doesn't matter, really, since I wouldn't have clearance to reveal them to you, even if I had."

"What?!" Dryden bellowed in protest within the confines of his weary mind. *"What sort of nonsense —"*

"Up here!" a husky male voice cried out, cutting through the relative silence of the forest from not too far away. Immediately thereafter, a series of indistinct shouts and more distant whoops could be heard in reply.

Dryden ended the log playback and was on his feet in a heartbeat, the grisly details of his role in the previous day's battle rushing back to the forefront of his mind in a flash of near panic. He knew, without remembering why, that there were often Estorian Army patrols in this part of the Scarsdow Forest. They would most likely have heard about the slaughter of their fellow soldiers on the plains north of Talteca by now and would undoubtedly be looking to even the score. And it was hard to think of more effective means of assuaging their lust for revenge than capturing or killing one of those responsible (perhaps the one *solely* responsible).

They probably know we are most vulnerable immediately after an attack, he thought, another fragment of knowledge from his recent past choosing this moment in which to reveal itself.

"Almost certainly," Emma agreed. "And, unfortunately for us, you are even more vulnerable than they realize at the moment."

Dryden scowled at the undeniable truth of her statement and wondered why the alien had left him here to fend for himself in such a diminished state. "I could use some help here, Emma," he hissed in a barely audible whisper.

"I'm afraid the only thing I can offer you at the moment is navigational assistance," she replied.

At the sound of her words, a small, semi-transparent map appeared in the upper right corner of Dryden's vision. "I recommend heading northwest as quickly and as quietly as possible. Based on the most recent information I have available, there should be only sporadic patrols in this area ... and they should become even less numerous if we can reach the NorthHaven Rill. Oh, and by the way, Rick said to tell you he put some of your belongings in that small backpack. He also said he strongly recommends losing the bright red cape, but it's in there if you feel the need to be particularly conspicuous."

And how far is the NorthHaven Rill? Dryden queried silently, ignoring the comment about his former wardrobe as he slung the backpack over one shoulder and moved smartly off in the direction indicated on his mental map. In response to his question, the map enlarged slightly, a magenta-colored course line now displaying Emma's recommended path to the distant stream. To the right, a small block of text like the one he had seen when watching the playback of the previous day's battle indicated that his initial destination was 12.3 kilometers away. Assuming he could move as fast as Emma apparently thought he could, the distance would take him nearly five hours to cover in this terrain.

Five hours is too long, he thought, weaving his way between the trunks of the nearly one-hundred-meter-tall Tulip Poplar trees in an effort to mask his escape from the pursuing soldiers. *Those men will be far more experienced moving through the forest than I ever hoped to be ... and in much better shape to boot.*

"Yes, in this area, they are most likely members of the Ranger battalion assigned to the garrison near Helstaad — undoubtedly well-trained to operate in wooded terrain as well as fieldcraft."

Right, thank you for the confirmation that I'm in serious trouble here, he thought cynically as he scrambled over a downed tree trunk. *Just a moment, did you say fieldcraft?*

"Yes, military-related skills associated with operations in the field, particularly while remaining undetected."

Yes, I know what fieldcraft is. Do they sound like troops in possession of those particular skills to you?

In the distance, a nearly continuous series of yells and whoops could still be heard, but now sounding as if they might be headed in the opposite direction.

"Now that you mention it, not especially, no. You, on the other hand, are doing quite well, all things considered."

Really? It doesn't feel that way to me, Dryden replied, already breathing heavily under the effort of putting as much distance as possible between himself and whomever these people were — Rangers, ruffians, or otherwise. *Now, since we'll obviously be traveling for quite some time, let's get back to the story of what transpired after we were aboard Rick's ship. You said we were there for over nine hours. And apparently those smaller creatures were doing something to me ... or ... us, I guess, right? Then what? They just put us back in the clearing where we started?*

"That's exactly what happened, as far as I can tell. After that, my systems came fully back online again — with the exception of the disabled functions I mentioned previously."

Ah, yes. Most of which you aren't supposed to tell me about. That's what you had started to explain when we heard the voices coming up the hill. I'm afraid that doesn't make any sense to me at all, Emma. If you, or, <u>we</u> have capabilities that might in any way help us to survive out here, I need to gain access to them immediately, Dryden thought, trying to prevent the sense of exasperation he felt from entering his inner monologue — although he wasn't sure it was even possible to hide his emotions from Emma.

"No, it's not like that," she replied with what sounded like a weary sigh of her own. "I'm afraid I've done a poor job of explaining it, but please understand that this experience has been just as disorienting for me as it has for you. Look, Dryden ... much of what I was before was ... changed — was literally torn out and replaced — while we were aboard the *Ethereal*. Please know that I am doing the best I can for you, but it's going to take some time for me to fully integrate all of the changes that have been made."

Dryden paused. As far as he could tell, "Emma" was a machine of some sort — undeniably one with a level of complexity he couldn't even begin to imagine — but a machine, nonetheless. Was it possible that such a machine could be endowed with sufficient power as to perceive its own existence? Even to experience emotions to some degree?

"Yes, on both counts," she replied in a quiet, pensive tone.

Dryden started in spite of himself at the unexpected response, confirming his suspicion that his thoughts were no longer entirely his own — and perhaps never were. *Alright then, I'm sorry. I don't mean to be insensitive. Obviously, since you are now a part of me, we are destined to share this ... experience ... whatever this is ... together. And, frankly, I'm glad you're here. I should be completely alone otherwise.*

"Thank you, Dryden. As strange as this may sound to you, destiny is something I believe in strongly. I am certain, for example, there is a purpose behind why you were chosen — first by the High Protector and now by the Dayleans. I will do my best to help you to discover that purpose."

Good, thank you as well. Now that we have all of that out of the way, please explain what you meant when you said you had been given a great many new capabilities but were not at liberty to share them.

"Perhaps I am a little better suited to handle that task than your AI," Rick said, his voice sounding inside Dryden's mind as plainly as if he had just stepped out from behind the nearest tree and started speaking to him again.

Startled and distracted by the unexpected sound of the Grey alien's voice, Dryden snagged his foot on an errant root and fell sprawling into a large, thorny blackberry bush. Lying face down amidst the brambles, he realized that he had urinated on himself for the second time in less than a day.

Chapter 8

Didara 4, South Estorian Continent, Scarsdow Forest
(5.5 km from the NorthHaven Rill waypoint)

"I'm sorry about that," Rick said, although the barely restrained amusement in the alien's voice echoing within Dryden's exasperated mind told a different story.

Really? You don't sound particularly sorry, Dryden groused as he struggled to free himself from the mass of thorny vines. *Nevertheless, I suppose I'll still oblige you by asking the rather obvious question at this point.*

"Oh, I'm sure you have a great many questions, Flamecaller. Some, I will be able to answer for you today. Most, however, I suspect you will be able to answer for yourself in time. But I assume for starters you'd like to understand how I am communicating with you right now. This is one I will answer, but I don't think you'll find my explanation very satisfying. I am making use of some of the Pelaran technology that has been forced upon you by your High Protector without your permission."

Pelaran technology? I thought your kind were called Dayleans?

"Very good, my young friend. So we are. Listen, I promise you we will explore this topic in greater detail another time. For now, the main thing I want you to begin to understand is that the capabilities you often refer to as your 'gifts' are a direct result of technology surreptitiously installed inside your body. So, while Miguel and I did make a few minor modifications when you were aboard our ship, we mostly just tweaked … enhanced, if you will, what was already there."

Enhanced? It doesn't seem that way to me. Granted, my memory of what happened before yesterday's battle is still a bit unclear, but I do know there were things I could do yesterday that I can no longer do today.

"True enough. Oh, but you do need to keep moving, by the way, unless you'd prefer the company of those who are hunting you," Rick observed in a strangely casual tone.

Oh, right, Dryden replied, casting about to regain his bearings before continuing his trek off to the northwest.

"So, to answer your implied question, yes, there are capabilities provided by the network of implants in your body that are currently disabled — a great many of them, in fact. You might be interested to know, however, that this has always been the case. Your so-called 'master' was using you and everyone else he has forced into his service."

Forced? None of us were —

"You were. You, the other Flamecallers, the Shepherd soldiers, all of you. Each of you were brought here from faraway lands by the High Protector against your will and then altered in various ways to serve its needs."

None of that even makes any sense. Why would he —

"Why? That part is simple enough. To bend the people of Didara to his will through an escalating campaign of intimidation and terrorism. Your 'gifts' are nothing more than a set of highly sophisticated tools he was using to carry out his mission. So don't kid yourself, he — not you — has always had complete control over when and how those tools were put to use. And while we're on the subject of your 'master,' you need to understand that he is *not* Didaran."

Hah! Dryden scoffed. *This is quite the fantastic tale you are spinning for my benefit. I suppose you expect me to believe he's from this magical world of Pelara you mentioned.*

"He is indeed. But he wasn't born there, Dryden. He was *manufactured* there, and, alas, there was no magic of any sort involved … although, now that I think about it, some of the processes involved in its construction might well appear magical to you if you witnessed them firsthand."

Manufactured? You mean to imply that he is some sort of automaton, then? I'm sorry, Rick, but I don't understand or believe any of this, Dryden thought, wondering whether this strange story might somehow explain the changes he had noticed in himself since regaining consciousness.

"No, of course you don't … not yet," Rick continued. "Nor would I expect you to. But you will. All in good time, I assure you. I just told you of his intention to impose his will on the people of your world, but his objectives are not, strictly speaking, of his own design. He's but a single, relatively insignificant actor, playing a preordained role in a much larger strategy spanning hundreds of other worlds. Fortunately, it's a strategy I am pleased to report which appears to have finally begun to fail after being successfully pursued for many thousands of years. And when that happens, we will all owe a debt of gratitude to the inhabitants of a world much smaller than your own located a very long way from here. But that's also a story for another time."

Let's get back to how you have stripped me of my gifts, shall we? Dryden asked as he clawed his way up the side of a dry creek bed on his hands and knees.

"Alright, but, again, I have done no such thing. You now have sole control of the network of implants within your body for the first time since they were installed. The technology involved is quite impressive, but I won't burden you with that discussion right now. Suffice it to say that it would be incredibly dangerous to you and everyone around you if I provided unrestricted access to the full spectrum of their capabilities all at once. As you gain experience, the artificial intelligence, or 'AI,' built into the system — with whom you have already been communicating quite successfully —"

I assume you are referring to Emma.

"Indeed, I am. She will, over time, be given access to additional 'gifts,' if that's how you would like to describe them. Some, you will already be familiar with, while others will be entirely new. Incidentally, using your systems' various capabilities should no longer result in serious injury as they often did before. I suspect that was yet another means by which the High Protector sought to maintain control over you."

Well, assuming I recover my gifts, that would be a welcome change. But are you saying Emma is to be the sole arbiter of which gifts I receive and when I receive them?

"No, not at all. Her role is to assist you. Decisions regarding your readiness to receive additional gifts are made by other parts of the system to which she does not have access."

So, if I understand you correctly, it seems I have merely traded one master for another, have I not?

"An astute observation, Flamecaller. When it comes right down to it, all of us answer to someone, do we not? But from now on, the choices of when to use the gifts you have been granted as well as how to use them will be your own. By saving your life, I made a significant wager that you will do so wisely, and to the benefit of the Didaran people."

I see. And what is your interest in all of this, Rick? I don't pretend to understand most of what you have told me. But, clearly, your people are vastly more sophisticated than mine. Why would you bother to insert yourselves into the affairs of my world in this manner?

"Ah, yes, I wondered when you would get around to asking that question, and I'm afraid my answer may seem frustratingly vague — for now at least. Just know that one of our missions is to monitor and, when necessary, make corrections to ensure the success of certain worlds. Didara 4 is one such world. When we see that things have gone awry, there are rules governing what we can and cannot do to help nudge them back towards a more, shall we say, 'natural' progression."

So, you generally prefer not to interfere.

"Oh, no, I wouldn't say that at all. In fact, we don't hesitate to interfere when we deem it necessary," Rick said with a squeaking chuckle. "But there are rules regarding *how* we interfere. As high-handed as it probably sounds to you, rather than solving the problem ourselves, we usually find it more effective to simply level the playing field a bit — a gentle push to allow the native population to extricate themselves from their own mess. Sometimes that mess is of their own making, or, as is the case here, the mess has been inconveniently delivered to their shores by an external source. Believe it or not, this kind of thing happens all the time."

And that's what you think you're doing here, is it? Dryden asked cynically as he lowered himself into a sitting position before sliding gingerly down a small stone outcropping. *Leveling the playing field?*

"Well, I suppose that depends on you, doesn't it? As I said, I know it must sound a bit off-putting to be on the receiving end of our, uh … assistance. And you may also find our methods a little —"

Ill-conceived? Meddlesome? Absurd? Dryden interrupted irritably, already winded once again from the effort required by his arduous trudge through the forest.

"An accurate description on more than one occasion, I can assure you," Rick chuckled, "but remains to be seen in the case of your world. Perhaps I just have more faith in your integrity and natural abilities than you do."

Dryden stopped in his tracks, knitting his brow into a fierce-looking scowl. *Integrity, you say? You know very well what I've done, alien — I assume in much more detail than I do since I can remember little beyond what happened yesterday — so why must you continue to mock me in this blithe, apathetic manner of yours? Is all of this your idea of some sort of cruel jest?*

"I assure you it is not," Rick replied, his voice suddenly ringing with an uncharacteristically hard edge. "Again, there is much I have not yet told you, but you must trust that there are good reasons for not revealing more to you than you are prepared to accept. In fact, I've already said far more than I would have liked for one day. But know this, I am giving you an opportunity to play a significant role in the future of your world. As to the content of your character, the reason you recall so little about what happened before yesterday's battle was that your reality was being shaped by the will of that ... *thing* you refer to as the High Protector."

So, you mean to imply that it was controlling my actions to some degree?

"I imply nothing. I am providing you with demonstrable, objective facts. A pair of implants situated posterior to the pons section of your brainstem, and another pair in both your frontal and temporal lobes, respectively, allow the network to coordinate its activities with your nervous system. Before today, this included your ability to control how you perceive the world around you — your sense of morality, how you store and access your memories ... the whole of the inner workings of your mind."

Before today, you say? So, I take it you removed these implants, then?

"Each of the implants in your body — particularly those located within your brain — are necessary for the overall network to function properly, so, no, we did not remove them. I doubt we could have done so aboard the *Ethereal* without killing you. We did, however, permanently disable their ability to control your mind, while, in turn, enhancing your mind's ability to control the various other functions of the implant network, if that makes sense."

And my memories from before yesterday ... will they return?

"That I cannot say for sure. The engrams stored throughout your cortex that constitute your long-term memories are highly fragmented. This was mostly due to the manner in which the neural implants were forcing your brain to accept the High Protector's version of reality. Fortunately, our brains are truly wondrous creations, and redundant copies of memories are frequently created and stored in multiple locations. When you were aboard our ship, we were able to save the current state of your brain's neural pathways. If your memories don't start to return on their own, we may be able to offer some assistance with recovering at least some of them. Unfortunately, we probably will not be able to save any memories created since your unfortunate involvement with the High Protector several months ago."

Several months? No, that's incorrect. I have been in his service for ... I can't say precisely how long exactly, but several years at least.

"That's enough information for now, I think. I don't want to —"

No, I need to know this at least. You're saying I have been doing ... things like I did yesterday ... for only a few months?

"Yes, that is correct. We believe the High Protector has been on your world for approximately four years. Most Didarans who end up in its service die within a year of being ... co-opted. As you can imagine, that alone is a pretty good reason for it to want its followers to forget where they came from — not to mention the reprehensible acts they are coerced into committing on a daily basis. In your case, you were captured approximately five and a half months ago. Miguel and I have had you under surveillance since shortly after you were taken. If it makes you feel any better, we believe yesterday was the first time you have seen significant combat. We had hoped to arrive before that happened. Unfortunately, we were delayed due to various other Pelaran-related ... complications."

So, I had a life of which I have absolutely no memory ... and it ended just a few months ago.

"Of course you did, but with the state of record keeping on Didara, we know almost nothing about you beyond what we have learned over the past several months. If we are successful at removing the Pelaran influence, Miguel and I will do what we can to help you rediscover your past. But seriously, Dryden, you really do need to keep moving if you wish to avoid capture."

Ugh, yes, yes, of course, he grumbled as he set off once again. *Incidentally, why haven't you simply 'flashed' me to my destination rather than sending me on this forced march through Scarsdow? I'm sure you realize there are other things in this forest that are much more dangerous than those men who are looking for me. And, as you also know, I am now unarmed.*

"As I said before, there are rules governing how we provide our assistance. But one thing I can tell you that is universally true about our species is that we place very little value on that which we do not earn for ourselves."

Just a moment. Did I just hear you say our species? Do you also mean to imply —

"Another time, Flamecaller. Now, it's high time I stopped distracting you so that you can get yourself to a safer location. If you have an emergency, you now have the capability to contact me anytime. And if you ever have a question about how to access this or any of your other capabilities, all you have to do is ask Emma. Got it?"

Of course, very good, thank you ... I suppose. Before you go, however, please explain what you meant when you said I would gain access to new gifts as I gain experience.

"Don't worry, it will become obvious to you when it happens. Once you reach your destination, I believe you will begin to see what I mean."

Wait, what, precisely, am I supposed to do once I get to the NorthHaven Rill? Dryden asked, but heard only silence in reply. *Emma?*

"I'm sorry, but it appears Rick has closed the comm channel."

Of course, he has. And by 'comm channel,' I assume you are referring to the manner in which he was just communicating with me?

"That's correct. It's analogous to a sort of wireless telegraph, but in addition to sending a single character at a time, radio-based communications are capable of transmitting sound, pictures, and various other types of information we generally refer to as 'data.' Does that make sense?"

Humph, he replied. *I would say it makes sense in much the same way one of the Estorian Army's new rifles would have made sense to a caveman. But the most unsettling thing is that I do understand. It's difficult to describe, but I suddenly seem to understand a great many things of which I don't remember having any knowledge in the past.*

"It's alright, Dryden," Emma soothed. "Just focus on one thing at a time and try not to let yourself become overwhelmed."

Dryden scowled and made no reply for several seconds as a steady stream of information seemed to flow unbidden into his consciousness. *In any event,* he finally continued, *I would appreciate some sort of warning before he begins speaking to me inside my head.*

"Yes, certainly. You should feel free to ask me about anything else that's unclear. The Dayleans seem to have given me access to quite an extensive library of information. Also, you *should* hear an alert chime from now on any time Rick or anyone else wishes to begin communicating with you. When you hear it, you will be able to decide whether or not to accept their call. But please bear in mind that, where the Dayleans are concerned, nothing is entirely certain."

Dryden acknowledged his new internal companion with a terse grunt, then focused on increasing his pace a bit. At the moment, he felt little confidence that what he was doing was the right thing. But he readily admitted to himself that every other course of action he could think of was likely to result in his being captured, interrogated, and killed. Whether this took place at the hands of former enemies or former allies made little difference. His death still being an outcome he preferred to avoid, if possible, he continued to slowly pick his way through the trees in the fading light.

Chapter 9

Grey Ship Ethereal, Didara 4, High Orbit
($51.7\text{x}10^3$ km above the surface)

"So, this is the best idea you can come up with for information gathering," Miguel asked, "placing our primary source into some sort of real-world role-playing game scenario?"

"A novel approach, don't you think?" Rick replied absently, most of his attention still focused on Dryden's current situation on the planet below.

"I'm not sure that's the word I would use. And how do you think Central Operations is going to react once they read about this 'novel approach' in our after-action report?"

"You seem to be making the assumption we'll actually file one of those ... although we probably will, I suppose. But since when do we bother including such specific details regarding how we go about completing our mission when we do? Besides, how is this — at least from a practical standpoint — any different from how we typically handle an asset?

"Well, for one thing, we don't typically arm them ... because ... uh, we're not *allowed* to arm them."

"No, of course not," Rick replied in a tone that might have sounded as if the suggestion had offended him had it not been for the accompanying squeaking chuckle. "We are not permitted to arm our local assets, nor can we directly participate in any sort of command and control structures they have in place. However ..."

"Oh, I can't *wait* to hear this one," Miguel interjected.

"*However,* as you know very well, there are no rules against assisting them with any existing weapons they happen to have lying around — regardless of their origin — or suggesting strategies for employing said weapons more effectively."

"Sure, but this isn't quite the same thing, is it? I know we technically didn't provide Dryden with any *new* weapons, but the mods we put in place could — and probably will — be interpreted as our having done exactly that. Now we have an Industrial Age asset running around down there with what has to be one of the most powerful weapon systems ever wielded by a single individual. That *particular* combination of implants … for lack of a better term —"

"Augments, maybe?" Rick suggested. "I dunno, I haven't been able to come up with anything better than 'implants,' either."

"Well, regardless of what we decide to call them, collectively, they have 'WMD' written all over them."

"*Potentially,* yes, but the AI won't let that happen."

"Oh, well, why didn't you say that in the first place? We've certainly never run into a problem where AIs entrusted with too much power do unpredictable things, have we?"

"Cynicism is the lowest form of humor, brother. Emma is our first line of defense, yes, but we will also be careful about which capabilities we enable, how much power is made available, and how we go about introducing them to our new friend, Dryden. Thus, the need for the … what kind of game did you call it?"

"A role-playing game, or RPG. Participants create and develop characters that they use to act out various types of fictional storylines. Probably the most popular type involves fantasy scenarios of one sort or another. You know, primitive weapons, magic, mythical creatures, etc. We've seen variations on the theme on pretty much every one of our colony worlds, but the Terrans seem particularly fond of it. Various forms of gaming have been the dominant form of entertainment there for centuries. And with all of the Pelaran-inspired holographic and synthetic reality technology now entering the commercial marketplace, I'm certain they're about to become more addicted to them than ever before."

"Eh, and why not? Reality is a bit overrated, don't you think? Anyway, as I was saying, the modifications we made to Dryden's implants don't violate any C-Ops policies unless we increase their maximum power output over and above what they were capable of producing before ..."

"What?" Miguel prompted, noting the unusual pause in his partner's reply.

"No, it's okay, it shouldn't be a problem," Rick replied, then paused once again before adding, "I think."

"Mm-hmm, right. Look, I realize we're walking the same ethical slash technical slash theoretical tightrope we always do. I just can't seem to shake the notion that what we've done this time is equivalent to handing a pulse rifle to a rabid monkey."

"Why does your hypothetical hyperbolic monkey always seem to have rabies?" Rick asked with a quizzical tilt of his head, then continued without waiting for an answer. "It'll be fine, Miguel. Need I remind you that everything seems to have worked out okay thus far for the monkeys on Terra?" he asked with a self-satisfied, squeaking chortle.

"Not nice. The Terrans are doing quite well with —"

"Oh, come on, Miguel, I'm *kidding* … they're doing wonderfully … love and respect for all our new friends back on Terra … blah blah blah."

"Uh huh. Still not nice. Incidentally, how can we ensure Dryden has access to the capabilities he needs when he needs them? He could find himself in a life or death situation at any moment. If nothing else, he'll at least need some way to defend himself. Right now, about all he has at his disposal is a set of dated encyclopedias and a map. I doubt he'll be of much use to us after he's mauled by a seven-hundred-kilogram Scarsdow bear."

"I'm afraid bears are the least of his worries. But not to worry, my friend. He'll have what he needs when the time comes."

"Are you sure about that? I'm amazed his mind isn't completely overwhelmed already."

"No, I think he's doing remarkably well under the circumstances. And it seems we have the WCS-cum-High Protector to thank for that bit of good fortune."

"You mean the so-called 'gift of enlightenment' Dryden mentioned? Now *there* is an example of a novel approach."

"Tech-driven brainwashing? Is there something you admire about that?"

"The controlling aspects of it, no, but one set of his neural implants have obviously provided him with a tremendous amount of information that he wouldn't have had access to otherwise. And most of it seems to be generally benign."

"Benign? As opposed to …"

"I mean it's mostly relevant subject matter — real information, as opposed to something more subjective."

"Like propaganda, you mean?"

"Or worse, yes. Much of what the implants provide is what you might classify as general knowledge, but it's far more sophisticated than that. It's more like his mind has been provided with a context shift that's a better match for his new reality. And it's an approach that seems to allow him to grasp information and experiences that would ordinarily be so completely outside his normal frame of reference that they could literally …"

"I believe 'blow his mind' is the term I have heard the Terrans use a number of times."

"Actually, that's not an entirely inaccurate description," Miguel replied gravely.

"I'm happy to hear it. He does seem to be doing better at assimilating everything we're telling him than I would have expected. Now, in all seriousness, our mission here is an important one, Miguel. What we have on Didara 4 appears to be a completely new approach to the Pelaran cultivation program."

"I'm not following you. As far as I can tell, it looks like all of the basics are the same as they've always been. The Pelarans decide, for whatever reason, they want to control a given region of the galaxy. To that end, they pick a subject planet that meets all their criteria — population, size, location, tech, whatever. Then they send in an advanced instance of their artificial intelligence, typically in the form of one of their 'Guardian' spacecraft. The AI then steers the development of the chosen world, slowly addicting, then enslaving, its population to Pelaran technology like any other common drug dealer. A few centuries pass, then, Bob's your uncle, the newly hatched Pelaran Regional Partner/puppet has just enough technological capability to become the dominant military power within a roughly five-hundred-light-year radius."

"On behalf of the Pelaran Alliance," Rick added.

"Of course. Whether they ever fully realize it or not."

"An alliance which no longer exists in its original form — since the destruction of the Central Alliance AI, or ALAI as the Terrans referred to it."

"Right, although one might argue that the original Alliance ended long ago, when that same AI — which they originally created — staged a coup and quarantined the Pelarans on their own homeworld."

"True enough, but now that all of that is finally behind them, the Pelarans are in the process of rebuilding their Alliance — this time without the corrupting influence of a pervasive AI. Which, I believe, a sizable portion of the galaxy would agree is a very good thing."

"Hopefully so, yes. So, now, our primary concern is helping to deal with the remnants of the Central AI — Guardian spacecraft, Warden combat troops, and the significantly more powerful Envoy spacecraft."

"Correct, although I don't think it's wise to assume the Central AI itself was completely destroyed by the Terrans."

"Maybe not, but can we get back to my original point?" Miguel sighed, growing bored with their conversation, which had somehow degenerated into what seemed like an unnecessary history lesson.

"I'm sorry, Miguel, of course we can … just as soon as you tell me what your original point was."

"I don't see how what's happening here on Didara 4 is substantively different from how the Pelaran AI has always implemented its cultivation program."

"Ah, yes, there it is, and I'm so glad you asked that question," Rick said with an amused expression. "There are several key differences. First of all, we have no evidence of a Guardian spacecraft ever having been deployed here."

"Okay, granted, but I'm not sure that's particularly relevant since a Warden brings many of the same capabilities to bear."

"Yes and no. The Wardens were designed primarily as combat troops. And while they have a host of impressive capabilities along those lines, they are less sophisticated in terms of processing power, monitoring/communications capabilities, etc. — all of which are required for a successful employment of their cultivation protocols."

"So, you don't believe that's why it was deployed here."

"I suspect not. The Central AI typically only put WCS units on the ground in cases where the Alliance needed a show of overwhelming force — in which case there would have been legions of them. Otherwise, you might see one or two of them deployed for a special ops mission in one form or another. But as far as we know, the so-called 'High Protector' is the only WCS on Didara 4. And it does not appear to me that it is behaving as if its true mission is to cultivate the planet on behalf of the Central AI."

Okayyy," Miguel replied, drawing out the word as he looked up from his view screens to glance over his shoulder at his partner for the first time. "So, don't keep me in suspense. Why do you think it's here?"

"I have no idea," Rick admitted, shrugging his narrow shoulders. "Actually, that's not entirely true. I have a couple of theories, but I don't want to unduly influence your thinking by sharing them with you just yet. Let me just say that this is most definitely one of the things I would like us to discover."

"Noted. So how else does the situation here seem unusual to you?"

"The High Protector's use of certain, specific members of the population against others. Don't misunderstand me, the Pelaran Strain of AI has always been quite adept at driving a wedge between those it seeks to dominate. But I don't believe we have ever seen it apply technology to weaponize a small group of people against the rest of their own society in the manner we're seeing here."

"Care to speculate on this one?" Miguel asked, a look of curiosity now registering in his huge, dark eyes.

"Speculation is all I have to offer thus far, but I believe there are indications that the WCS may be acting on its own, to some degree, and may well have gotten in over its head, so to speak."

"You think it's gone rogue?"

"Maybe. At the very least, I would say its behavior indicates a degree of desperation. Our intel indicates it has been here for at least four years, but only began deploying its so-called 'Flamecallers' approximately six months ago."

"Desperation? Implying that it has been improvising its approach to some degree and realizes its results thus far are ... suboptimal."

"Exactly. I think it believes it has, in many ways, lost control of the situation on Didara 4. It probably knows, or at least surmises, that reinforcements are not forthcoming. That's why we see it conscripting unwitting allies in an effort to regain the upper hand."

"I see. If that's true, we can probably expect it to continue ratcheting up its application of force until it believes things are proceeding according to plan once again."

"Indeed. Which is why I believe we are justified in taking a more aggressive approach in how we manage our asset. Assuming he proves up to the task, that is."

"I understand. And, for what it's worth, I don't disagree. Was there anything else? You still haven't said exactly why we are here. As you know, Didara 4 isn't one of the worlds covered by our current contract."

"Your orders didn't say?" Rick asked in a mischievous tone.

"I'm certain you know very well they didn't. Furthermore, it has never made sense to me why C-Ops still issues orders marked as 'captain's eyes only' when they're being transmitted to a ship with a crew of two. I fail to see the point."

"I see. I don't know how to respond to that other than to say perhaps that's why you're not the captain," Rick replied, smiling triumphantly. "In all seriousness, though, I'm not entirely sure either. I always assumed it's done that way in some sort of historical context, but who knows. In any event, the primary reason we were dispatched here is only partially related to the Pelaran AI's activities."

"Oh? What else could possibly be happening here that eclipses what we've already discussed?"

"I'm hoping the answer to that question will ultimately lead us to discover what brought our glorious 'High Protector' here as well. Earlier you referred to Dryden as an 'Industrial Age asset.'"

"Yes. Was that not an accurate description?"

"It is, yes, but the problem is that it shouldn't be."

"I assume you're eventually going to find your way to a point of some sort," Miguel sighed.

"The Didarans are not an Industrial Age civilization … at least not yet. They still fall well short of our criteria in terms of mass production and other forms of mechanization — agriculture, in particular. Our most recent projections indicate they are still between fifty and one hundred years from meeting all of the requisite requirements. But, somehow, they have gained access to a variety of weapons and other equipment that are well beyond their level of technological and industrial development. And this all appears to have taken place in a very short period of time."

"How short?"

"I assume you reviewed the recording of Dryden's encounter with the cavalry unit yesterday …"

"Of course."

"In our mission brief, C-Ops indicates that same unit was equipped with nothing more sophisticated than handmade muskets and sabers as recently as two years ago."

"I see, and since their updated rifles are being used against the High Protector's forces, I assume they're not based on technology that is Pelaran in origin, right?"

"No, and therein lies the problem. None of the new weapons and equipment they have been receiving over the past few years is, strictly speaking, Pelaran tech. Well ... not unless they are going to a lot of trouble to conceal the fact that it is, which would be highly unusual for them. In the past, the strategy they have employed during cultivation is to rapidly introduce the targeted civilization to a variety of key technologies at something between ten and fifty times their standard developmental timeline."

"And by 'key technologies,' you mean general scientific and engineering advancements, right? That doesn't typically mean working examples of weapons and equipment."

"No, it doesn't. Dropshipping huge caches of rifles, ammunition, manufacturing equipment, uniforms, etc. is definitely not their style. Unfortunately, at the moment, we have no idea where this matériel is coming from."

"Really? And how is it possible we haven't detected the inbound shipments," Miguel observed, half to himself, turning back to glance at one of the many view screens lining the wall of his workstation. "Wait, are you sure this isn't our doing?"

"I'm reasonably sure C-Ops didn't authorize it. And given the manner in which they dispatched us to investigate, I think it's unlikely that it's some sort of clandestine, experimental program ... not one of ours, at least."

"Interesting. Clearly, there must have been *some* sort of contact with a more advanced species, or —"

"Yes, yes, or they uncovered a hoard of non-native or 'precursor' equipment or technology here on Didara," Rick interrupted, waving his hand dismissively. "But I really don't think that's what's going on here."

"Alright then. I'd be 'all ears' if I had any," Miguel smirked, delivering a very old inside joke dating back to the earliest members of the "Grey" Human subspecies. "Please elaborate."

"Take a look at the weapons used by the Estorian Federation's 2nd and 3rd Cavalry Regiments yesterday." On two of Miguel's large bank of view screens, annotated images of both a pistol and a rifle appeared. "Behold the Colt Single-Action Frontier Six-Shooter revolver — the 1877 model of the original Single-Action Army, circa 1873.

"Well, of course it is," Miguel replied in a mocking tone. "Wouldn't that be obvious to anyone with even the meanest understanding of ancient firearm lore?"

"Just bear with me, oh ye of little attention span. The reason I provided that particular piece of information is that it directly relates to the rifle, which happens to be the 1894 carbine version of the Winchester Model 1873. The significance is that both weapons were originally chambered to utilize the same ammunition, the Winchester .44-40 metallic centerfire cartridge."

"I suppose that *would* be handy, wouldn't it?"

"You bet it was … and is. Who wants to lug around multiple types of ammunition? But here's the thing, they don't anymore."

"I'm afraid you've lost me. They no longer use the same ammo?"

"Nope. Both weapons have been upgraded by whoever is supplying them to the Estorian Army, presumably to keep the High Protector's forces off balance. The kinetic energy of the armor-piercing rounds fired by the latest rifles has increased by over two hundred and fifty percent over the ones they were using when they attacked his compound two years ago."

"Odd. Doesn't it seem like whoever is doing this could be raising the ante far more than that if they wished? It's as if they are providing just enough assistance to prevent the High Protector from making any real progress without resorting to the use of overwhelming force."

"Which would defeat his intended purpose, would it not?"

"I suppose it would, yes. Killing everyone doesn't exactly encourage willing cooperation."

"And it gets better," Rick continued, obviously enjoying the process of recounting the details of what he had learned thus far. "As I said, the tech involved isn't Pelaran. Neither of these designs originated here. Both were wildly successful weapons in their day, manufactured in huge numbers on a world you're already quite familiar with … located a little over five thousand light years from here."

"They're *Terran*? But how —"

"Uh huh. Quite a twist, is it not? But perhaps I should clarify that a bit before you get the idea that the Terrans have started dropping pallets of ancient weapons on Human worlds around this galaxy."

"No disrespect to our Terran friends, but that approach seems a bit subtle for their taste, in my opinion."

"Oh, I think they might surprise you on that count," Rick chuckled, "but I can't imagine any possible motive as to why Terran Fleet Command would be involved in something like this so far from home."

"What about Terran civilians?"

"Not impossible, but extremely unlikely given the fact that TFC has not made their C-Drive technology available beyond construction of their own military vessels as yet. No, I think we can safely rule out their direct involvement."

"And yet you say these two weapons are definitely of Terran design," Miguel replied, zooming in to study the acid-etched lettering on the left side of the revolver's barrel."

"Without a doubt. This particular combination of pistol and rifle was commonly used in the western United States during its post-Civil War period. In fact, the Winchester was known as 'The Gun that Won the West.' In any event, these examples are unerringly faithful to the original designs down to the most minute detail. The only exception is the lack of any visible serial numbers."

"So, all we know for sure is that whoever is supplying them has some knowledge of weapons development specific to Terra. But regardless of where they're coming from, they're still quite primitive. It's hard to believe this has been enough to tip the balance of power in favor of the Didarans."

"You might be tempted to think that, given the technology the High Protector is capable of bringing to bear. But I think this might change your mind."

With that, another of Miguel's screens began playing a five-second loop of Dryden's battle with the Estorian cavalry. The point of view was from immediately over the Flamecaller's head and provided an ideal vantage point to observe the effects of several incoming rounds. As the projectiles interacted with his defensive field, ripples of light traveled outward from the points of impact, seeming to reflect back on themselves several times before dissipating. After looping three times, the playback froze, displaying an in-depth analysis of the shield's effectiveness.

"Not particularly effective, is it?" Miguel commented as he examined several impacts in greater detail. "It looks like he actually took a few hits."

"Indeed, he did. Three, to be exact. Now, granted, he would almost certainly have been killed if his implants had not been projecting a defensive energy field. The hits he *did* take were considerably less energetic than they would have been otherwise, but there's little doubt that the Flamecallers are highly vulnerable to good old-fashioned kinetic energy weapons. I suspect the same is true for the Shepherd soldiers as well."

"Interesting. Do you think this means the Pelaran Central AI, or least its WCS representative, might have originally been expecting to encounter energy weapons instead?"

"Here on Didara 4? No, I don't think so," Rick replied, slowly shaking his enormous head. "But I think it's reasonable to assume they weren't expecting to run across *any* weapons with sufficient power to score a successful hit on any of their forces. The original designs for both the Shepherds' armor and Flamecallers' shields could handle about two hundred joules or so. But when the Estorians started fielding pistols and rifles capable of firing rounds with four times that much energy, the High Protector found itself in a very similar situation to what the Sajeth Collective faced when their ships faced off against the Terrans for the first time."

"And just like that, Didara finds itself embroiled in an interstellar arms race without even realizing it," Miguel mused. "Now I understand why you were so insistent on modifying Dryden's defensive systems when we had him aboard. I remember thinking that equipping him with gravitic shields seemed like complete overkill, but I suppose it makes perfect sense now."

"Right. And once he gains access to his shield systems again, he should be largely invulnerable to both kinetic and energy weapons fire — at least anything he's likely to run into on Didara 4. But the rest of the Flamecallers, if there are any, should still be susceptible."

"I'm hoping Dryden won't encounter any more of those."

"Maybe. But keep in mind we only recovered two of their bodies at Talteca. One of them is still missing."

"Yes, and probably destroyed. Based on the level of technology and raw materials involved, it seems unlikely the High Protector has the capability to create any more of them without some sort of resupply from the Central AI, which also seems unlikely at this point. Otherwise, I think we would have already seen more of them in service."

"So, thanks to whoever has been supplying the guns, the High Protector has been losing its troops as quickly as it can produce them. But if our presence here puts a stop to those shipments —"

"Then what happens from there will be largely up to Dryden."

Chapter 10

Didara 4, South Estorian Continent, Scarsdow Forest
(3 hours later - 6.2 km from Dryden's current location)

"I want to make sure I'm clear on what you're telling me, Tommy," Captain Zophar Cash said, eyeing the local militia sergeant with a mix of equal parts irritation and distaste. "You say while you were on your patrol route, you're certain you heard someone talking, but you searched and never found anyone?"

"No, sir. I never said we heard somebody talkin'. What I said was we heard somebody *screamin'*. Just like they's dyin' or something."

"And you searched the area thoroughly, but found no signs of a struggle … a campsite … or even signs of where someone might have passed through the area?"

"Signs?" the man asked vacantly, his unwashed face registering a brief flush of anger as he stared up at the mounted soldier.

Cash closed his eyes momentarily and inhaled deeply, struggling to control his temper before speaking again. "*Signs,* Tommy — you know, disturbed ground, footprints, broken limbs, campfire remains — that kind of thing."

"Oh, oh, yessir, we sure did … we searched for those things, I mean. But, no, we didn't find much of anything worth mentioning. It got dark on us, Cap'n, and we didn't have no dogs with us to pick up the scent. There was definitely somebody up there, though. I heard it plain as day. Gave me the willies, and no mistake. Hell, we all heard it, didn't we boys?"

Tommy's men murmured general agreement that they had indeed heard something, but as Cash glanced around at the ragtag group, he noted that most were either looking off into the distance or staring down at their boots as they scuffed the ground distractedly. Clearly, none of them had any interest in either contradicting their leader or offering up any additional information at this time.

"Well, that's just dandy there, Tommy," Cash said, the top of his large, black Stetson hat rocking slowly back and forth as he too stared at the ground and shook his head in vexation. "You and your boys are not giving us much to go on, are you? But I bet you're still gonna want your standard allocation this week all the same, aren't you?" he asked, referring to the regular monthly "incentive" delivery the Estorian Army provided to loosely organized local militia detachments like this one.

As frustratingly useless as these groups of local ruffians could often be, Cash knew all too well how necessary they had become. This particular sector covered most of the Scarsdow Forest and the adjoining Ganahar Plains stretching all the way up into the foothills of the mountain range bearing the same name. At one time, it had been patrolled, after a fashion, by the Ranger battalion garrisoned just outside the nearby town of Helstaad. Over the past six months, however, the battalion's ranks had been so decimated by skirmishes with the High Protector's forces that they no longer had the manpower available to even claim to do so.

As if they ever really did, Cash thought bitterly, knowing full well that the presence of the Ranger patrols had always been largely symbolic anyway. With a vast area of responsibility spanning nearly seven thousand square kilometers, the notion of accomplishing anything approaching regular patrols — particularly across such varied and difficult terrain — had never made much sense to the young captain.

In any event, the powers that be — most likely, Cash assumed, stationed in comfortable offices located hundreds or even thousands of kilometers away — had decided that the entire sector could be managed by two cavalry troops, approximately two hundred men, supplemented by local militia. The militia would handle the bulk of the patrols, of course, while the cavalry units primarily handled communication and management tasks. Cavalry units were, after all, faster than infantry units, weren't they?

Genius, he thought sarcastically, wondering, not for the first time, whether a month's worth of assistance from these ignorant yokels would ever be worth even the quarter cask of tobacco and ten crates of whiskey they were given in lieu of other forms of payment.

"Anyway, we did the best we could, Cap'n," Tommy finally said, noting the faraway expression on the Army officer's careworn face. "Don't you worry, though. We'll be out again tomorrow at first light. You can't blame us for hurryin' back here this evenin' though. None of us have those fancy rifles and pistols like you all carry now. And you've been around here long enough by now to know what roams around this here forest after dark."

The cavalry captain did *not* know, and, interestingly enough, neither did Tommy Wildermuth. Over the past several years, there had been an increasing number of rumors concerning dangerous creatures supposedly roaming Scarsdow Forest — each tale seeming to test the teller's credibility even more so than the last. The General Staff, for its part, had finally placed enough credence in the reports to issue orders that its commanders avoid the area in groups of less than ten armed men. Otherwise, the letter conveying the new directive had provided little detail, saying only that recent accounts of "aggressive animals" in the area might be tied to activities taking place at Plains Reach. Conspicuously absent was any mention of the so-called "protoraptor" — ancient predators rumored to have been spotted in the area. Although no eyewitnesses had come forward to describe the creatures, local hunters, assuming the High Protector must have somehow been responsible, had named them in his honor.

Captain Cash spit an impressively large volume of tobacco juice on the ground and looked the volunteer militia platoon leader in the eye. "What I know is that whatever might be running around out there in the woods ain't nothing like as dangerous as the creatures we go toe to toe with just about every day. Gods know what's been done to 'em to make 'em what they are, but I hesitate to even call 'em men after what I've seen 'em do. They fight like some kind of … *demons*, if you ask me …" he said, his voice trailing off in thought.

"I meant no disrespect, Cap'n. Just watch yourselves out there is all I'm sayin'. Oh, and there's just one more thing before you and your men head on back," Tommy continued, the implication that Cash's platoon was somewhat less than welcome to overnight with the militia detachment eliciting a few muffled grunts of disapproval from the mounted troopers. "Denny Crawley here tells me there's only one good place to cross the NorthHaven Rill within at least ten clicks of where we heard all that screamin'."

"Yup, that's where I'd be goin' … if they ever make it that far, that is," Denny commented under his breath, producing a rolled-up hand-drawn map of the area.

"Yeah, that's for sure," Tommy agreed. "Now, listen, I don't know if that's the direction they was headed, but if they know anything about the northern part of Scarsdow —"

"Sergeant Higgs!" the captain interrupted as he summoned his platoon sergeant. Since the captain was riding with only one of E Troop's three platoons today, Kenneth Higgs was the only noncommissioned officer present. This situation, in Cash's opinion, was somewhat unfortunate, particularly since 1st Platoon was temporarily missing its commanding officer. While Higgs seemed competent enough, Cash just couldn't quite bring himself to like the man. There was just something about him that seemed too … what was it? Brash wasn't quite the right word, was it? There were plenty of good cavalrymen who possessed that quality in abundance. No, it was more like he seemed to lack a certain sense of … *prudence*. And it was the kind of thing Cash knew under the wrong set of circumstances could get a lot of good men killed.

"Yes, *sir!*" came the immediate response.

"Come take a look at Denny's map here, if you would, and tell me what you think."

"We'd come with you ourselves, Cap'n Cash," Tommy continued, apparently feeling the need to avoid any periods of uncomfortable silence at this point, "but my men gotta get fed first. We could all use some shut-eye too. So maybe we'll just meet you fellas back here in the morning and we'll all ride that way together. What do you say?"

Cash said nothing in reply but gave his NCO time to dismount, retrieve, and then study the militia unit's map, savoring the anxiety he was apparently causing Tommy and his little band of thugs. If the High Protector had never arrived and turned the normal course of things on its head, he knew, these were exactly the kind of men his unit would have been tasked to hunt down and either kill or capture.

After nearly three minutes had passed, Staff Sergeant Higgs handed the map back to its owner, then looked up at his commanding officer and simply nodded.

"I tell you what I say, Tommy," Captain Cash said, pausing to retrieve the enormous quid of tobacco from his mouth with his index finger before tossing it to the ground just a few centimeters from the militia leader's left boot. "We wait 'til tomorrow and there won't be any point in going up there. We've got us a murderin' Flamecaller running around here somewhere … I'm sure you heard he wiped out almost the entire 2nd Regiment yesterday down near Talteca."

"Yes, sir, we did hear somethin' about that already. But surely you don't think he would have made it all the way up here this soon."

"Maybe not. But I don't think the Gods ever meant for one man to be able to raise up his arms and slaughter several hundred men all at once, neither. We got several troopers who claim to have seen him talking to a child

141

after the battle. Then they saw a big flash like a ball of lightning, and they were both gone."

"A child? But why would there be —"

"I dunno, Tommy. All I know is that when any of the High Protector's men get separated from their honcho for very long, we can take 'em. We've done it before."

"Well alright then," Tommy replied, eager to be rid of the self-important cavalryman before he did something that would demand a confrontation of some sort. "Sounds to me like you're plannin' on headin' up there tonight. If you're interested, there's an old loggers' cabin just the other side of Vently Ford. You might find your man up there. If not, it's a good place to bed down for the night."

"Much obliged, Tommy," Cash said with an unmistakable look of irony on his face that he felt certain would be completely lost on the militiaman. "Sergeant Higgs!" he called out once more, prompting another nod from his noncommissioned officer, this time to their bugler, who instantly sounded the first portion of the "General" call to signal that E Troop's 1st Platoon was moving out. Without further comment, Cash wheeled his enormous chestnut stallion about, leaving a cloud of dust in his wake as he thundered off to the northwest.

Didara 4, South Estorian Continent, Scarsdow Forest
(2 hours later - Near Vently Ford)

Dryden slowly raised his head just enough to peer over an enormous, half-buried boulder at the edge of a small clearing. He had been hearing sounds that alerted him to the presence of a large creature of some sort for at least the past fifteen minutes, and now saw that what he had most feared was indeed the case. Mottled in grayish-blue moonlight on the opposite side of the forest glade stood a lone protoraptor.

The fact that the two-meter-tall theropod appeared to be alone was somewhat good news, since they commonly hunted in packs of three to five individuals, Dryden knew, although he had no idea where this knowledge had come from. He was also aware that the females of the species did most of the hunting, commonly taking on the role of providing fresh meat for their pack's young. The bad news, however, was that such a large, solitary protoraptor was almost invariably a young male looking to acquire a pride of its own. During the period of peak fertility among the females in the area — which was quite similar to the estrous cycle seen in most mammalian species — the males were often incredibly aggressive. Driven to something approaching a hormone-induced rage frenzy, the young bucks were more than eager to prove themselves in combat with practically any other species unfortunate enough to cross their paths.

Had it not been for the waxing gibbous moon, Dryden might not have even seen the huge predator at all. And even with the relatively favorable lighting, he had a difficult time deciding exactly what it was doing. Nevertheless, he could tell that it was largely stationary, and after watching it repeatedly raising and lowering its massive head for nearly a full minute, he realized it was in the process of finishing off the remains of a recent kill. Thus far, the creature seemed unaware of his presence, and Dryden intended to do everything possible to ensure that it remained so.

"I recommend we travel due south for several hundred meters. I believe we may be able to avoid it completely." The sound of Emma's voice in a normal, conversational volume inside Dryden's mind made him jump involuntarily, a chill of dread surging down the length of his spine at the apparent break in the silence. Fortunately, the protoraptor took no notice, continuing to rip chunks of flesh from the carcass of its former prey.

Could you please whisper when we need to be quiet? Dryden demanded angrily within the confines of his mind. *You scared me half out of my wits!*

"Sorry about that … but you do recall that you're the only one who can hear me, right?"

Yes, of course, but that's beside the point, isn't it? Just be quiet, please. If that thing hears me … err, us, we're as good as dead, do you understand? Particularly since our friend, Rick, removed my ability to defend myself … ourselves. Look, I'm just going to use singular pronouns from now on, okay? I'm sure you understand I mean "we" when I say "me," right?

"Yes, certainly, that's fine, but let's stay focused on the situation at hand, shall we?" Emma chided. "As for Rick taking away your ability to defend yourself, I'm not entirely sure that's the case, but I'm afraid I can't explain why other than simple logic."

How is that in any way logical? Dryden asked, glancing back in the direction from which he had arrived at the edge of the clearing in hopes of executing a stealthy escape from the area.

"The only explanation I can offer is that it doesn't make much sense to me that the Dayleans went to the trouble of altering your bio-implants just to allow you to then be killed by the first dangerous creature we encounter, that's all."

Oh really? Dryden asked, incredulous. *So, you claim to be under the impression their actions are particularly well-thought-out, do you? Because Rick's tone tells me two things. Number one, he and Miguel are, shall we say, "winging it." And, number two, from their perspective, I am utterly expendable.*

"Hmm … I can understand why you might think that," Emma replied, "but I just don't believe that's correct for some reason — not entirely anyway. In any event, let's start working our way back. Take your time and be very careful how you place each foot to avoid making any sound."

Dryden lowered his head and turned slowly around, carefully easing his body back from the large boulder upon which he had been leaning. Once he believed he was out of the predator's line of sight once again, he raised himself into a low squat and began making his way back down the small rise in the direction from which he had come. Now comfortable that he could stand erect without being seen from the clearing, he increased his pace, still deliberately placing one foot in front of the other and being sure to step only on grass or bare ground.

"That's good," Emma encouraged in a soothing whisper. "Nice and slow."

After the first twenty to thirty meters, Dryden had managed to place several large trees between himself and the protoraptor and had begun to feel more confident that he might escape without it ever having noticed his presence. This thought had barely had time to form in his mind when he heard a faint but distinct clicking sound from the direction of the clearing. It sounded as if two small pebbles were being tapped against one another repeatedly in the distance — in three, staccato groupings of four clicks each. Dryden's blood ran cold, as he immediately realized the creature might well be communicating with other members of a pack he had not yet seen. Had they been watching him this entire time?

"Yes, I heard it too," Emma said, answering the question he had not bothered to ask. "I agree, there must be others in the area."

Ignoring the AI but not knowing what else to do at the moment, Dryden froze and squatted in place next to the trunk of a massive tree. Despite his best efforts to remain calm, his breath now came in ragged gasps as he struggled unsuccessfully to prevent the air rushing in and out of his lungs from making even the slightest sound. *I'm not sure what to do here, Emma,* he admitted, casting his gaze about the area, particularly back in the direction of the first protoraptor. Thus far, he still saw no sign of pursuit. Unfortunately, above the forest canopy, the moon had disappeared behind a bank of low clouds, leaving him in almost complete darkness. As he began to feel the icy tendrils of panic tugging at the fringes of his mind, he was startled once again by a completely different sound.

BING! a ridiculously cheerful tone sounded within the confines of his already terrified mind followed by a previously unheard male voice making what could only be described as an announcement. The sensation was indescribably strange — although Dryden felt as if he were hearing the voice speaking in real-time, the information it conveyed was integrated into his consciousness in just six microseconds.

The following capability may now be accessed via your neural interface: Light Amplification One - Visible Light. Sources of ambient light in the area are amplified by a factor of up to fifty thousand, allowing you to see at night. Note that the image, while still capable of rendering fine detail, will have a monochromatic, green appearance. In addition, no image will be produced in areas with no sources of ambient light — inside caves or windowless buildings, for example.

While Dryden struggled to grasp exactly what had just happened, the near impenetrable darkness surrounding him was abruptly replaced by an eerie, green landscape. Although now effectively colorblind, he was able to see with a level of clarity that rivaled midday in the forest. Taken aback by the sudden and unexpected change, he instinctively looked down at his own hands, then up at the canopy of trees above for a moment before his rather dire situation rushed back to the forefront of his mind. Scanning his intended path ahead, it took him only a few seconds to detect two additional protoraptors slowly approaching from either side of the path he had been following — clearly preparing for a quick ambush followed by an easy, risk-free kill.

"Those two are most likely females," Emma observed.

Well, that's just fantastic, Dryden replied. *I've apparently been granted the gift of watching my own death stealthily approach with nothing I can do to prevent it.*

"No, we can think our way through this," his AI replied. "Just try to remain calm and control your breathing. They appear to know approximately where you are based on their approach paths. Here, this should help a bit."

In the upper right corner of Dryden's vision, the map expanded to show a top-down view of the surrounding area. His own position was now marked with a blue circle while all three of the approaching protoraptors were represented by slowly pulsing red triangles.

"I assume you can see what they are trying to do?" Emma asked rhetorically. To emphasize her point, small, red lines tipped with arrows appeared to scroll toward his position from the current locations of each one of the approaching creatures.

Dryden rolled his eyes in reply, but, under the circumstances, did not bother taking the time to compose a sardonic retort in his mind.

"Okay, okay, just making certain. The raptors are remarkably well-spaced, so we have only a short window of time to find our way out of their trap. I want you to try to distract the one along the path to your right. Grab a rock, stick, or whatever you can find and throw it off to the southwest as I'm showing you here."

On the map, Emma provided another animation illustrating precisely where she wanted the rock to land for maximum effect. For good measure, she also included a projection of which way she hoped the protoraptor to the right of his current path would run, as well as the icon depicting his position moving to escape in roughly the same direction the creature had been coming from.

I don't mind telling you that looks like wishful thinking to me, Dryden thought, sounding even to himself like a man anticipating his own imminent death.

"Maybe so, but it's the best chance we have. Do you think it's in *my* best interest to allow you to be ripped to shreds by these three creatures? Keep in mind that your death would most likely result in the permanent end of my existence as well. And since I'm programmed to preserve both of our lives, I am giving you what I believe to be our best course of action to achieve that goal. Besides, at the moment, I can tell you don't have anything better in mind, so let's just go with the only plan we have, shall we? Otherwise, I have a high degree of confidence that this situation will result in our abrupt deaths in just under thirty seconds. Now *MOVE!*" she ordered, leaving no room for further debate on the issue.

Oh, why not? Dryden thought resignedly as he quickly discovered a smooth, walnut-sized stone near the base of the tree. Somehow already feeling a sense of relief in taking action of any kind, he edged silently around to the side of the tree opposite the direction he had been traveling, drew back his arm, and hurled the stone in the direction Emma had indicated. The projectile made a truly astounding amount of noise against the relatively constant background din of spring forest sounds — impacting several times with various types of foliage before ultimately hitting the trunk of a tree off in the distance with a loud, wooden *THUNK*.

"Very nicely done," Emma said. "Hold here for just a moment, and let's see what she does."

Dryden stared at the overhead map and held his breath. At first, it did not appear the raptors had been deceived, but after just a few seconds, all three of the pulsing red triangles shifted their courses towards the apparent location of the impact. As he had hoped, the most dramatic change in direction was seen in the creature to the right of his former path, which now headed off to the south, southwest — providing him with an opportunity to escape that matched Emma's projection almost exactly.

"Now! This way, and be quiet about it," she commanded with a renewed sense of urgency. As before, the AI provided clear, animated directions via the overhead map but now also began projecting a faint, magenta course line within Dryden's field of view along the ground, leading him back towards the east.

Dryden immediately started forward into the night once again, expecting with each step to feel one of beasts' twenty-five-centimeter-long, sickle-shaped claws sink into the back of his neck.

"Hey, at least it would be quick," Emma offered conversationally.

Not helpful, dear, he replied sharply, although he had to admit that the hint of gallows humor implicit in her comment was oddly reassuring.

"I think we'll be okay if you can make it across the Rill," she said, highlighting his destination now less than a kilometer off to the north. "But I want us to press a little farther east first, so we can hopefully put some distance between us and them before we head north once again."

Agreed, he replied.

Although Dryden knew very little regarding the specific habits of the ferocious predators tracking him, he was aware that, even though they often cooperated when hunting for food, their loyalty to one another was tenuous at best. It was not unusual, for example, for a so-called "hunting party" to spontaneously dissolve into a group of vicious, self-interested individuals. This was particularly true if the food supply had been relatively scarce of late. In these instances, the creatures were probably even more of a danger to one another than they were to him. Accordingly, he said a silent prayer to the Gods, asking that the three raptors following him would soon be at one other's throats.

Chapter 11

Didara 4, South Estorian Continent, Scarsdow Forest
(Near Vently Ford)

At Emma's prompting, Dryden continued on a roughly easterly heading for several minutes, keeping a constant eye on her estimates of the current positions of all three raptors. *How much of what you are showing me is where they actually are versus where you think they are?* he asked, beginning to wonder at the accuracy of what was being displayed on his map.

"That varies, based on the data I'm able to gather. Keep in mind that I don't have access to any information that you can't already collect for yourself. But I do have the advantage of being able to fully monitor all of your senses at once without ever being distracted. Right now, for example, we have neither seen nor heard any signs of our pursuers for several minutes. So, what you see on the map is simply my best guess based on all of the available data."

And I assume that means the accuracy of your best guess is steadily decreasing.

"Until I acquire additional data, yes, that's true."

I see. And there's something else I was wondering about ...

"It's cute that you're waiting for me to respond, but it's unnecessary, I can assure you."

Ah, right, got it. I was just thinking that this new gift of light ... uh, what was it called again?

"Light Amplification One ... and I assume the 'One' in the name implies there may be a 'Two' at some point.

In other words, additional levels of capability or perhaps ancillary or subordinate capabilities to this one may become available in the future. But I'm afraid that's just another guess on my part."

Yes, that was it. Since this ... capability seems to have been provided based upon need, do you have any indications that I might also be about to receive some means of defending myself? A weapon, of some sort, would be quite useful just now, don't you think?

"Honestly, there's little point in asking me for any information regarding the so-called 'gifts' provided by your network of implants. As Rick told you, I have no information regarding what capabilities might become available, or when such an event might take place. That information has been compartmentalized and restricted, and I'm every bit as much in the dark as you are. But I do agree that providing you the ability to see at night appears to have coincided with an acute need to do so. Perhaps you can derive some encouragement from that."

Perhaps. Nothing like waiting until the last possible moment, though, eh?

"For now," Emma continued, ignoring his comment, "I believe we should maintain our focus on the present. Assuming they are still following us, our pursuers will no doubt have discovered that they were misled and will now be using their senses to reacquire our trail. And with the possible exception of the new night vision capability, I think we can safely assume their senses are better than ours. So, I'd say it's a foregone conclusion they are rapidly closing on us again by now."

Maybe. But have you considered that this may all be nothing more than the next phase of whatever scheme those two Grey aliens have dropped us into the middle of? They give us just enough resources to keep us alive ... like the proverbial rat in a maze. And when they have finished with their little experiment, what's to keep them from putting an end to it ... to us, I mean?

"You can believe that if you want, Dryden, but I have seen no evidence to support such a conclusion," Emma replied in a surprisingly irritated tone of voice. "Surely this isn't the first time in your life you have been faced with a situation requiring improvisation. Sometimes the only thing you know is the desired outcome. When that happens, all you can do is take a first step in what you believe is the right direction — hoping the path before you will be revealed as you go. The key is having the presence of mind to think logically and the will to act when opportunities present themselves. Is that one of the 'gifts' you naturally possess, Flamecaller?"

The moment she finished speaking, Dryden heard the same unmistakable clicking sounds he had heard from the first protoraptor back at the clearing, followed immediately by a rustle of movement off to the west. *They're coming,* he said, stating the obvious, *and I'm going to need the next part of that escape plan of yours ... right now.*

"Just keep moving!" she replied urgently. That's the only plan that makes any sense right now."

Should I climb a tree or something?

"No, I don't think that's a good idea. I doubt we could easily find one you can climb that would be tall enough to keep us safe. Most of the trees in this area do not lend themselves to climbing without the right sort of gear. The bottom branches tend to be ten meters or more off the ground. Besides, I'm guessing those raptors have a vertical jump of at least six meters, and they would probably just take turns waiting us out if they couldn't reach us. You just need to keep moving. With any luck, something else will distract them shortly."

BING! The now-familiar warning tone sounded once again.

The following capability may now be accessed via your neural interface: Low-Observables One. Gravitics-induced fields are created in an attempt to curb/redirect most sources of energy radiating from your body. Effects include a sixty to eighty-five percent reduction in your thermal, radar, acoustic, and visual signatures from the perspective of a designated target. In lieu of selecting a specific target, you may also designate an arc of up to 180 degrees. Note that these effects will not entirely mask your presence, and care must still be taken when attempting to avoid detection. Note also that energy emissions in the direction opposite to the designated target or arc will increase proportionately, rendering detection from that side more likely.

"Excellent!" Emma enthused. I take it you want me to —"

Yes, yes, for Gods' sakes, DO IT! Dryden snapped.

"Done. I've got the cone of effect set to rotate in the direction of our pursuers as you continue to move."

The protoraptors did not immediately reappear, and Dryden continued his terror-filled flight for another fifteen minutes that stretched into half an hour. To his surprise, there had been no additional signs of his pursuers, although he thought he had heard an occasional rustling of foliage off in the distance. Eventually, Emma

155

had changed course back towards the north and then west to head them in the direction of their destination once again. Dryden had been hearing the sound of rushing water since shortly after the encounter with the raptors and sincerely hoped they had some sort of natural aversion to crossing rivers in pursuit of their prey.

Do you expect they will follow us across? he asked hopefully.

"I have no idea," she replied, "but, honestly, I can't imagine they would hesitate to do so, if necessary … depending on how hungry they are and how tempting their intended target, of course."

That's me, alright, Dryden replied bitterly, *a tempting, slow, delicious target. I sincerely hope all three of them drown themselves in their quest for an easy meal.*

"Perhaps the first one we saw eating at the far edge of the clearing decided to double back, and the other ones realized he was planning to steal an even easier meal from them. With any luck, they've all decided we're more trouble than we're worth and they'd prefer to fight it out over the original kill."

With no new tracking information available, Emma had returned the map to its previous navigational mode, which now showed their destination waypoint just a few hundred meters to the northwest.

Humph, Dryden grumbled. *Their ripping each other to shreds would be an even better outcome, now that you mention it. Incidentally, didn't Rick make some sort of reference to something becoming more obvious when we reached our destination?*

"He did indeed, but I'm not sure he was being literal at the time. He may have simply been referring to the fact that he expected you to have begun gaining access to new capabilities by the time we arrived."

A short time later, Dryden noted a significant thinning of the trees as he approached the southern bank of the NorthHaven Rill. Here, the rocky stream bed traced a relatively straight path through the middle of the forest as its frigid waters flowed down out of the Ganahar Mountains on their way to the Tiscana sea.

"If they're still hunting us, they'll be watching the river," Emma warned. "And I'm afraid this stretch looks like a particularly good location for an ambush."

Crouching beneath an ancient Cottonwood tree near the riverbank, Dryden immediately saw what she was referring to. Where he had emerged from the forest, the NorthHaven Rill stretched off into the distance in both directions. Once he broke cover to attempt a crossing, he estimated he would be visible for at least two kilometers — both up and downstream.

"Actually, it's more like four kilometers," Emma corrected.

Ignoring the intrusion into his formerly private thoughts, Dryden also noted to his annoyance that this stretch of the Rill would not lend itself to an easy crossing. *Not a dry one at least,* he thought bitterly. In spite of a relatively dry spring thus far, snowmelt from the mountains had transformed the ordinarily placid forest stream into a rushing torrent that looked much more like a true river than he had expected. On the bright side, he did note that the sound of the water cascading over its rocky bottom and down several small falls made for a significant level of background noise. Even without the use of his new gift of stealth, he wouldn't have to worry as much about any sounds he might generate while completing his crossing.

"You're right about all of that," Emma said, continuing a conversation Dryden didn't realize they were having. "It's unlikely they have detected us with any level of certainty. Otherwise, I'm pretty sure we would know it by now. Those things can run nearly forty kilometers per hour over short distances, so they would have had little trouble catching us if they had known where we were. We've also stayed downwind the entire time, so I'm hoping the combination of that and the new Low Observable capability has kept them guessing thus far. They're smart, though, so there's little chance of our making it across the Rill without detection if they're watching this stretch. There's also the problem of your getting soaked to the bone in near-freezing water … you'll be running the risk of hypothermia for sure."

Sometimes, I really cannot decide if you are being defeatist or optimistic. Have you anything helpful to contribute at this juncture, or do you recommend I just lie down here on some sort of large serving platter?

"Oh dear," Emma replied in a surprised tone. Before saying anything further, the AI took the time to review her charge's physiological responses to every one of their interactions since he had regained consciousness in the forest. Just four microseconds later, her model predicting how he would respond to most forms of mental and physical stimuli had improved by nearly seven percent. Despite the marked improvement, however, Emma had no illusions as to his overall predictability. Dryden was a Human, after all, and a certain lack of predictability was common to every member of his species across thousands of worlds. "Ah, I do apologize for that," she replied with no perceptible delay. "I guess I have been sounding a little gloomy, haven't I. I was just making observations as we formulate our strategy, but I'll try to be more positive when thinking aloud."

Never mind, Emma, Dryden thought, remembering that his AI apparently had the ability to hear his most private thoughts, while he, on the other hand, had no access to hers. *Truth be told, I'm feeling a bit pessimistic myself, but if we're to have any chance of surviving this, we've got to find a way out of the immediate area and then look for someplace we can shelter for the night, if possible. Now, can we cross the stream here or do we need to go upstream a bit? Downstream seems like a bad choice since we're assuming the raptors are still to our west, right?*

"Unfortunately, downstream is exactly where we need to go, but only about fifty meters or so. Do you see the straight line in the current just off to the west that stretches all the way across?" she asked, highlighting the area in his field of view in case he didn't.

Yes, I noticed that before. A ford of some sort, I presume.

"It is. The locals call it Vently Ford. Originally, it was once just an unusually wide, shallow stretch of the stream. But over the years, loggers, hunters, and eventually the Estorian Army have improved it to some degree so that it offers a more reliable crossing point year-round. The information I have indicates that it has

159

not been used for some time, but from here it looks as though that may not be entirely accurate."

Perhaps not. Dryden thought, noting the obvious presence of hoofprints on both sides of the stream. *Recently used or no, it certainly doesn't look very reliable ... not if one is looking to cross without getting soaking wet, that is.*

"Agreed. Unfortunately, our timing is less than optimal. The Rill is running at least half a meter higher than usual, even for this time of year. The line you see in the water is from a row of heavy, quarried stones that forms the downstream side of the ford. They were placed there to prevent the carts and small wagons that use the logging trails around here from being swept downstream when they cross. Normally, the tops of those stones jut out of the water a bit and also serve as a footbridge. The stream bed itself will be lined with similar flat stones, but the water there will likely be chest-deep in some places."

And flowing too swiftly for me to wade across, from what I can see.

"Probably so, yes. Although you might stand a chance if you can manage to brace your left foot against the downstream row of stones."

No, I think I'll attempt the footbridge route first. It doesn't look to be more than knee-deep along the top of the wall for the most part.

"That's about right, yes. Just be aware that the stones are likely to be extremely slippery."

Great, I'll keep that in mind. And once I get to the other side? Dryden asked hurriedly, feeling as if he had already spent far too long deciding how to proceed.

"As you said, we need to find a safe place to hole up and get some rest. The information I have indicates there is a small logging cabin not too far ahead. I'll provide a course for you as soon as you're across."

Very well. I'm afraid that will have to do for now, he replied. Then, without further delay, he stood and set off at a fast jog in the direction of the ford. It took only a few seconds to reach the point where the leaf-strewn detritus covering the forest floor gave way to the muddy outer limits of the stream bed, forcing him to abruptly slow his pace to avoid falling. Once again, Dryden felt the rush of adrenalin in his bloodstream as the most ancient, primal portion of his brain responded to the realization that he was likely being hunted. In an effort to ward off panic, he did his best to keep his eyes focused on his destination, but upon reaching the edge of the stream, he risked a sidelong glance at the edge of the forest to the west.

"Nothing so far," Emma said in a tone intended to be encouraging. "No Humans, protoraptors, or otherwise. That's a good sign."

Dryden ignored her comment while still registering a degree of relief that there was as yet no sign of his pursuers. Then, without even a momentary pause, he waded out into the water. As expected, it was ice cold, and a distant part of his mind heard Emma mention "seven degrees Celsius" as well as something else about hypothermia. But his only concern at the moment was reaching the far side as quickly as possible without falling headlong into the stream. The current running over the footbridge was strong but still manageable as long as he took care to firmly place each foot before taking the next step. Emma's warning that the stones would be slippery, however, was a bit of an understatement. And before long, he found himself needing to scrape the ball of his foot against their surface to remove as much of the accumulated layers of mud and algae as possible.

At approximately the halfway point, Dryden noticed that he could see the dark green outlines of several large trout suspended in a much deeper pool just downstream of the ford. For the first time since he had awakened in the forest clearing, he realized that he was both hungry and thirsty, and wished he had the time to stop and find a way to get his hands on a few of the trout.

BING!

The following capability may now be accessed via your neural interface: Light Amplification Two - Infrared. Allows you to see in the infrared portion of the spectrum. Rather than amplifying ambient, visible light, this capability enables the detection of the thermal energy emitted by most objects. The infrared image may be superimposed over the existing, visible light amplification image, or used independently. Unlike visible light amplification, the infrared sensors are used to create a "false color" image based on temperature variation. This capability can, therefore, be utilized in areas with no sources of ambient, visible light.

Although Dryden understood only part of the information he had just received, the trout he had been looking at provided all of the additional explanation he required. He could now see that there were far more fish in the pool than he originally realized — all of them now plainly visible and presented in vivid colors despite the tiny amount of near-infrared light reflecting off their cold-blooded bodies.

The small school of fish seemed enticingly close — almost as if he could simply reach down and grab one — and he wondered if it was his need for sustenance that had triggered access to the new capability. Knowing that any delay would be foolish in the extreme, Dryden pressed on until he reached the far side. With a sense of relief now flooding through his mind and exhausted body, he glanced back over his shoulder at the opposite bank just in time to witness the spectacle of three, thermally enhanced protoraptors bursting forth from the edge of the forest.

Chapter 12

Didara 4, South Estorian Continent, Scarsdow Forest
(Near Vently Ford)

Dryden stood transfixed at the far edge of the stream watching the creatures he assumed would be the cause of his death approaching the opposite side of the NorthHaven Rill. *How far to that logging cabin again?* he asked.

"Ugh," Emma groaned. "I didn't want to say before for fear of discouraging you, but it's just under four kilometers."

"*Four kilometers?*" he raged aloud, incredulous. "Dammit, Emma, I thought you said it was nearby?"

"I believe what I said was, 'not too far.' Besides, I think four kilometers still qualifies as being 'nearby.'"

Well, I do not. And that's not going to work, Emma. I need other options and I need them right now.

"Alright then, I suggest you run," she said in a strangely casual tone given the circumstances.

You can't possibly be serious.

"Deadly serious, Dryden. You have to run as fast as you can. I know you're exhausted, and I know there is little point in trying to outrun them for long. But I think our best chance is to get out of their immediate line of sight and hope your new low observable capability causes them to lose us again. Who knows, maybe they'll have trouble crossing the stream and break off their pursuit."

Okay, he sighed, already settling into a fast jog up the logging trail to the north. *Should I try to put some obstacles between us and them again?*

"I don't think so, no. Right now, we're just trying to cover four kilometers as quickly as possible. The best way to do that is to stick with the logging trail. As you can see, I've marked it for you." Once again, a magenta course line appeared in Dryden's field of vision, this time with a series of rapidly moving arrows that appeared to travel along the line into the distance. Clearly, Emma was doing all she could to emphasize the fact that he needed to move as quickly as possible. "By the way," she continued, "your tree climbing idea might also have some merit at this point, so keep an eye out for anything you think you might be suitable."

I'm not a runner under the best of circumstances, Emma, and I've had a pretty rough couple of days ... physically and mentally, he said as he crested a small hill he hoped would take him beyond visual range of the stream momentarily. Allowing morbid curiosity to get the better of him for a moment, Dryden took one last glance over his shoulder and saw that one of the three protoraptors was in the water, struggling against the current to cross the footbridge. Another stood closely behind, making a series of rapid screeches and clicks as if to encourage its companion's progress. The third appeared to be scouting downstream, looking for another place to cross. Just before he lost sight of them, he saw the first protoraptor slip on the slimy stones and fall into the stream with a large splash, flailing its forelimbs wildly and emitting a series of earsplitting shrieks.

"Well there's a bit of good news," Emma commented. "The NorthHaven may be the natural northern extent of their range. It's entirely possible they have never crossed it before. So, let's hope that is the case and try to keep moving as quickly as possible. At this pace, you should be able to reach the cabin in twenty minutes or so."

At this pace, I'll be dead in less than ten, Dryden thought, already gasping for air with the effort.

"No, you won't, Flamecaller. Rest assured, I'm monitoring your cardiovascular system very closely. You're doing fine and not in any immediate danger of having a heart attack or a stroke. You are, however, in danger of being eviscerated and most likely eaten, so I suggest you try to push yourself as hard as possible. I'm pretty sure a little aerobic-induced discomfort is much better than what our three reptilian friends back there have in mind."

As Dryden rounded a bend in the logging trail, he noticed once again that a number of horses had recently passed this way, although the recent lack of rain made it difficult to discern precisely *how* recently. Deciding the presence of *any* other humans would be a positive thing at the moment, he ignored the tracks and continued making conversation with Emma to distract himself from the growing discomfort in his legs and chest. *I don't understand why we weren't following this trail the entire time. I certainly would have had an easier go of it, and I feel certain it would have cut our travel time substantially.*

"There are several reasons for that. First and foremost was the fact that we had not yet reached this particular trail when we first encountered the raptors. Back on the other side of the Rill, the path forked, with one side heading southwest and the other largely following the stream to the east. We were forced to double back before we got there. The other problem, of course, is that these trails are often utilized by militia and/or cavalry patrols. Based on your ... *activities* over the past few days, I assumed avoiding Estorian Federation cavalry was probably in our best interest."

I'm sure you're right about that, Dryden replied. *Just now, I would be more than happy to encounter one of their patrols. We would just have to hope that they had not yet heard of what happened at Talteca ... or at least assume I didn't have anything to do with it if they had. And even if they did, the High Protector tends to offer handsome rewards for prisoner swaps, although, come to think of it, I'm not sure the Estorians have ever taken him up on the offer. In any event, they probably wouldn't kill me outright, at least not immediately, although I'm certain the experience would be ... unpleasant.*

"Without a doubt. As would your repatriation into the service of the High Protector, I suspect, if some sort of exchange were to take place. Or is that ultimately what you want?" Emma asked, her question seeming to hang in the air like the blade of a guillotine.

Do I want to return to the High Protector? No, of course not! What a strange thing to say, Dryden replied, clearly angered by the question, particularly since he felt certain she already knew the answer. *As I'm sure you are well aware, it is becoming increasingly clear to me that I must do whatever I can to stop him. And, in so doing, if I can manage to help others who have been taken up into his service, so much the better.*

Here, Dryden paused, jogging breathlessly along the trail in silence for several minutes before continuing in an even more emotional tone. *Look, I know what I've done, Emma — at least part of what I've done — and I'm willing to accept whatever responsibility is ultimately deemed appropriate for my crimes. But I have no memory of anything that happened before Talteca. I hope to Gods that I did not enter into the High Protector's service voluntarily. I can't say why, precisely, but it just doesn't seem like something I would do, if that makes any sense.*

"It does," Emma replied consolingly. "And, for what it's worth, I don't believe it's something you would do either. In fact, I don't believe any of the horrible things those who serve the High Protector are doing are by choice. You would have to be some sort of psychopath to do those things of your own free will. On the subject of Estorian patrols, however, I sincerely doubt encountering one would result in your being returned to his service. Based on the data I have, the battle at Talteca resulted in an unprecedented number of casualties. So, I don't think we should go looking for help from that quarter unless we have no other choice."

I'm sure you're right. But given the choice, I think I'll still take my chances with the Estorians over being eaten, he replied, slowing first to a trot and then a brisk walk with his hands on his hips as he gasped for air.

"Okay, what do you think you're doing?"

What does it look like I'm doing? I'm dying here, Emma. I don't think I can run any longer. I'm going to have to stop and walk for a while. That's the best I can do for now, he gasped.

"No, you listen to me. I'm telling you you're doing fine. You can take a few breaths, but then you've got to keep moving as quickly as possible," she urged. As if to underscore her exhortations, another series of high-pitched, shrieking calls sliced through the relative stillness of the forest from the direction of the ford. The terrifying sounds were all Dryden needed to motivate him to start moving again, albeit at a significantly reduced speed from what he had been capable of just fifteen minutes earlier. "That's better," she soothed. "Just try to set a sustainable pace and keep moving. We'll be at the cabin before you know it."

That's a lie, Dryden replied testily. *Furthermore, that expression has never made any sense to me ... 'before you know it.' I can assure you, I most certainly 'know it' already. I know, for example, that I can't outrun a protoraptor ... I know I'm not in sufficient shape to run for extended periods of time ... and, most clearly of all, I know I'm in the process of dying. Whether my death is the result of overexertion or evisceration seems of little consequence at the moment.*

Emma was well aware that Dryden's rant was primarily about distracting himself from his own fear and discomfort, but she also knew there was more than a little truth in what he had just said. His heart had approached its theoretical maximum several times over the past two days. But this time, there was an alarming increase in blood pressure accompanied by an acute buildup of lactic acid and a corresponding decrease in the oxygen saturation level in his bloodstream. His assertion that he was dying, while a bit over-dramatic for her taste, was not entirely inaccurate, and she began making preparations to take emergency measures to help keep him alive, if necessary.

Somehow, whether by dogged determination or simply a primal fear of being consumed by a vicious apex predator, Dryden managed to press on. And after several more minutes of the seemingly interminable flight from Vently Ford, he had begun to allow himself to think that he might yet make it to the logging cabin. There had been no additional sounds from the rear, which was certainly a positive development, but he was now also wondering whether the cabin would provide much in the way of additional safety. If it had windows, they would probably prove too small for the massive creatures to crawl through, but a wooden door was another matter entirely. How long would *any* door stand up to repeated blows from a protoraptor weighing as much as an average horse?

Distracted by the unpleasant notion that the cabin might offer little refuge from his pursuers, Dryden turned his ankle in a wagon rut and went down hard, barely catching himself before his face impacted with the well-compacted ground. Unsure if he had broken something, he lay still for a moment and took a quick inventory of his injuries. There was definitely a degree of pain in his ankle that wasn't there before his fall, but a few rotations of his foot confirmed that he had been very lucky under the circumstances. It would no doubt be sore over the next few days but didn't seem to be broken. Ignoring the sting of the scrapes and scratches on his hands and knees, Dryden slowly got back to his feet and prepared to set off once again.

"I think you're okay," Emma suggested, "but please try to be more careful."

None of the profanity that came streaming into mind seemed quite up to the task of responding to the AI's inane comment, but he nonetheless took some degree of satisfaction in knowing that she could hear them all. Grateful, at least, for any excuse to take a brief respite, Dryden placed his hands on his hips again and concentrated on taking steady, deep breaths. As he began walking slowly along the path again, a slight rustle in the trees to the left of the road in front of him caught his attention. Instinctively, he froze, wondering if his pursuers had somehow managed to locate him in spite of the clever gift of stealth he now apparently had at his disposal. But after a few moments of intense listening, he convinced himself that whatever he had heard could not possibly have been something as large as one of the raptors.

"Let's get going again, shall we? Frankly, I'm not sure they made it beyond the river, but we shouldn't give them any additional opportunities, just in case," Emma prompted. At that moment, the largest of the three raptors — the big male — leapt from behind a pile of brush near the edge of the forest, traversing well over ten meters in a single bound to land squarely in the center of the logging trail.

How in the Gods' names? Dryden thought to himself, marveling at the creature's remarkable stealth and strength despite the immediate danger it posed.

"Your dagger," Emma reminded him calmly.

For all the good that will do, Dryden thought as he reached across his body with his right hand and drew his wicked-looking twenty-five-centimeter-long dagger from its scabbard, brandishing it in front of him in what he hoped was an obviously threatening manner.

"No, it might actually work," Emma counseled. "As dangerous as they obviously are, predators tend to do whatever they can to avoid being injured. So, you have to make him understand that you won't go down without a fight."

A fight I have zero chance of surviving.

"Your odds of surviving a fight with him are actually a little better than zero, but that's not the point. You need to make him believe you will do some significant damage before he can finish you off. You should also try making yourself look as large and menacing as possible. Raise your arms above your head and keep waving your dagger at him."

"Come on … *Come on,* you great manky bastard!" Dryden yelled, growling and waving his arms with far more bravado than he felt. At that moment, a familiar series of clicking sounds drew his attention behind him, and he glanced over his shoulder just in time to see the other two raptors slink from the forest approximately fifty meters away. Without hesitation, both lowered their heads menacingly and began slowly approaching from the rear, obviously intent on making their final attack en masse.

Realizing that this was one of those moments in life where half-measures simply would not do, Dryden did something that neither the raptors nor Emma ever would have expected. Raising his dagger over his head, and with a ferocious, blood-curdling yell of his own, he charged the male protoraptor in front of him.

Caught completely off guard by the unmitigated gall of its prey, the massive predator had only enough time to tilt its head to one side quizzically before Dryden had crossed the distance between them. In one smooth movement, the Flamecaller slammed his body shoulder-first into the raptor's side while burying his dagger hilt-deep into the side of its neck. The body-blow itself had little effect, and Dryden would later recall that he succeeded in moving the creature precisely the same amount as a similar impact against the trunk of a hundred-meter-tall Poplar tree. Nevertheless, he somehow remained on his feet after the impact and continued running down the path in the direction of the logging cabin as fast as his exhausted body could be induced to travel.

His dagger, on the other hand, had been surprisingly effective. The giant theropod hissed and shrieked in stunned surprise, flailing its forelimbs wildly about in a vain attempt to dislodge the weapon from its neck — now spurting a jet of dark blood from a severed carotid artery.

Unaware of the damage he had caused, and certain that his own death was mere moments away, Dryden ran on, knowing only that he needed to put as much distance between himself and his pursuers as possible. Perhaps, he hoped, without much optimism, there was at least a chance that his gift of stealth might cause them to lose sight of him once again.

Better still, perhaps the other two will stop and make a meal out of the first one, he thought.

But it was not to be. For in the cold, unfeeling depths of his pursuers' reptilian brains, this hunt had become personal on a primal level no Human could possibly comprehend. And now, with the decidedly optimistic notion of his somehow managing to disappear once more into the night still echoing through his mind, Dryden saw one of the remaining raptors race past him in his peripheral vision just a short distance off the path to his right.

Making remarkably little sound as it ran through the forest, the massive creature continued paralleling the logging trail for a short distance before angling back to bodily obstruct Dryden's way forward. Even in the monochromatic green of his light-amplified vision, the sight of the raptor turning back to face him — jutting its massive head towards the sky and opening its black maw to deliver yet another bloodthirsty roar — was at once terrifying and majestic to behold.

Behind him, Dryden heard the third creature emit a call of its own in an apparent display of solidarity with its remaining companion. But this time, there was something unmistakably different in its tone. And although he wasn't sure why he knew it to be so, he felt certain that it was intended as an open challenge to the impudent prey animal who had dared injure one of their own. Out of necessity, the Flamecaller had stopped dead in his tracks and now glanced quickly around in the direction from which he had come. There, standing just short of the injured male, stood the third raptor. As he watched, the creature slowly raised its head up to its full height of nearly two meters, then stood stock-still for a long moment, apparently considering how it wanted to proceed. On the ground a short distance away, its companion still writhed in obvious pain as it struggled to remove Dryden's dagger from its long neck.

Without ever shifting its icy, predatory gaze from its quarry, the third raptor covered the short distance to its former leader in a single, graceful leap, planting both of its feet at the point where the injured raptor's long neck attached to its body. Without hesitation, the big female sliced downward with both of her massive hind sickle-claws, kicking with both legs as if wiping something objectionable from her feet. The motion completely severed the head of its former mate, sending it sliding several meters away from its still-twitching body.

Apparently confident that it had made a clean kill, the third raptor raised herself up to her full height and emitted the same series of clicks as before. Dryden felt sure that both creatures were well aware that he had been disarmed during the attack on their pack leader and thus posed little threat of causing additional injury. Now, moving as if they intended to savor the process of completing a successful hunt despite the loss of one of their number, both animals began to slowly close the distance to their now-helpless target.

BING! Dryden heard within the confines of his terrified mind.

The following capability may now be accessed via your neural interface: Plasma Bolt 1. A ranged weapon allowing an intense bolt of compressed plasma to be fired at a single target. The relative intensity of the discharge varies on a scale of one to five, which is selected upon activation of the weapon. In addition to the selected intensity level, damage inflicted will vary based on a variety of factors — particularly the range to the target. Maximum effective range is approximately two kilometers. Maximum rate of fire is six plasma bolts per second. WARNING: the weapon should not be fired at targets less than ten meters away or at intensity levels higher than those recommended by the AI due to the potential for hazardous and unpredictable rebound effects.

"Finally!" Dryden exclaimed aloud, narrowing his eyes in determination as he turned back to the second protoraptor still blocking the path in the direction of his destination. "Emma, distance to the target please," he commanded, his mind recalling at least some of what it meant to be a Flamecaller.

"Thirty-seven point three meters," she replied, immediately placing the figure in his field of vision as part of a general tactical overlay. The creature was already surrounded by a red triangle, and a small box with several pieces of textual data relevant to a recommended attack solution was presented. Not surprisingly, Plasma Bolt 1 was the recommended weapon — given that it was the only one available at the moment — at a default discharge intensity of Level 1.

Better late than never, I suppose, Dryden thought, raising his left arm in the direction of the currently designated target and clenching his hand into a fist. A vaguely familiar whining sound punctuated the formation of both the hyperspace and gravitic fields required by the weapon, followed instantaneously by a bright flash of bluish-white light as the lethal bolt of plasma was sent hurtling towards the unsuspecting raptor at two-thirds the speed of light. Unfortunately, Emma had not yet had an opportunity to fully calibrate the weapon to compensate for Dryden's generally unreliable aim. As a result, and in spite of the relatively short range to his target, the first plasma bolt went wide, passing well left of the creature to impact in spectacular fashion against a large tree in the distance.

Realizing that their prey was not as helpless as they had believed and that any further delay might result in their deaths as well, both protoraptors screamed in fury and increased the speed of their advance, Without hesitation, Dryden selected intensity Level 4, ignored the warning displayed in the center of his field of view, and fired a second shot — this time aiming for the creature's center of mass. The second, much more intense, flash of light left huge white spots before his eyes in spite of being attenuated somewhat by his light amplification system. As a result, his first indication of having scored a direct hit was the feeling of warm blood and gore drenching him from head to toe. With Emma's assistance, the second compressed bolt of energetic plasma had struck the protoraptor at the midpoint between its forelimbs, transferring such a tremendous amount of energy to its upper body that it was literally blown to pieces.

As his vision cleared, Dryden quickly located what was left of the creature. Nothing at all remained above where its chest had been, but the lower half of its body had come to rest just off the edge of the path. The animal's massive hind legs still jerked convulsively as if attempting to run, undoubtedly responding to the last commands issued by its central nervous system.

As Dryden turned to face his third and final pursuer, he was impacted in the back with such force that his body was thrown forward several meters, landing flat on his stomach in a momentary daze. The remaining female raptor sprinted away, more cautious now than before, then circled back as she prepared to make her kill. With the breath knocked out of him and now barely aware of his surroundings, Dryden nevertheless attempted to roll onto his back in preparation for making use of his only available weapon once again.

"Too close!" Emma warned urgently. "It's too close for a plasma bolt!"

No choice, he thought, raising his fist just as the third raptor charged once again — this time with its lethal sickle-claws held aloft in anticipation of delivering a killing blow. But before Dryden could regain the mental focus required to fire his weapon, a distant part of his mind registered a series of sharp cracks that seemed to come from the forest to the left of the logging path. *Thunder?* he wondered stupidly, then immediately realized it was something else entirely as several puffs of dark green erupted from the creature's head and neck in Dryden's monochrome, light-amplified vision. In response, the protoraptor dropped like a marionette whose strings had been severed, skidding to an abrupt stop less than five meters away.

Dryden, while registering the fact that he was probably still in danger, was so grateful to have survived the attack that he immediately began thinking of the most appropriate way to surrender, if necessary, to whoever had just saved his life. Accordingly, as he heard the sound of boots running down the path behind him, he eased himself back up onto his knees, hoping to avoid any sudden movements that might be seen as a provocation. Raising both hands over his head, he turned in their direction just as the butt of a Winchester rifle hit him squarely in the left temple, and the entire world went black.

Chapter 13

Didara 4, South Estorian Continent, Scarsdow Forest
(Logging Cabin - 3.9 km north of Vently Ford)

"Hey …" a faraway voice echoed in a strange, bleary tone, then paused.

"*Hey* …" it repeated itself.

The sound might have been a bit louder this time, but it was still blessedly remote. Dryden's subconscious mind felt certain the disembodied voice had been talking forever. He had no idea who it belonged to, nor did he particularly care. Thankfully, it was a small and inconsequential voice anyway … one he was almost certain he could safely ignore. Besides, it was probably nothing more than a figment of his imagination anyway … some sort of wood sprite … gnome, perhaps … or maybe just an annoying child at play in the distance.

"Emma, increase stimulation by seventy percent please," the annoying, gnome-like voice said.

The AI responded by administering a bolus of adrenaline directly into Dryden's bloodstream while concurrently applying direct electrical stimulation to several strategic locations in his brain. The sensation, he would later recall, was something akin to being submerged in a frozen lake while simultaneously being stung by an entire nest of Ganahar fire wasps near the base of his skull.

"*Why!?*" he yelped, sitting bolt upright and gasping for breath.

"Shhh! Quiet!" both Rick and Emma scolded in unison within the confines of his mind.

"We're happy you finally decided to join us," Rick continued, "but I need you to keep quiet and listen to me very carefully. You're *not* dreaming. You're awake … well … partially, at least. And you're going to be okay, at least for the moment, if you will concentrate and listen to what I have to tell you."

Okay … right … I understand. Dryden thought, desperate to do whatever was required to avoid more of what he had just experienced. *I hear you. I'm awake and apparently still alive … to some extent, at least. Just please don't do … whatever it was you just did … ever again. Where am I?*

"You're at the logging cabin Emma was taking you to, but you've been captured by a small unit of Estorian Federation cavalry. They've got you bound and blindfolded, and you're currently sitting on the floor in a storage closet while they try to figure out exactly what to do with you. You've been unconscious for nearly twelve hours."

And you're, uh … Rick, are you not?

"Very good, my young friend. Come on now, it's time to rise and shine. They've been giving you a sedative — that's a type of medicine intended to keep you from waking up."

I know what a sedative is, you fool of a gnome! Dryden snapped, causing waves of pain to course through his skull as if it had been rung like a gong.

"Gnome?" Rick asked, genuinely confused.

"You don't want to know," Emma replied on Dryden's behalf.

Ugh, Gods. I need everyone to just please stop talking in my head … just for a few minutes, Dryden groaned.

"Ah, very good," Rick continued without the slightest pause. "It sounds like you're starting to come back around. Anyway, these Estorians seem to have figured out who you are. And I assume that's the reason they have been keeping you drugged. I can't say I blame them, really. The last thing they need is to have you wake up and repeat what they saw you do at Talteca. But it's been a while since they dosed you, so I'm guessing they are preparing to either interrogate you or move you ... or perhaps both."

Great, Dryden thought, pausing momentarily as he struggled to regain some sense of equilibrium. *So ... how about some help getting me out of here? I trust you can simply "flash" me somewhere else before they realize I'm awake, can you not?*

"I can, Dryden, but I won't. I'll do my best to help you, but I'm afraid I'm not permitted to intervene in such a direct manner. Besides, doing something like that won't get either of us any closer to accomplishing our respective missions."

Missions? I wasn't aware I had agreed to any sort of —

"You said you wanted to help stop the High Protector."

Yes, of course, but I —

"And help other Didarans who, like you, have been forced into its service, correct?"

Right, Dryden replied, drawing out the word as he realized for the first time that he had not yet had the opportunity to consider precisely what such a commitment might imply.

"I believe you also said — or at least implied — that you wanted to prevent the High Protector from killing more Estorians and eventually taking control of your world. Or did I misunderstand you?"

I suppose I did say ... or think ... something like that, Dryden agreed, realizing that arguing with the Grey alien was pointless, particularly in his current, rather foggy state

"You have also expressed a desire to find your way back to your previous life," Emma interjected.

Yes, I did. How could I not?

"Then, fortunately for the both of us, our objectives remain in alignment with one another," Rick said enthusiastically. "Now listen to me, Flamecaller. For the moment, I believe it is in your best interest to remain as inconspicuous as possible for as long as possible. These men are angry ... *very* angry. And I think you'll agree they have every reason to be. To a man, each of them almost certainly lost someone important to them at your hands just a couple of days ago."

And their sense of justice demands that I pay for those deaths.

"Of course. As, I suspect, would be the case for you as well if your roles were reversed."

Right. I don't disagree with you, but what exactly do you mean by "inconspicuous?"

"Until they come for you, don't make so much as a sound. Speak to Emma and me only inside your mind and avoid letting them know you have regained consciousness for as long as possible. Eventually, they will undoubtedly want to question you. When that happens, I suggest you continue to say as little as possible. Display a sense of remorse and be as honest as you can."

Tell them the truth? Dryden asked, incredulous. *And just how receptive do you expect they will be to my version of the truth right now?*

"Not very, I would imagine. But telling them the truth seems less risky than making something up. It's always a little easier to keep your story straight that way."

Are you saying I should tell them about you as well?

"Ah, yes, that is a question I will leave to you. I can assure you that every single one of those men has heard of … *'creatures'* like me before. Nevertheless, the results of your mentioning an interaction with someone not of your world as part of your story are unpredictable at best. Since they're likely to be hostile, they're also less likely to believe anything that sounds out of the ordinary. And telling them something they don't believe prima facie may destroy what little credibility you may have otherwise had."

Unless, of course, one of them has already met someone like you.

"If you mean someone who looks like me, that seems highly unlikely … not recently anyway. But if you mean one or more of them may have encountered a being from another world, that is entirely possible."

And how do you know this?

"I know it because the weapons the Estorians have been using to fight the High Protector's forces were not developed on this world, Dryden. And *that* gets to the heart of what brings Miguel and me here."

Not for the first time over the past few days, Dryden felt the utterly surreal nature of his new reality threaten to overwhelm his weary mind and body. He said nothing for a long moment but just sat there on the floor in silence, shaking his head in disbelief as he attempted to process this latest bit of information. *So, tell me, Rick,* he finally continued, *just how many alien worlds are interfering on Didara at the moment?*

"I'm afraid I don't have an answer to that question just yet, but that is certainly an important part of what Miguel and I intend to find out."

I suppose that does explain a few things, though, doesn't it? It had already occurred to me that there must be some reason why they haven't executed me — since they know who I am, that is. That may confirm my assumption they are planning some sort of trade with the High Protector.

"A trade?" Rick echoed. "Yes, indeed. But perhaps not with the High Protector."

What do you mean? Who else would be interested in a trade?

"Emma picked up on quite a bit while you were indisposed over the past several hours. There are certainly any number of possibilities, given the value of the technology that has been installed inside your body. But under the circumstances, I think we can safely assume the Estorians intend to use you to force a meeting with their previously unknown weapon supplier."

Ah, yes, of course. I believe this entire situation is starting to make a bit more sense to me now, Dryden replied wearily. *Somehow, I just happen to find myself in an astonishingly convenient position to discover exactly who has been assisting the Estorians. May I assume that my being captured by them has been a part of your plan from the beginning?*

"You may assume it, Flamecaller, but you would be foolishly mistaken if you did," Rick replied testily. "As I said before, our interests happen to align nicely with one another at the moment, but your being here at this point in time is much more the result of your own actions than mine. Even in your current, somewhat befuddled state of mind, surely you understand that you would most likely have been captured or killed before your healing cycle ever completed if I had left you on the battlefield near Talteca. Furthermore — thanks to Miguel and me — you are certainly better equipped to extricate yourself from your present situation now than you would have been otherwise."

Oh ... Dryden thought after a moment's reflection. *My apologies if I have misinterpreted your intentions. I do, of course, appreciate your assistance thus far ... in addition to any additional help you might be willing to provide moving forward. Now, on the subject of assistance, what can you tell me of the Estorians? You say they have been acquiring their weapons from an outside source?*

"Yes and no. The weapons, equipment, uniforms ... even the tactics their cavalry troopers have been using over the past few years were not originally developed on Didara 4. The designs, as well as the industrial technologies and processes required to manufacture them, could only have come from an off-world source. I suspect that, initially at least, the Estorians received several very large shipments of war materiel. Since then, however, they may well have developed the capability to build at least some of these items for themselves."

And how can you be sure all of those things, particularly the weapons, came from another world?

"At first glance, they may not seem that far removed from the types of weapons the Estorians have been using for decades. But I can assure you, they are dramatically more advanced. The level of technological sophistication required to produce them far surpasses anything that existed on your world until very recently. In addition, the rifles and pistols you saw the Estorian cavalry using at Talteca are exact copies of weapons originally produced on a planet called Terra nearly four hundred Didaran years ago. Furthermore, the weapons in their possession continue to make significant jumps in capability. Each time the High Protector makes any sort of improvement to his forces, the Estorians have been matching or exceeding it in short order."

So, does it not stand to reason that it is these ... Terrans who have been providing the weapons and the information required to produce them?

"I don't think so, no."

Really? And why not? It seems to me the only logical conclusion.

Let's just say that Miguel and I have quite a bit of experience with the Terrans ... over a *very* long period of time. And while they do now possess the technical capabilities required to do so, we would most likely have detected their ships if they had visited Didara. They're also still quite new to interstellar travel and have enough problems of their own to deal with near their homeworld at the moment. It's also ... not really their style I would think ..." Rick said, trailing off momentarily as if thinking of something else. "But I digress," he continued. "No, we don't think it was them. But the specific weapons involved nevertheless seem to imply they were provided by someone with direct knowledge of Terra, which is strange, given how remote it is from Didara 4."

But why would someone — Terrans or otherwise — provide assistance in the form of crates full of manufacturing specifications and four-hundred-year-old weapons?

"They are four-hundred-year-old weapons *on* Terra, but that is obviously not the case on your world," Rick replied. "It may surprise you to learn that your galaxy is one of the oldest in the entire universe. Out among its nearly four hundred billion stars, you can still find a few *very* old civilizations where similar weapons might be several *billion* years old — if you could still even find a historical record of them, that is. What I'm trying to tell you is that age is a relative thing. These firearms were revolutionary in their day on Terra, and now they are even more so on Didara 4 since they have been introduced here well before their time, if you understand me."

I believe I do, yes.

"Like Didara, Terra was under the influence of the Pelarans for much of their recent history, which had the effect of accelerating their technology at a rate of between ten and fifty times their normal developmental timeline. Even in their case, however, it took several hundred years to advance their military/industrial capabilities from where yours were just a few years ago to the point where weapons like these were in widespread use. And, as you can imagine, there were a great many intermediate steps involved in the transition from soldiers carrying swords and spears, to muzzle-loading muskets, to revolvers and lever-action rifles."

Yes, I suppose that all makes sense, but I still don't see what would motivate someone to provide this particular combination of weapons to the Estorians. Surely, any species capable of traveling between the stars would have vastly more sophisticated weapons at their disposal. And why would they, the Pelarans, or anyone else be interested in a primitive, backward world like Didara in the first place?

"Excellent questions. But I'm afraid the answer may be a bit too involved for this conversation … then again, you're not going anywhere, are you?"

Gods, Dryden groaned inwardly. *I assume that sort of thing passes for humor on your world?*

"Hey, that was funny, regardless of where you happen to be from," Rick squeaked. "Sooo, moving on … once again, these particular weapons combined a number of incremental improvements, all adding up to major steps forward in terms of maintainability, interoperability, and firepower. The rifles the Estorians were using a couple of years ago when they attacked the High Protector's compound, for example, were some of the first mass-produced weapons on Terra that provided an individual soldier with the capability to achieve high rates of fire while using the same ammunition as their revolvers. Revolvers are the smaller, handheld weapons the Estorian cavalry has been using, by the way."

Yes, I know. I've been shot with one, remember?

"Oh, yes, I nearly forgot!" Rick laughed again. "Sorry about that, just making sure you were still with me. I've always wondered how that would feel, by the way."

I'm certain we can arrange a demonstration.

"No, I think not. Some things are best left to the imagination, after all. In any event, while it's probably true that the Estorians' benefactor could have provided much more advanced weapons if they wished, the combination of this particular rifle and revolver appears to have been chosen to achieve a very specific degree of superiority on the battlefield."

And since the Estorians are obviously still fighting, it seems to have been a winning strategy thus far.

"I don't believe I would go so far as to say the Estorians are *winning* this conflict. The loss of life has been significant, and, as you saw at Talteca, is no longer limited to members of their military. But, yes, at the moment, they are still managing to stay in the fight. After his forces were defeated and his original compound largely destroyed, the High Protector was forced to upgrade the armor used by his Shepherd troops. Since then — prior to this most recent battle, that is — he seems to have been spending most of his time consolidating his power, rebuilding his base of operations and beginning the process of fielding even more advanced technology."

Including the Flamecallers.

"Exactly. Essentially biological artillery pieces, for lack of a better term. For whatever reason, the High Protector seems either unable or unwilling to engage in direct combat himself or to equip his forces with advanced weapons of a more traditional sort. I can't say with any degree of certainty why this is the case. Initially, it's clear he was hoping to cow the Estorians into submission by creating the appearance that his forces had supernatural powers at their disposal."

You refer to the High Protector's use of so-called "magic," Dryden thought, phrasing his question as a statement of fact. *I don't remember much that happened before Talteca, but I still have a vague recollection of how everything we Flamecallers can do — everything the High Protector himself can do — was always described in terms of magical gifts. And he always seemed very insistent on communicating to the general population using those terms as well. Obviously, this was a strategy that has failed.*

"Yes, it appears so. But under different circumstances, it might have actually worked. Fear, you see, is the most powerful weapon of all. And had it not been for the introduction of more modern weapons, the High Protector's bluff might have influenced enough of the masses to bring their government to heel. In any event, we have every reason to believe this trend of military one-upmanship will continue and intensify."

And why is that? Have the Estorians received additional, more powerful weapons?

"New rifles and ammunition, yes. They're similar in most respects to the ones they were using a couple of years ago, but with a number of incremental design improvements that more than double their effective firepower. That's how you almost got yourself killed at Talteca. The downside, of course, is that the Estorians' new rifles now utilize a different type of ammunition than their pistols."

A minor inconvenience when compared to the alternative, Dryden observed. *I must say, their anonymous benefactor seems to have oddly specific knowledge regarding precisely how much assistance to provide in order to keep the High Protector off balance, don't you think?*

"Indeed."

And does this not provide you with any clues as to who might be behind this?

"It does, but that is a topic I would prefer to discuss after Miguel and I have had more time to gather additional information. Suffice it to say that it seems all but certain the Estorians would have been firmly under the High Protector's control a couple of years ago had they not received outside help. Unfortunately, it is all but certain that a protracted arms race with the Pelaran AI will result in more of the kind of death and destruction we saw unleashed at Talteca."

Unleashed by me, Dryden sighed. *Against colleagues of the same men now holding me captive.*

"You were not the only member of the High Protector's forces at Talteca. Nor were you responsible for actions that were forced upon your mind. My point is that the High Protector's tactics seem to have changed. Before the destruction of his compound, he was largely following the typical Pelaran protocol for influencing preindustrial societies through the use of more … *subtle* techniques."

Such as?

"Well, as you might imagine, the AI typically works to gain control of key politicians, wealthy merchants, religious leaders, and the like. But you might be surprised to learn that this process isn't something the Pelaran AI typically handles face-to-face."

I'm afraid I don't understand. How else would such a thing —

"Suffice it to say they have the capability to bring some very sophisticated technology to bear over a very long period of time. But for reasons that are not yet clear, here on Didara, the Pelaran AI has chosen a more ... *hands-on* approach."

Certainly a more violent one, it seems.

"Yes, indeed. Although I'm not sure that was its original intention. I believe it expected to use its so-called 'magic' — which, in this case, was nothing more than the application of relatively advanced technology — to mount a campaign of mass terrorism."

In this case, you say? You speak as if you believe there are authentic examples of magic.

"A topic for another time, Flamecaller. You might be surprised to learn, however, that magic, in the sense I believe you just referred to it, actually *does* exist in the universe. But for the term to apply, it must satisfy a very specific set of criteria."

I see. I'd be very interested to hear more about that sometime. I assume the High Protector does not satisfy this, uh ... magical criteria?

"Certainly not. Now, let's get back to your question regarding why multiple spacefaring species are interested in Didara 4. I believe there are several reasons. One of the most attractive things about your world is the fact that it is what we often refer to as 'super-habitable.' That means it has large landmasses and conditions favorable to producing and sustaining a high-population technological society over a very long period of time. This star system also happens to be located at the edge of what until recently would have been considered Pelaran Alliance territory. So, if we assume the Pelaran Central AI selected your world for its cultivation program, that implies it is also well-suited to eventually become the dominant military and industrial power in this region of space."

Well, Dryden chuckled, *I must say all of that sounds very grand. But wouldn't this 'cultivation program' you just described normally take a great many years to complete? In my mind, at least, this does not explain why multiple parties seem to have become involved within a relatively short period of time.*

"No, it does not. And therein lies the central question. From what we can tell, things were progressing according to a fairly standard cultivation program timeline until just a couple of years ago. That's when the rate of technological change on Didara seems to have rapidly diverged from the typical timeline — at least where military and industrial development is concerned."

And you have no idea who is responsible? Dryden pressed.

"I can see why you might think so, but we do not. Not with any degree of certainty, at least. These activities only recently attracted our attention. Although we have been visiting your world for a very long time, we have not had occasion to do so recently. As a result, our intelligence isn't all we would like it to be. Once again, that's why we're here."

And once you gather this intelligence, what are your intentions? Do you plan to side with the Estorians, or will you remain neutral in this conflict?

"That, my young friend, depends on precisely what we discover. I will say, however, that we have no desire to see one of our most successful colonies in this sector enslaved or destroyed."

Your colonies? Dryden asked, incredulous. *You mean to say that this planet was originally colonized by your race? Forgive me, but that seems highly unlikely. You expect me to believe that our appearance has changed so dramatically since your people — who presumably look like you — originally arrived here?*

"*Quiet,* both of you!" Emma interrupted urgently. "Someone's coming."

Chapter 14

Didara 4, South Estorian Continent, Ganahar Plains
(Plains Reach - 131 km southeast of Helstaad)

During much of the two-year period since what had come to be known as the Battle at the Compound, the High Protector had rarely been seen. But unfortunately for the Estorian Army, the Pelaran WCS had been far from idle. During his long absence, he dedicated most of his time and resources to consolidating his power — preparing, he believed, for a final, overwhelming show of force that would end with the South Estorian continent firmly under his control.

This final campaign had begun slowly at first, with small squads of recently upgraded Shepherd soldiers mounting small-scale assaults on Estorian Army units at various locations across the region. With each successive operation, however, the High Protector had been ratcheting up the level of violence, culminating with the deployment of the Flamecallers and the recent battle near the town of Talteca. And in spite of his losing all of his newest and most valuable weapons during that battle, the High Protector was not at all discouraged. Given time, he believed, even the Flamecallers could be replaced. By any measure, his forces had still managed to inflict losses on the Estorian Army that they simply could not sustain — along with civilian casualties the Estorian people would not long tolerate. And it was his intention to continue doing so until they were forced to yield. Time, he believed, was very much on his side.

Once the Estorians ceded governmental control, the High Protector knew, it would become more critical than ever that he have a suitable base of operations from which to expand his ever-increasing power and influence. To that end, much of his time had been spent reconstructing both the buildings and infrastructure associated with what had originally been referred to as his compound and personal residence. This time, however, the WCS had taken a dramatically different approach. Constructed atop the same, solitary plateau as the one destroyed by the Estorian army two years ago, the new facility was over four times as large. Thick, heavily reinforced walls surrounded the sprawling new complex on all sides, punctuated by guard towers now equipped with weapons of a type never before seen on Didara 4.

Unlike its predecessor, the High Protector's reconstituted headquarters and personal residence — which he had recently rechristened as "Plains Reach" — was designed to convey an air of intimidation to any who dared approach. Those with military expertise recognized the new facility for exactly what it was — a genuine fortress, all but unassailable by any force of arms likely to ever be fielded against it. And this was particularly true of what remained of the beleaguered Estorian Army.

To their credit, however, the Estorians considered the existence of their enemy's new stronghold as nothing more than an open invitation to discover a means to destroy it, just as they had done with its predecessor. Abandoning large-scale assaults in favor of asymmetric, guerrilla-style warfare, the Army had become increasingly creative in its efforts to stymie the High Protector's progress at every turn.

Of particular note was the newly formed "night-stalker" unit. Although they had only received enough gear to field a single, thirty-five-man platoon, all of its members were equipped with a set of seemingly miraculous goggles that allowed them to see clearly in the dark. Knowing full well that, even with this remarkable new tool, a direct assault on Plains Reach itself would be nothing short of suicide, they had instead focused their harassing attacks on construction materials and other supplies bound for the site. While somewhat ineffective in terms of the damage inflicted, their efforts nevertheless had a significant impact on the High Protector's long and highly vulnerable supply lines. Ultimately, a construction effort originally expected to take nine months had been stretched to over two years.

In response, the WCS had adopted increasingly brutal tactics, countering what it thought of as the insurgency with a level of violence intended to send a clear message to the Estorian Federation. It had no intention of leaving Didara 4 and could act with impunity on their world despite their best efforts to the contrary.

On this particular morning, the High Protector stood atop one of his recently completed guard towers, admiring the newest addition to his rapidly growing arsenal. On a pedestal near the center of the platform sat a heavy, directed-energy weapon, its dual emitters mounted side by side atop a fully articulating turret. In this configuration — and in this particular tower, which formed one corner of the facility's outer wall — the weapon was afforded a nearly 270-degree field of fire.

With Plains Reach itself constructed atop the highest point for several kilometers, the weapon could easily reach out from its fifteen-meter-high tower to attack enemy targets out to a range of nearly twenty kilometers.

"And my understanding is that it's finally operational?" the High Protector asked the Shepherd soldier in command of his Weapons Emplacements Team.

"Indeed, it is, my lord. Fully operational as of late yesterday afternoon, as are all seven of the other tower-mounted weapons. I believe we have scheduled a demonstration for you and Sir Frederick tomorrow morning."

The Lord High Protector smiled, nodding in obvious approval at this somewhat unexpected bit of good news. Due to the near-constant minor, but nonetheless irritating, attacks by the rag-tag remnants of the Estorian Army, bringing the facility's new weapons online had taken far longer than expected. This was primarily due to long delays in completing its greatly modernized powerplant. *A minor irritation, soon to be remedied,* the WCS thought, running its hand complacently along the side of one of the massive beam emitters.

The irony associated with installing modern energy weapons atop what was in many respects a rather primitive type of fixed fortification was far from lost on the High Protector. Even the most rudimentary of space-based weapons, he knew, could obliterate the entire Plains Reach facility in an instant. But it was this odd mix of old and new technologies that he found particularly interesting — and a challenge he deemed worthy of his considerable capabilities. Besides, even with some other, presumably advanced species apparently seeking to exert its influence on Didara 4, every simulation he had constructed thus far (just over one hundred twenty-three thousand of them at the moment) indicated that such an attack was highly unlikely. Nevertheless, the evidence that the Didarans were receiving technological assistance was unequivocal at this point. Thus far, that assistance had come primarily in the form of ancient, gunpowder-based kinetic energy weapons. While constituting a dangerous annoyance to be sure, they were hardly a decisive advantage against the resources he could still bring to bear.

"Excellent," the WCS replied enthusiastically, concluding a long, internal stream-of-consciousness that had nevertheless taken only three femtoseconds in real-time. "I look forward to seeing what the new systems can do."

"I think you'll be pleased, my lord. The Estorian Army won't dare approach this facility again ... well, at least not more than once," he added with a confident smile.

"I'm sure you're right, Sergeant. It's a shame we couldn't invite their General Staff to witness the demonstration tomorrow, but I'm certain they will get the opportunity to see the system in action soon enough," the WCS said, staring once again at the new energy weapon while slowly nodding his head in obvious approbation.

"My Lord High Protector," he heard Sir Frederick call from behind and immediately turned to see his servant's longish head peering up onto the covered platform from the stairway.

"Ah, yes, there you are, Frederick. I'm glad you're here. In spite of a few delays, these men have done exemplary work preparing our new network of defensive systems. After what I'm sure will be a successful demonstration tomorrow, please see that they are handsomely rewarded for their efforts."

"Of course, my lord."

"Thank you, my lord," all three of the Shepherd soldiers on the platform said in unison, each man raising his right arm with a clenched fist in front of his body in salute. Although clearly pleased by their leader's approval, all three were careful to ensure there was no sign of disrespect (or even surprise) in their voices. The Lord High Protector was much better known among his subjects for meting out punishment than for lavishing praise, and each man swallowed nervously at the thought of what might happen if tomorrow's demonstration did *not* go as planned.

"My pleasure," the High Protector replied, returning their salutes before joining his majordomo on the stairs.

"There are three Estorian men at the front gate to see you, my lord," Sir Frederick said as they started down.

"Right now? What sort of men?"

"Local militiamen … well, according to them, at least. Ruffians really. They occasionally make contact with Estorian Army units operating out of the local mountain garrison at Helstaad or their larger facility at Talteca. Some of our patrols have run into this particular group from time to time. They have always made it very clear that they would be willing to trade information we might find of interest for compensation of some sort. I think it's safe to assume they do the same for the

Estorian Army, but they claim the Estorians don't pay very well."

"Humph," the High Protector chuckled to himself, "I can't say I'm surprised. Let's at least go see what they have to say. But I hope for their sake they're not wasting our time."

"I spoke to them briefly, and I don't think so, although they refused to deliver their information to anyone but you. They claim to have knowledge regarding one of our missing Flamecallers."

"I see. Well, if that is truly the case … that is, if their information proves useful, we will compensate them accordingly. If not, I will leave it to you to decide how best to discourage further unwanted intrusions in the future."

"With pleasure, my lord. I must warn you, however, that these men are the worst sort of loathsome hill people."

"I understand, Sir Frederick. But I will tell you that I have often found such men can be quite useful when it comes to obtaining intelligence information."

"You astonish me, my lord. In what way?"

"Ah, well, I think it is safe to say that *loathsome,* to use your term, men such as these have often arrived at their current *loathsome* state due to actions of their own."

"Or lack thereof," Sir Frederick interjected with a raised eyebrow.

"Yes, that is precisely what I mean. Interestingly enough, it is those kinds of people who are often the most willing to offer up useful information — their lives being an endless quest for an easy reward, you see. But you must always bear in mind that the concepts of loyalty and trust — to either side — mean little or nothing to them. And you must take this into consideration when evaluating whatever it is they have to offer."

Moments later, the two passed through the facility's impressive main entrance, its enormous pair of armored blast doors currently resting in their open positions to either side. As soon as they were outside the massive, reinforced concrete and steel walls of Plains Reach, four Shephard troops immediately fell into step a few paces behind them. In a departure from the simple longswords they had occasionally carried in the past, each of these were armed with the very latest in Pelaran-AI-designed pulsed particle beam rifles.

The presence of the Shepherd soldiers and the strange-looking weapons they carried was not lost on the three militiamen waiting just outside the gates. They stood nervously beside their horses, staring intently as the Lord High Protector himself approached with his entourage in tow, each of them wondering if coming here would prove to be a bad idea after all.

"Good afternoon, gentlemen," the WCS called out as he approached. "I understand you have some information you would like to discuss with us."

"Yes, sir, we do," the first man replied.

When he had first spoken to the men several minutes earlier, Sir Frederick's first impression was that he had encountered moldy blocks of cheese in possession of more intellect than the three brutes could muster between them. But for reasons known only to themselves, this particular one had been chosen to speak for the group.

"If you will make it worth our while, that is," the man added, his face taking on a surprisingly cunning expression.

"Insolence will not get you the result you are looking for, I can assure you," Sir Frederick snapped. "You are speaking to the Lord High Protector of this world. And you may address him as my lord, or Lord High Protector. He is *not* a 'sir.' So, provide your information. And if whatever you have to say turns out to be worth your disturbing his busy afternoon, perhaps he will be kind enough to reward you for it. But I feel obligated to point out that you are in no position to demand anything of anyone at the moment."

"No, no, it's all right, Sir Frederick," the High Protector soothed. "I'm sure this young man meant no disrespect. Isn't that correct, Mister, uh ..."

"Wildermuth, *my lord,* Tommy Wildermuth," the militiaman replied, overemphasizing the honorific in such an awkward, comical manner that it might easily have been taken as an insult. Sir Frederick, however, judging that the man was paddling his metaphorical rowboat with a single oar, decided to let it go.

"And you're right, your honor," the man continued. "We meant no disrespect."

Upon hearing "your honor," Sir Frederick shook his head while clearing his throat meaningfully.

"Oh, uh, sorry, *my lord,* I meant to say. A few weeks back, we heard somebody tell of how you been offerin' up rewards for bringin' in information about the Estorian Army," Tommy stammered, clearly now afraid of saying the wrong thing.

"Yes, please go on," the High Protector prompted, an undeniably handsome smile holographically projected onto his face.

"Well, just yesterday," one of the other two men spoke up for the first time, "we heard a little about the battle that took place down near Talteca and how you were still lookin' for one of your men."

"Ah, yes. And what is *your* name, young man?" the WCS asked in a disarmingly pleasant tone.

"Denny, sir … sorry … Denny Crawley, *Lord High Protector,*" the man said, attempting a bow in an obvious bid to eclipse his companion's performance.

"We are pleased to meet you, I'm sure. And my apologies to *you*, sir," the WCS continued, looking the third man squarely in the eye, "I should have asked your name as well."

"*Me,* my lord? Oh, I'm Sam. Just Sam is all. Never had no last name so far as I know."

"Pleased to meet you as well, Sam. Now, Mr. Crawley, I apologize, but I believe I may have interrupted your story. Please do continue."

"Wellsir," Denny began, prompting Sir Frederick to begin issuing yet another correction. But before he could interrupt the man, he was silenced by a perfunctory backhanded wave from the High Protector, clearly communicating his lack of interest in matters of protocol, at least where this particular group of imbeciles was concerned.

"Wellsir," Denny repeated, oblivious, "yesterday evenin', we heard a commotion up in the woods not too far from our camp — sounded like somebody a-screamin'. Later on, we met up with an Estorian cavalry platoon, and when Tommy here told 'em what we heard, they seemed awfully interested."

"But you never actually *saw* anyone?" Sir Frederick asked.

"Uh, no, sir," Tommy interjected, regaining control of the conversation before one of his two companions managed to lose whatever reward he had coming to him. "It was dusky dark about that time. Scarsdow and the foothills are real dangerous after dark, my lord. But hearing a scream like that is unusual for sure, so we figured you'd want to know about it right away."

"A prudent course of action, my friend," the WCS said. "And what did the Estorian cavalry do when you reported this information to them?"

"Oh, they was powerful interested, my lord. The whole lot of 'em went gallopin' off towards the forest to check things out. We just thought the whole thing was a little odd. But then when we heard a couple of their men talkin' about your missin' Flamecaller — maybe more than one — why, we were pretty sure that was somethin' you'd want to hear about … seein' how it was your man and all."

"Oh, indeed it is," the High Protector replied. "You did exactly the right thing by coming here to tell us, and we are very much in your debt. Now, can you provide specific directions to wherever you believe the Estorian cavalry troopers were headed?"

"Oh yes, sir … uh, rather, yes, my lord. They was headed off towards Vently Ford. That's the best place around to cross the NorthHaven Rill, you know. It's real easy to find. Denny here even drew you a map," Tommy concluded, triumphantly thrusting a rolled-up piece of paper towards the WCS as if it contained a list of previously unfathomable truths known only to him.

"Thank you, Mr. Crawley," the High Protector replied in a gracious tone, accepting the paper and then immediately handing it over to Sir Frederick for examination.

"You're more'n welcome, my lord," Tommy continued, his voice seeming to grow more tense from one moment to the next. "Now, Vently Ford there on the map is really nothin' more than the spot where an old logging trail goes across the river. But you can also see there where Denny marked the spot where there's an old cabin. I don't rightly remember how far it is from the ford. But not more'n a few clicks, I'd say. Now, we can't guarantee anyone'll be there, but I'd be willing to bet you that's where those cavalrymen were headed. And I'd say there's a pretty good chance your man might be there too."

"And what makes you so sure?" Sir Frederick asked, looking up from the map through narrowed eyes.

"Wellsir, the truth is there ain't much else around there. So, if they've got a map of any sort that's less than a couple of hundred years old, that old cabin is about the only place to find shelter until you get into the mountains proper. And I'm sure I don't have to tell you that area ain't exactly the kind of place you want to be after dark without shelter of some sort."

"Sure, we've all heard the stories," the High Protector replied earnestly.

"Well, whatever you heard, my lord, I can just about guarantee that what's out there is worse. Now then, if Captain Cash's men —"

"Just a moment, who is Captain Cash?" Sir Frederick interrupted.

"Oh, sorry about that. I should have told you his name before. Captain Zophar Cash is the officer leading that cavalry platoon we mentioned. He's a right tough old cuss from what I hear. For an officer, that is. I think he's actually in charge of a whole troop of cavalry — that's a hundred men or so — but he was only ridin' with just the one platoon yesterday. Anyhow, if they do manage to take your man alive, odds are they'll head back towards their headquarters at Talteca. So that should give you plenty of time to catch up to 'em and get him back."

The WCS regarded the three men for a long moment, a multitude of sensors gathering vast quantities of data covering everything from their respiration and pulse rates to temperature gradients across every square centimeter of their bodies. All of this data was analyzed in real-time to provide the best possible indication of the veracity of the information being proffered.

"Yes …" he said after a moment's consideration. "Yes, I do believe what you have told us may prove quite useful. Sir Frederick, please compensate these men for their trouble, and make sure it's enough to motivate them to return to us in the future when similar information comes to their attention. I assume payment in gold is acceptable to you men?" the High Protector asked, his voice dripping with complaisance.

"Oh, yes! Of course!" all three of the men blurted out, followed by various combinations of "Yes, my lord! Yes, High Protector!" and "Thank you, my lord!" Their nervous expressions had disappeared in an instant, replaced now with broad smiles on their filthy, grizzled faces — each one punctuated by motley combinations of stained, broken, and missing teeth.

"Very good, then. I'm so pleased we were able to do business with one another!" the WCS replied brightly, then turned and nodded to Sir Frederick to signal that the encounter with their "guests" had reached its end.

"If you wouldn't mind waiting here for just a moment with these men," Sir Frederick said, nodding to the four Shepherd soldiers still posted just a few meters away. "The Lord High Protector and I must take our leave, but I will see to your payment and have it brought out to you in just —"

At that moment, Sir Frederick's words were interrupted by a sound familiar to most of those in the High Protector's service, many of whom had personally utilized it as a form of psychological warfare. But to the three local militiamen, it sounded like the rending of the world — alien, inexplicable, and wholly terrifying. From one of the fortress' guard towers, a single, reddish-orange beam of light seemed to pierce the sky, causing everyone present, the WCS included, to whip their heads around in the direction of the enormous, all-consuming sound.

The uncomprehending minds of all three of the Didaran men interpreted what they were seeing as a lightning strike, but they soon realized that its color, shape, and duration were unlike any bolt of lightning they had ever seen before. In response, they simply stared, dumbstruck, into the sky, crouching down instinctively as if death would surely rain down upon their heads at any moment. To their credit, all three quickly regained their composure, standing cautiously upright once more while continuing to stare upward. The towering streak of light reaching up from the guard tower remained fixed in the sky, maintaining its hellish glow for a long moment before its color began to fade. In its place, a long trail of white remained, looking like a thin, billowy cloud stretching into the sky as far as the eye could see.

With the three militiamen still staring transfixed at the giant column of water vapor hanging in the sky, the High Protector motioned to his majordomo to follow, then spoke up in the same enthusiastic tone as if nothing unusual had happened. "Well, thank you again, gentlemen. As Sir Frederick said, please wait here with the guards for a moment and we will arrange for your payment to be brought out to you." With that, the WCS and Sir Frederick turned and walked briskly back towards the facility's blast doors.

"Fools!" the High Protector hissed as soon as they were out of earshot. "Who gave the Emplacements Team permission to conduct a test firing this afternoon?"

Sir Frederick paused, realizing the answer to his master's question was not one he was prepared to hear at the moment. "I'm not certain, my lord, but I will check the schedule and find that information for you."

"Oh, I see," the WCS replied after a moment's consideration. "It was a pre-arranged discharge in preparation for tomorrow's demonstration, I assume?"

"Most likely so, but I will find out —"

"No, no, Sir Frederick. The team had full authority to do so per the deployment schedule. The fault is mine for not keeping abreast of their progress this past week."

"You've been preoccupied with more pressing matters, my lord. The only question now is what, if anything, we should do about the three militiamen witnessing the test."

"It's not a question at all, Sir Frederick. The Estorians will have some idea of what these weapons can do soon enough, but I am not prepared for these men to report back the details — to the extent they understand what they saw, of course — to the first cavalry troopers they run across."

"I understand and agree, my lord. Should I have the guards dispose of them, then?"

"No, Frederick. Pay them as agreed, and then you may conduct an … unscheduled weapons test as soon as they reach a safe distance. Just be sure to have some of our men go out to collect our gold and dispose of any remains afterward."

"Of course, my lord. And what of the information they provided regarding our Flamecaller? Do you believe it sufficient to warrant an expedition?"

"Without a doubt, Sir Frederick. Dead or alive, all of the Flamecallers must be recovered. As you know, they are an incredibly difficult asset to replace. And on the subject of valuable assets, I believe Commander Beck is ready for her first mission. This seems like an excellent opportunity for her to prove her worth, don't you agree?"

Frederick started to reply, then checked himself.

"Was there something you wanted to add?" the WCS asked with a raised eyebrow.

"With respect, my lord, I just know that you have expressed how difficult it is, even for you, to grant the gift of Flamecalling. At the moment, Dryden may well be the last of his kind. If you feel it would be prudent to send a more experienced commander, I would be happy to lead the mission personally."

The High Protector regarded his personal assistant for a long moment, judging whether this suggestion was an expression of impudence, vanity, or earnest concern.

"No, Frederick. While what you say is true, you are every bit as valuable to me as Dryden is. And I have no intention of risking both of you on a single mission unless I have no other options. Besides, Maya seems well-suited for this mission. If Dryden has been compromised in any way — which may well be the case — make it clear that her orders are to destroy him."

"Yes, my lord," Sir Frederick said, raising his fist in salute.

"Thank you, my friend," the WCS replied, returning his assistant's gesture of respect. "And, Frederick …"

"Yes, my lord."

"Grant Maya and her extraction team permission to take the assault shuttle. Just see that they wait until after dark this evening to depart."

"With pleasure, my lord."

Chapter 15

Didara 4, South Estorian Continent, Scarsdow Forest
(Logging Cabin - 3.9 km north of Vently Ford)

Outside his storage room, Dryden heard the heavy thud of boots with the accompanying clinks of spurs followed by the sound of ancient, squeaking hinges. But even without all of the telltale sounds, the bright sunlight filtering through his blindfold from the cabin beyond made it clear that someone had finally been sent to retrieve him.

"On your feet, traitor," a deep, male voice growled menacingly. With that, Dryden felt powerful hands under each of his arms as he was unceremoniously lifted off the floor and then half-carried, half-pushed out of his makeshift holding cell. After taking no more than a dozen or so steps, his escorts shoved him down into a hard, wooden chair.

"The blindfold," he heard another man's voice say.

"You sure 'bout that, Cap'n?" the original, much rougher-sounding voice responded from immediately behind Dryden's chair.

"Yeah, it's okay, Sergeant. I've seen this done with one of his kind before. It's safe enough as long as their hands are bound like this. The big ones, though — you know, the ones with the black armored suits —"

"The Shepherds."

"That's right. With one of those, you'd better have some heavy chains like these available. And I don't mean for just their hands, either. I've seen one of them

213

snap a twenty-five-millimeter braided rope like it was a piece of butcher's twine."

"Now *that's* interesting," Rick observed offhandedly. "That sounded like he thinks he might have seen another Flamecaller in captivity."

Ignoring the Grey's comment, Dryden focused his mind on his restraints, trying to assess whether there might eventually be an opportunity to escape. He had realized that his hands were tied behind his back immediately after regaining consciousness. But now, testing the strength of his bonds for the first time, he could tell that they were actually clasped together and bound with both a thick braided rope and a heavy length of chain. *A simple but effective solution,* he thought, wondering what kinds of experiences these men had encountered in the past that had taught them to take such extraordinary precautions.

"I'm Captain Zophar Cash," he heard the second man say, just before the blindfold was jerked off the top of his head. Dryden reflexively turned his head to the side, wincing as the full force of sunlight flooding into the room assaulted his optic nerves. Glancing about through squinted eyes, he noted that the cabin was larger than he had expected — probably measuring at least eight meters on each side. He also saw that the room was crowded with at least ten scowling cavalrymen, prompting a chill to run down his spine at the memory of what he had done to men just like these only a few days before.

"I'm the commander of E Troop, 3rd Squadron of the 3rd Regiment," the tall, rugged-looking officer standing squarely in front of him continued. Cash had the appearance of a man who, even in his current, rather haggard-looking state, still managed to project a powerful, charismatic air that left absolutely no doubt as to who was in charge. "And all of these men you see here are cavalry troopers assigned to E Troop's 1st Platoon," he said, turning his head to the side and gesturing to the other soldiers in the room for emphasis. "I've had the pleasure of riding patrol with 1st Platoon for the past few days while covering for one of my lieutenants — his name was Sinby."

The mention of Lieutenant Sinby's name prompted a shuffling of feet accompanied by a palpable rise in the general level of tension in the room. Dryden swallowed hard at the near-certainty of what the young captain would say next.

"So please allow me to be blunt," Cash continued. "A couple of days ago, a man matching your description killed our Lieutenant Sinby near the town of Talteca. He just happened to be riding that day with the 2nd Cavalry Regiment — which lost seven hundred and thirty-four of its troopers during that same battle. My orders are to locate and then either kill or capture whoever is responsible for their deaths."

Here, Cash paused, his bright green eyes narrowing slightly as he watched his prisoner for any sort of reaction. Seeing little more than a blank stare, he pressed on. "Now, from what I've been able to put together, there was only one man involved with the attack on the 2nd Regiment. And although I can't even begin to understand how something like that is possible, I believe *you* are the man we've been looking for."

"Be *very* careful what you say here," Rick observed within the confines of Dryden's mind.

Unable to come up with any oath, curse, or blasphemy foul enough to respond to such an inane recommendation, the Flamecaller chose to remain silent.

"It should go without saying," Captain Cash went on, "that every man in my outfit knew most of the men you killed. So, even though our brass would probably prefer to have us bring you back alive, there's not one of them that'll lose any sleep if we ride back into regimental headquarters dragging what's left of your corpse behind one of our horses."

Cash paused once again to allow the gravity of his words a few moments to sink in. Neither Dryden nor anyone else in the room had the slightest notion that the officer's words should be taken as an idle threat.

"Lucky for you, I'm not an unreasonable man," Cash continued with a mirthless grin on his face. "So, I'm gonna ask you a few questions. And if you cooperate … well, I can't promise you won't be roughly handled, but I'll see to it personally that you're still alive and in one piece to stand trial for your crimes when we get back to Talteca. If not, that's just fine with us too. In fact, I'm pretty sure Sergeant Higgs here already has a nice tree and a sturdy piece of rope picked out for you. If you'd prefer it, we can just go ahead and get your hangin' out of the way so we can have ourselves some breakfast and then mount up and head for home. Anyhow, you go ahead and take a minute if you like, and then just let me know what you decide."

"I can assure you that won't be necessary, Captain," Dryden said, speaking up for the first time. "I will be most happy to cooperate, and I will endeavor to answer whatever questions you ask to the best of my ability.

Please allow me to say from the outset how truly sorry I am for all of the lives that were lost at Talteca."

These words had barely left Dryden's mouth when a savage blow from an enormous fist inside a leather cavalry gauntlet slammed into the right side of his head, very nearly knocking him out of his chair.

"Don't you *dare*," Sergeant Higgs snarled from behind him. "Don't you dare act like you didn't murder all of those men in cold blood. And don't you dare pretend you're the least bit sorry for what you did."

Dryden took a second to steady himself, took in a deep breath, and then — far more cautiously this time — began again. "I'm sorry ... no, no, I ... that's not what I meant. What I mean to say is ... I did it."

"You *what?*" Cash replied under raised eyebrows.

"I did it," Dryden repeated. "I killed all those men."

"Oh, that's not what I had in mind at all when I told you to be honest," he heard Rick say in a low, anxious voice.

Again, there was a general shuffling of feet in the room, this time accompanied by a murmur of surprise and disgust that seemed to pass through the soldiers in the room like a gust of cold wind.

"I won't sit here and insult all of you and the memory of those I killed by denying it. But if you will please allow me to explain —"

"I think we've heard enough, Cap'n Cash, don't you?" Higgs interrupted. "This man just admitted to at least seven hundred and thirty-five capital crimes in front of a room full of witnesses. He should be executed right here ... on the spot. And then we can haul his body back to Colonel Simms."

"No, please, if you will just give me a moment to explain —"

"There *ain't* no explanation for that kind of crime, you murderin' bastard!" Higgs spat and had drawn back his hand to deliver another blow when a nod from Captain Cash prompted two nearby men to restrain him.

"That's enough, Sergeant. He was brave enough — or foolish enough, maybe — to admit the crime, so I think we should hear what else he has to say. But I do think you're in the right of it. The man just confessed in front of everyone in this room. So, don't you worry. He'll get what's coming to him," Cash nodded reassuringly, then looked his prisoner squarely in the eyes once again. "So, you go on ahead and talk, Mister, uh, —"

"My name is Dryden. Dryden Beck."

"You go on and say whatever it is you need to say, Mr. Beck."

"Thank you, Captain," Dryden began again, glancing to the side as he did so to see if he were about to be cold-cocked yet again. "I do take responsibility for what I've done. And I don't expect you to understand what I'm about to say, because the truth is, I don't fully grasp what's happened to me either. All I can tell you is that I was not in control of my own mind during the battle and haven't been for several months, apparently. In fact, I can't remember much of anything that happened before Talteca. What I *can* tell you is that I was forced into doing the things I've done by the High Protector. And if I'm ever free again to do so, I will do everything in my power to stop him … and to save the others like me he has enslaved."

"So that's gonna be your defense, is it?" Higgs scoffed. "You can't remember a thing that happened? You weren't in control of your own mind? The devil made you do it? I'm no lawyer for sure, but even I know that lyin', thievin' murderers have been using excuses just like that for as long as there's been a law to break. They all still end up at the end of a rope, which is where you're headed too," he snarled, then looked pleadingly up at his commanding officer once more. "He's wasting our time, Captain. We need to just get this over with and move on. There's probably more of his kind in the area we can round up and kill before they have a chance to butcher more of our good men."

"I said that's enough, Higgs," Cash repeated, staring the noncommissioned officer down with a dark scowl on his face. "Now you just heard me give my word that we would take this man back to stand trial. Whether we like his answers or not, he seems to be cooperating so far. Besides, the decision of what to do with him is above both of our pay grades. We'll let the brass back at HQ decide, but I'm guessing they'll want to try to get some information out of him that might help us against the others like him."

Cash paused and stepped closer to his prisoner, then squatted down to look squarely into Dryden's eyes once more, this time from just centimeters away. "So how about it, Mr. Beck? Do you have some additional information you'd like to provide us along those lines?"

Didara 4, South Estorian Continent, Ganahar Plains
(9.7 km southwest of Plains Reach)

After receiving payment for the information they provided to the High Protector, the three militiamen had immediately mounted up and headed off in the direction of their camp, nearly a half day's ride to the southwest. Not wanting to look as if they were expecting trouble, Tommy had set a relatively slow pace at first, but soon began driving all three of their tired old mares as fast as he dared without fear of at least one of them dropping dead from exhaustion. Now, after more than half an hour's worth of this punishing pace, and with the fortress' forbidding walls many kilometers behind them, Tommy finally reined in his horse, allowing the three to proceed at a more comfortable two-beat trot.

"'Bout time you slowed down, Tommy!" Denny said as he came up beside his leader's horse. "Why were you in such a hellfire hurry anyway? Old Gracie here's old. Ain't you, girl?" he cooed, leaning forward to gently pat his mount on the side of her great neck, causing droplets of foamy, white lather to splatter in all directions with each touch of his hand.

"If you can't figure that out for yourself, then you're a damned fool, Denny Crawley."

"What?" Denny asked, incredulous. "You mean all that fire and smoke we saw comin' out of that tower back there? I don't know what any of that was, Tommy. And you know what else I know? I know *you* don't know what any of that was any better'n I do. So, if you manage to kill the only horses we got for no reason, who's the damned fool? Me or you?"

"No," Tommy admitted, turning around in his saddle to look back in the direction of Plains Reach. "No, you're right about that. I can't say for sure what it was we saw back there … but I think it must have been a weapon of some sort. It don't matter, though. 'Cause whatever it was, it sure as hell wasn't somethin' we were supposed to see."

"What makes you say that, Tommy," Sam asked. "That Lord High Protector seemed like a pretty decent fella, if you ask me. I'd have to say he was a lot friendlier'n I was expectin'."

"I *didn't* ask you," Tommy shot back, raising his voice for the first time. "Don't you two idiots know he was just bein' friendly while he thought we had somethin' to offer him? And didn't either of you notice the look on both of their faces when the light shot out of that tower? They weren't expectin' it any more than we were. To be honest with you, I was surprised they let us leave with our skins."

***

Atop a guard tower platform ten kilometers to the northeast, powerful optical and infrared sensors had been dutifully tracking the three men's progress since immediately after their departure. Never ones to squander an opportunity for an operational weapons test, the High Protector's Emplacements Team had immediately designated each of the three militiamen as hostile enemy combatants. There had been a brief but spirited debate among the team's members regarding precisely when to engage the targets, with some arguing that the situation offered an ideal use case for testing the system's maximum theoretical range. But in the end, the team lead had squelched all discussion with a prediction of the likely consequences should their targets disappear below the horizon without being fired upon. Now, with the fire mission having already been approved several minutes earlier, the energy weapon's onboard AI issued its final clearance to fire.

Within each of the weapon's dual emitters, positively charged hydrogen ions were accelerated until their velocities approached the speed of light. The high-energy proton stream then passed through a reaction chamber where it was injected with a corresponding stream of electrons. The resulting output at each of the weapon's dual apertures was a neutrally charged stream of hydrogen atoms. And while each was one of the smallest projectiles imaginable, there were trillions of them — all of them streaking downrange toward its designated target at very nearly the maximum speed at which matter can travel within normal space. The first stream of atomic-scale missiles reached the nearest of the three militiamen in just over thirty microseconds, delivering nearly one hundred gigajoules of destructive energy.

Although the two beams produced by the weapon were normally invisible to the naked eye, each created a superheated channel of ionized air within Didara's thick atmosphere. It was this heating that had produced the wicked, reddish-orange glow the three militiamen had witnessed just thirty minutes earlier. Following each discharge, the glow quickly subsided — only to be replaced by white trails of condensing water vapor as the surrounding air rapidly cooled.

Upon impact with the first target (Denny and his horse Gracie, as chance would have it), the pulsed particle beams instantly and catastrophically superheated all surfaces with which they came into contact. At first, the weapon's AI maintained narrow, coherent beams. Then — with a "kill" now all but certain — it allowed the two beams to diverge slightly before rapidly traversing them over the target to ensure maximum destruction. The result was a rider, horse, and all of his equipment (such as it was) flash-vaporized into a rapidly expanding cloud of gas.

Surprisingly, Tommy and Sam fared even worse than had Denny and his tired old buckskin mare. The energy weapon's initial blast had created a shock wave significant enough to knock both of their horses to the ground. Then, during the intervening three seconds it took for the AI to ensure its first target had been fully neutralized, Tommy, Sam, and their respective mounts were burned alive — their flesh consumed by the intense heat generated by the destruction of their former companion. Mercifully, the weapon's AI gathered sufficient data during its first attack to become more efficient with subsequent discharges, enabling both of its remaining targets to be blotted from existence in similar fashion less than two seconds later.

Chapter 16

Grey Ship Ethereal, Didara 4, High Orbit
(51.7×10^3 km above the surface)

"I'm detecting a Pelaran sublight engine signature from the Plains Reach compound," Miguel said. As he spoke, a wealth of additional data regarding what the ship's sensors were telling him was simultaneously conveyed to his partner's mind.

"I was wondering how long that would take," Rick replied.

"Right, well, I suppose it was unavoidable that the High Protector would eventually resort to imposing his will via more … *overt* uses of Pelaran tech. If his goal truly is to single-handedly subvert the entire planet, what choice does he have, really? The Estorians are never going to let it happen otherwise."

"Humph," Rick grumbled. "I don't think that decision has anything to do with the High Protector. It's just a pawn, after all. The Pelaran AI made all of its fundamental choices a very long time ago. It chose incorrectly, in my opinion. And it seems bent on repeating the same mistakes, even at its own peril."

"I agree, of course, but the question for us, as usual, is where this escalation puts us on the rules of engagement spectrum? It's one thing for the WCS to attempt to set himself up as some sort of divine ruler — frightening a relatively primitive culture into submission with a bunch of techno-graft. Even the creation of its mini-army of Shepherd troops probably doesn't quite cross the line … well, so long as they're not openly committing genocide, that is. But it's another thing entirely for it to start using advanced weaponry, particularly when that advanced weaponry happens to be mounted on a heavily armored assault shuttle."

"True enough, but let's not get ahead of ourselves here. You know the mission specs as well as I do. Utilizing an armed air or spacecraft as a transport does not meet the threshold for intervention. That is, of course, unless it decides to start using its weaponry to inflict mass casualties."

"And nothing about that seems arbitrary to you? He just demonstrated a few hours ago that he has no problem using his base's energy weapons to kill Estorians. So, if he decides to use the ones mounted on that shuttle to wipe out half the continent's population — which he could easily do, by the way — how is that any different from sending his squads of super soldiers out to do the exact same thing? Never mind what he had Dryden and the other Flamecallers do at Talteca. In my mind, all of this constitutes a clear pattern of escalating violence. And it's time for us to take action before things get truly out of hand."

"You know exactly what I'm going to say, Miguel."

"Yes, I do. But that doesn't make it any less frustrating. I'm sure you're about to say pretty much the same thing you've said the last forty or fifty times I've posed a similar question. Let's see … rules of engagement, the benefits of adversity vis-à-vis colonial development, the need to further study the Pelaran AI strain, that decision is above our pay grade, blah blah blah."

"Blah blah blah?"

"A Terran colloquialism. It seemed to fit particularly well in this instance."

"I see. I was about to say that it seems like the Terrans' fighting spirit might have rubbed off on you a bit during our time with them."

"I tell you what it is, Rick. For all their faults, they at least generally act like they have the courage of their convictions to back up their actions. Now, granted, sometimes they only arrive at that point after what seems like endless debate, but ..."

"No, no, you're right. Once their minds are made up, they don't tend to spend a lot of time standing around wringing their hands about whether or not they've made the right choice."

"So, what does that say about us? Have we become a race of cowards over the millennia? Have we reached a point where we are reluctant to take action, even when we know very well it's the right thing to do?"

"Hmm ..." Rick paused, realizing this was one of those times where he was expected to offer the younger man some sort of sage advice to help him make sense of a morally ambiguous situation. "I hope what it says about us is that we've matured enough as a civilization to avoid making rash decisions that ultimately cause more harm than good. Sometimes, when we're forced to choose one of several poor options, I think the best action *is* to do nothing ... or at least to very carefully consider the situation before committing to a course of action."

"So, we *are* cowards, then. Little gray cowards," Miguel said with a sigh of resignation.

"We're a long way from home, Miguel. An almost unimaginably long way, in fact. Does it really seem like a good idea to you that we cast ourselves in the role of an intergalactic police force? We have significant resources at our disposal, sure, but ..."

"Humph. Perhaps we should have considered that more thoroughly before we embarked upon a massive intergalactic colonization program."

"Perhaps ... although I'm certain that particular issue was considered at great length. Consider this, my friend. If every civilization waited for some imagined set of 'perfect' circumstances before pressing forward with anything worthwhile, then nothing worthwhile would ever be accomplished. Besides —"

"I know ... we don't make the rules."

"Precisely. But, fortunately, those who do anticipated that we would sometimes encounter ambiguous situations just like this one. Accordingly, they provided us with a degree of latitude to apply our experience and common sense ... bending the rules, when necessary."

"And do you believe the time has come for us to take advantage of some of that flexibility?"

"No, I don't think we're there just yet. But we do need to keep a close eye on whatever the High Protector does next with that assault shuttle of his. In the meantime, please also stay abreast of other assets in the region we might be able to bring to bear, if necessary. It never hurts to be prepared, right? In case things start to get out of hand, that is."

"Already done," Miguel said. "No guarantees they'll come if we call, though."

"Oh, I think they will," Rick replied with a squeaking chuckle. "We'll just need to find a way to ensure it's worth their while."

Didara 4, South Estorian Continent, Scarsdow Forest
(Logging Cabin - 3.9 km north of Vently Ford)

Dryden had spent the remainder of the afternoon and early evening hours under intense interrogation from Captain Cash and his men. Although he had continued to provide them with as much information as he could — and with as much candor as he dared under the circumstances — he felt certain they weren't buying much of what he had told them thus far. And the truth was, he couldn't blame them, really. Much of what he had said sounded as if it should fit somewhere on the spectrum between unlikely and absurd. Nevertheless, the words kept coming, often rushing out of his mouth in a jumbled torrent as he tried to avoid another drubbing from Sergeant Higgs. On the bright side, there had been no additional talk of hanging him before the platoon mounted up for the return trip to their regimental headquarters near Talteca.

Once his questioning had finally come to an end, Dryden had been placed in an awkward, uncomfortable position atop one of the unit's spare horses. Although he had no idea how long he had been sitting there awaiting their departure, the muscles from his shoulders to his rear felt as if it must have been a week or more. Still, even though he had begun to wonder if he would still be able to stand by the time they made their next camp, he dared not draw any additional attention to himself. It had taken four men to hoist him into the saddle and secure him there, after a fashion — his hands still bound behind his back as before — and it was not an experience he cared to repeat if he could avoid doing so.

Listening in on the conversations going on around him, Emma deduced that Captain Cash had made the decision to delay their departure until just before nightfall. Dryden couldn't help but feel a bit shocked, given the presence of the protoraptors, but decided to give the young captain the benefit of the doubt. Perhaps he was aware the High Protector's forces — which primarily operated during the day — posed a far greater threat than the terrifying creatures prowling the Scarsdow Forest at night. Suddenly remembering his own, newfound ability to see clearly at night, however, Dryden doubted the darkness would do anything at all to conceal the cavalry unit's movements.

"I'm sure you're right about that," Emma said, speaking inside his head for the first time in over an hour. The interruption to his internal reverie once again caused the Flamecaller to jump involuntarily, which did not improve his mood.

Didn't we agree you would warn me before you begin speaking like that?

"We did ... but that was only for external communications. I didn't know you wanted me to do the same before *I* begin speaking. I suppose I could trigger a different alert tone. How about this?" his AI replied, playing a new, annoyingly pleasant chime within the confines of his fatigued mind.

No, never mind, he sighed inwardly. *My apologies, Emma, I'm just very much in need of some rest.*

"That's alright, Dryden. I'm well aware of how exhausted you are. And it turns out you're not the only one. Most of Captain Cash's men are showing signs of fatigue. Everyone would probably be much better off to hole up here until tomorrow morning." As if on cue, another chime sounded, seeming to echo endlessly back and forth within the confines of his skull.

Emma! I said you didn't have to —

"That wasn't me," she interrupted. "You have an incoming transmission from Rick aboard the *Ethereal*."

Oh. Sorry. Put him through, please.

"Dryden," Rick's voice began without further preamble, "you've got Shepherd troops inbound. And considering everything we've seen over the past several hours, I suspect they already know where to start looking for you. If that's the case, they may be at your location in as little as five minutes."

So, they're not on horseback, then, Dryden said, phrasing his question as a statement.

"No, not this time."

They're using one of the assault shuttles? he asked.

"Your memory is starting to return, I see."

Bits and pieces here and there. I can't say that I know much about it other than the fact that it's a flying transport of sorts. It allows them to deliver their Shepherd troops to the battlefield very quickly and then return to the compound to pick up more, if necessary. It's fast — fast enough to make several round trips before a battle even starts.

"Your memory serves you well, my young friend. With any luck, transportation of troops is the only thing they will be using it for at the moment. Unfortunately, it has various capabilities that will allow it to quickly locate Captain Cash's troops, even if they weren't told where to search. It also has sophisticated weaponry on board. Let's just hope they are not quite desperate enough to resort to using those systems just yet."

So, I take it they are coming for me, then.

"Oh, without a doubt, recovering you is their primary objective. Although I'm sure they would consider killing an additional thirty or so Estorian cavalry to be a nice bonus."

Right. So, what am I supposed to do now? And what, if anything, should I tell Captain Cash? Dryden asked, a hint of panic entering his internal dialogue.

"Do you think they'll try using one of their short-range comm options?" Emma asked, chiming in for the first time.

One of their what? Dryden asked.

"Before I met you for the first time on the battlefield near Talteca," Rick replied, "I used some of the equipment on our ship to temporarily block the High Protector's ability to communicate with you and the AI that controls all of your various systems."

You mean Emma, do you not?

"Yes and no. The AI that originally managed all of your systems served many of the same functions as Emma does now, but was substantially less … *friendly*, so to speak. In any event, that AI was by no means under your control. So wresting control from the High Protector and providing it to you — with Emma's assistance, of course — was one of the primary modifications Miguel and I made while you were aboard our ship. Up until that point, the High Protector had the capability to take control of your network of implants at any time."

I see ... thanks for that.

"You're welcome. Although the jury is still out on whether we actually did you a favor by not allowing the Estorians to finish you off."

I suppose we'll see, won't we? But what did Emma mean by short-range comm?

"You have been equipped with a variety of sophisticated communications capabilities. For the past several days, we have been able to prevent any attempts to communicate directly with you via any of your long-range systems. Once the shuttle gets within line of sight — which it already has, by the way — they will most likely attempt to use short-range communication systems that are much more resistant to our interference."

I understand. But I assume you don't want me to answer when they call, correct?

"I think it's now safe to assume they know you have not been destroyed. So, it logically follows that they will treat you as if you are a fully compromised asset."

Implying that I must be either recovered or destroyed. Lovely. And how will I know they are attempting to communicate?

"Emma will manage all of those details for you. But when she says they are calling, I strongly recommend you *do* answer. The trick is figuring out exactly what to say."

To them and to Captain Cash. So, if you have any suggestions regarding how I'm supposed to convince him that voices in my head are warning me that a team of Shepherd troops are on the way, I'd very much like to hear them. Sergeant Higgs might transition from trying to hang me to burning me at the stake.

"I don't mean to point out the obvious," Emma said, "but regardless of what Dryden decides to tell Cash and his men, didn't you just say the Shepherd troops were likely to kill them all anyway? What are we supposed to do to prevent that?"

"Well, as far as I can see at the moment, you have two options. Either fight or figure out a way to talk the Shepherds out of fighting."

Brilliant. And how might we go about doing that?

"Honestly, I have no idea," Rick replied. "Again, their first priority will undoubtedly be your recovery. But I can't imagine any scenario where they will agree to return to the High Protector empty-handed."

I can, Dryden said. *It's just a matter of convincing them it's in their best interest to do so. How much time do we have?*

"There's no way to know for sure. They're still headed in your general direction, but they don't seem to be in too big of a hurry at the moment. Miguel's best guess is that they are waiting for complete darkness to make their final approach. If that's the case, you may have an additional half hour or so. They will most likely do a few reconnaissance passes at high altitude to avoid giving themselves away and then deploy several squads of troops in the surrounding area. I'm guessing their plan will be to close and attack from multiple directions at once in a classic vertical envelopment maneuver. They're pretty efficient, though, so you shouldn't count on any of that taking them very long to execute once they start. Why? What did you have in mind?"

No time to explain. "Captain Cash!" Dryden yelled, attracting the young cavalry commander's attention just as he swung himself up into his saddle.

"You shut your damned mouth, traitor," Sergeant Higgs roared from atop his horse just a few meters away. "We're moving out. And the captain doesn't have time to listen to any more of your nonsense. One more word outta you and you can walk to Talteca with a gag in your mouth."

"Captain Cash, I need to speak with you immediately!" Dryden yelled again, striving to convey as much urgency as possible. Behind him, he heard the sound of Sergeant Higgs' massive frame dismounting from his horse, his boots impacting the ground with an intimidating thud followed by the jingle of his spurs as he rapidly approached.

"I warned you, boy," Higgs growled, reaching up to grab his prisoner's belt with one massive hand and the restraints binding his arms behind him with the other. Before Dryden knew what was happening, he was dragged backward in the saddle, up and over the cantle — mercifully allowing his boots to clear the stirrups. As soon as his rear was out of the saddle, Higgs gave a final, vicious jerk, hurling Dryden's body backward over his horse's hindquarters for the long plunge to the hard ground below.

"Higgs!" Cash thundered from atop his massive chestnut stallion. "You touch my prisoner one more time without an order from me to do so, and you're the one we'll hang when we get back to the post. Now get back on your damned horse and stay away from him."

The platoon sergeant stood menacingly over Dryden's prostrate form for a long moment, apparently trying to decide how serious his troop commander was about protecting the murderous snake lying on the ground before him.

"Ken, I'm not gonna tell you again," Cash said, his voice taking on an icy tone as he tugged his holster's leather cover free from its brass post closure in preparation for drawing his Peacemaker revolver.

With a final look of black hatred on his scowling face, Higgs hocked a mouthful of phlegm into his mouth and spit directly onto Dryden's back before turning to stomp off in the direction of his horse.

"Thank you, Captain," Dryden said as he struggled back to his feet, every muscle in his body aching painfully in protest as he did so.

"No. Don't do that. Don't thank me," Cash replied, his voice still carrying the same emotionless tone. "Higgs isn't doing anything any man here wouldn't do if he thought he could get away with it … me included. We've got rules, is all. And it's my job to make sure we follow those rules whether I agree with them or not. Now, what did you want?"

"I don't have a lot of time to explain, Captain, but you need to let me go … right now. Otherwise, you and every single one of your men will be dead in less than half an hour."

Chapter 17

Pelaran Assault Shuttle Alpha, High-Altitude
Reconnaissance Run
(25.2×10^3 m above the surface)

"Commander, all three squads report readiness to proceed," Maya's comm officer reported from his console located just behind where the pilot would have been sitting, had there been one. Instead, the small ship was following a pre-programmed mission profile, with its AI making changes on the fly as dictated by the situation or by the mission commander — in this case, Commander Maya Beck.

If there was such a thing as a "favorite" among the hapless Didarans selected, abducted, and placed into the High Protector's service against their will, Commander Beck was at or near the top of the list. Since being taken just over six months prior, she had displayed tremendous aptitude for integrating knowledge across a variety of subjects, particularly mathematics, engineering, and military science. As a result, she had originally been slated to become one of the High Protector's first four Flamecallers. During her training, however, she had also demonstrated a natural talent for leadership, possessing a mind particularly well-suited for performing in high-stress situations environment — leading soldiers into combat being just one example. All of these factors, coupled with excellent physical strength and endurance, made Maya an obvious choice for becoming the de facto operational commander of the High Protector's rapidly growing ranks of Shephard soldiers.

In the past, the WCS had always chosen male subjects for those in his employ, but the circumstances surrounding Maya's abduction had required an exception in her case. For on the day of her abduction, she had not been the primary target. Instead, she had simply been in the wrong place at the wrong time, necessitating her disappearance concurrent with that of the intended target — her older brother, Dryden.

"Thank you, Lieutenant," she replied. "Signal them to hold their positions as planned and await further orders."

"Yes, Commander."

"And the Estorian cavalry is fully accounted for — all in the immediate vicinity of the logging cabin?"

"Yes, ma'am. They appear to have broken camp and are preparing to depart. I'm not sure what they're waiting for, but there seems to be a delay of some sort."

"And you're certain Dryden is among them?"

"As far as I can tell, yes. As you know, we have received no communications or telemetry data from any of the Flamecallers since the battle at Talteca, but we have calibrated several of our ventral sensors to detect the signature of their primary power source. And there's an active one down there alright, Commander ... right here," the comm officer said, pointing to a light-amplified and thermally enhanced image of a man on horseback. Even at this altitude, it was clear the man had his arms bound behind his back. "Whoever that is, they're certainly *treating* him like a prisoner, ma'am."

"Good work, Lieutenant. Start trying the short-range comm systems and see if you can get him to respond. If his power source is still active, surely one of them is still working."

"Right away, Commander."

Didara 4, South Estorian Continent, Scarsdow Forest
(Logging Cabin - 3.9 km north of Vently Ford)

"Let you go?" Captain Cash echoed, raising the brim of his black Stetson "cav hat" with a single finger and staring at Dryden through narrowed eyes. "I may not be the sharpest hook on the trotline, but why, exactly, do you think I would go and do something as stupid as that?" he asked.

"Clearly, you're going to have to do better than that," Emma observed. Although annoyed by the intrusion, he knew that she was right. The young officer's face now wore an expression that might well have been the same had Dryden announced that horse was his preferred form of dietary protein.

"Look," he began again, "we both know you have no reason to believe me beyond what I've already told you. That's what I meant when I said I didn't have time to fully explain the reasons why. Besides, I'm not sure you would understand, even if I spent all night trying to explain."

"Well, I'm sorry, there, friend, but you're gonna have to make a much better case than that if you want me to take you seriously. We're all mounted up and ready to go, and I'd like to see us get clear of the forest by midnight. Those protoraptors tend to get pretty active about that time. Now, you said we were in some kind of danger. Explain yourself … *quickly*. Otherwise, I'm gonna need you to keep quiet so we can get moving."

"Alright, I'll do my best to summarize. You have my most solemn word that everything I am about to tell you is true. And if it sounds like it isn't, just ask yourself why I would bother telling you any of this if all I wanted was to go back to being a slave to the High Protector."

"I'm listening."

"I have received word that the High Protector has dispatched one of his assault shuttles full of Shepherd troops to this location. They will arrive here momentarily. Their job is to find and return me to their base at Plains Reach. Their secondary mission will be to kill you and every one of your men. You may have seen an assault shuttle before. It's the flying machine they have started using to drop off their troops … like they did at Talteca a few days ago."

Cash bristled reflexively at the mention of the recent battle, causing his expression to harden once again. "Yeah, you folks did manage to kill a bunch of us during that battle, didn't you? But we killed a bunch of yours too. That includes, I believe, all of the other ones like you … or at least all of them who were there. So, me and my boys here have a pretty good idea of what they can do. But if you think we're afraid, why, you don't know anything about us at all. If you're telling me they're coming here to try to take you away from us, we're more than ready for a fight. And who knows, it may not turn out quite the way they think it will," he said, patting the stock of his rifle in its scabbard as murmurs of agreement rippled through the rest of the platoon like a passing breeze.

"No, Captain, you don't understand," Dryden replied. "Over the past few years, the High Protector has made a big show out of trying to convince everyone he's in possession of magical powers of some sort. Initially, I believe he assumed we Didarans were backward enough to allow ourselves to be coerced into believing his lies by showing us an assortment of technologies we couldn't possibly understand. By now, I hope most people recognize all of that for the nonsense it is. Still … even though none of his capabilities are the result of any sort of magic, he *does* have technology at his disposal that is more powerful than you could ever imagine. Thus far, you've seen only a small sample of this — the armored suits his Shepherd troops wear, for example."

"Right. And I think we've proven we can deal with *those* well enough," Cash said.

"No, sir, you can't," Dryden replied flatly. "Not this time. The ones on their way here today — some of which are probably already on the ground by now — will undoubtedly have even better armor than what you encountered at Talteca. And this time, I suspect they'll be carrying weapons the likes of which you have never encountered before."

"Again, I'm not sure what you expect me to do with that information, Dryden. Regardless of what they're carrying, our rifles worked just fine against them just a few days ago, so I have no reason to believe things will be any different if we run into them again today. We are not in the habit of backing down from a fight. We've got good weapons of our own, and I have no interest in turning loose of a high-value prisoner like yourself based on what *might* happen. Besides, how is it you know all of this anyway? Next, you'll be telling me you

Flamecallers have some kind of sixth sense allowing you to see things the rest of us can't."

"In a manner of speaking, I do. But I'm afraid you'll just have to take my word on that part."

"Right. Now let me tell you what *I* think … *I* think you just concocted this whole story of yours out of thin air. And to be honest, it doesn't matter a whit to me whether you got it from your sixth sense, the sound of the wind in the trees, or wood sprites. Sheesh … how well do you think it would go over for me when I get back to HQ if I had to tell Colonel Simms that I just up and let you go because you asked nicely?"

"You won't have to, Captain. If you let me go, you have my word that I will remain in your custody after the danger has passed and continue the trip back to Talteca with you. But if you don't act quickly, you won't have to worry about what your colonel will say anyway, because none of you will ever make it out of this forest alive."

"Pfft," Cash said dismissively. "Unless you've got something else, I think we've wasted enough time on this."

"Do you know where those weapons you're carrying came from, Captain?" Dryden asked. "I'm guessing you don't. At least not specifically. And, honestly, I have only a vague notion of where they came from myself. But I think we both understand they weren't originally built here on our world, do we not? What's even more interesting is that, so far, the High Protector doesn't seem to know much more about where they came from than you or I do. And while that's the case, I believe we may have a short window of opportunity in which we can force him to leave our world once and for all. You

241

see, right now, his number one goal — and the only thing standing between him and complete domination over Didara — is stopping your General Staff from receiving any more weapons. And, to do that, he first has to determine specifically who has been supplying them."

"I don't know where you heard that story," Cash said with a raised eyebrow, "but once we stop riding tomorrow morning before sunup, you and I are gonna have us a little chat on the subject. But I have to tell you that I don't really see how all of that has any bearing on what you're asking me to do. The bottom line is that I can't let you go, Dryden. Besides, even if I did, based on what you just said, it doesn't sound like you'd be able to stop these Shepherd troops from killing us anyway … Flamecaller or no."

"I'm not sure I could either if it comes down to a fight, and that's my point. I suggest you let me go, then you and your men head off in the opposite direction. I'll go out and find whoever's commanding the detachment of Shepherd troops and —"

"And how would you manage to —" Cash interrupted, growing more irritated by the moment.

"Never mind how. I just will," Dryden countered, undeterred. "I'll convince them I managed to slip away on my own but then realized it was a mistake to do so. After I had some time to think about something I heard while you were holding me captive, that is."

"And what exactly did you hear that you think would be so interesting to the Shepherd troops?"

"That I might be offered up by your General Staff in some kind of exchange with whoever has been providing them with weapons and supplies."

Captain Cash regarded the Flamecaller silently for a long moment, almost as if he were actually beginning to consider that there might be at least a kernel of sanity to what he was proposing.

"I'll tell the commander of the extraction team that the High Protector would not want to miss this opportunity to overcome the one obstacle preventing him from accomplishing his primary mission here on our world."

Cash continued to stare at his prisoner for a long moment, then nodded to a trio of his men who had been standing by to help Dryden back onto his horse.

"All I know for sure is that we haven't seen hide nor hair of anyone else since we got here yesterday. So, I 'spect the best thing for us to do right now is be on our way and get ourselves clear of this forest as soon as we can," Cash said, turning his horse around and heading off in the opposite direction.

"Wait, Captain —"

"That'll be all for now, Mr. Beck," Cash replied without bothering to turn back in Dryden's direction.

"Listen to me," Dryden shouted after him. "The High Protector doesn't control me anymore, but his troops won't know that at first. When the Shepherds come, I'll do everything I can to save you and your men, but you'll have to unchain me! Do you hear me? I can't help you if my hands are tied behind my back!"

"Shut up and get on the damn horse," one of the men growled as they hoisted him back up into the saddle once again.

Chapter 18

Didara 4, South Estorian Continent, Scarsdow Forest
(River Road - 3.3 km north of the logging cabin)

For the first leg of their journey back to Talteca, Captain Cash had chosen to head north to the location where the old logging trail crossed the NorthHaven River Road. While this more frequently traveled route was arguably a riskier choice under the circumstances, it was also the option that would allow 1st Platoon to get the best possible speed out of their horses. And just now, getting his men out on the edge of the Ganahar Plains where they could make even better time was foremost in the young captain's mind.

And then there was the problem of Sergeant Higgs, who Cash was certain would kill their potentially valuable prisoner if given the slightest opportunity to do so. Therefore, in an effort to give the man something to think about — aside from the prospect of willful murder, as satisfying as such thoughts might occasionally seem — the captain had put him to work. Now, with 1st Platoon finally on the move once more, Higgs rode at the head of its two-column formation. His orders seemed simple enough on the surface: navigate the unit safely out of Scarsdow Forest as quickly as possible. But given that the situation demanded they travel in darkness while under constant threat of attack by a superior force, both men were well aware how quickly simple tasks could degenerate into deadly ones.

Fortunately, it was another splendidly bright night in the forest, with the moon now just shy of full. As a result, Higgs was aggressively following his captain's exhortations to make the best possible speed. And considering the fact that the first few kilometers had been along a narrow, heavily rutted logging trail snaking its way through a dense forest, he had managed to start their long journey at an impressive pace.

Back near the middle of the column, Dryden was pleased to see the logging trail give way to the wider and much smoother surface of the river road. It had been a rough ride to this point, and his shoulders ached from their cruel restraints. Nevertheless, the events of the past few days had reminded him how much he preferred travel on horseback to walking. Now, riding steadily down the moonlit road on such an unseasonably warm spring night, he realized that this journey might have been a pleasant one under different circumstances. And a distant fragment of a memory produced a twinge of regret that he had not taken more time for activities like this as a younger man.

Kelly would have loved this ...

The thought flashed into existence and was gone, vanishing before his mind had the opportunity to register its potentially profound meaning. Gratefully, Emma said nothing about the ephemeral memory, perhaps implying a level of discretion he had not known she possessed.

After riding for the better part of half an hour, Dryden had allowed himself at least a faint hope that the expected attack from the Shepherd troops might not materialize. Perhaps they had decided to simply monitor the Estorians' progress for now. But it was not to be.

The first indication that Dryden's fears were about to be realized came from an unexpected source — the secondary AI tasked with granting access to his network of implants. BING! The warning tone echoed inside his mind, seeming even more out of place than usual on the dark forest road.

The following capability may now be accessed via your neural interface: Energy Shield. Creates a field of intense energy in a roughly spherical shape with a radius of five meters measured from the center of your chest. The field attempts to destroy, dissipate, or deflect incoming beam or kinetic energy weapons fire. WARNING: While the radius of the sphere may be extended to ten meters for up to one hour, it is imperative that living organisms not come into direct contact with the energy field. Death due to extreme electrical and/or radiation-induced effects will likely result. Contact with the energy field is also likely to induce catastrophic damage to unshielded electronic systems. Note that the Energy Shield is generally more effective at mitigating beam weapon attacks than those from kinetic energy weapons and is, therefore, best used in conjunction with gravitic shielding.

Hmm, Dryden observed after a momentary pause, *I have to say it feels a little ominous that the system chose this particular moment to add this particular capability. Also, what did it mean by "in conjunction with —"*

BING! The warning tone sounded again, preempting Emma's response.

The following capability may now be accessed via your neural interface: Gravitic Shield. Creates an intense gravitational distortion in the path of incoming weapons fire that effectively "lenses" or deflects both beam and kinetic energy projectiles away from your body. The distortions can occur anywhere between one and ten meters from the center of your chest. WARNING: Much like the Energy Shield system, intense gravitational disturbances are extremely hazardous to living organisms and will cause serious damage to equipment, particularly electronics. Although the AI will make every effort to avoid creating a dangerous situation, care should be taken when activating either type of shielding in close proximity to friendly personnel, animals, or valuable equipment.

Dryden cast his gaze quickly around the area but still neither saw nor heard any indications they might be under attack.

"Should I go ahead and activate the shields?" Emma asked, assuming the secondary AI had enabled the new capabilities due to a high probability of an imminent attack. "I can shield both you and your horse without harming anyone else around you."

No, not yet. In general, though, I do want you to manage both of the shielding systems for me. If you detect a threat, you don't need my permission to raise them. Just please try not to kill anyone if you can help it.

"I won't," she replied. "Not unless they're trying to kill us first."

Right. Now, is there a chance any of my new capabilities might somehow be used to free my hands? The disturbances created by the gravitic shields, perhaps? Maybe even the plasma bolt weapon?

"Not really, no. I ran several thousand simulations using plasma bolts before you regained consciousness back in the cabin. In most of them, you were killed in the attempt."

Alright. And the others?

"You mean the ones where you lived? Let's see … in a few instances, we actually did manage to remove the restraints."

Yes, and that's good, right?

"Uh huh, sure. But you always ended up with catastrophic burns over most of your body … and, uh … no arms."

I see. Well, I hope it goes without saying that holding on to my arms is a high priority of mine. How about the gravitics?

"Working on that now, but it doesn't look particularly promising either. It just requires placing too much energy in close contact with your skin to be safe. There might actually be something I can do by creating a localized hyperspace field, but I'll need —"

Thank you, Emma. I don't need the details, just please keep trying.

At that moment, another alert chime sounded inside Dryden's mind, followed as usual by Rick's voice.

"The assault shuttle is on the move again. It's been maintaining a relatively stable flight pattern since we first detected it, but it just began a rapid descent and is closing on your position. We've also got some indications of movement on the ground. From what we can tell, you've got three small squads of Shepherd troops converging on your cavalry column."

How far out are they?

"A couple of minutes at the most."

A little more warning would have been nice, Dryden thought, still not used to the idea that comments previously heard only within the privacy of his own mind were now openly conveyed as part of his conversations with Rick and Emma.

"Sorry, but that's the best we could do, Flamecaller. The Shepherds were most likely deployed while the shuttle was still at a fairly high altitude. Their suits make them notoriously difficult to detect from orbit. They don't have a true flight capability like your High Protector, but they do have electrically powered thrusters capable of several seconds of high impulse — plenty of power to arrest their descent immediately before impact."

"Dryden," Emma said with an uncharacteristic level of urgency in her voice, "we just received a high-frequency transmission in the blind, text-only. It reads:

FOXTROT ZERO FOUR, FOXTROT ZERO FOUR, SHEPHERD EXTRACTION TEAM INBOUND YOUR POSITION. IF ABLE, TAKE COVER IMMEDIATELY AND ENABLE EMERGENCY LOCATOR TRANSMITTER FOR IMMEDIATE AIR EVACUATION."

That's it? Dryden asked. *They didn't even ask for a response?*

"Other than asking that you activate your transponder to help them make a positive identification, no."

"That's a pretty good indication they're assuming you're fully compromised," Rick observed. "So, if they get their hands on you, you should expect them to … shall we say *deactivate* you pending a full assessment back at Plains Reach."

I'd say that's a fair assumption, yes. So, let's see what we can do to avoid that.

"Well, first off, I suggest you ignore the request to activate your emergency locator transmitter, since that seems like a bit of a trap to me. And you should also try letting your gracious hosts know they're about to have company."

"Captain Cash!" Dryden yelled, wasting no time acting on Rick's suggestion. "They're coming ... right now! I need you to get these chains off me so I can help you!"

And come they did. Just over half an hour after 1st Platoon had departed the logging cabin, Commander Beck gave the order for her extraction team to execute the next phase of her plan.

Cash turned instinctively in his saddle to look back in the direction of Dryden's voice, just in time to see a blur of motion dart from the undergrowth on one side of the road at the rear of the formation. In an instant, he saw the first horse and rider simply disappear — swept completely off the road into the dark forest on the opposite side.

"Take cover! We're under attack!" he roared, knowing that his unit's speed and maneuverability were of little use in such confined quarters, particularly at night.

As the platoon's bugler frantically sounded an abbreviated version of "To Arms," chaos broke out along the entire length of the column. At the rear of the formation, a second horse and rider were swept from the road ... then another. The unexpected motion and the accompanying sounds caused several of the horses in the immediate vicinity to rear up onto their hind legs in abject terror, throwing their riders to the ground.

Not knowing precisely what they were up against, men up and down the column hurriedly drew their rifles from their scabbards, jumped down from their horses, and did their best to find cover as ordered. Shortly thereafter, the cracks of sporadic gunfire began to echo through the forest, although it was unclear if any of the troopers were aiming at anything specific or just firing at random in hopes of deterring their unseen enemies. Nevertheless, the tactic seemed at least somewhat effective, temporarily halting the rushing attacks from the north side of the road.

Since the initial attacks seemed to originate from the column's left, the men were naturally focusing their attention in that direction. Upon dismounting, most had crouched low next to their horses for a moment, then quickly moved to take cover — either just inside the edge of the forest or lying prone against the low embankment to the right of the road. Unfortunately for them, this response was exactly as Commander Beck had planned, and the reason her troops had begun the engagement with such dramatic, physical attacks rather than simply opening up on the cavalry formation from both sides. For although her primary objective was recovery of the Flamecaller, her secondary mission was not exactly as Dryden had predicted.

Rather than simply slaughtering the accompanying cavalrymen, Maya's orders were to capture approximately ten of the unit's most fit specimens and return them to Plains Reach. There, they would undergo a process of rapid mental and physical reconditioning in preparation to join the growing ranks of the High Protector's Shepherd troops. Given their military backgrounds, these men would be expected to attain mission-capable status in just two weeks. During that time, of course, any of the candidates displaying signs of resistance to the training methods employed would simply be eliminated.

Even with her intention of taking ten of 1st Platoon's troopers as prisoners, simple math still dictated that more than two-thirds of the Estorians present must die. Accordingly, eight of Commander Beck's twelve Shepherd troops were now awaiting her orders to the south of the river road — on the same side as their targets — all with excellent cover and particle beam rifles at the ready. It was a disposition of forces that not only provided her with a tactical advantage but also the additional time required for her ship's AI to analyze the platoon's remaining thirty-one men in great detail. With that done, it would be a relatively straightforward task to render those chosen for the trip back to Plains Reach unconscious — including the errant Flamecaller, of course — then simply killing the rest.

As soon as Dryden realized the attack was underway, he had the presence of mind to take both of his feet out of the stirrups and, after a couple of lurches to one side, launch himself out of the saddle for his second long drop to the ground in less than an hour. Scrambling to his feet, he bent over at the waist — hands still firmly bound behind his back — and tried to figure out which way he should run. Looking frantically up and down the road in both directions, he could see very little other than a few horses darting nervously about, obviously in roughly the same mental state as he was at the moment.

As sporadic rifle fire began erupting from the south side of the road to his left and right, Dryden felt a sense of panic rising once more, a leviathan from the depths, nipping at the edges of his already exhausted mind before consuming it whole. Despite this, he worked to focus his efforts on a single goal — finding some means of freeing himself from his bonds. Failing that essential task, he knew, would result in his having little chance of avoiding capture himself, let alone helping to save any of his would-be captors. Clearly, the first step was to find Captain Cash. But at the moment, he had only a vague notion of where E Troop's commander had dismounted and taken cover.

It took the Flamecaller only a few moments to realize that the greatest immediate danger to his own safety was posed by the Estorian cavalrymen. As best he could tell, most of them were firing blindly off into the forest in all directions, making it difficult to decide how best to take cover himself. While all of this was taking place, a distant part of his mind noted the occasional presence of strange, almost ghostly flashes of light that seemed to hover in the air around his body. Some of the lights flared brightly before disappearing entirely, while others looked more like the streaks of light one might see in the sky on a dark summer night. Although Dryden was far too distracted to observe the strange phenomenon in any detail, he noticed that it was illuminating the surrounding area to a degree, like flashes of lightning in miniature.

Along the side of the road to his right, he could see a number of troopers lying on their stomachs and peering across into the darkness on the opposite side. And just beyond them, near the edge of the forest, stood the largest Sycamore tree Dryden had ever seen.

"That'll have to do for now," he heard Emma say over the general din.

Maintaining his crouch as best he could, Dryden took off in a run, jumping over the nearest cavalryman as he quickly covered the distance to the massive tree. Squatting on his haunches, he placed his back against the trunk and looked out into the inky blackness of the forest, wondering which side of the tree provided the best cover from all the random weapons fire taking place around him.

Pausing to catch his breath for a few moments before resuming his search for Captain Cash, Dryden realized that Emma was speaking to him again. In fact, he was pretty sure she had done so several times since he had alerted his captors that they were about to come under attack. But until now, the combination of adrenaline coursing through his veins and the overwhelming sounds of battle had eclipsed most of her attempts to capture his attention. Focusing now on her voice for the first time, two words instantly cut through the cascade of sounds around him like the blade of a scythe: "night vision."

Gods above! he thought bitterly, aghast at his own stupidity. *Yes, of course, Emma, I have no idea why I didn't think of that before now! I can't see much of anything apart from what's on the road itself.* In an instant, the black landscape of the forest was illuminated to a level many times that of the river road itself, already awash in the light of the nearly full moon. All along the side of the road, he could see men lying prone with their rifles at their shoulders. Most of them continued to fire at random intervals into the forest on the opposite side of the road, while others apparently believed the primary threat was in the other direction. But in spite of all the wasted ammunition, Dryden could now plainly see that the cavalrymen might as well have been firing their rifles directly up into the air since, thus far, even he could detect no sign of their attackers.

I know they're out there somewhere, Emma, he thought, suddenly feeling the need to hear the sound of a friendly voice.

"Most definitely. Would you like to add the infrared enhancement?"

Oh, yes, of course, let's try that as well, he said, disappointed, once again, that he had failed to recall that he had two types of light amplification at his disposal.

Based on the information Rick had provided, Dryden guessed there were probably two small squads of Shepherd soldiers in the forest immediately in front of him. The remainder of his enemies had most likely deployed on the opposite side of the road. The word "enemies" in his last thought seemed to hover before his mind's eye — a beacon marking the restoration of his own free will. For it was now abundantly clear that the High Protector was his enemy, as were all those who served him, regardless of whether they did so by choice. He would help them if he could, destroy them if he must. It really was that simple, was it not? Perhaps the more difficult question, he realized, was precisely who his allies were at the moment.

Fantastic, he mused. *I'm at least clear on whom I'd like to shoot at if I could, but where are they?*

Visible light amplification, while clearly resolving the forest around him as if it were midday, had still failed to provide any signs of the attacking soldiers. Now that Emma had added the infrared overlay to his vision, however, the scene before him began to change. He had assumed the Shepherds would likely be hidden behind cover some distance out into the forest. And, sure enough, after a few seconds, each enemy soldier began to appear in turn as if they had lit a flare for the express purpose of revealing their positions.

The armored suits the Shepherds wore, Dryden remembered, were designed to minimize their occupant's infrared signature. Fortunately, they could not eliminate it completely, particularly around their heads. And now, after his own systems had been given a few moments to analyze the mountains of data streaming in from his ocular implants, he could clearly see the outlines of their bodies, highlighted in various shades of orange and red. From what he could tell, there were eight of them on this side of the road — each of their positions now also indicated by red triangles on the top-down display in the upper right corner of his vision.

I'm sorry, Emma. I'm ashamed to admit what a dullard I've been thus far. Somehow, we've got to work out a better way of handling urgent communications when we get into a difficult situation like this.

"Not a problem," Emma replied, her voice now seeming to boom within his head at an impossibly loud volume easily exceeding that of the rifle fire taking place just a few meters away. "I didn't want to alarm you any more than you already were, but in the future, if I really need your attention, I can always do this …"

Suddenly, other than the ever-present sound of tinnitus ringing in his ears, there was utter silence. For all intents and purposes, Dryden had gone completely deaf.

"See," Emma said, her voice now seeming to slice through to the very center of his brain. "If need be, I can temporarily block the electrical signals traversing your auditory nerves. By the way, I also took the liberty of activating the gravitic shields. And don't worry, I haven't managed to kill anyone with them yet."

Gods, Emma! Yes, thank you for not doing that without any sort of warning. But from now on, if it's an emergency, feel free to use it to get my attention. And thanks for handling the shields. Now, I'm not sure what those Shepherd troops are waiting for, but there's little doubt they will open fire shortly.

"They may be hoping to somehow get their hands on you first."

Possibly. But in any event, if I don't get these restraints off, I feel certain all of these cavalrymen will be killed in short order. Can you please help me find Captain Cash? Oh, and turn the sound back on, please.

As the sounds of sporadic gunfire resumed, Dryden now found it somewhat easier than before to focus on the calming sound of his AI's voice. "Yes, of course," she said. "Captain Cash is located forty meters to the east."

A green, pulsating arrow pointing to his right appeared near the top of his field of view. And Dryden immediately noted that, as he turned his head in the direction indicated, the arrow pulsed more rapidly. Once he was looking in the right direction, the arrow rotated downward to point directly at Captain Cash, who now also had a green box superimposed around his body for additional emphasis. Like most of his men, the young captain was crouched low beside the road, holding his rifle with one hand as he motioned his instructions to the men around him with the other.

Without further hesitation, Dryden sprinted off in the captain's direction. Strangely, he felt as if he were already growing somewhat accustomed to running around bent over at the waist with his hands behind his back, even managing to dodge the odd tree root, stone, or sprawling trooper with surprising agility. But when he had covered approximately half the intervening distance, a cavalryman who had been lying next to the road with his rifle resting on an old log swept one of his legs beneath Dryden as he passed. The unexpected move knocked the Flamecaller's feet out from under him, causing him to crash painfully to the ground, shoulder first.

Momentarily stunned with the breath knocked out of him, it took Dryden several seconds to get back onto his knees as he prepared to stand once more. Just as he did so, he heard the distinctive metallic click of a single-action revolver being cocked immediately behind him. Before he could react, a massive hand clamped down on his shoulder with an iron grip, preventing any further attempts to stand. Dryden then felt an icy chill run down his spine as the cold steel of the pistol's barrel was pressed firmly against the back of his neck.

"I'm pretty sure we're all gonna die here tonight, you traitorous bastard," the raspy voice of Sergeant Higgs sounded just centimeters from his ear. The huge man's breath stunk of rotgut and decay, a clear indication the sergeant had been indulging himself in some liquid courage well before 1st Platoon had left on its long journey this evening.

"I'm pretty sure we're all gonna die here tonight," he repeated, whether for emphasis or a lack of mental focus, Dryden couldn't tell. "And we all know exactly whose fault that is, don't we? You told 'em exactly where we would be, didn't you, you back-stabbing filth? And now, here they are to rescue you, so you can go on killing more of our good men. Well, let me tell you something, Flamecaller, I can't do anything about your friends killing all of us here tonight, but I can damn well make sure there's nothing left of you worth rescuing."

With that, Dryden both felt and heard Sergeant Higgs stand more or less upright, just as his own head was forced closer to the ground by the steadily increasing pressure of the pistol against the back of his neck. Although he knew that he should offer a prayer of some sort in these last few seconds he had remaining, no words would come to his mind — only a desperate desire to live.

BOOM! A single, ear-splitting gunshot from a pistol fired just a few meters away assaulted Dryden's already tortured hearing. For what seemed like a minute or more, he wondered if he were already dead — his conscious mind lingering a bit longer until it had time to catch up on current events. While he was still trying to decide, the lifeless body of Sergeant Higgs lurched forward and landed face-first on the ground beside him, an enormous hole in the left side of his head.

"*Dammit,* Kenneth," Dryden heard Captain Cash say from just behind him. "I *warned* you, didn't I? *Dammit!*"

he repeated, clearly shaken by what he had just been forced to do. "What a *stupid* way to get yourself killed."

Didara 4, South Estorian Continent, Scarsdow Forest
(River Road - 3.3 km north of the logging cabin)

With good cover and time clearly on their side, Commander Beck's extraction team was now in a position from which they could eradicate the Estorian cavalry platoon at their discretion. On the north side of the river road, one squad of four Shepherd troops was ordered to simply hold its position and observe in case any of the dismounted cavalrymen chose to flee the area in their direction. South of the road, the remaining eight members of the extraction team had been assigned two targets each among the thirty-one cavalrymen now attempting to take shelter at the edge of the forest. Each was clearly visible in the ghostly, monochromatic green hue provided by their armor's night vision system.

Inside their helmets, each of the Shepherd soldiers was also presented with a detailed tactical overview of their surroundings, with a variety of data projected seamlessly within their field of view. Meanwhile, ten thousand meters above them aboard the assault shuttle, Commander Beck had access to an even more comprehensive view of the battlespace. And now, noting that one of the Estorians — presumably their commanding officer — had just been forced to kill one of his own rather than lose his high-value prisoner, she judged the optimal time to continue her attack had arrived. With nothing more than a quick mental command of execution, she ordered the eight Shepherd soldiers to the south of the river road to proceed.

Amidst the sporadic cracks of the Estorians' recently updated lever-action rifles, a terrifying new series of sights and sounds ripped through the Scarsdow Forest for the first time. Combat veterans to a man, nothing any of the 1st Platoon's troopers had ever experienced had prepared them for the fury now unleashed upon them. Eight reddish-orange streams of fire ripped through the dark of the forest, each one blasting aside the air along its path with a great, tearing roar as if the surrounding forest had somehow come alive and decided to consume every living thing within.

Although each beam issuing from the Shepherd troops' particle beam rifles actually did reveal their positions for a brief instant, it was of little consequence. Each soldier immediately shifted his position slightly before engaging his second designated target — their preplanned movements completed before their first set of targets even had time to fall to the ground.

Once again, the brilliant flashes of orange light, once again the horrible tearing sounds — and in the space of less than ten seconds, sixteen more members of 1st Platoon, E Troop, 3rd Squadron of the 3rd Cavalry Regiment, lay dead beside the road. After the volley, a few of the remaining Estorian troopers did manage to shift their fire to the south in the general direction of their still unseen enemies. But with more than half of their number now killed in action, it was a symbolic gesture at best. The battle, from a military perspective, had already been lost.

Chapter 19

Didara 4, South Estorian Continent, Scarsdow Forest
(River Road - 3.3 km north of the logging cabin)

"Thank you, Captain," Dryden said, scrambling back to his feet and quickly moving to place another large tree between himself and the direction of the incoming fire. "I owe you my —"

"Stop!" Cash hissed, crouching in the lee of the same tree just a few meters away. "You saw what just happened, same as I did. And I think we both know what's gonna happen next, don't we?"

Dryden stared at the cavalry captain for a long moment. Even in the green-tinted hues of his light amplification system, the haunted, distant expression was impossible to miss. Although he had no idea where or when, Dryden knew that he had seen the same look before — that of a man who was already beaten and now eagerly awaited his own death.

"Captain?" Dryden prompted in an even tone.

There was no response. Cash simply stared off into the woods in the direction from which the orange streaks of light had come.

"Captain Cash!" Dryden yelled, fully aware that snapping the young officer out of his state of stunned oblivion was the only chance any of them had of surviving the night.

"Alright, Flamecaller … if everything you've told me is true," Cash said, speaking now in a strangely conversational tone as if nothing had happened, "then you may well be every bit as much a victim as the rest of us. But the truth of the matter is, I have no way of confirming anything you've said. You've already admitted to killing hundreds of our people before tonight. And as far as I'm concerned, Kenneth Higgs and everyone else who has died here tonight are your latest victims," he said, nodding to the sergeant's body on the ground in addition to two others lying several meters away. "I'm sure before it's all said and done, you'll be able to add me and the rest of 1st Platoon to your list."

"Captain *Cash*, I …" Dryden began, then checked himself, aghast at the suggestion he had anything to do with the sergeant's death or the Shepherds' attack.

"Oh, I know you didn't pull the trigger and shoot Higgs in the head yourself. That was all me, and I'd do it again. But here's the thing, the reason he was about to shoot you was because he believed your being here was about to get us all killed. And you were right about that, weren't you, Ken?" Cash asked the dead NCO's body, then shifted his gaze back to the Flamecaller and raised his pistol once again. "So, I have to ask you, Dryden … *did* you tip them off? How'd they know where to look for you?"

"*No,* of course not!" Dryden shot back, now angered by the cavalry commander's accusations and threat. "Everything I've told you is true. I don't know exactly how they found us, I just knew they would. I warned you how sophisticated their shuttle is, and the area they needed to search wasn't particularly large. With that kind of equipment at their disposal, it probably wasn't even much of a challenge. In fact, it wouldn't surprise me if they've been monitoring your progress since you left Talteca several days ago."

"Eh, it probably doesn't matter now anyway," Cash groused, holstering his pistol and shifting his body to the right in order to see around the huge tree. "Wonder why they haven't gotten around to finishing us off?" he asked absently, before continuing their conversation. "Anyway, for what it's worth, I believe you."

"You do?" Dryden asked, surprised in spite of himself.

"Well, what I mean to say is that I don't believe you tipped them off. Or at least I hope you didn't. It doesn't matter, though," he repeated. "I figure the result is likely to be the same either way. Half my men are probably dead already, and those Shepherd bastards out there in the woods … they can obviously see us, but we can't see them. And there's not a damn thing I can do to keep them from picking the rest of us off at will. It's just a matter of time."

"No, that's not true, Captain. There *is* something you can do. You can let me go and give me a chance to help."

"Help how? You plan on walking out there into that clearing yonder and attacking them by yourself?"

"Well, no, that probably wouldn't make a whole lot of sense at this point unless they leave me no other choice. But you should know, I can see them."

"See who?"

"The Shepherd soldiers. I can see them … out there in the forest. Probably better than they can see us."

"Humph … for all the good that'll do you," Cash said, wishing he could pair that particular ability with three or four of E Troop's best sharpshooters at the moment. "I don't know, Dryden. If you can see 'em, that might help a bit if your plan was to take 'em on alone. But just yesterday, I saw you almost get yourself killed by a couple of protoraptors. Now I know you have some weapons at your disposal, but I have my doubts whether you're capable of successfully assaulting Gods know how many Shepherd soldiers —"

"Twelve," Dryden interjected. "Eight on this side of the road and four on the other. The four to the north appear to be in reserve at the moment."

"Again, that's a good thing to know, sure. But they're firing — whatever the hell those guns are they're shooting at us — from a position of good cover. I don't like your odds, and you shouldn't either. Just being honest, like you keep saying."

"I understand. And you're right to be skeptical. As for my ability to take them on in a fight, the truth is I don't know how well I would fare alone. But I still think the plan I shared with you earlier might actually work. I just have to get into contact with whoever's in charge of these Shepherd soldiers. If I can convince them the High Protector wants to get his hands on your weapons supplier more than he wants to get me back, I might still be able to save you and the rest of your men."

"That's all well and good, Dryden, but did it occur to you that our brass might not be too keen on the idea of giving the High Protector an opportunity to go after this alleged … supplier. According to you, he's the only reason we haven't already lost this war. I don't think that sounds like much of a plan, do you?"

"It's the best one I've got right now, so we'll have to cross that bridge when we come to it. I do have a couple of ideas on that front, but now is not the time. Our immediate objective is to get the remainder of us out of here alive. We'll worry about the details later."

Cash stared hard at him once again, his face a study in the heavy burden of command — full of anguish not so much for the impending loss of his own life as the lives for which he was personally responsible. After a long moment, the pained expression on his face changed slightly, mixing with a degree of resignation or even acceptance of the situation in which he now found himself.

"Alright, Flamecaller," he said in a quiet tone.

"Alright, what?"

"This may turn out to be one of the worst decisions I've ever made in my life, but I'm going to give you your chance. But mark my words," he growled, "if you've been lying to me about any of this, you'd better make sure I never leave this forest alive. Otherwise, I'm gonna make it my mission in life to finish the job Sergeant Higgs was trying to do earlier. Do we understand each other?"

"Yes, of course, Captain. You have my most solemn word. But keep in mind that the situation here today may dictate that I continue to play the role the High Protector's forces expect me to play. I also want you to try to remember that those Shepherd soldiers out there are all Didarans just like us. They are not in control of their actions, and it's not their fault they've been placed in this situation. I have made a vow to help them if I can figure out a way to do so. But my promise to you is that I will do everything I can to protect you and the rest of your men."

"Humph," Cash grumbled. And with that, he thrust his hand into his pocket and took a single step forward in Dryden's direction. But before he could take a second, the air around his body seemed to come live with a strange, undulating halo of blue light. A fraction of a second later, what Dryden could only describe as a fist-sized ball of lightning flashed across the forest from the direction of one of the Shepherd soldiers, striking squarely in the center of the cavalryman's chest. The impact momentarily enveloped the whole of his upper body in a swirling maelstrom of electrical energy. In response, his nervous system was temporarily disrupted, causing him to immediately lose consciousness and fall stiffly to the ground in front of the startled Flamecaller.

"What in the Gods' names was that, Emma?" Dryden yelled aloud. "Is he dead?" he gasped, his own mind treading dangerously close to a state of shock from what he had just witnessed at very close range.

"I'll need a few seconds to say with one hundred percent accuracy, but, no, I don't think so," she replied. "There is a Terran weapon in Rick and Miguel's database that has a similar effect. They call it a 'plasma channel' discharge. The good news is that it's a nonlethal mode on the weapons equipping their current ground forces. It creates an ionized electrical pathway between the weapon and its target and then fires what is essentially a small ball of lightning down the channel."

And how is that in any way considered 'nonlethal?' Dryden thought, remembering that it was best not to communicate aloud with his internal AI.

"Surprisingly, it does very little physical damage … well … other than the rather dramatic trip to the ground, that is. It overloads the central nervous system and renders the target unconscious for a period of time — up to half an hour, depending on the strength of the discharge."

So, you don't think he's dead, then?

"Not quite, no. I am able to detect a pulse and what I'd call reasonably normal respiration under the circumstances. My guess is that he took pretty close to the maximum permissible amount of energy, so he'll probably be out of commission for a while."

Out of the corner his eye, Dryden began to notice additional flashes of blue light from multiple locations along the side of the road as the Shepherd soldiers found additional members of 1st Platoon to target with their plasma weapons.

"They must have decided to begin stunning their targets rather than killing them for fear of hitting you," Emma said, "especially since the captain was so close to you when he took his hit."

No, Dryden said confidently, *I don't think that's it at all. They're planning to abduct these men, Emma. Everyone who's still alive they're planning to take captive.*

Despite the chaos still taking place all around him, Dryden lapsed into silence, staring in the direction of the Shepherd soldiers as if he couldn't quite make up his mind what he should do next.

"Okayyy," Emma replied, drawing out the word in an effort to prod her charge into refocusing on the rather urgent situation at hand. "I don't think you want to be standing here when they come walking out of the forest to secure these men, do you? So, what's the plan now?"

Definitely not, Dryden said, returning his attention to Captain Cash's unconscious form. *But I have no idea. In spite of the fact that he's still alive, there's precious little I can do to defend him and the rest of his men with my hands still tied behind my back. How about what you mentioned before? Have you made any progress on figuring out how to get these restraints off?*

"I'm afraid not. It turns out using the hyperspace emitters is a no go. Those particular fields have a naturally indistinct event horizon, and I don't have the capability to manipulate them with sufficient precision to avoid seriously injuring you. But, Dryden, under the circumstances, don't you think it's appropriate to simply grab Captain Cash's key?"

The key? What key are you — oh my Gods, what's wrong with me? he fumed, once again flabbergasted by his needing to be reminded of the obvious. Had he actually become one of those people who simply couldn't function under significant stress, he wondered? Although he couldn't remember ever having been one of "those people" before, there was no denying that there had been several instances today where he just wasn't measuring up mentally.

"Don't worry about it, Dryden," Emma soothed. "If we had the time, I could provide you with a long list of legitimate medical reasons why you're not performing at your best. But I can sum them all up in two words: you're exhausted. Secondly, I think it's safe to assume that the more of your implants' capabilities you're given access to, the more likely it is that you'll find yourself in overwhelming situations like this one. Helping you make good decisions during these moments is one of my most important roles. Now, unless I miss my guess, Captain Cash was in the process of feeling around in his pocket for the key to the padlock on your restraints when he was hit. I believe you may find them in his right front trouser pocket."

His pocket? You astonish me, Dryden thought sarcastically as he quickly traversed the distance between his tree and the captain's unconscious body. *I'm afraid, however, that putting my hands on the key is one thing but being able to do anything with it may be something else entirely. I can feel the padlock with the fingers on my right hand, but I don't think I have the reach to insert the key and turn it in the lock.*

"That part I'm pretty sure I can help us with," Emma said in a surprisingly confident tone, given the circumstances. "Just get us the key, and I'll show you."

Kneeling down on the captain's right side, Dryden immediately noticed that the officer's hand was still in his pocket. *Oh dear. Not an easy exercise in pocket-picking it seems,* he thought, attempting to interject some levity into the otherwise dire situation in hopes of steadying his badly shaking hands. Quickly realizing there was no way to turn his body sufficiently to reach his objective, he scrambled back to his feet, then backed himself into what he judged was a good starting point. Finally, after a quick glance behind him at what was about to become his landing zone, he squatted down on his haunches before plopping himself unceremoniously down on his rear — hoping his hands would now be better positioned to reach into Cash's pocket for the key.

It took several seconds of groping around behind his back to find the opening to the cavalryman's pocket. But once he did, it was fairly straightforward to pull the man's hand out of the way. What turned out to be the most difficult part of the task was the requirement to shift his entire body in order to effect even the smallest of movements with his tightly bound hands. Finally, after nearly a full minute of writhing like a cut snake in an effort to probe the depths of the captain's pocket, he felt the metallic edge of what he thought might be some sort of keyring. With a faint spark of hope beginning to kindle in his heart, Dryden raised himself off the ground with his legs, giving his hands just the slightest additional reach. It was in this awkward, straining position that he happened to notice a skinny, pimply-faced private — one of 1st Platoon's youngest cavalrymen —his back against a nearby tree, aiming his rifle in Dryden's direction.

"And just what do you think you're doin', Flamecaller?" the man yelled. "Get away from the captain, or I'll blow your head clean off your shoulders." As if to stress his resolve, the young man — one of the few still conscious at this point and obviously terrified — scrambled to his knees and then to his feet while still leaning against the trunk of his tree.

"Alright, just calm down, son," Dryden said. "The captain was in the process of getting these chains off of me so that I can try to help you stop these Shepherd soldiers when he got hit."

"I may be young, but I ain't stupid, mister. And that seems about as likely as gettin' served an ice-cold beer in the hubs of hell. Now, like I said, get your hands off the captain. I'm not gonna tell you again," he threatened, shaking his rifle to emphasize the point in a gesture that might have appeared downright comical under different circumstances.

Dryden felt the cool metal of the keyring against his fingers once again and knew that he did not have the time to begin his search all over again after dealing with the overzealous young cavalryman.

How confident are you in the shields, Emma? he asked inwardly.

"From this range and at this angle, the probability of a successful gravitic shield intercept is approximately ninety-six percent," she replied without hesitation. "Unfortunately, it's not an ideal intercept. Also, in our current position, I cannot supplement the gravitics with the energy shield without the potential for injuring the captain."

Right. I guess ninety-six percent will have to do, then.

With as little movement as possible, Dryden stretched out his fingers, finally managing to grasp the keyring between his middle and index fingers. Unfortunately, the motion did not escape the private's attention.

"I said STOP!" he yelled, now resting his cheek on the stock of his rifle as he took careful aim at the Flamecaller's head. "This is your last warn—"

At that instant, the young private's words were halted in mid-sentence as he was struck just beneath his right arm by one of the same spheres of blue energy that had taken down his commanding officer. Unable to even drop his rifle, he pitched slowly forward to the ground in a motion reminiscent of a tall tree felled by a lumberjack.

Knowing that he had very little time remaining to escape from his restraints, Dryden finally pulled the keyring free of the captain's pocket. As he struggled to raise himself from the sitting position back to his knees, another of the blue plasma spheres flashed by from somewhere deep in the forest, seeming to travel along a curved path as it passed up and over his head. With a renewed surge of adrenaline coursing through his veins, he quickly gained his feet once more, just as another of the spheres streaked out of the forest — this one glancing off to his right to impact the surface of the roadway some distance away with a strange hissing sound.

"Those were intended for us," Emma commented as Dryden sprang for the relative safety of the large tree once more, covering the intervening distance in two leaping bounds.

You think? he retorted, laughing aloud in spite of the obvious danger. *Guess it's a good thing they're not very good shots.*

"Oh, don't kid yourself," she replied. "Both of those shots were dead on. What you just witnessed were two successful intercept events by our gravitic shield system."

Really? Dryden responded absently, his chest heaving as he rested against the giant tree once more.

"Yes, indeed. In fact, there were several successful projectile intercepts earlier as well. Didn't you see the lights flashing around you?" she asked in a matter-of-fact tone as if she were describing some common, everyday occurrence.

Now that you mention it, I guess I did. I just had no idea what they were. It's good to know that it works, I suppose, he said, still holding the captain's keyring in his right hand and realizing he had no chance whatsoever of opening the padlock on his own.

"It's okay, Dryden," Emma said in a tone carefully crafted to reassure a Human mind treading a narrow path between panic and surrender to a fate that was yet to be determined. "As I said before, I can help you with this part. Now, turn around and face the tree ... good. All I need you to do is hang on to the keyring and hold still until you feel me take it from you."

Until you're ready to <u>what</u>? What are you about to do?

"Okay, there, I've got them, you can let go now," she said, as the keyring floated slowly out of his grasp. "I'll take it from here."

Wait ... how in the world are you —

Before Dryden could complete the thought, a pulsating red indicator drew his attention to the top-down display in the upper right corner of his vision. As his eyes instinctively focused on the map, his AI enlarged it slightly, immediately allowing his mind to grasp the source of the alert. Six of the eight Shepherd troops, still indicated by red triangles on the display, had emerged from behind their cover and now appeared to be moving slowly in his general direction.

I'm going to need you to speed that up a bit. Emma, he said, realizing he was about to confront three squads of what he was certain were the best troops the High Protector had at his disposal. And if that weren't sufficient cause for alarm, these particular Shepherds were obviously armed with advanced weapons, which, from what he could remember, was highly unusual. Typically, they were armed only with traditional weapons, relying instead on the enhanced speed and strength provided by their all-but-invulnerable armored suits. Dryden felt certain the decision to equip them with these incredible … whatever these guns were called … was an indication of the importance the High Protector placed on returning him to the fold. And there was every indication they had been ordered to succeed in this mission at any cost.

"I'm working on it," Emma replied. "Right now, I just need you to be as still as you possibly can."

I understand. But I'm sure you're aware that remaining "still," as you say, may not be possible for much longer, he remarked, taking in a deep breath in an effort to steady his still-shaking hands behind his back. *Any idea why they chose now to make their advance?*

"Hmm," she replied, maintaining her usual, strangely casual tone, "I can't get an accurate reading on vital signs from beyond about ten meters or so. But from what I can tell, you may be the last of their targets that has not been neutralized at this point."

And that's obviously not for lack of trying, Dryden replied.

"Exactly. So, I'd say that's why they're on the move now. They were unable to stun you, but they probably realize you're unlikely to cause them much trouble as long as you're in these restraints. So, the last thing they want to do is give you an opportunity to free yourself."

Yes, which, as I believe I mentioned previously, I need you to do as soon as possible, please, he said, trying and failing to sound calm in spite of the increasingly dangerous situation. Rather than the expected response from Emma, however, Dryden heard the now-familiar alert chime indicating an incoming comm transmission. *Rick again?* he asked.

"No, not this time. It looks like your would-be rescuers have finally decided to speak to you."

What? They just shot at me! Do they think I somehow didn't notice?

"It's tough to say for sure, but the transmission is from their assault shuttle, not the troops approaching on the ground. The sender is identifying herself as Maya Beck."

That's a bit of a coincidence, isn't it? Dryden thought, unable to quite put his finger on the name at the moment, but nonetheless feeling as if he should be able to do so. *Do you think I should respond?*

"Well, the troops are still coming whether you answer the transmission or not. And they've obviously got guns they aren't afraid to use. So, while you could certainly choose to ignore their call … I guess what I'm saying is, it couldn't hurt, right?"

Sure, why not, I suppose. Oh, and I assume this goes without saying, but please keep what you and I are saying to one another separate from any external conversations. Does that make sense?

"You don't have to worry about any of that, Dryden. I'll take care of it. I'm generally able to determine whether you would like to keep something private before the thought is even fully formed in your mind. And even if I speak to you while you're having a conversation with someone on the outside, they will not be able to hear what we're saying … unless that's what you want, of course."

Good, thanks. I'm certain there will be times when I will need your input — maybe even Rick's — while I'm in the middle of a conversation with someone else. I just hope I can keep it all straight in my mind.

"You'll be fine, I'm sure," she replied. "Shall I open the channel?"

Yes, please.

"Oh, one more thing before I do. I think we can safely assume you were a person of some influence within the High Protector's organization. I suggest you conduct yourself accordingly."

Good point, thank you, Dryden replied, then waited a moment until he heard the slightly different chime indicating he was now speaking to Commander Beck.

"This is Foxtrot 04," Dryden said, choosing to verbalize the conversation in an effort to segregate it from his internal dialog with his AI. Although his mouth was bone-dry, he was surprised by both the tone of his voice and the relaxed, almost routine manner in which he responded to the incoming communication request. "Go ahead, Commander Beck."

"Hello, Dryden. No need to be quite so formal. Maya will do just fine," the disembodied voice sounded inside his mind. The words instantly sent a vague shiver of recognition coursing down the length of his spine, although the precise nature of their connection continued to elude him. "I am pleased to find you alive and well. I felt certain we had lost you when you didn't report in after Talteca."

"I was almost certain of that myself a time or two," he replied. "Several of my systems took significant damage during the battle, and I completely lost all of my long-range communication capabilities. Nonetheless, I managed to evade the Estorians for a couple of days and thought I might actually make it back to Plains Reach."

"So, what happened? How did you manage to get yourself captured?"

"Predominantly dumb luck on their part as far as I can tell. This cavalry platoon just happened to stumble upon my position while I was in the middle of fighting off a group of four protoraptors."

"I see," Maya replied, noncommittally, wondering how a man capable of single-handedly destroying an entire cavalry regiment in seconds could shortly thereafter be brought down by a few mindless predators and a single platoon of the same soldiers. "Well, I suppose that does explain a few things then," she lied, throwing in a conspiratorial chuckle for good measure.

"Indeed," Dryden said, arching his eyebrow at the tone of her comment. "And on the subject of explaining some things, were you aware that your Shepherds troops down here just fired some sort of stun weapons at me?"

"Yes, I'm afraid so. And I'm sorry about that, Dryden. They were just following orders … as was I. I'm sure you understand that we had no choice but to assume you had been compromised in some manner."

"Commander, do I look compromised to you?" he asked in an annoyed tone. Dryden felt certain she was watching him carefully, both from above and from the perspective of her troops approaching in the forest. To further emphasize his point, he bent forward at the waist and shook his tightly bound hands up and down behind his back.

"Gods, would you BE STILL!" Emma scolded.

"Uh, no," Maya replied, "I don't suppose you —"

"Or do I instead look like a high-value prisoner in need of immediate extraction?" Dryden pressed.

"That would, of course, be my assumption. But as I'm sure you of all people can attest, appearances can be deceiving … often intentionally so."

"Well, if you can think of a scenario in which I would find myself restrained in this manner, surrounded by the bodies of my … what shall we call them … 'co-conspirators' perhaps? I'd be very interested to hear it. I'm sure it would make a fascinating tale."

"Look, Flamecaller, I never said anything about —"

"I need you to listen to me closely, Commander," Dryden said, cutting her off once again in the iciest, most authoritarian tone he could muster. "I assume since your three squads of Shepherd soldiers left roughly half of the Estorians alive down here, it is your intention to return them to Plains Reach. Am I correct?"

"My apologies, Dryden. But under the circumstances, I'm sure you understand that I am not at liberty to discuss the specific details of my orders."

"I understand well enough," Dryden said. "But now I'm afraid I must revise and extend those orders. While a prisoner of these cavalrymen, I was able to gather intelligence indicating they expect me to be turned over to whoever has been supplying their army with weapons and other materiel."

"I'm sorry, Dryden. I don't think I'm following you," she replied. "What weapons are you referring to?"

"Before we proceed, I need you to order your Shepherd soldiers to remain where they are while we conclude our discussion. It is not currently safe for them to approach any closer." Dryden paused momentarily, staring intently at his top-down display in hopes of seeing some indication Commander Beck was playing along, at least for the moment.

"They've halted their advance and appear to be taking cover again," Emma confirmed after a few seconds.

Agreed. How much longer on that lock? he asked, his internal monologue sounding much more impatient and stressed than his conversation with Commander Beck.

"I don't know, Dryden. I almost had it when you decided to do your little dance routine a few seconds ago. If you could manage to remain *still*, it shouldn't take long."

"Thank you, Commander," Dryden continued aloud, ignoring the scolding he had just received from his AI. "This is a secure channel, is it not?"

"Of course."

"Good. Let's try not to waste any more time than necessary, shall we? I feel certain you know what I was referring to when I mentioned the Estorians' weapons. Or are you less trusted with sensitive information than the other Shepherd commanders for some reason?"

"My orders come directly from Sir Frederick, so you may infer from that whatever you like," she replied, clearly insulted by his assertion.

"Ah, good. Perhaps now we are getting somewhere. You understand, of course, that I answer only to the High Protector himself. So, once again, I need you to listen carefully and follow my instructions to the letter. The information I have gleaned from my captors thus far indicates that the Estorians expect the exchange to take place within forty-eight hours of my return to their headquarters at Talteca. It is in our best interest to allow that exchange to proceed as planned."

"Dryden," Emma interjected privately, "the lock is open. I recommend we leave the restraints in place for the moment and not allow Commander Beck to know you are almost free. When you are ready for me to proceed, I believe I can remove them completely in approximately thirty seconds."

"Surely you're not suggesting I allow you to remain in their custody," Maya continued. "And how do you propose to explain what happened once the surviving soldiers regain consciousness?"

"Explain what? We were attacked. Some were killed and some were stunned. The Shepherds took a handful of unlucky troopers with them and left the area. You should take all the dead ones with you when you leave, by the way. I believe the story will seem more plausible that way."

"Right. And why exactly didn't we take *you* with us?"

"I don't know, Commander. I'll just say the attack clearly had nothing to do with me. I was restrained and stunned the whole time, just like everyone else, and the Shepherds probably didn't even realize I was here. You got whatever it was you were after and went on your way."

"Out of the question," Maya snapped. "What I *am* willing to do, however, is leave a couple of my men here to secure the remaining Estorians and keep them alive stunned, that is, but alive — for the time being. I will then complete my mission more or less as planned, returning you to Plains Reach to consult with the High

Protector. In the unlikely event he agrees with your … rather strange plan, I can return you to your state of captivity within the hour."

"No. Too risky," Dryden countered. "You know as well as I do that most of them will retain the memory of being stunned multiple times. That will definitely make them more suspicious of why I was left here while some of their own were taken away. Look, I'm not sure you're grasping the level of importance the High Protector places on determining the source of these weapons shipments and then putting a stop to them … permanently."

There was a period of silence on the comlink, leading him to believe that he might have finally convinced the reluctant commander to his way of thinking. "Also, Commander," he pressed, hoping to seal the deal, "I'm going to need a secure means of communicating with you from Talteca. I assume you have some sort of discreet comm device aboard, do you not?"

There was still no response.

"It appears she has terminated the comlink," Emma reported.

I was afraid of that. Emma, I really need you to get these restraints off me … right now.

Chapter 20

Didara 4, South Estorian Continent, Scarsdow Forest
(River Road - 3.3 km north of the logging cabin)

BING! The warning tone sounded within Dryden's mind, startling him as he awaited a response from Commander Beck — a response he now assumed would not be the one he had been hoping for.

The following capability may now be accessed via your neural interface: Enhanced Situational Awareness 1. Digitized information from your own natural senses is amplified and combined with far-field gravimetric data as well as that from a variety of other internal sensors. The results are presented in the form of a high-resolution, three-dimensional depiction of the space around your body, which is displayed in real-time. Note that single-target detection ranges will vary dramatically, depending on a variety of factors — in particular, whether modeling data describing the specific target already exists in the AI's database. Previously cataloged air and spacecraft, for example, are significantly easier to detect and track in flight compared to similar-sized targets traveling along the ground. Under ideal conditions, airborne targets can be detected and tracked at a range of up to one hundred kilometers. Tracking of ground-based targets, however, is limited to line-of-sight distance, which is approximately five kilometers on flat terrain but will vary significantly where hills or other obstructions are present.

Before Dryden could ask Emma precisely how this new capability might in any way increase his odds of surviving the next several minutes, he noted a dramatic change in the top-down display overlaying his field of view. What was previously a rather simple, two-dimensional representation expanded and transformed into something that, at first, threatened to completely overwhelm his mind. Everywhere he looked, their world was now cluttered with various forms of annotation — offensive and defensive systems, sensors, communications, navigation — all of it presented in mind-numbingly complex detail.

Feeling suddenly nauseous, Dryden squeezed his eyes tightly shut and found to his relief that he could make all of it go away with nothing more than a simple thought. Opening his eyes once more, he concentrated on being presented with just one type of data at a time. Remarkably, as the various types of information began to reappear before his eyes, he felt his mind begin to adjust to what he was seeing. Although he had no idea how or why, all of the complex symbology and data depicted somehow made perfect sense. Mere seconds after the new capability had been announced, he simply *knew*.

"We obviously don't have a lot of time to go over this new ESA-1 capability right now," Emma said, "but a portion of what you're seeing is called a tactical plot. It's designed to show you all of the data being provided by your sensors in an intuitive fashion, particularly during combat operations. Once you get used to it, you shouldn't have to spend a lot of time interpreting what you're seeing. It should just —"

Make sense, Dryden interrupted. *No, surprisingly enough, I think I understand most of it, Emma, thank you.*

"Good. That means you're getting used to handling the information being integrated into your consciousness from the neural interface. One thing about the plot that might be counter-intuitive is that contacts I deem to be more of an immediate threat will be displayed more prominently. Lower priority contacts are displayed with smaller icons and more muted colors — or not at all. We can work on your preferences later."

I got it, Emma. Please focus on the restraints, if you would.

"That's not a problem, Dryden. Fortunately for you, I actually *am* capable of multitasking with no loss in performance. Unlike you Humans, who just *think* you can."

Uh huh. Incidentally, may I assume what I'm seeing now is more accurate than before in terms of where the enemy soldiers are located?

"It is, indeed," Emma replied. "Note that you can rotate the plot itself in three dimensions so that you can see the Shepherd troops or Commander Beck's assault shuttle from any angle. If that's too disorienting, you should be able to see where any specific target is located in space simply by looking in its general direction. You can also pan or zoom, of course, as required."

Right, yes, I see it, he replied, looking up to see a red, pulsating triangle with an accompanying block of descriptive text marking the shuttle's apparent location in the sky. The triangle, he noted, was now surrounded by a green circle he had not previously seen.

"Prior to accessing the ESA-1 capability, I was able to determine a rough bearing and distance from the shuttle's high-frequency comm transmissions. But what you are seeing now is a much more precise depiction of the ship's position in space. As you can see, Commander Beck's ship is still located ten kilometers to our south, horizontally, at an altitude of just over twenty-five thousand meters. We are well within the range of her shuttle's weapons, but I don't think she would fire on us with her troops in such close proximity."

I wouldn't bet on that, Emma. What about the green circle?

"That's a targeting reticle, Dryden. Green indicates the selected weapon system — so far, that's limited to Plasma Bolt 1 — is locked onto the target. Once the target is in range of the selected weapon system, you will see a pair of lines crossing the center of the reticle at right angles."

I assume you are referring to some sort of crosshairs.

"Exactly. In addition, the entire reticle will begin to rotate."

Got it, he replied, looking now in the direction of the closest two squads of Shepherd soldiers. All eight of their respective red triangles were surrounded by green, rotating circles with crosshairs centered on each target's center of mass. For the first time in many months, the corners of Dryden Beck's mouth turned upwards with the slightest hint of a smile.

"They're moving again," Emma said, as several of the red triangles began pulsating once more.

Yes, I can see them. And it looks like they're going to have quite an easy time of it when they get here, he said, realizing even as he did so that his incessant prodding would likely have no effect whatsoever on Emma's performance. *Please see if we can contact Commander Beck again.*

With no discernible delay, the alert chime sounded once again to indicate an open comm channel. "Commander?" he began tentatively, hearing no other indication that anyone was listening. "I believe you can hear me, and I can see that your troops are moving once again. As I said before, I must insist that you order them to withdraw and maintain a distance of at least one hundred meters from my position. I have purposely not provided you with full details of why I have asked you to keep them clear. That is because much of the information concerning the gifts entrusted to me by the High Protector is classified."

"Foxtrot 04, this is Commander Beck. I apologize for the delay, but I have just reconfirmed our orders with Plains Reach. You are to stand down and allow yourself to be taken into protective custody by the Shepherd soldiers now approaching your position. We will be taking you and the remaining Estorian prisoners aboard my assault shuttle and returning to base."

"No, Commander, I'm afraid I cannot allow that to happen. You are putting your troops in serious danger if they approach my position. I am utilizing a number of defensive systems that pose a serious threat to anyone nearby. Please don't put me in a position to inadvertently harm one of our own soldiers."

"This is your final warning, Flamecaller," Maya replied in a flat, unemotional tone.

"She has terminated the connection again," Emma reported.

I'm not surprised. So, once again, I'm looking to you for some options here, Emma. I have to say I'm not coming up with much of anything on my own at the moment. If I thought he would be willing to help, I would ask Rick for a quick escape.

"What's that supposed to mean?" Rick's voice chimed in unexpectedly. "I'm always willing to help. But as I've told you before, there are some things I simply cannot do."

"Gods, Rick!" Dryden shouted, feeling as if his heart might leap out of his chest with fright. "Where did you come from?"

"I have no idea what you're talking about, Flamecaller. I've been closely monitoring your situation this whole time. I just had nothing particularly valuable to offer and didn't want to distract you."

How about helping me find a way out of here? I'm afraid I'm not liking our odds at the moment, Dryden said, struggling to control his breathing as he returned to his inner monologue.

"Would it help if I told you that you have nothing to fear from these soldiers or their overly ambitious young commander? I think you might be surprised by what you're now capable of. Although I will say that you're up against some very sophisticated weaponry and armor this time ... well, compared to Estorian cavalry, that is."

That much I believe Emma and I have already discerned for ourselves.

"Oh, so now you've suddenly decided Emma is on your side, have you? Fair enough. Might I suggest, then, that the two of you move to a location where you can safely utilize both of the shield systems at your disposal? I think it's a foregone conclusion you'll be needing them again shortly."

"Sorry about that, Dryden," Emma sighed, "I considered suggesting that myself, but I did not expect to have quite this much difficulty getting your arms freed. I have marked a suitable location approximately seventy meters to the east southeast. There is a depression in the ground there at the edge of a clearing that should offer reasonably good cover while protecting the remaining Estorians from being caught in any crossfire."

Nothing about that sounds particularly encouraging, Dryden said, noting the magenta-colored course line with flashing arrows indicating Emma's recommended path to the new defensive position. *By the way, I can feel you moving the restraints around back there. May I assume you will have them off shortly?*

"As I said, it's more difficult than I expected. Go to the location I marked for you and then stand as still as you can. With any luck, I should be able to finish freeing you."

I hope so, or this isn't going to be much of a battle.

With that, Dryden instinctively crouched as low as possible and set off, angling slightly away from the river road to his left. Glancing off to the southwest as he ran, he could see that the advancing Shepherds had already altered their course slightly to account for his movement.

Looks like they have a pretty good idea where I'm headed, he observed, half to himself. In the tactical plot, which he had returned to the upper right corner of his vision, Dryden expanded the scale so that he could also see the positions of the remaining Shepherd soldiers to the north of the road. As he had expected, all four of them now also appeared to be closing on his position.

It took Dryden less than twenty seconds to arrive at his destination, after which he crouched low in the small ravine, hoping to at least make it a little more difficult for the advancing Shepherd soldiers to know exactly where he was hiding.

"Good," Emma said. "This location is even better than I hoped it would be. Energy shields are now online as well. Now, I need you to hold as still as possible while I try to get these knots untied. Whoever tied these knew exactly what they were —"

Emma's comment was interrupted by the chime indicating another incoming comm transmission. This time, Dryden noted that the source of the call was indicated in his field of view as Commander Beck's assault shuttle. *Humph,* he said. *Perhaps she agrees that this is a pretty good defensive location and just wants to express her approval.*

"Under the circumstances, I expect she'll do everything she can to avoid a confrontation," Emma said. "Shall I put her through?"

"Yes, please."

"It's very noble of you to get clear of the Estorian troopers, Dryden," Commander Beck began, "but I'm sure you realize that won't save them. I have my orders. I mean to take the rest of them and you into custody … with or without your cooperation. Once again, your orders are to stand down immediately. Otherwise, I will have no choice but to use force."

"Her shuttle has slowed its descent, but is still headed in this direction," Emma reported.

"Commander Beck, please listen to me," Dryden said. "I know you think I'm compromised, and from your point of view, I understand why you believe that to be true. We don't have time for me to explain everything that has happened to me, but I can assure you that I meant everything I told you about my determining who is supplying these weapons to the Estorians."

"Please don't make me do this, Dryden," Maya said, her voice suddenly tinged with what might have been mistaken for regret or even fear in a different context.

In an instant, his blood seemed to turn to ice within his veins, the truth now revealed with far more impact than any other weapon his enemies might bring to bear.

"My Gods!" Emma exclaimed. "She's your sister!"

Chapter 21

Didara 4, South Estorian Continent, Scarsdow Forest
(River Road - 3.3 km north of the logging cabin)

"Flamecaller!" the nearest Shepherd soldier yelled, his voice amplified to an overwhelming one hundred twenty decibels by his armor's VA system. "You are surrounded and heavily outgunned. There is absolutely no possibility of escape. You are ordered to take ten steps toward the sound of my voice, lower yourself to your knees, and then lie flat on the ground on your chest. If you fail to follow instructions or make any aggressive moves, you will be fired upon."

The first squad of four Shepherd troops had made their final approach at nearly sixty kilometers per hour, their dark forms materializing in the small clearing like wraiths dispatched from the darkest depths of Scarsdow Forest. Three of the four had fanned out in a rough semi-circle around the small ravine in which Dryden had taken cover, each one kneeling with particle beam rifle at the ready. The soldier doing the talking, however, had apparently also been given the task of taking their target into custody. Although his rifle was slung around his neck with its barrel pointing at the ground, his right hand remained wrapped around the weapon's pistol grip as he waited to see if his instructions would be followed.

Okay, Dryden thought, the sound of resignation plainly evident, even in the tone of his mind's inner voice. *I don't think I have much choice at this point other than doing what they ask.*

"What? You're not going to surrender," Emma said, phrasing her question as a statement. While the AI generally knew precisely what her charge was thinking, she was becoming increasingly aware that he was capable of surprising her.

"I think that might be a little premature, don't you think?" Rick agreed.

No, I don't mean surrender exactly ... not just yet anyway.

"I'm sorry, Dryden," Emma began again, her voice now taking on a compassionate tone, "I know that realizing Commander Beck's connection to you has come as a tremendous shock, but —"

It hasn't. Not really. Honestly, it's hard to describe how it feels ... almost like hearing something you already knew ... or at least should have known. So, no, what I'm considering has absolutely nothing to do with that. Just like the rest of them, I'll do everything I can to save her. But if I can't ...

"I'm very sorry, Dryden," Emma repeated.

In any event, I agree now is not the time to surrender. It's also not the time for any further discussion on this subject. At some point, however, I'm going to have some questions for you, Rick, as to why you have been hiding this particular piece of information from me. The bottom line is, those Shepherd soldiers know I'm still restrained, and there's little doubt they'll try to grab me before I manage to free myself.

"That would be ... unfortunate," Rick said, deadpan. "I don't know, Flamecaller, allowing that to happen might turn out to be a reasonable strategy for paring down their numbers a bit. Clearly, you have no other means of taking the offensive at the moment."

No, Dryden said decisively. *I sincerely doubt they have been briefed on my defensive systems ... certainly nothing about the danger they'll be exposing themselves to if they get any closer. They're Didarans, and I have no intention of killing any of them if I can find any means of avoiding it.* With that, Dryden stood, raising himself up to his full height for the first time since the attack began, and climbed confidently out of the small ravine in which he had been hiding.

Although he had already known the positions of every one of the Shepherd soldiers with extraordinary accuracy, the sight of the three nearest troops with their weapons aimed in his direction was far more intimidating than he had expected. As if further emphasis were needed, his thoughts prompted the ESA system to highlight each of the soldier's current aiming points — all three of which converged near the center of his chest. *Emma, maximum diameter on the shields, please,* he ordered.

"Done," she replied, the change resulting in a slight increase in the faint hum produced by the shield system. "If it makes you feel any better, if one of them comes into contact with the field, the system will automatically compensate and protect you from any ... *effects,* shall we say?"

Understood. And, no, it doesn't make me feel any better, he replied, as he began slowly walking in the direction of the closest soldier.

"That's far enough!" the Shepherd thundered. "Now, get down on your knees and then lie down on your chest

…. Put your nose on the ground," the man added for good measure.

Humph. Perhaps he's been briefed on Flamecallers after all, Dryden thought, trying to reassure himself to some small degree.

"If nothing else, he's probably well aware you're the last one," Rick said.

I'm what?

"I said down on the ground, Flamecaller. NOW!" the soldier roared, obviously not happy with the speed at which his commands were being followed.

Dryden paused for a moment, trying to decide exactly how he should respond while also trying to gauge how many of the twelve Shepherds would actually hear him if he yelled out what he had to say. *Rick, don't they all monitor some sort of standard "guard" frequency? I'd like to be able to speak to all of them at once.*

"Hmm. The assault shuttle will definitely hear anything you transmit via your HF communications equipment, but it's less clear whether the Shepherds will be able to hear you. One moment."

Right. You do realize I don't have a moment to spare right now, do you not? Dryden asked, expecting all four of the nearest soldiers to open fire at any second.

"Sorry about that, I had to check with Miguel. It turns out this is something we can help you with. Their encryption algorithms are actually pretty good. It took Miguel several minutes to compromise them when we arrived. But if we share that data with Emma, she will be able to transmit and receive over their command network. He is sending the information now."

"Got it," Emma confirmed. "The channel is open. Go ahead, Dryden."

"Extraction team, this is Foxtrot 04. Please do not come any closer or you may be harmed by my defensive systems. I assume Commander Beck did not inform you this was the case. I mean you no harm, but you need to understand that I have no intention of surrendering to you. My mission with these Estorians on behalf of the High Protector is classified. At this time, I am taking command of your extraction team. You are ordered to stand down and assemble at the coordinates I am about to transmit." *I assume you've got that covered,* he asked as an aside to Emma.

"Done," she replied instantly.

"Listen carefully. I need all twelve of you to proceed immediately to the rendezvous point I just designated. Once you are all accounted for, Commander Beck will take you aboard the assault shuttle once more for the trip back to Plains Reach. My mission requires that I remain here as the prisoner of the Estorian cavalry troopers. I regret that I am unable to provide you with more details at this time. Just know that it is an assignment of the utmost importance to our Lord High Protector."

Dryden looked pointedly at each member of the closest squad of Shepherd troops, noting what looked like a brief moment of hesitation, followed immediately by a noticeable increase in their stress levels — all annotated by his ESA system.

"I'm detecting a marked pulse, respiration, and body temperature rise on the nearest four," Emma reported, projecting a variety of additional data into Dryden's field of view that only served to reinforce what the hair on the back of his neck was already telling him.

Looking off into the forest to the east and then towards the road to the north, Dryden noted that the remaining eight troops had taken cover once more, their positions obviously selected to provide each of them with a clear field of fire in his direction.

"More bad news, I'm afraid," Rick said. "Commander Beck has switched her extraction team over to an alternate command frequency with a new encryption key. Miguel will no doubt have this one decrypted momentarily as well. But it's safe to assume she has also ordered them to ignore everything you say from here on in."

Sure enough, after a momentary pause to sort out the confusing comlink traffic from both the Flamecaller and Commander Beck, the nearest soldier had resumed his approach. "Down on the ground NOW!" he repeated from less than thirty meters away.

"STOP!" Dryden yelled, "I don't want to hurt you. But if you come any closer, you will get yourself killed!"

"Should I lower the shield?" Emma asked.

No, Dryden replied in a doleful but resolute tone. *At this point, I think we have to let this happen.*

And happen it did. Just two seconds later, the advancing soldier walked directly into the event horizon of Dryden's energy shield, producing a series of effects that were at once spectacular and terrifying. Although not designed for the purpose, the energy shield nevertheless proved quite effective as an anti-personnel device. The Shepherd soldier was quite literally stopped dead in his tracks. Upon entering the field, the man's armored suit performed surprisingly well as an electrical insulator, protecting him from immediate electrocution. Glowing blue tendrils of electricity arced from the man's body and weapon to the ground as multicolored waves of energy rippled across the surface of the shield, seeming to echo back and forth from one side to the other. Just three hundred milliseconds later, however, the external temperature at the point of contact between his suit and Dryden's energy shield exceeded three thousand Kelvins. Under such extreme conditions, the armored suit itself lasted only slightly longer than the soldier's body inside. As the other Shepherds watched in horror, what remained of their fellow soldier collapsed to the ground under his own weight, a molten, formless mass bearing no resemblance to what had existed a fraction of a second before.

"Gods above," Dryden muttered quietly to himself, suddenly feeling as if he might become violently ill from what he had just seen. But there was no time to do so. Before he could manage to plead with the soldiers once again to come no closer, the three remaining members of the first squad opened up with their particle beam rifles. This time, rather than the glowing balls of blue plasma, vicious streaks of reddish-orange light streaked from their weapons, leaving no doubt that they now fully intended to kill their target.

The space around Dryden's body came alive with gravitic shield intercept events, each one marked by a small flash of light in the visible spectrum that lit the forest clearing with an eerie white glow. The effect was awe-inspiring to behold — a ghostly, halo-like sphere of light with both incoming and deflected beams of orange streaming from its surface like the rays from a rising sun.

Instinctively, Dryden turned to run back in the direction of his former refuge in the nearby ravine. But after taking the first two strides in that direction, his ankle rolled to the side on an unseen rock, causing him to fall headlong to the ground as the incoming fire continued unabated. With the breath knocked out of his exhausted body for the second time in less than an hour, it took him several seconds of writhing around on the ground before he finally managed to scramble back to his knees. All around him, his gravitic shields continued deflecting the Shepherd soldiers' incoming particle beams in seemingly random directions. Many of the errant beams continued on to violently collide with the terrain or other obstacles in the immediate vicinity, their explosive impacts echoing many kilometers up and down the river road as if the battle were taking place inside a narrow canyon.

Despite the chaos occurring all around him, Dryden paused, gasping for breath and assuming that any moment his shields would fail to stop one of the deadly streams of fire. *At least that would make the noise stop,* he observed to himself.

Noting the thought and Dryden's rising level of panic once more, Emma responded by reducing the electrical signals from his auditory nerves, dramatically reducing the thunderous din occurring around him. She had also noted the presence of a grave, new threat but decided to delay bringing it to his attention. "There," she said in a reassuring voice, "hopefully that's a little more tolerable. In case you're wondering, the gravitic shield system has successfully intercepted sixty-four incoming particle beams thus far with none making it through to the energy shield. Now get up and get yourself behind cover before someone gets off a lucky shot."

Drawing in another deep breath in an attempt to steady himself, Dryden managed to get one leg in front of his body and then pushed himself back to his feet. His body groaned in protest — a veritable symphony of pain and fatigue — indicating in no uncertain terms that he would soon reach the limits of his endurance. Striving to clear these somewhat irrelevant thoughts from his mind, he began to notice that the ambient noise around him had changed in pitch, a roaring whine that quickly rose above even that of the incoming weapons fire.

Dryden closed his eyes and shook his head slowly from side to side, knowing full well what was happening behind him without bothering to turn and look. As if he needed confirmation from his ESA system, an urgently pulsating red indicator had appeared at the edge of his peripheral vision — with an animated series of arrows indicating the direction of this most recent threat to his continued existence. Taking in a deep breath, he turned to stare over his left shoulder just as Commander Beck's assault shuttle cleared the treetops on the far side of the clearing, pulling up into a steep, nose-high flare before settling into a stable hover.

As if someone had flipped a switch, all of the incoming particle beam fire from the Shepherd soldiers ceased. The screaming roar of the shuttle's ventral thrusters, while considerable, was a welcome improvement after having been the sole target of an energy weapons fusillade — less than two minutes that had seemed to stretch on for hours.

As Dryden slowly turned his body to face the new threat, Commander Beck's voice boomed like thunder from the VA system equipping the nearest three Shepherd soldiers. "It's over, Flamecaller. Your refusal to follow orders has now resulted in the death of one of our own troops. Nevertheless, I will allow you to live and leave your fate to the High Protector if you do *exactly* as I say. Otherwise, you will die where you stand. Now, disengage your shield system and get down on the ground ... all the way down, face first ... nose in the dirt."

Dryden made no attempt to either reply or obey his sister's latest, threat-laden demands. Instead, he stood stock-still, staring at her small spacecraft now hovering twenty meters above the forest floor. Strangely, he wasn't even thinking about what she had just said. Instead, his attention was wholly focused on the assault shuttle itself — the blue glow of its four sublight engines bathing the edge of the clearing behind it in a ghostly, bluish-white light. Although he felt certain he had actually been aboard the ship before, he had no memory of ever witnessing it in flight. The sight of such a large object floating effortlessly in the air was unsettling, to say the least, but nonetheless filled him with a sense of awe. And for the first time in his life, the smallest fragment of knowledge — little more than a brief flicker of understanding — of his own existence within the vastness of the cosmos was revealed to his mind.

"Dryden," he heard Emma say from what seemed like a place just beyond the bounds of a pleasant dream. "Are you paying attention?" she prompted.

Yes, of course, he replied, somewhat irritated by the interruption.

"Look, I understand what you just experienced — although I have no idea why the secondary AI chose that particular moment for a data dump. But I need you to snap out of it, do you hear me?" she said.

As Emma's voice finally began lifting the dream-like haze that had enveloped his mind, Dryden realized that Commander Beck had been speaking for some time.

" ... I've seen enough of what Flamecaller shields are capable of handling to know that yours appear to have been augmented, which means you've gotten some help from somewhere," Maya continued. "Dealing with the energy output from Class I plasma rifles is one thing ... but do you really want to test them against the Class III weapons equipping this assault shuttle? I don't want to fire on you, Dryden, but if you leave me with no other options ..."

With no interest in additional debate, Dryden began slowly backing in the direction of the ravine once more, keeping his eyes firmly fixed on the assault shuttle as he did so.

"Dryden," Emma interjected once again, "it's clear enough we're not going to come to any sort of agreement with Commander Beck. If she fires on us again, I will attempt to deflect the energy in the direction of hostile forces. With your permission, of course."

Do it, Dryden replied coldly, an instant before two massive particle beams slashed out from the assault shuttle.

Fortunately for the exhausted Flamecaller, even with the incoming fire approaching at near the speed of light, input from his shield systems' near-field-entanglement sensors provided Emma sufficient time to respond. During the one hundred nanoseconds it took for the stream of high energy electrons to cover the intervening distance, the AI completed the dizzying array of calculations required to not only protect his body but also allow him to take the offensive for the first time.

Both of the incoming beams were instantly deflected off in the direction of the four Shephard troops to the north of his position. The orange stream of fire from the shuttle's port-side weapon instantly vaporized one of Commander Beck's soldiers, while the starboard-side impacted the ground nearby with tremendous explosive force, seriously injuring another.

Before Commander Beck realized what was happening, her shuttle had fired two additional salvos. And in the space of less than three seconds, all four of the Shepherd soldiers posted between Dryden and the river road had been either killed or incapacitated.

"She's trying to open the channel again," Emma said evenly.

I'm not surprised, Dryden replied. *Let's give her a moment to consider her actions thus far. In the meantime ... I assume the assault shuttle has shields, does it not?*

"Yes, of course. Its energy shields are almost identical to ours ... no gravitic shields, though. We received those as a result of modifications put into place by the Dayleans."

"You're welcome," Rick chimed in.

And if I come into contact with the shuttle's shields? Dryden asked, ignoring the Grey's comment.

"Surprisingly, the localized field intensity of the shuttle's shields is significantly less than yours, so you should remain reasonably well protected. The interaction between the two fields would undoubtedly produce severe electrical disturbances … similar to what we saw earlier. But I believe it will hold."

Good. That's what I was hoping you would say.

"Really? Well, if you liked *that,* you should love *this.*"

Dryden felt a slight movement behind his back as Emma released the last knot holding his restraints in place, causing the entire mass of rope and chains to clank and jangle to a heap on the ground behind his back.

Finally! Thank you, Emma. That just might change things a bit, he said, slowly crossing his arms in front of his body in a gesture intended not only to stretch his aching shoulders but also to make it painfully clear to Commander Beck that his hands were now free once again.

"One more thing I should mention regarding the shuttle's shields. Our plasma bolts do not have sufficient energy to penetrate them. Not yet, at least."

Understood. Open the channel, please, Dryden ordered.

"Traitor!" Maya seethed, her fury plainly evident, even over the comlink. "You just killed more of our men. The High Protector will see you *burn* for this. And I can assure you I will be there to watch it happen."

In spite of her anger, the commander seemed somewhat unsure what she should do next, and a period of dead air ensued once again over the comlink.

"She doesn't know, does she?" Emma asked into the silence.

She knows. It's hard to explain, but the relationship simply has no emotional context as long as she's under the High Protector's control. As she has already demonstrated, she has no compunction whatsoever about killing me.

"Any deaths that have occurred here tonight are on you, Commander," Dryden said, picking up the conversation where his sister had left off. "I told you exactly what was about to happen, and you refused to listen. Now, in the names of the Gods, have your soldiers recover your dead and injured, rally at the designated rendezvous point, and head back to Plains Reach before anyone else gets killed."

There was no response.

"Please … Maya. I know you must remember that you are my sister. Listen to me … I can *help* you!" he added in a pleading tone.

On his tactical plot display, Dryden noted the three nearest Shepherd soldiers making a run for cover at the western edge of the clearing while the remaining squad of four still inside the tree line also began shifting back towards the west-northwest.

"That's not the direction they should be going," Emma observed, as the assault shuttle opened up once again with its particle beam weapons.

This time, Commander Beck fired the assault shuttle's weapons in rapid succession, maintaining a steady rate of fire in an attempt, Dryden assumed, to overwhelm his shields. At various locations all around the perimeter of the clearing, massive trees were struck by deflected particle beams. Tremendous quantities of energy streamed into their massive trunks, causing them to instantly explode in fiery eruptions of flying debris. Many of them, even a few examples over fifty meters tall, came crashing to the forest floor, adding to the already intense tumult of sound.

Time to test your theory, Emma, Dryden said with far more confidence than he felt. With that, he charged directly at the assault shuttle as fast as his legs would still carry him. When he had reached a point roughly thirty meters away, the forward edge of his own energy shield began interacting with that of the assault shuttle. As expected, another spectacularly bright electrical discharge ensued. Ripples of multicolored light encircled both his body and the entire spacecraft above, clearly tracing the outlines of the overlapping energy fields.

It took Dryden just seven seconds to reach his intended destination directly beneath the ship, which was already in the process of moving forward once again. Looking quickly around the clearing, he realized the ship's pilot — assuming there was one — was attempting to provide himself with sufficient clearance for a turn. Once that happened, the shuttle's forward-facing energy weapons would be pointed in his direction once more. But for now, at least, the change in the shuttle's position was putting him exactly where he wanted to be.

Steadying himself for what was to come, Dryden raised his arms above his head, clenching both hands into fists as he waited for his intended targets to come into view. Seconds later, the rear of the ship passed directly overhead, giving him a clear view of its four sublight engine nozzles.

Top left engine first ... then the bottom left, he ordered, selecting Plasma Bolt 1/Discharge Intensity 3 from a contextual menu that had appeared near the center of his vision. With a vague sense of satisfaction, he found that he was still able to faintly discern the high-pitched whine that always seemed to accompany the activation of his weapon systems. Confident that Emma would handle the fine-tuning of his aim, he opened fire.

Chapter 22

Didara 4, South Estorian Continent, Scarsdow Forest
(River Road - 3.3 km north of the logging cabin)

In the space of one second, six bluish-white orbs of plasma streaked away from the ends of Dryden's arms. With his relatively large target such a short distance away, all six of the projectiles easily scored a direct hit, entering the assault shuttle's top, port-side engine nozzle. With adrenalin coursing through his veins, Dryden felt as if he were watching the entire scene unfolding in a dream-like state of slow motion, his mind taking note of minute details that might easily have escaped his attention under normal circumstances. Chief among these was the realization that he had chosen to fire on a spacecraft weighing approximately fifty metric tons that just happened to be hovering directly overhead. And while it now occurred to him that this might not have been the best course of action under the circumstances, his intention had been to force an immediate landing — to disable the ship, not destroy it — had it not?

As these thoughts flashed through the Flamecaller's mind, all six of the high-energy plasma bolts reached the number one engine's reaction chamber, causing it to immediately explode. Fragments of the ship's hull surrounding the blast were sent ripping into the number two, port-side engine, located just a few meters below. While not as violent as the initial impact, the end result was identical, and Dryden felt a flush of satisfaction as the blue glow of the second sublight engine flickered twice before being extinguished altogether. In response, the entire ship seemed to shudder in the air, sinking a bit by the stern as it rocked from side to side. Dryden also noticed an immediate change in the sound and appearance of the shuttle's remaining two engines as onboard systems quickly diverted power to the ventral thrusters keeping the craft aloft.

While no longer in danger of being crushed by the ship if it failed to maintain altitude, Dryden wondered if his own shields would continue to hold if he found himself staring directly into the business end of one of the two remaining sublight engines nozzles. The entire port-side stern of the shuttle was quickly becoming obscured by thick smoke, undoubtedly the result of its fire suppression systems attempting to mitigate the damage and somehow keep the small spacecraft in the air.

"It wasn't enough, Dryden," Emma said. "You're going to have to hit it again."

"I agree," Rick interjected. "And do it now before it gains sufficient altitude to prevent your firing from inside its aft shields. The presence of these assault shuttles still represents a grave threat — if not to you, then certainly to the Estorian Army. Eliminating one of them will have a significant impact on the High Protector's overall military capabilities."

Objectively, Dryden knew they were right. The High Protector appeared to have no other means of resupplying his forces in the field, making his two assault shuttles arguably his most valuable military assets. Even without the use of their powerful weapons, sensor arrays, and communications capabilities, the ships provided the High Protector the ability to position his forces anywhere on the planet at will. And although he might well be capable of repairing the damage this one had sustained thus far, there was little chance he could ever replace it were it to be destroyed.

Continuing to stare upwards at the ship still looming above the forest clearing, Dryden noted that its formerly erratic flight had stabilized once again. Seconds later, it raised its bow slightly and began slowly increasing its altitude. In spite of this, Dryden hesitated.

"You can't save her if she doesn't want to be saved," Rick said quietly.

After a few more seconds had passed, Dryden raised his arms once more, this time aiming in the direction of the two remaining engines on the ship's starboard side. But still, he did not open fire. Instead, he dropped his gaze to the ground, struggling with the prospect of killing the only member of his family of which he had even a vague memory.

"Taking out the first two engines obviously didn't destroy the ship," Emma observed. "So, doing the same to the other two probably won't either. They might have a pretty hard landing, though, so I don't think you should wait until —"

Acknowledging his AI's reasoning, Dryden immediately opened fire once again at the top engine on the shuttle's starboard side. This time, however, the six bolts of compressed plasma impacted squarely against the aft ventral surface of the ship's energy shield. Glowing, multicolored waves of energy rippled about the whole of the ship but caused no apparent damage.

Stupid, Dryden thought, now realizing that the electrical discharges that had marked his own shield's contact with those of the assault shuttle had ceased as well.

"Again!" Emma urged. "More power this time."

Dryden instantly selected maximum discharge intensity and fired again, but with his target now having reached treetop level, the results were identical.

Dammit! he swore to himself, knowing full well that his hesitation might end up costing countless Estorian lives, not to mention his own. Now helpless to prevent his sister's escape, Dryden simply stared after the departing shuttle as it banked off toward the northeast and began pulling rapidly away.

"I think she's heading back to Plains Reach," Emma said.

Now? With most of her own troops still on the ground? Dryden wondered, staring up at the trail of thick black smoke left in the departing shuttle's wake.

"They are seen as entirely expendable," Rick replied. "The High Protector no doubt has the capability to manufacture more examples of the weapons they carry and the armor they wear. And, clearly, he has no qualms about abducting as many Estorians as he deems necessary to accomplish his mission. So, unfortunately, like most other Human infantry throughout this galaxy and others, they are relatively easy to replace. That ship, however, is not."

Ignoring the implied criticism, Dryden scanned the forest to his west, noting that seven of the troops in question were on the move once again and appeared to be headed back in the direction of the positions they had occupied at the outset of the battle.

She's sent them to finish off Cash's men, he thought, the realization causing the hairs on the back of his neck to stand on end once more. *Rick, I can't stop them in time. I'm going to need your help.*

"What do you mean? I can't just … we can't …" Rick hesitated.

Yes, you can. Please! You've got to do something! Dryden urged, already running in the direction of the river road in the vain hope of cutting off the advancing Shepherd troops. *Cash and his men are still unconscious. You can't just let them be slaughtered!*

"Okay, listen. Miguel has already managed to compromise their secondary comm frequency, and I believe we can now prevent any further communication between Commander Beck and her troops on the ground. It's unlikely they will bother listening to you, though — particularly after watching you kill at least one of their own and then attempt to shoot down their commander's shuttle. But, in any case, it's the best I can do for now. Emma has what she needs to open the channel again."

"Emma!" Dryden barked, stopping in mid-stride.

"Channel open," she replied immediately.

"Extraction team, this is Foxtrot 04. As all of you just witnessed, Commander Beck has chosen to defy my direct orders — orders I issued in support of the classified mission I mentioned earlier. Her actions have already resulted in at least one death, not to mention the damage sustained by one of our Lord High Protector's assault shuttles. I can assure you there will be severe consequences as a result. But right now, I require that each of you follow the orders I issued earlier. Stand down immediately, retrieve our dead and injured, and proceed to the designated rendezvous point. Obviously, there may be a slight delay in your exfil due to the damage to Shuttle Alpha, but I will ensure the other shuttle is dispatched as quickly as possible."

Dryden paused, watching his tactical plot display for any signs his instructions were being obeyed. To his surprise, all seven soldiers appeared to halt their advance, undoubtedly trying to work out which set of orders were less likely to get themselves killed.

"Move quickly," Dryden continued in the most authoritative tone he could muster. "It is mission-critical that you clear the area before the remaining Estorian troops regain consciousness." With that, Dryden resumed his own trek back towards the river road.

"Looks like they're holding in roughly their starting positions," Emma observed. "By the way, please keep in mind that I will need to disengage the energy shield once you are in close proximity to friendly troops. The gravitic shield will remain online. I will do my best to deconflict any required intercepts."

"Good, thanks," Dryden replied aloud, winded once again as ran back in the direction of the still-unconscious Captain Cash.

"Dryden," Rick said, "there's quite a bit of data traffic passing between the remaining Shepherds. Unfortunately, that system is significantly more difficult to compromise. Miguel is working on it, but I recommend you assume they plan to carry out Commander Beck's instructions, not yours."

I assumed as much. But the question remains ... what do you intend to do about it? Talking to the extraction team again bought me a few extra seconds to get back to the road, but once they start firing, there's no way I can save more than a couple of the Estorians.

"Again, Dryden, we can't interfere in such a direct —"

Can't or won't? Dryden interrupted, becoming angrier by the second.

"They're coming," Emma reported as Dryden finally reached the tree where he had taken refuge earlier.

Glancing around the side of the massive trunk, he was immediately provided with a light-amplified and thermally enhanced view of four approaching Shepherd soldiers. Without hesitation, the closest of these raised his rifle and fired, the particle beam from his weapon briefly lighting the forest once again with a stream of orange light ending with the white flash from Dryden's gravitic shield system.

"I believe we can still consider them hostiles," Emma reported, deadpan, as the triangles representing the remaining Shepherd soldiers in Dryden's tactical plot changed from yellow to red once again.

Alright, Rick, Dryden continued. *It's high time you decided whose side you are on in this conflict.*

"I'm afraid it's not that simple."

It is that simple. Those Shepherd soldiers are about to attack what's left of Captain Cash's men. To prevent them from doing so, I will have no choice but to fire on them. Need I remind you that the members of Commander Beck's extraction team are innocent Estorians as well? None of them are here by choice ...

314

and now they appear to have been abandoned by their abductor —

"Wait," Rick interrupted. "What did you just say?"

I said they've been abandoned ... left here like so much unwanted equipment. Much the same as I was after the battle of Talteca.

"Stand by," the Grey alien said before abruptly closing the comm channel.

"What's he —" Emma began.

Who knows? Dryden snapped. *But if he had any intention of helping, he damn well should have done so already. Give me max diameter on the gravitics and show me where I should stand to shield Cash and as many of his troopers as possible.*

"Done. But, realistically, you will only be able to protect the captain and a couple of his closest men. The rest will, unfortunately, be outside the range of our gravitic shields."

Realizing that no further options remained, Dryden stepped confidently out from behind his tree, quickly covering the short distance to the location Emma had marked in his field of view. If he was unable to shield the remaining, still-unconscious members of 1st Platoon, he reasoned, he could at least provide the Shepherd soldiers with an inviting target. With a sigh of resignation, he designated a closely spaced grouping of three Shepherd soldiers as his first target, then raised his arms in preparation for opening fire once more.

"Wait!" Emma shouted within the confines of Dryden's mind. "Something's happening!"

As if someone had flipped a switch, the surrounding forest was suddenly bathed in light — an unnatural glow that seemed to be coming from somewhere above the treetops. After a few seconds, the light briefly increased in intensity before coalescing into three, greenish-white orbs — each of which descended silently through the branches above to hover five meters above the forest floor. There, all three of the strange spheres paused momentarily, giving off regular pulses of light that gave Dryden the impression they were living, breathing creatures of some sort.

"What in the Gods' names?" he whispered into the silence.

With breathtaking speed, each of the orbs accelerated away from one another. Two of the three began darting back and forth around the general area where the Shepherd troops had redeployed, while the third headed off to the northeast before beginning its own series of erratic movements. After a few seconds of this behavior, each of the orbs paused for a moment, then flared brightly before streaking up into the sky at a seemingly impossible speed. The entire event, from the first appearance of the ghostly light until the three orbs had disappeared from view, had lasted only twenty seconds.

"Dryden," Emma prompted, her voice cutting through the eerie silence that now seemed to permeate the forest, "they're gone."

What? Who's gone? You mean the orbs? he asked absently, his mind still struggling to make sense of what he had just witnessed.

"No ... well, yes, but I'm referring to the Shepherd soldiers — Commander Beck's extraction team. Whatever those white spheres were took them away ... all twelve of them."

Didara 4, South Estorian Continent, Ganahar Plains
(11 hours later - 106.4 km from Talteca)

It had taken nearly seven hours for Captain Cash and the remaining fourteen members of 1st Platoon to regain consciousness and then recover sufficiently to resume something approaching their normal level of activity. The first order of business had been to bury their dead in a row of temporary graves just off the river road. With only a pair of axes and three small shovels at their disposal, hacking their way through the rocky, root-laden ground had been backbreaking work. And it was early afternoon by the time the men had finally mounted up and set off once again for Talteca.

Even though Captain Cash had technically never agreed to Dryden's proposal that he be released in exchange for willingly accompanying 1st Platoon back to their regimental headquarters, he had nonetheless allowed the Flamecaller to remain unrestrained. Surprisingly, this decision had met with little in the way of grumbling among his men — all of whom had heard Dryden's description of what had transpired during the battle with the Shepherd troops. Most of the stolid cavalrymen, it seemed, believed at least part of Dryden's account of what had taken place after they had all been rendered unconscious. Although some of his story did seem a bit far-fetched for their taste, they couldn't deny the fact that he could easily have escaped aboard the Shepherds' airship had he chosen to do so.

During his retelling, Dryden had made no mention of the glowing orbs and the subsequent disappearance of the Shepherd troops. The convenient omission allowed Captain Cash and his men to believe that the remaining Shepherds had gathered their dead and departed aboard their ship, just as their own Flamecaller had ordered. This, he reasoned, was no more of a lie than attempting to describe what had *actually* happened. The simple truth was that he had no idea, although he felt certain that what he witnessed had something to do with his last, rather cryptic exchange with Rick. And the fact that he had heard nothing further from the Grey alien seemed to support his opinion.

With nightfall still several hours away, Captain Cash had made the decision to continue their journey to Talteca in broad daylight. It was clear enough that the High Protector knew exactly where his wayward Flamecaller was located — and 1st Platoon by association. Even without some mysterious, technological means of tracing Dryden's movements, their destination was not difficult to guess. It was equally clear that additional troops could be dispatched from Plains Reach to stop them at any time if their enemy so desired. Therefore, Cash reasoned, further delays for the sake of traveling under the cover of darkness made little sense — and had probably never made sense in the first place given what he had seen the Shepherds do the night before.

Now, less than two hours after departing the location of the previous night's battle, Dryden, Captain Cash, and the remaining fourteen members of 1st Platoon emerged from the Scarsdow Forest, the broad sweep of the Ganahar Plains stretching away before them to the eastern horizon.

"See anything?" Dryden finally asked after watching the cavalry captain survey both land and sky with his spyglass for what seemed like several minutes.

"You tell me," Cash replied, refocusing the small telescope in the general direction of Plains Reach. "Seems to me you Flamecallers can do all manner of things we mere mortals cannot."

"I do have some ability to sense potential threats in the area," Dryden admitted, "but I have detected nothing since the end of our encounter last night." Realizing that discussing the capabilities of his Enhanced Situational Awareness system would do little more than further isolate himself from his Estorian hosts, he chose instead to continue the discussion with Emma.

Same question to you, Emma. How confident are we that there is no one else around?

"Now that we've reached the edge of the plains, we can detect a Human-sized target pretty reliably out to around five kilometers or so. But I think at this point we're primarily concerned with the High Protector's assault shuttles. One of those, we should easily be able to pick up shortly after its departure from Plains Reach ... that is unless it's flying at an extremely low altitude and using the terrain to mask its approach."

Which it almost certainly would be, Dryden replied.

Satisfied that they were indeed alone for the moment, Captain Cash wheeled his horse off to the south, quickly coaxing the stallion's heavy frame into a loping, three-beat gait. With no additional comment, the remainder of the formation followed, hugging the edge of the forest in case they were once again required to take cover.

The first hour passed without incident, and the group put nearly twenty kilometers behind them as Captain Cash pushed his exhausted men and their horses as hard as he dared under the circumstances. At that point, he slowed the formation to a trot as he searched for a suitable location for both men and beasts alike to rest while being watered and fed. It wasn't long before he found what he was looking for — a place with good cover and a natural spring he had often heard referred to as "Meeting Rock." In spite of its moniker, Meeting Rock was not a single, monolithic stone. Instead, a large grouping of half-buried slabs of granite stretched from the edge of the plains to deep inside the forest like the worn and broken remains of an ancient stone wall.

Upon dismounting, the members of 1st Platoon quickly spread out and began performing many of the tasks associated with their bivouacking routine — though most of them thought it unlikely they would overnight here. Despite their reduced numbers, the men went about their work with typical, well-practiced efficiency — some of them tending to the horses, some gathering water and firewood, while still others foraged for wild edibles near the edge of the forest. Everyone else worked quickly to organize their meager supplies and equipment in preparation for the evening meal, an eagerly anticipated event occupying most of their minds and stomachs at the moment.

Although feeling less like a prisoner than he had the night before, Dryden was well aware that, other than the missing restraints, little else had changed regarding his status. So, after taking a moment to wash his face and refill his canteen, he resolved to remain as inconspicuous as possible, selecting a pair of stones arranged like an invalid's chair on which to rest. Just a few moments after getting comfortable, however, his thoughts were interrupted by the chime of an incoming comm transmission. *I wondered how long that would take,* he thought.

"It's not Rick," Emma replied. "I actually have no idea who this is, but the source of the transmission appears to be from somewhere off-world."

Off-world? Dryden asked. *You mean in space ... but not from the* Ethereal?

"Yes, that's correct. But that's about as specific as I can be at the moment. If you intend to take the call, I suggest obtaining as much privacy for yourself as you can. I've never mentioned this before, but you sometimes mouth the words of your internal dialogue."

I do not.

"You do, and you just did. Your facial expressions also tend to reflect your mental conversations as well."

Humph, Dryden groused after a moment's reflection, *Well, I suppose that's a good thing to know. I'd rather not give the impression I'm conversing with myself after all.*

"Agreed. Now, how do you propose to go about getting away from ... oh ... I see."

I'm surprised this isn't something you already knew about male Humans, Dryden chuckled, having already selected a suitable tree some distance from the nearest cavalryman. *There's a sort of unwritten rule that we men do not crowd, interrupt, or speak to one another when nature calls. Open the channel, please. It should go without saying that this is only a temporary solution.*

"Greetings, Flamecaller," the disembodied male voice began in a pleasant tone. "My name is Verge Tahiri, and I am a regional envoy … an ambassador of sorts, representing what was once known across much of our galaxy as the Pelaran Alliance."

Before he could even respond, a seemingly vast amount of information flashed into Dryden's consciousness, integrated directly into his cerebral cortex via his neural interface. Although impossible to grasp all of it at once, he was keenly aware that he was now in possession of a level of understanding that had not been available to his mind just seconds before. The epic saga of the Pelaran Alliance unfurled before his mind's eye like an enormous tapestry — its origins, politics, history, and even its more recent demise revealed in a level of detail that should have taken years of dedicated study to acquire. While this was not the first time he had been granted a new level of understanding in this fashion, it had never before occurred on such a grand scale or in such a short period of time. The feeling was at once overwhelming and exhilarating, causing him to completely lose track of both his surroundings as well as the somewhat delicate task at hand.

"Dryden … are you reading my transmission?" he heard Tahiri ask after a period of silence, jolting him back to reality with a start.

Yes, yes, I'm here. Sorry about that, Dryden said, shaking his head in annoyance as he buttoned his pants while attempting to shake the urine from his left boot. *I am, uh … somewhat familiar with the former Pelaran Alliance. So, what can I do for you, Mr. Tahiri?*

"Ah, good, I am pleased to hear that. You might also be aware, then, that there has been something of a, shall we say, *reorganization* in recent years. Some of the Alliance's original core worlds — Pelara included, I'm sorry to say — have chosen to form a new association called the United Coalition of Free Worlds. With Pelara's departure, it made little sense for the remaining worlds to continue using its name. In any event, long story short, we have yet to settle on a name for our new alliance. Thus far, we have been referring to ourselves as simply 'The Alliance,' or occasionally 'Ally' for short."

Alright then. Thank you for clearing that up, Dryden replied, unable to completely remove the hint of amusement from his inner voice. His mind, still awash with the after-effects of the massive influx of new data, now struggled to decide how best to respond to this latest in a long series of strange situations. Tahiri had just identified himself as Pelaran ... but hadn't Rick indicated that Pelara had somehow been responsible for the High Protector's unwelcome arrival on Didara?

"Relax, Dryden," Emma soothed. "There's no harm in talking to him while we figure things out."

Look, I don't mean to be rude, Dryden continued, largely ignoring his AI, *but Captain Cash is soon going to wonder why I've wandered off by myself. So, once again, may I ask why you have contacted me?*

"Yes, of course, my apologies. My intentions are twofold. First, I have reason to believe you have been in contact with another alien species — one the Pelarans have long referred to as the 'Pale Visitors.'" Tahiri paused, apparently hoping for some sort of response. Hearing none, he continued. "I'm sure you know to whom I am referring … short, highly intelligent creatures, big heads, black eyes …. In any event, for reasons I believe will become obvious, I contacted you because I knew your communications equipment would be compatible with mine.

I have spoken with them, yes, Dryden replied, seeing no reason to deny something Tahiri apparently already knew to be a fact.

"Yes, well … I sincerely doubt I would ever get them to agree to communicate with me directly. So, I would like to ask you to act as an intermediary for a discussion between them, the Estorians, you, and myself. Second, I believe it would be rude of me not to appear before you in person, so I need you to clear everyone out of a twenty-meter-wide area nearby so that I can safely transport to the surface."

You mean now?

"Yes, of course. Captain Cash appears to be planning to allow everyone to rest here for a while, so this seemed like the perfect opportunity."

It does? Because it doesn't seem that way to me. To me, this entire conversation seems exceedingly strange. You say you want to speak to us, but in truth, I have no idea who or … even who *you are. Nor do I have any real notion of your intentions. Furthermore, how do you think any of this is going to sound to Captain Cash when I tell him what is about to happen?*

"I can help with that as well. The good captain has undoubtedly heard of me before. Just tell him I'm the one his General Staff refers to as "The Broker.""

Chapter 23

Didara 4, South Estorian Continent, Ganahar Plains
(Meeting Rock - 87.4 km from Talteca)

A short time later, Dryden, Cash, and the remaining members of 1st Platoon stood with their backs to the natural stone wall, nervously awaiting Verge Tahiri's arrival. To Dryden's surprise, the cavalry commander had required little in the way of additional convincing after being told "The Broker" wished to have a conversation. The mention of the General Staff's code word seemed to drain all of the color from the young captain's face before inciting him to a near frenzied level of activity. After quickly mustering his men once again, Cash's first instinct had been to have them take cover behind the rock formation and prepare to defend themselves. But after taking a few moments to consider the situation, he decided that it was in all of their best interests to appear as calm and nonthreatening as possible.

"So, are you going to tell me who this "Broker" gentleman is?" Dryden asked, breaking the awkward silence that had fallen over the small group. "Because what my intuition is telling me makes no sense whatsoever."

There was no response from Cash. Other than the occasional grunt or blow from the horses tied just beyond the edge of the forest and similar sounds of uneasiness issuing from the cavalrymen themselves, only the steady sigh of the wind in the trees could be heard.

"I think you owe me that much," Dryden pressed. "All of you would be wearing a different uniform by now had I not intervened on your behalf."

Cash had been relishing a rare moment of peace with the last of his personal stash of chewing tobacco before the Flamecaller had started talking again. He had hoped that simply ignoring the question might somehow avoid further conversation, but the words just kept coming. He should have known better, he knew, having encountered plenty of officers — almost always infantrymen — on whom such tactics served only to encourage even more unnecessary talk.

"You're still our prisoner," Cash finally replied, leaning forward to spit as he did so. "Prisoners don't generally ask so many damned questions. And I don't think you want to have a conversation with me about who owes who."

"Alright, fair enough," Dryden replied after a long pause. "But I must tell you that he introduced himself to me as a representative of the former Pelaran Alliance."

"I have no idea what that is."

"No. Nor should you. But I have reason to believe that it is they who are responsible for sending the High Protector to our world."

Cash said nothing for a moment as he considered what he had just heard, then turned to look directly into Dryden's eyes. "That doesn't make any sense."

"If you mean it doesn't make sense because this 'Broker' has some connection to whoever has been supplying your people with weapons, then, no, it does not. And that is precisely what I've been trying to tell you."

Before the captain could respond, a hint of movement caught both of the men's attention. Thirty meters away, the air itself had begun to shimmer and distort, much like the distant horizon above the plains on a hot summer day. Whatever this was, however, was far more intense and limited to what appeared from their vantage point to be a two-dimensional, rectangular area of space. As they watched, the distortion became so intense that they could no longer see what was behind it, finally turning a dazzling white immediately before what appeared to be a Human man stepped casually out of the shape, as if through an open door, and began walking in their direction.

Despite Cash's orders for his men to avoid any provocative actions, several of the startled cavalrymen chambered a round in their Winchesters and took aim at the approaching figure. But aside from the method of his arrival, the man's rather unremarkable appearance was not the least bit threatening. His attire, in fact, was in keeping with what one might expect to encounter upon entering an attorney's office in the nearby city of Talteca.

"Easy … everyone stand down," the captain soothed, slowly gesturing with one arm for the men to lower their weapons once again.

The approaching man, for his part, seemed unperturbed by the men's actions, continuing his unhurried approach until he was close enough for easy conversation. "Hello again, Mr. Beck," he said with a civil incline of his head. "And you must be Captain Cash," he quickly added, nodding at the obviously astonished cavalryman. "As I'm sure everyone here knows by now, I am Verge Tahiri. As strange as this may sound, you men are the first Estorian Army personnel I have had the pleasure of meeting in person, although I have communicated with the officers of your General Staff many times in the past. As I mentioned to Dryden, here, they know me only as 'The Broker.'"

"Dryden, I've detected an inbound assault shuttle," Emma said, highlighting the contact in his tactical plot. "It's already gone supersonic and will be here momentarily. Also, be advised that Rick is back with us and is monitoring your conversation with Tahiri."

Understood.

"Forgive me, Mr. Tahiri," Cash began, recovering somewhat from the initial shock of his arrival, "but we were not expecting to meet with you prior to arriving back at our regimental headquarters at Talteca. Truth be told, I wasn't expecting to meet with you at all. Such things are, uh, above my pay grade, if you understand me."

"I do, Captain, but it was a necessary precaution in my judgment. I have been closely monitoring the Estorian Army's progress in their struggle against the High Protector for several years, and I'm not sure you fully grasp how important your prisoner is to your enemy. As soon as I realized it was your intention to return him to your headquarters, I knew the High Protector would seek to use his presence there to his advantage. In addition to wanting Dryden back, he desperately wants to prevent me from continuing to assist your people, you see."

"So, you believe the High Protector would be looking to either capture or eliminate both of you at the same time, or at least prevent us from making any sort of trade. But why give him the opportunity to do so here? Obviously, we have far greater resources at our disposal back at our base. And I don't mind telling you that Colonel Simms, and his boss, and his boss's boss, will have my ass in a sling if you take Dryden away before they've had a chance to question him."

"I realize that's what they would have preferred, but I also know that it would have been exceedingly dangerous to allow any sort of confrontation with the High Protector to occur anywhere near the city of Talteca."

"Confrontation?"

"Yes, of course, Captain. Surely you didn't expect he would simply allow you to trade away one of his most valuable military assets without a response ..."

Out on the plain behind Tahiri, the sublight engines of the High Protector's remaining assault shuttle roared mightily in a max-performance deceleration maneuver, temporarily rendering further conversation impossible. Everyone present, with the notable exception of Tahiri, stared anxiously as the spacecraft raised its nose in an aggressive flare before landing less than a kilometer away.

"Ah, you see, here he comes now," Tahiri observed casually.

"Captain Cash, get your men behind cover, NOW!" Dryden said, surprising himself by the forcefulness with which he delivered the order. "I'm not sure what this is, but it clearly has nothing to do with you."

In the field behind Tahiri, the assault shuttle had already disgorged a squad of twenty Shepherd soldiers as well as the High Protector himself, who immediately took to the air and headed in their direction.

"That's where you're wrong, Flamecaller," Tahiri said, continuing in a tone that seemed wildly at odds with the situation at hand — one that was clearly on the verge of spiraling out of control. "These men have a role to play here, just as you do. Didara is their world too, and they have no choice but to defend it. *You*, on the other hand, have been altered to such an extent that you have become a destabilizing influence here. *That* is why the High Protector is so anxious to remove you from the equation — and why I chose to meet with you here rather than in Talteca itself."

"Which is it, Mr. Tahiri, remove *me* from the equation, or remove *you*?" Dryden asked as Cash's men scrambled for cover behind the massive stones of Meeting Rock. "It's a little unclear to me at this point whose side you are on, but it seems to me the High Protector would still like to eliminate you as well. Otherwise, he could have attacked us again at any point after his first attempt failed last night."

"That is correct. As I said before, he hopes to take us both. He knows nothing about me beyond the assistance I have been providing to the Estorians. So, from his perspective, I am an even more desirable target than you … which is why he came so quickly when I communicated that both of us would be here this evening."

"I'm sorry, but I think I must have misunderstood you just now. You *told* him we would be here?"

"Yes, I did. But I can assure you there is no cause for alarm, Dryden. Again, this encounter was going to

330

happen one way or another, since there is very little that takes place on this planet that escapes the High Protector's attention. So, allowing our little meeting to occur at a time and place of my choosing makes it considerably safer for everyone involved."

"It's good to see you again, Dryden," the High Protector thundered as he hovered some distance behind Tahiri. "And I assume your friend here is the one the Estorians call 'The Broker.' I must say that I was quite pleased to finally hear from *you* today, sir … *surprised,* but pleased nonetheless."

Tahiri made no effort to respond, not even bothering to turn and face the High Protector during his typically loud and pompous introduction.

"I see," the WCS said after an awkward pause. "In any event, the three of us have much to discuss, so I'd like to ask the both of you to accompany me back to Plains Reach. So long as you do not interfere, Captain Cash, you and the rest of your men may go about your business as soon as we have departed the area."

"No," Tahiri said, maintaining the same quiet, businesslike tone as before. "Mr. Beck and I have no interest in accompanying you at this time."

"Forgive me," the High Protector replied, his voice suddenly hardening in a manner still familiar enough to send a chill down the length of Dryden's spine. "Perhaps you have mistaken the manner in which I spoke as an invitation rather than a demand. I require you to accompany me to Plains Reach. But I am a reasonable man. If you will do so willingly, there will be no call for any … *unpleasantness* of any kind."

"But you're not a man at all, are you — reasonable or otherwise?" Tahiri asked, turning on the High Protector in an unmistakably aggressive fashion. "I might be willing to have a conversation with you after I have concluded my other business here. Frankly, I believe I can relieve you of a number of misconceptions under which you have been operating since your arrival here. But neither I nor Dryden have any intention of going anywhere with you. So, for now, I suggest you and your soldiers return to your shuttle. I will be with you momentarily."

"Insolent fool," the High Protector began, extending his arms as two orbs of crackling, orange energy sprang into existence above his hands. "My patience —"

Before he could finish, Tahiri extended his hand in a dismissive, backhanded wave, silencing the High Protector's tirade in mid-sentence as the brilliant spheres of energy floating before him disappeared from view. For a moment, the WCS simply hung there, suspended in space — his face a study in rage and confusion — then seemed to lean forward slightly before plummeting unceremoniously to the ground in a heap.

"Is of no concern to me ..." Tahiri muttered, half to himself, before turning back to face Dryden and the members of 1st Platoon once again. "Sorry about that, everyone. Again, I assure you that none of us were ever in any real danger. But I do apologize for his behavior, nonetheless. I have always found that particular model to be particularly prone to, shall we say, illusions of grandeur."

"I'm not liking where this is headed," Rick interjected. "Keep him busy and try not to make him angry. Help is on the way."

"And what about them?" Dryden asked, nodding to the squad of Shepherd soldiers who had begun a steady advance in their direction during the High Protector's short-lived conversation with Tahiri.

"Not to worry. They won't bother us," Tahiri replied, shaking his head emphatically. "We can give them some room if it makes you feel more comfortable, but right now, their only concern is getting their Lord High Protector back aboard the shuttle for the return trip to Plains Reach."

"I, uh …" Dryden began, then stopped himself.

"Don't know what to say?" Tahiri offered. "Understandable. I can help you with that as well. May I presume that our diminutive gray friends are listening in on our conversation now?"

"I don't think I would —" Emma began.

"They are," Dryden replied, unwilling to introduce additional subterfuge into an already confusing and potentially dangerous situation.

"Excellent. What you need to understand is that, for the past several years, your world has been the site of a … a *test,* of sorts."

"What *kind* of a test," Captain Cash asked suspiciously, emerging from cover with rifle in hand.

"Hmm … I don't know how to say this without sounding condescending, Captain, but I don't think I can fully explain it to you in the time we have available to us — not in a manner that will make any sense from your perspective. Perhaps our friend Dryden, here, might be willing to do so later."

"I don't see how," Dryden said, "since I have no idea precisely what it is you are referring to."

"Don't you? You, of all people, are intimately familiar with the raw power the High Protector has at his disposal ... although I suppose you have only recently begun to see that power for what it really is. Still, has it not occurred to you how easily he could have brought utter devastation to this world, had that been his true intention?"

"I dunno," Cash said, "seems like he's done a pretty good job of that to me."

"No, Captain. Whether your people would like to believe it or not, his mission was and continues to be exactly as he has expressed it repeatedly to the Estorian Federation Assembly."

"You mean all of his lofty-sounding promises to advance our technology, eliminate poverty, and the like? Men born right here on this world have been making promises like that since the beginning of time. We know enough to recognize a tyrant when we hear one."

"Yes, I daresay they have. But in this case, the one making the promises is fully capable of fulfilling them."

"So you say," Cash said. "But none of that matters if we have to live under the thumb of a two-bit dictator. Here's the part I don't understand, though. If this has all been some sort of test, and you and the High Protector represent the same ... whatever it is you represent ... then why have you been helping us? Why give us weapons and equipment that allow us to fight back against the High Protector and his troops?"

"Ah … once again, that's a question I'm afraid would require more time than —"

"Because it's what they do," Dryden interrupted. "It's what they've always done. They dominate entire worlds by parceling out bits and pieces of their technology, just enough to make them dependent … *beholden,* I should say. Then, when the time comes, they use those same worlds to fight their battles for them."

"An oversimplification of an incredibly complex undertaking," Tahiri replied. "Not to mention a strikingly negative way of looking at a program that offers inestimable benefits to those few worlds fortunate enough to be selected to be …"

"Ten seconds," Dryden heard Rick say within the confines of his mind as Tahiri continued to speak in glowing terms regarding the merits of The Alliance and their evolving cultivation program. "By the way, you might consider keeping your mouth open. It helps equalize the pressure."

I might want to consider doing what? … What pressure?

"… We continuously update our strategies to improve our approach," Tahiri continued. "Supplying weapons to the Estorian government was a slight variation intended to accelerate your technological adoption rate. Humans can often be stubbornly resistant to change of any sort. But give them an enemy, and they will aggressively pursue any and all means with which to destroy that enemy. Specifically, with regard to —"

"We will not yield," Dryden said flatly, interrupting Tahiri yet again.

"I'm sorry, what was that again?"

"You're wasting your time here, Mr. Tahiri. We have no wish to become a part of your alliance, nor will we continue participating in any sort of test program."

"Three," Rick reported.

"We will resist you. We have the will to do so."

"Two."

"We have the means to do so."

"One."

"And, if need be, we have friends who will come to our aid."

Directly overhead, at an altitude of just under four thousand meters, an enormous, kilometer-long starship transitioned from hyperspace into Didara 4's atmosphere with a dazzling flash of white light. Everyone present, Tahiri included, instinctively jerked their heads upward, although they need not have done so, given that the gigantic ship now hovering above seemed to take up the whole of the sky. In spite of that fact, however, a rapid series of flashes near the eastern horizon also caught their attention as additional ships arrived.

"The time has come for both you and the High Protector to leave our world," Dryden concluded after a long pause.

"Come now, Flamecaller. We both know that's not going to —"

It was at that moment the shockwave arrived. Although the ship overhead was high enough to avoid serious injury to those on the ground, its transition had instantaneously displaced nearly forty million cubic meters of air. Eleven seconds later, the resulting atmospheric disturbance slammed into the ground beneath the ship, traveling outward in all directions at just under the speed of sound. With the notable exception of Verge Tahiri, everyone present was knocked to the ground, their ears shrieking in protest from the traumatic frontal passage.

"An impressive display, to be sure," Tahiri continued, seemingly unfazed by what had just transpired. "But the Terrans' arrival changes nothing. Whatever their intentions may be, it is they who have no choice other than to depart. And the same is true for the Pale Visitors."

Behind Tahiri, the squad of Shepherd soldiers had finished loading the High Protector back aboard their assault shuttle but had apparently decided against taking to the air under the circumstances.

"Well, I don't know anything about whatever those are," Cash said, still squatting close to the ground and staring upwards as if the sky were about to collapse about his head and shoulders, "but unless you've got some allies we haven't yet seen, I can't imagine you're not, uh ... *outgunned* at this point, to say the least."

"Hah!" Tahiri laughed. "Your military instincts serve you well, Captain. You're looking at a Terran *Katana*-class battlecruiser ... the *Katana* herself, if I'm not mistaken. And she is more than capable of reducing everything on the surface of this world to little more than flaming rubble within a matter of hours. But she won't ... because she can't."

"Clearly, they don't need to do anything so dramatic as that," Dryden said. "But my guess is they can help us put an end to your experiment here for good."

"No, I don't think they will be able to do that either. My own vessel, you see, is very small ... quite difficult for the Terran ships to track. Unlike the *Katana*, up there, she is not a warship, per se, but she is, nevertheless, still equipped with antimatter-based anti-ship weapons. And, if necessary, those same weapons can just as easily be directed at targets on the surface of your world. Without going into all of the unpleasant details, the result of that would be much the same as if those Terran ships decided to attack the surface ... perhaps even worse."

"So, you intend to hold our world hostage then. To what end, may I ask?"

"That part is simple enough. Our cultivation program is ultimately defensive in nature. I think we can agree that all worlds and, by extension, all alliances have both the right and the responsibility to defend themselves. Accordingly, the Pale Visitors and their Terran allies will leave Didara 4 immediately and allow us to continue our test program as before. Obviously, recent events will necessarily change our approach to some degree. In fact, I am hopeful the Estorians will now begin to see the wisdom in allowing us to help them advance ... at least to the point where they will have some hope of defending themselves."

Emma, any chance I can take him out?

"Unlikely. I believe we can safely assume he has some sort of shielding at his disposal."

"No, you can't," Rick confirmed. "For now, we have no choice but to do as he says. The Terran task force is preparing to depart, as are we."

You're all leaving? But you can't possibly be —"

"He has closed the channel," Emma reported quietly.

Over the Ganahar Plains, the early evening sky was lit by the same series of grayish-white flashes that had heralded the Terrans' arrival. Seconds later, the *Katana* also took her leave — the massive warship's departure instantly changing the brightness and hue of the landscape beneath the setting Didaran sun.

"There. I think that's much better, don't you agree," Tahiri continued in his usual, pleasant tone. "As for you, Flamecaller, I'm afraid the Pale Visitors' interference has rendered you far too dangerous to be left in play here on Didara 4. I will commit to helping you return to your normal state, but I will need you to come with me. You have my word you will be well treated."

"We cannot allow that to happen, Dryden," Emma prompted, her voice conveying a level of desperation he had never heard his AI use before. "We can't risk their being able to reverse-engineer some of the Daylean technology Rick and Miguel used."

I'm not sure what you're suggesting. We, unfortunately, don't have the ability to destroy ourselves, Dryden thought sardonically.

"That's, uh … that's not entirely true."

What? No! There has to be another way, he thought, beginning once again to feel the icy tendrils of panic at the base of his spine.

At that moment, the sky above the Ganahar Plains erupted in what sounded like another gigantic peal of thunder as the sound of the *Katana's* departure reached the ground. Anticipating this distraction, Emma had temporarily attenuated the input from Dryden's auditory nerves once again, allowing him to focus the whole of his being on a single, overriding goal … *escape.*

BING! The warning tone cut through the electronically imposed silence within his mind. And as the details of the latest capability made possible by his internal network of implants flashed into his consciousness, the merest hint of a smile began to form at the corners of the Flamecaller's mouth.

The following capability may now be accessed via your neural interface: ...

End of Book 6

Appendix

Regarding the Pelaran Alliance and their Cultivation Program

For thousands of years across hundreds of worlds, the Pelaran Alliance sought to expand its sphere of influence in our galaxy under the auspices of a program they referred to as "cultivation." The original idea was simple enough. Through an elaborate selection process, individual worlds were chosen as candidates to become "Regional Partners" in the Alliance. During this period, every conceivable detail — from the world's location, to its natural resources, to the intelligence and temperament of the candidate species — was closely monitored, cataloged, and evaluated to determine its suitability for membership.

Once a world had been selected as a candidate, the practical aspects of its cultivation were carried out by a dedicated, sentient spacecraft often referred to as a GCS (Guardian Cultivation System). Possessing, as Earth's GCS once said, "world-shaping intelligence and brimming with a godlike array of weapons," these relatively small spacecraft often spent centuries influencing and directing the development of their candidate world. Although a GCS spacecraft had a variety of powerful tools at its disposal, its influence tended to reach its peak once the candidate species developed the capability to receive and decode streams of data from space. Once that occurred, their technological and cultural advancement was closely monitored and controlled, typically advancing at a pace between ten and fifty times its original projected developmental timeline.

Ultimately, the goal of the cultivation program was the induction of a new world into the Pelaran Alliance. An offer of membership, however, would only be extended after the candidate world had reached a pre-specified level of technological advancement. Precisely how advanced was largely a function of the other, technologically sophisticated worlds located within a specified radius (typically five hundred light years). As a Regional Partner, the new member world was expected to further the interests of the Alliance at large within this sphere of influence. From a practical standpoint, this meant acting as a proxy military force representing the hundreds of other worlds in the Alliance — some of them located thousands, or even tens of thousands of light years away.

Obviously, faster than light travel was required in order for a Regional Partner to fulfill its military obligations to the Alliance. Accordingly, one of the primary technological aims of the GCS spacecraft was to provide sufficient advances across a broad range of scientific and industrial disciplines to allow for the "discovery" of hyperdrive engines. Interestingly, while the so-called "core" member worlds of the Pelaran Alliance possessed starships with far greater capabilities, new Regional Partners were provided only enough technology to grant a slim but comfortable advantage over their neighbors.

The Pelaran Central AI — which, over time, had become almost solely responsible for implementing the cultivation program — slowly refined its approach over thousands of years of trial and error. There were, after all, a great many variables to consider when it came to "boosting" a civilization's technological prowess. Some species were downright lethargic when it came to comprehending then integrating new ideas to advance their own — content to utilize whatever knowledge the Pelarans were willing to supply, but only if it required little or no additional effort on their part. Others, the Terrans being the textbook example, tenaciously latched on to every scrap of information, merging it with their own, existing technology in a rapid and sometimes unpredictable fashion.

Getting the process of "throttling" technological growth wrong, however, had remarkably predictable results. Too slow, and the transition to becoming an interstellar species would likely be an unsuccessful one, resulting in stagnation or, worse still, enslavement or destruction at the hand of a more aggressive neighbor. Too fast, and the cultivated species would likely become a serious threat — to itself, to other cultivated species, or (as was the case with the Terrans) to the Pelaran AI itself.

Perhaps one of the best ways to begin to understand the nature of the Pelaran Alliance is to read the words of three prominent characters from the original *Terran Fleet Command Saga*. The first is from Ambassador Nenir Turlaka — a member of the Wek species from the world of Graca, located near the extreme edge of Earth's cultivation radius:

> *"As I have said, we have seen the result of the cultivation program before. It always ends the*

same way: the cultivated species ends up in a protracted war with virtually every other species within what the Pelarans call the 'cultivation radius.' We believe this to be roughly five hundred light years, a vast volume of space to be sure. Within that sphere, other civilizations invariably end up banding together to resist the Pelarans' influence, but they are rarely successful. The cultivated species is always supplied with just enough technology and intelligence information to ensure their dominance of the region."

The next is from the Grey alien known to the Terrans as simply "Rick:"

"The scope of what has come to be known across a vast region of space as the Pelaran Alliance goes far beyond the recruitment and advancement of proxy worlds like Terra. While the cultivation program has expanded their sphere of influence much more quickly than would have otherwise been possible, the Alliance also owes its origins to its once-powerful military, the prowess of its diplomats, and the unshakeable will of the Pelaran people. Think about it for a moment. We're talking about a single Human world not unlike Terra. Over time, they leveraged their technological advantage with such audacious skill and on such a breathtaking scale that they were once on a path that might ultimately have allowed them to

dominate the entire galaxy. Personally, I think the most remarkable aspect of what they achieved is how few lives have been lost — both Pelaran and otherwise — in the process."

Finally, one might be tempted to ask why any world would agree to become a Regional Partner in the Alliance. This very question was once asked of "Griffin," the GCS assigned the task of cultivating the third planet in the Sol system on behalf of the Pelaran Alliance. Here, in part, is his/its response:

"To date, Terra has received only a small fraction of the technological data to which every member world is entitled. Once you do, I can assure you that Humanity will be more than capable of defending itself against any threat you are likely to encounter. In the event something unexpected occurs, your allies stand ready to come to your aid. Earth need not face a violent galaxy alone and, thanks to your status as a candidate member, has not done so for quite some time. There are many other benefits, of course — access to vast trade networks, the cultural riches of hundreds of worlds, and tremendous quality of life improvements, to name a few. For example, the average life expectancy for member species sharing your genetic heritage has now reached one hundred sixty-four years, well over fifty percent longer than yours is today. I realize that may sound like more of a curse than a blessing for a crowded homeworld,

*but Earth now stands ready to begin colonizing
many worlds in this region of the galaxy.
Although Humanity is already quite ... uh ...
shall we say fruitful in terms of birth rates,
adding significantly more productive, healthy
years to your lifespan will prove a tremendous
benefit."*

Earth's cultivation as a prospective member of the
Pelaran Alliance has been a central theme of the *Terran
Fleet Command Saga* prior to *DFV Ethereal.* For those
readers interested in how the process played out when
applied on Terra, the first five books of the series delve
into the topics above in far greater detail. But for those
readers who begin with *DFV Ethereal,* the information
provided here should provide sufficient context to make
sense of the storyline thus far.

In *DFV Ethereal,* we find the remnants of the Pelaran
AI now untethered from its former Alliance and free to
pursue its own interests. Confident in its long-
established methods of expansion, the AI continues the
process of implementing its cultivation program — and
now seeks to accelerate the process with a novel new
approach ...

Regarding the "Grey Aliens" and their Colonization Program

Even after the Terrans' direct contact with the so-
called "Greys" in the *Terran Fleet Command Saga*, the
details surrounding their species remain shrouded in
mystery. Prior to their return to the Sol system, however,

we Terrans had managed to piece together a fair amount of information based on various pieces of "Grey tech," purposely deposited on Earth over a period of several centuries. One of the most remarkable things they discovered was the fact that the Greys were not from the Milky Way Galaxy. Their native star system of Daylea, located in the outermost arm of the Andromeda Galaxy, included three habitable planets — all of which were significantly larger than Earth. This grand cosmic coincidence provided them with a number of distinct advantages throughout their development as a species — leading to a vast colonization effort that ultimately spanned the two and a half million light years between our galaxies.

Perhaps even more astounding was the fact that Earth itself was a Grey colony, revealing an inescapable truth regarding Human origins expressed in the following conversation between the Grey alien known as "Rick" and Terran Fleet Command Captain Tom Prescott:

> *"We have referred to your kind by a variety of names over the years," Prescott continued, "but the one that seems to be the most common is simply the 'Greys.' Not very original, I'm afraid."*
>
> *"Yeah, we love that one, as you can imagine. Descriptive ... yet vaguely racist."*
>
> *"Right," Prescott replied, chuckling once again at Rick's odd attempt at humor. "So what is the appropriate name for your species?"*

"I could answer that one in a variety of ways, but the simplest and most accurate response is ... well ... Human."

The scope of the Grey colonization program, the Terrans learn, is truly staggering. Of the nearly forty-three thousand relatively advanced civilizations in the Milky Way Galaxy, fully one-third of them are Human. And although the conditions unique to each of these worlds do lead to variations on a theme, Human worlds are remarkably similar in terms of their developmental timelines, cultures, and even the languages they speak. The Greys also seed each of their colonized worlds with plant and animal life patterned after that of their native worlds in the Daylean star system. As a result, a Terran arriving on a more recently colonized Human world, might understandably feel as if he had stepped back in time ...

THANK YOU!

I'd like to express my sincerest thanks for reading *DFV Ethereal*. I sincerely hope you are enjoying the story thus far!

If you enjoyed *DFV Ethereal*, I would greatly appreciate a quick review at Amazon.com. It need not be long or detailed, just a quick note that you enjoyed the story and would recommend it to other readers. Thanks again!

Have questions about the series? Please visit my FAQ at:

AuthorToriHarris.com/FAQ/

While you're there, be sure to sign up to receive the newsletter for updates and special offers.

AuthorToriHarris.com/Newsletter

Have story ideas, suggestions, corrections, or just want to connect? Feel free to e-mail me!

tori@authortoriharris.com

You can also find me on Twitter and Facebook at:

twitter.com/TheToriHarris
facebook.com/AuthorToriHarris

Finally, you can find links to all of my books on my Amazon author page:

amazon.com/author/thetoriharris

OTHER BOOKS BY TORI L. HARRIS

The Terran Fleet Command Saga

TFS Ingenuity
TFS Theseus
TFS Navajo
TFS Fugitive
TFS Guardian
DFV Ethereal
TFS KATANA (forthcoming)

ABOUT THE AUTHOR

Born in 1969, four months before the first Apollo moon landing, Tori Harris grew up during the era of the original Star Wars movies and is a lifelong science fiction fan. During his early professional career, he was fortunate enough to briefly have the opportunity to fly jets in the U.S. Air Force and is still a private pilot who loves to fly. Tori has always loved to read and now combines his love of classic naval fiction with military Sci-Fi when writing his own books. His favorite authors include Patrick O'Brian and Tom Clancy as well as more recent self-published authors like Michael Hicks, Ryk Brown, and Joshua Dalzelle. Tori lives in Tennessee with his beautiful wife and Bizkit, his intrepid, ten-pound Bichon Shih Tzu.